Christmas Cove

REBECCA YORK
ANN VOSS PETERSON
PATRICIA ROSEMOOR

MILLS
BOON

Published in Great Britain 2014
by Mills & Boon, an imprint of Harlequin (UK) Limited,
Eton House, 18-24 Paradise Road, Richmond, Surrey, TW9 1SR

CHRISTMAS AT JENKINS COVE © 2014 Harlequin Books S.A.

Christmas Spirit, Christmas Awakening and *Christmas Delivery* were first published in Great Britain by Harlequin (UK) Limited.

Christmas Spirit © 2008 Ruth Glick
Christmas Awakening © 2008 Ann Voss Peterson
Christmas Delivery © 2008 Patricia Pinianski

ISBN: 978-0-263-91210-4
eBook ISBN: 978-1-472-04505-8

05-1114

Harlequin (UK) Limited's policy is to use papers that are natural, renewable and recyclable products and made from wood grown in sustainable forests. The logging and manufacturing processes conform to the legal environmental regulations of the country of origin.

Printed and bound in Spain
by CPI, Barcelona

CHRISTMAS SPIRIT

BY
REBECCA YORK

Award-winning, bestselling novelist **Ruth Glick,** who writes as **Rebecca York,** is the author of more than one hundred books, including her popular *43 Light Street* series. Ruth says she has the best job in the world. Not only does she get paid for telling stories, she's also an author of twelve cookbooks. Ruth and her husband, Norman, travel frequently, researching locales for her novels and searching out new dishes for her cookbooks.

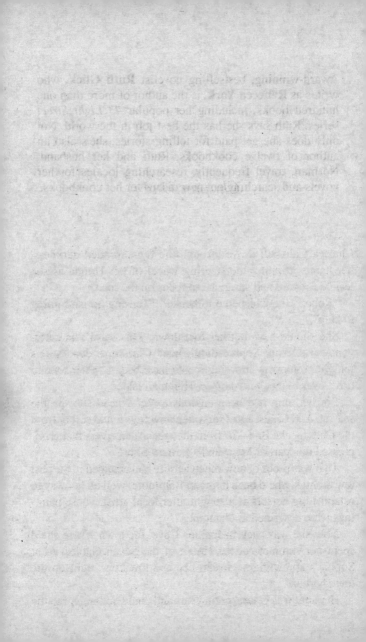

Chapter One

Chelsea Caldwell drove through the fog-shrouded darkness, her hands gripping the steering wheel of her Honda as she leaned forward and struggled to focus on the road.

"Relax," she whispered to herself. "Tensing up isn't going to help."

She should have put her foot down. This wasn't an emergency trip. Aunt Sophie didn't need Christmas decorations tonight. Tomorrow morning would have been a better time to drive over to the craft shop on Tilghman Island.

But her aunt had been anxious to get a head start on the season. And Chelsea had forgotten how fogs could roll in from the Chesapeake Bay—or from the creeks and rivers that crisscrossed this part of Maryland's Eastern Shore.

That was proof of how much her life had changed in the past few months. She'd been living in Baltimore, well on her way to establishing herself as a sought-after local artist whose paintings were described as "haunting."

Now she was back in Jenkins Cove, the town where she'd spent her summers at the House of the Seven Gables, Aunt Sophie's sprawling Victorian bed-and-breakfast right on the town harbor.

Her aunt was getting on in years and could no longer run the

B & B by herself. Chelsea knew that if her aunt was forced to sell the business she'd run for the past forty years, her reason for living would be gone.

Chelsea simply couldn't let that happen to her only living relative. So she'd done what she'd sworn she'd never do. She'd moved to Jenkins Cove.

Once, she'd loved the town and the House of the Seven Gables. Now it felt like foreign territory. She was struggling to settle into the rhythm of life in the quaint little community whose main business was tourism.

Every year the merchants sponsored a contest for the best and most tasteful holiday display. Aunt Sophie wanted to win—which was why she'd sought out a woman known for the specialty garlands she created and why the trunk of the car was full of holiday greenery.

Chelsea felt her shoulders begin to tense again. It was spooky along this stretch of four-lane highway. She could imagine ghosts weaving their way through the trees.

"Stop it!" she ordered herself, firming her lips as she kept driving. "Don't think about that now. Just get home, and you can have a cup of hot chocolate in the parlor."

A car honked and passed. A fool going too fast for the foggy conditions.

When a noise in the trees to her left made her jump, she took her eyes from the road for a moment.

"It's only an owl," she muttered, then flicked her gaze to the blacktop again—just as her headlights illuminated a shape on the pavement. Gasping, she slammed on the brakes.

In the swirling mist, she saw what looked like a person huddled on her side, lying on the pavement. A woman with long dark hair fanned out behind her head.

Easing the car to the gravel shoulder, Chelsea sat with her heart pounding for several seconds.

Though she wanted to stay in the car where it was safe, she knew she had to get out and help the woman. With an unsteady hand she cut the engine, then reached toward the glove compartment and got out a flashlight.

Gripping the barrel like a club, she stepped out, shivering in a sudden gust of wind that rattled the bare branches of the trees. During the day, the weather had been warm for the last days of November, but after dark the temperature had sharply dropped.

After glancing up and down the highway, she walked back toward the place where she'd seen the woman. But when she shone the light on the ribbon of macadam, she saw nothing.

"Hello? Where are you? Are you okay? Can I help you?" she called out.

When no one answered, her fingers tightened on the flashlight and her throat clogged. Maybe she'd been mistaken, she thought as she swung the beam along the road, then onto the far shoulder, the mist distorting the light.

As luck would have it, no other cars passed. With a quick glance back at her car, she walked along the shoulder, shining the light into the underbrush.

Again, nothing.

Finally, she returned to the vehicle and fumbled in her purse for her cell phone. But when she opened the cover, it made a beeping sound and went black.

She muttered something very un-Christmas-like under her breath and put the phone back. Who was she going to call, anyway? Police Chief Hammer? And tell him what? That she thought she'd seen a body on the road to Tilghman Island and now it was gone—vanished like a ghost?

The lazy old bulldog would really thank her for that.

Charles Hammer must have had some kind of pull to get voted into office. Too bad the town couldn't get rid of him for another couple of years.

Or maybe most of the people in Jenkins Cove thought he was doing a fine job.

After casting one last anxious glance at the spot where she thought she'd seen the woman, Chelsea started the engine again. The mist was thicker now, and she drove more slowly, afraid to hit a deer leaping across the highway.

Maybe that's what she'd seen earlier. A deer, hit and momentarily stunned. There hadn't been anybody lying on the blacktop, after all. It was just her imagination working overtime.

She'd started to relax a little when a flash of movement made her brake again.

This time she didn't see a body lying across the blacktop. This time, in the moonlight, she saw a woman running through the woods at the side of the road. And a man chasing her.

Her long black hair was streaming out behind her, and she looked as though she was wearing a dark coat that hung loosely on her body.

The woman screamed, then screamed again as the man caught up with her, catching her by the hair.

Chelsea pulled to the shoulder once more. Grabbing the flashlight again, she leaped from the car.

"Get away from her," she shouted as she charged into the underbrush.

She heard the woman whimper and thought she saw the man raise a knife. Then they both disappeared into a thicker patch of woods. When Chelsea tried to follow, she splashed into cold water that slopped over the tops of her shoes. As she pressed onward into sucking mud, she floundered into a water-filled hole and almost fell on her face. She was in one of the swampy areas so common around Jenkins Cove, and if she kept going, she was liable to end up waist-deep in freezing water.

Heart pounding, she stared into the bog. The woman and the

man had vanished into the darkness as though they had never been there.

As Chelsea replayed the scene in her mind, she realized she'd never heard anything besides the woman's scream. Shouldn't they have been splashing through the water? And how had they gotten through the swamp, anyway, when she had ended up knee-deep in frigid water almost immediately?

She backed up, feeling her way carefully, trying not to step into another hole. She'd only been out of the car for a few minutes, but her pant legs were soaked, and her legs and feet already felt like blocks of ice.

As she retraced her steps, she wondered what she had seen. Had her overactive imagination combined with some trick of the moonlight to make her think that a woman was running for her life?

Chelsea made it back to her car and stamped her feet to shake off some of the mud. Climbing inside, she closed the door and sat behind the wheel, shivering.

She started the car and turned up the heater, thinking that she had to report this to the police. Even if it turned out to be nothing. Even if the last thing she wanted to do was tell her tale to the cops.

She raised her head, looking around for a landmark. A few yards away was a sign advertising a restaurant in Jenkins Cove. Now she knew how to find this spot again.

While she stared at the sign and the blackness beyond, she thought about something that had happened when she was ten. Something she could block out of her mind most of the time. But not now.

She'd been at a friend's house out at Mead's Point, on a farm that bordered the bay. She and Amanda had been playing outside down near the water. When it got dark, neither one of them wanted to come in, so they went over to the old icehouse to look for fireflies.

That was where it had happened. Amanda was looking out toward the bay, while Chelsea was staring at the icehouse, trying to figure out why the shadows seemed so strange around the little building and why the air felt so cold.

Then a young woman stepped out of the doorway and stood facing Chelsea. She held out her hand, her face pleading as though she wanted something urgent.

Her lips moved, but Chelsea couldn't hear what she was saying. She only felt a terrible pressure inside her own chest and horrible waves of anguish coming off the woman.

She moaned or screamed something, because Amanda came running. But her friend didn't see anything.

When Chelsea looked up, the woman had vanished.

"She was here. I saw her," Chelsea insisted.

"You're making it up."

"No, I'm not. I saw her."

Maybe it was fear that made Amanda start teasing her.

"Liar, liar. Pants on fire."

The next thing Chelsea knew, she was in tears. She'd been looking forward to spending the night at Amanda's, but she was too upset for that. She ended up going back to the House of the Seven Gables, where Aunt Sophie did her best to find out what had happened and then to comfort her.

But Chelsea was beyond comfort. She knew with a strange certainty that the woman she'd seen was a ghost. A ghost who was depending on her to set things right—whatever that meant. But Chelsea simply hadn't been able to understand her. And she felt like a failure.

It was a lot to put on a ten-year-old girl. So much that the experience changed her whole feeling about Jenkins Cove. Until then, she'd loved spending the summer down on the Eastern Shore. It had been a child's dream vacation.

After that incident, though, she'd only come back for short

visits with her parents—until they'd been killed in a car accident right after her senior year of college. Then she'd come back from time to time to visit Aunt Sophie, her father's older sister.

Now she was back in town again—for the time being.

At first she'd felt a vague sense of foreboding. When nothing upsetting had happened, she'd started hoping that living with Aunt Sophie would work out for her. She'd taken over a third-floor room in the House of the Seven Gables for her art studio, where she worked most days. She was still sending some paintings to galleries in Baltimore. She was also selling at some of the galleries on Main Street right here in town.

And now this.

But what was *this,* exactly?

She took her bottom lip between her teeth. Had she seen another ghost?

She didn't want to talk to anyone about it, least of all Chief Hammer. But she knew she had to—in case this was something real, and she could save the woman's life. Or help the police find her body. That last thought made her shudder.

With shoulders hunched, she drove into Jenkins Cove, past the town square and all the shops and restaurants to the side street where the police station was located. Once it had been housed in an ugly redbrick building on Main Street. Now it was on a parallel street and it looked like a two-story beige clapboard house with a gable in the center of the front, a wide front porch and a red front door.

Pulling up in the parking area beside the building, she sat for a moment, steeling herself, picturing the chief in his rumpled navy-blue uniform.

He'd been here fifteen years ago when she'd seen the ghost out at Mead's Point. He hadn't been in charge then, just one of the deputies. But, like everyone else in town, he heard about her ghost sighting. Back then, everyone was talking about her.

Which was one of the reasons she'd wanted to get away from Jenkins Cove.

She tried to shove all that out of her mind as she climbed the three steps to the porch and pushed open the door.

Since it was after hours, the receptionist's desk was empty, but a light was on in the back, and Chief Hammer called out, "Who's there?"

"Chelsea Caldwell."

She must have sounded pretty shaky, because he came barreling out of his office, faster than she'd thought the squat bulldog of a man could run.

He took one look at her and helped her into one of the wooden chairs against the wall, his gaze taking in the water that sopped her shoes and slacks.

"What happened? Did you drive into a ditch?" he asked.

She shook her head. "No. It wasn't that. I...saw something when I was driving back from Tilghman Island. I got out, but...then I stepped into a hole full of freezing water."

He looked at her through small blue eyes. "Take your time, and tell me what happened."

She gulped in air, then blurted, "First I thought I saw a body in the middle of the road."

The sharp look on the chief's face made her cringe.

"Thought you saw?" he asked.

"Well, I stopped, but there was nothing there. It was foggy, so I guess it was just a trick of the light. But then a little ways up the road, I saw a man chasing a woman through the bog."

"Where was this, exactly?"

"Near the sign advertising the Crab Pot. Do you know where I mean?"

"Yeah."

"I got out and chased them."

"Bad idea," he muttered.

"But I…" She stopped and pointed down toward her wet feet. "But I stumbled into a hole full of water. Sorry. I tracked mud all over your floor."

"Don't worry about that." He stood there staring at her and tapping his finger against his lips.

Holding herself very still, she waited for him to make a smart remark about the ghost she'd seen all those years ago.

When he finally spoke, he said, "It would help if you could come out there and show us the exact place where you saw the woman and the man."

She nodded. She'd hoped she could go home, now that she'd done her duty. But she knew he was right. "Okay."

He looked down at her wet shoes and pants. "We keep clothing at the station in case an officer needs to change. I hope you don't mind wearing uniform pants and rubber boots."

"Thanks. I'd appreciate it."

"While you change, I'll contact a couple of my deputies."

She waited while he produced a pair of navy-blue uniform pants and a pair of rubber boots. The boots were much too big, but three pairs of heavy wool socks helped hold them on her feet.

When she came out of the ladies' room where she'd changed, two uniformed officers were conferring with the chief. Hammer made the introductions but the deputies—Sam Draper and Tommy Benson—had little to say to her. She wondered what the chief had told them while she was changing her clothes. Had he confined himself to tonight's incident, or had he told them about her misadventure fifteen years ago?

"Sorry about the boots," Hammer said as she clumped into the room.

"I'm fine."

They all left the building together, and she looked toward her car. "I'll lead you out there."

"I'd prefer that you ride with us so you can show us where to stop."

I could have done that from my own car.

When she answered with a quick nod, they walked around to where the police cruisers were parked, and Hammer opened the front passenger door of one.

She climbed into the cruiser, and he shut the door firmly behind her.

Hammer drove. The two younger officers sat in the back section that was walled off with a wire cage.

As they left the city limits behind and drove into the foggy countryside, Hammer said, "The weather's pretty bad. How did you happen to be out here?"

"My aunt asked me to pick up some Christmas decorations from a woman on the island."

"Okay."

The conversation died, and Chelsea leaned forward, looking for the restaurant sign. When she finally saw it, she tried to gauge the spot where she'd seen the couple.

"Right there, I think," she murmured, pointing into the swamp.

Hammer pulled the cruiser to a stop and switched on the red and blue flashing lights, which cast an eerie glow on the bare winter landscape.

The three men got out and shone their flashlights on the ground, searching for signs of her earlier visit.

Hammer handed her a light, and she also shone it on the gravel. At first she saw nothing, and she was starting to think this might be the wrong place. Then, to her vast relief, she spotted her own muddy footprints several yards beyond the car.

"Up there." She gestured with her flashlight beam.

"You get back in the cruiser and wait," the chief instructed. "We'll take care of this."

She shuddered as all three men drew their weapons. Then

they started off in the direction she'd walked earlier. Thanks to their rubber boots, they kept going through the mucky area.

Once back in the police car she ignored good judgment that told her to lock the doors and keep the windows closed. Instead she leaned over and rolled the passenger window down so she could hear what was going on in the bog.

With the flashlight gripped tightly in her hand, she listened to sounds of feet splashing and watched lights bobbing in the moonlight. The beams moved away from her, sometimes jerking as the men struggled across the uneven ground.

Minutes ticked by as Chelsea waited, sure she was going to hear the cops come splashing back to her with disgusted expressions on their faces. Finally one of them shouted in the darkness.

"I've got a body."

Chapter Two

Chelsea gasped as the impact of the statement hit her like a blow to the chest. She had been prepared for something bad. But, to her own chagrin, she'd seen it in personal terms. She'd assumed that they weren't going to find anything real—and that once again she'd be ridiculed. Instead, someone was dead.

As she stared toward the swamp, a male figure came looming out of the fog. She dragged in a breath, holding it until she saw he was wearing a police officer's cap.

Seconds later, Draper was beside the cruiser.

"Who is it?" she asked.

"A woman."

"Did you find any identification?"

"This is a crime scene. We haven't searched her."

"Do you know what happened?"

"Not yet."

Before she could ask more questions, another beam of light came out of the darkness. From the bulky shape that approached, she knew it was Hammer.

Draper moved deferentially out of the way so the chief could step up to the window of the cruiser.

"I understand you found a woman's body," Chelsea said.

"Yeah. I'm going to call in the state police. Since this is going to be a murder investigation."

As he pulled out his cell phone, he walked several yards up the road. She could hear him talking in a low voice, but she couldn't make out what he was saying.

"They'll be here soon," he said when he returned, then shifted his weight from one foot to the other. "I'd like to know if it was the female you saw."

Chelsea sucked in a sharp breath. "You mean you want me to look at the body?"

"Yeah."

"Is that standard police procedure?"

"That's *my* procedure," he growled, and she knew he wasn't pleased that she'd questioned his judgment.

"This way," Hammer said when she'd climbed out of the cruiser. "Best take my arm. It's slippery in the bog."

She didn't want to touch anyone right now. But she knew it was prudent to accept the chief's offer, particularly since her too-large boots were already making it hard to walk. So she grasped his arm and let him lead her into the bog, with Draper splashing along behind them.

Benson was waiting for them in the gloom. When they approached, he shone his flashlight onto a black shape on the ground. The beam illuminated a young woman lying on her side, her body half in and half out of a puddle of water. She was wearing a worn navy-blue or black coat and a shapeless gray dress that looked several sizes too big for her. Her eyes were closed and her dark hair was spread out in back of her as though she were still running through the bog, trying to get away from the man chasing her. A bloodstain spread out from below her body.

"I think that's the woman I saw," Chelsea whispered. "At least the hair and the coat look the same. I didn't get a good look at her face."

"Do you know who she is?"

"No." The wind had started to blow, and she had to clamp her jaw to keep her teeth from chattering.

"We'll want you to make a statement."

"I understand."

"And the state police will need to question you."

She looked back toward the road, sorry that she hadn't brought her own car. "Do I have to stay here?"

"When the state police get here, we'll take you back to the station where you can make your statement."

Chelsea gave up the battle to keep her teeth from chattering.

"Yeah, it's cold out here," Hammer agreed. "You can wait in the patrol car."

Of course, she wasn't only reacting to the cold. Seeing the woman up close had affected her deeply.

The victim looked so lost and alone out in the swamp. She'd been running from a man. Who was it? Her husband? Her lover? A guy she'd met in a bar?

No, she didn't look like the bar type. In fact, she looked strangely out of place in any context Chelsea could think of— except maybe a movie about displaced persons.

That was a strange thought. But she simply couldn't imagine this woman's life.

Chelsea and the cops started back across the muddy ground. When they reached the cruiser, she climbed into the passenger seat again. Draper slid behind the wheel, while Hammer went back to join Benson at the crime scene.

"Is it okay if I call my aunt?" Chelsea asked. "She's probably wondering why I'm not home yet."

"Go ahead."

She pulled out her cell phone—then remembered why she'd driven to the police station in the first place.

"Can I borrow your phone?" she asked Draper. "Mine's dead."

"Sure."

Aunt Sophie answered on the first ring. And her voice sounded worried.

"Chelsea, where are you? I was expecting you back an hour ago."

She'd wanted to reassure her aunt; now she realized she should have planned what she was going to say. Certainly not that she'd led the cops to a dead body outside town.

"I ran into a little delay," she temporized.

"A traffic accident?" her aunt asked immediately.

"Nothing like that. I'll be home as soon as I can. Please don't worry about me. I'm fine."

She could have added that she was with the police. But she decided that would be going too far.

How long was she going to have to sit here before they drove her back to town? Damn. Why hadn't she insisted on taking her own car? Then she could go home and explain this to Aunt Sophie.

That thought didn't exactly calm her nerves. She didn't want to talk to her aunt about ghosts. She'd ignored the subject since coming back to Jenkins Cove. Now she was going to have to face the inevitable. And the worst part was that she hadn't chosen the time and place. This situation had been thrust upon her by circumstances.

MICHAEL BRYANT SWIVELED his desk chair toward the French doors and stretched out his long legs, crossing them at the ankles as he looked out the window of his comfortable office into the paved courtyard between the back of his two-story brick house and the detached garage. The large patio was surrounded by raised beds with small shrubs and perennial flowers that had gone underground for the winter.

Some people would have called it a charming little retreat. He called it low maintenance—the perfect balance in his life.

An outdoor space he could enjoy when he wanted to get some fresh air, but at the same time, a garden he could maintain with very little effort.

Though born and raised in Chicago, he now lived in Washington, D.C., in the same house he'd rented a few years ago while working on a book about behind-the-scenes life in the White House. He liked the quiet, tree-lined street off Connecticut Avenue so much that when he'd gotten a chance to buy the property during a slump in the housing market, he'd jumped at it.

He shuffled through the stack of newspaper clippings on his desk, until he found the piece from the *Jenkins Cove Gazette,* a weekly paper published in a small town on the Eastern Shore of Maryland. His dark eyes narrowed, he reread the story that his clipping service had sent him.

Local Woman Leads Police to Mystery Body
By Helen Graham
The body of an unidentified woman was found three days ago in a bog along the highway between Jenkins Cove and Tilghman Island. Police got the tip from Jenkins Cove resident Chelsea Caldwell, who recently moved to town to help run the House of the Seven Gables Bed-and-Breakfast. She led police to the body late in the evening.

Ms. Caldwell said she was returning from an evening trip when she saw a man and a woman struggling in a boggy area near the highway. When standing water prevented her from investigating, she alerted Police Chief Charles Hammer, who returned to the highway with her, accompanied by two patrol officers, Samuel Draper and Tommy Benson. After Ms. Caldwell showed them the location of the incident she had witnessed, the officers investigated and discovered the body of a woman about fifty feet from the road.

Upon finding the body, Chief Hammer turned the investigation over to the state police.

The unidentified victim is described as a young woman or a teenager, possibly a runaway.

Michael looked up from the text and slicked back the lock of dark hair that had fallen over his forehead while he'd been reading.

He'd wondered at first why the clipping service had sent him the article. Then he'd gotten to the next paragraph and figured it out.

Sources close to the police department note that when Ms. Caldwell made her report of the incident, she mentioned seeing a woman's body on the road prior to witnessing the assault. According to her statement, she got out of the car to look for the body, but it had vanished. A few hundred feet down the road, she witnessed the man and woman struggling in the bog.

Longtime local residents remember that as a child, Ms. Caldwell frequently spent summer vacations with her aunt, Sophie Caldwell, in Jenkins Cove. On one of those visits, she claimed to have seen a ghost near a playmate's house, but no one else could turn up any evidence of the visitation.

When asked if the long-ago ghost sighting might have any relationship to the current case, Ms. Caldwell refused to comment. Several witnesses report hearing Ms. Caldwell discuss the possibility that the victim on the road could have been a ghost.

Michael studied the picture that accompanied the article.

Chelsea Caldwell looked petite, with a face he'd call appealing. She had large light-colored eyes, a small upturned nose and chin-length wheat-colored hair. Not the sort of woman he'd think of as a liar. She looked too cute.

But Michael had learned that you couldn't make such assessments from a photograph. Sometimes it was even hard to do in person.

But from where he sat, the case was a perfect example of the kind of story he was looking for in his research. It was about a woman who needed to feel she was important, so she was making up ghost stories.

The body she'd found had obviously been real. But had she portrayed her part in the incident accurately? Why would she have said she'd seen a body on the road that conveniently vanished? To deflect attention from what had really happened?

He got up and stretched his long, lean frame, then strode to the French doors, picking up the basketball in the corner of the office on the way out.

After crossing the patio, he stepped into the alley, where he'd installed a hoop over the garage door. The air was nippy, but the alley was sheltered from the wind. He bounced the ball several times, then tossed it toward the hoop, made the shot and dribbled again.

Fifteen years ago, he'd been recruited out of high school by several colleges, but he'd turned down the basketball scholarships in favor of focusing on academics. He'd played for fun in college, and he still did some of his best thinking when he was on the court.

He thought about Chelsea Caldwell as he shot some more. A while later he went back inside, then sat at his desk again.

He'd started working on this ghost project several months ago, after Jeff Patterson had called him in a panic. Michael had grown up with Jeff, and they'd kept in touch over the years. Jeff worked for an investment firm, and he'd become alarmed when he'd found out several of his customers were taking financial advice from a medium—and losing a great deal of money in the process.

Michael had never believed in ghosts or anything else super-natural. In fact, Jeff's call had brought his own childhood experiences slamming back to him.

Apparently, he'd been so traumatized that he'd repressed some very unpleasant memories. After talking to Jeff, however, he'd recalled that his mom had often spent the grocery money on psychic readings while trying to contact his dead father.

Michael had gone to bed hungry and gone to school in clothing from the Salvation Army store because a series of psychics had gotten their hooks into his mother. Back then he'd vowed never to let himself be taken in by supernatural nonsense. His mom's mania had made him test everything—and believe in only what he could learn from his own senses.

Jeff's phone call had done more than bring back Michael's unpleasant memories. He wasn't a powerless kid anymore. He was a journalist with a national reputation. So he'd come back to Chicago, investigated the scam and exposed it in a major piece for a national magazine. The heady feeling of evening the score had made him want to do more. Now he was expanding his research into a book proposal.

His gaze came back to little Ms. Caldwell. She intrigued him. He'd already dug into her background and found that she'd been selling paintings in Baltimore. Did she think her ghost stories would add to her cachet as an artist? Or had she tapped out artistically and was looking for another way to get some attention?

He wondered if the aunt was in on it. Were they using the ghost nonsense to get more customers for the B & B?

Well, finding out what made Ms. Caldwell tick wasn't going to be difficult. All he had to do was call up and make a reservation at the House of the Seven Gables.

He'd written exposés of the mob and helped get some wise guys put away in jail where they belonged. He'd accompanied an expedition down the Amazon and survived a very nasty spider bite in the process. He'd gotten in and out of a major African civil war without getting either of his arms lopped off.

Compared to that, investigating ghost stories on Maryland's Eastern Shore was going to be a piece of cake.

When he dialed the number of the B & B, a female voice answered, "House of the Seven Gables."

She sounded pleasant and professional—and just a little bit guarded. Odd for someone who made her living dealing with the public.

Was it her? The voice seemed too young to be the aunt, but he wasn't going to ask her name, because that might tip her off that he had more than a casual interest in meeting the woman who had been written up in the paper.

Assuming that she wouldn't recognize his name, he said, "This is Michael Bryant. I'm hoping I can book a room for some time in the next few days."

"Have you looked at our Web site?"

"Yes."

"What room are you interested in?"

He hadn't made a thorough study of the photographs, so he said, "I don't really care. They all look nice. I'd just like to get away for a few days."

"The Preston Room is one of our best, and it's available starting December second."

"Just a moment." He looked at his calendar. December second was the day after tomorrow. Well, he was anxious to get this started, and the timing was perfect.

"That date works for me," he said, keeping his voice bland though he felt an unexpected jolt of excitement.

"The room has a private bath with a tub and shower combination. And it's in the front of the house, with a view of the harbor."

He leaned back in his chair, a smile flickering on his lips. "It sounds very appealing." Of course, he wasn't simply talking about the room, but he wasn't going to tell her that.

"Do you have any special dietary needs?" she asked.

She was efficient. For a moment he toyed with the idea of giving her something to worry about—then decided that telling her he needed a gluten-free diet would only make his stay at the inn less enjoyable.

So he answered, "No."

"How long will you be with us?"

"Let's say…a week."

"Fine," she said again. "We like to keep things quiet during the Christmas season, so you may be the only guest by the end of the week."

"That's perfect."

They transacted the rest of their business, and he hung up with the smile still on his face. If he was lucky, Chelsea Caldwell would end up as a chapter in his book—whether she liked it or not.

Chapter Three

Chelsea woke with a start, every muscle in her body instantly tense. Lying in the dark, she strained her ears. She'd thought she heard the sound of a voice whispering urgently to her.

Reaching for the bedside lamp, she pushed the switch, flooding the side of the bed with a pool of yellow light.

As she huddled under the covers, she scanned the room with her anxious gaze. There was no one in here. Had she dreamed someone was calling her?

She'd wakened like this more than once since the incident on the road.

The incident! That's what she'd been calling it, because she didn't want to think about murder. Or about ghosts.

Or discuss them, either. It wasn't like what that horrible newspaper article had said. She hadn't been blabbing to anyone. It was everyone else who was talking. But what was she supposed to do, write a letter to the editor in protest? That would only make things worse. Instead, she'd gone about her business and hoped the town would stop talking about her.

When she heard the sound of something clattering outside, she breathed out a sigh of relief. It wasn't a voice at all. It was real. But what was it?

Simply a raccoon trying to get into the trash cans? Or was somebody sneaking around the house?

"Stop jumping to the worst possible conclusions," she muttered. When she'd come back to Jenkins Cove, she'd convinced herself that life here was going to be normal and uneventful. Ever since she'd seen the woman lying in the road, nothing had felt normal.

If she'd been free to leave, she would have gone back to Baltimore. But she'd given up her apartment. And she'd made a commitment to staying and helping Aunt Sophie.

Now she hoped she wasn't making things worse for her aunt. Sometimes Chelsea would turn her head and catch Aunt Sophie staring at her. But then she would quickly look away.

Chelsea was pretty sure her aunt was worried about her. So she was doing her best to make it seem as though everything was okay. She could do that during the day, but at night she couldn't control where her unconscious mind took her. Apparently now she was translating sounds outside into nightmare whispers.

She swung her legs out of bed and tiptoed to the window, looking out. A streetlight illuminated the side of the bed-and-breakfast. Down by the dock, another light shone on the small craft that were spending the winter in the sheltered harbor at the center of Jenkins Cove.

Fog wafted through the lights. As she stared at those spots of brightness, she thought she saw shapes swirling in the mist, shapes that took on human form.

No. That was ridiculous. It was just air moving.

She shivered, her eyes still fixed on the scene beyond the window as she imagined phantoms drifting through the town.

Damn!

Since her trip to Tilghman Island, ghosts had been on her mind. And she couldn't get them to go away.

She looked around the room. Well, the good news was that she wasn't seeing them in here. And she didn't want to. Which was why she hadn't gone near the third-floor room that Aunt Sophie called her "psychomanteum."

Chelsea made a sound low in her throat. Aunt Sophie had always been a little off-the-wall, but in the years since Chelsea had been away from Jenkins Cove, her aunt had let her eccentricities run wild. Now Chelsea had to cope with that, too.

She glanced at the clock on the nightstand. It was four in the morning. She should go back to bed, because she had to be up at seven to prepare breakfast for their guests. At the moment, they had three couples staying with them. One from Baltimore, one from Boston and one from Cleveland. The Cleveland couple were retired and traveling around the country, taking in holiday celebrations at various locations. The other four visitors were younger, and they had come to House of the Seven Gables for a weekend getaway.

Chelsea was about to climb back into bed when the same rattling sound made her stop in her tracks.

This time she thought it might be in the house.

Refusing to call the police, lest they think she'd gone hysterical, she pulled on her robe and grabbed the gun she'd started keeping in her bedside drawer. After slipping the weapon into the pocket of her robe, she scuffed her feet into bedroom slippers, stepped into the hall and started down the stairs, her hand in her pocket and her fingers wrapped around the butt of the gun.

The house was dark and quiet. All the guests were in their rooms, sleeping. The two weekend couples were leaving in the morning, and the maid would get the Preston Room ready for Michael Bryant, who was coming from Washington, D.C. He'd said he wanted to get away for a few days, but she'd wondered if he had more than that in mind.

Something in his voice had made her think he had a hidden agenda.

Silently, she admonished herself. Now she was getting suspicious of Michael Bryant. Lately, it seemed, she didn't trust anyone.

But look what had happened with the cops. She'd made a report about the incident on the road, and because she'd wanted to be absolutely honest, she'd put in the part about the body she'd thought she'd seen on the road.

She was sorry she'd been so scrupulous, because evidently someone who had read the report had started talking about it. Was it Hammer? One of the patrolmen? Or a detective from the state police? Whoever it was, the breach of police confidentiality had led to talk about the ghost incident fifteen years ago.

She sighed. Since that article had come out in the local paper, she knew people were looking at her with curiosity in the grocery store and in the shops on Main Street. And she was sure they were talking about her behind her back.

Or was that just her own paranoia?

She had the number of that detective from the state police, Rand McClellan. Maybe she'd ask him if he knew something about the leak. Or maybe it was better to keep her mouth shut, hold her head up and ignore the town gossip.

She walked across the front hall, where the light had been left on to illuminate the steps.

She had reached the dining room and was just walking between the sideboard and the long Chippendale table when the kitchen door opened and a figure filled the doorway.

Chelsea started to draw the gun.

Then the man's shape registered. He was lean and stoop-shouldered, and she realized it was Mr. Thackerson, from Baltimore, wearing a T-shirt and jeans and bedroom slippers. He was coming out of the kitchen with a plate and a cup in his hand.

"Oh," he said. "Sorry to startle you."

"What…what are you doing down here?" she asked.

"I got hungry in the middle of the night, and I remembered

that you had some delicious banana bread left over from yesterday's breakfast. It's one of my favorites. I hope you don't mind my helping myself to a slice—and some cranberry tea."

"No. That's fine," Chelsea allowed, seeing that he actually had two slices. Extra cake in the middle of the night wasn't really part of the deal, but she wasn't going to lecture him about it. She didn't want him bad-mouthing the House of the Seven Gables to his friends back in Baltimore. Instead, she stepped to the side, letting him pass her.

"I'll see you for breakfast in the morning," she said.

He mumbled an answer, his mouth already stuffed with Aunt Sophie's banana bread.

When he was gone, she leaned against the wall, breathing hard, thinking that she'd almost shot one of their guests.

She should get rid of the gun. But she couldn't do it. It was too much of a comfort to her.

After waiting a few minutes, she followed Mr. Thackerson back upstairs. In her room, she lay down and ordered herself to relax. She was going to look like hell if she didn't get some sleep. And instead of painting after lunch, she was going to have to take a nap.

She closed her eyes, thinking about all the things she had to do in the morning. Then she pushed them aside and focused on the painting that was half-finished in her studio upstairs. It was set in downtown Jenkins Cove, along Main Street.

Not one of her moody landscapes. It was for a holiday auction, so she'd deliberately painted a Christmas scene and set it at twilight so that she could show off her talent for bringing out the holiday lights.

As she let her mind picture the touches she was going to add tomorrow, she felt herself relax. Thinking about her work always soothed her. A good thing, because she needed to defuse her tension.

THE BRIGHT AFTERNOON SUN turned Jenkins Cove postcard perfect, Michael Bryant thought as he drove the length of Main Street, getting the lay of the land. This was definitely a tourist town. Very different from the gritty inner city where he'd grown up.

Most of the businesses that lined the street were decked out for the holiday season. Scattered among the shops were restaurants and real-estate offices—in case the tourists wanted to buy themselves a place in the land of pleasant living.

He circled the town square, where artificial icicles dangled from the roofline of a wooden gazebo, then passed two churches— one a Gothic stone and the other brick—on opposite sides of the street. They seemed to be in competition for the most elaborate crèche scene.

When he got to the outskirts of town, he turned right, heading down a residential street until the road stopped at the bank of what the locals probably called a creek. They used the word around here for bodies of water that he would have called rivers.

The creek was a surprise. He'd seen rivers and coves as he'd driven toward town, but he hadn't realized how much water hemmed in the community. Apparently you couldn't get very far without driving over a bridge—or into the water.

He turned around in the last driveway before the drink, then started back down Main Street. Consulting his computer-generated directions, he turned on Center Street, which dead-ended at Laurel. As he'd been instructed, he parked in the nearby public lot and wheeled his suitcase across the street toward the House of the Seven Gables.

The front garden was nicely tended, although winter obviously wasn't the best season to view it. The house itself was a white clapboard building, three stories if you counted the dormer windows under the gabled roof. It looked as though it had been built in two or three stages.

Like every other building in town, it was adorned with Christ-

mas decorations. The wreath on the front door was decorated
with miniature duck decoys, and the garlands twined around the
porch posts were studded with small sailboats and something
red that he at first took for ribbons. Then he saw they were
Maryland crabs.

Leaving his suitcase near the front entrance, he walked
around to the water side and saw a long, two-story porch facing
the harbor. Careful not to end up in the water, he turned and
looked at the house. Shading his eyes for a better view, he
counted at least five chimneys, hinting that the building had been
constructed before central heating.

The inn had a prime waterfront location on the sheltered
harbor at the center of town, directly across from a rambling
seafood restaurant. Probably it was noisy in summer, but there
weren't that many people operating boats at this time of year.
For that, he was grateful.

A KNIT CAP COVERED the watcher's wiry brown hair. His jacket
and pants were brown, too, giving him the appearance of a
workman who had some off-season business at the dock area.

Yeah, he had business, all right. But it didn't have anything
to do with repairing boats.

He was here to keep an eye on the House of the Seven Gables.

It was a boring job. But it paid well, and he wasn't complain-
ing.

When the B & B guests were out, and the two ladies had gone
out to get groceries, he'd used his lock picks and slipped inside
the house to have a look around.

After helping himself to one of Aunt Sophie's chocolate-chip
brownies, he'd looked at the guest book and snooped in some
of the rooms. Back in the kitchen, he'd taken a long look at the
step stool pulled up at the side of the cooking island.

He'd seen Chelsea climb up on it to get something from a

high cabinet. Maybe if he loosened the leg a little bit, she'd fall and break her neck. He'd be rid of one problem.

Now he leaned forward, zeroing in on the tall, dark-haired man prowling around the house. From his perusal of the guest book in the office, he suspected it was Michael Bryant, who was scheduled to arrive that afternoon. His build was athletic, and he was wearing dress slacks and an expensive V-neck sweater over a dress shirt. Not the grubby attire of some of the tourists who showed up in town.

The watcher noted the man was prowling around. Not your typical guest behavior. But he'd already looked up Bryant on the Web, using the computer at the library.

Apparently, the guy was an investigative reporter. So what was he investigating?

Murder in Jenkins Cove?

That was a good bet. Bryant definitely didn't look as though he was just here on vacation. At least, most people who came to a B & B didn't start by poking around the outside property. They introduced themselves first and got settled in their rooms—then went exploring.

Or maybe he was interested in ghost stories.

The watcher snorted. Well, he'd come to the right place, if town gossip was any indication.

The porch door opened, and Chelsea Caldwell stepped out, dressed in jeans and a cable-knit sweater. After watching her for days, he knew she'd be casually dressed, even when she was expecting guests.

He liked the way she filled out the jeans. Too bad the sweater covered her curves.

She stood for a moment with her hands on her hips, observing the nosy guy. Then she dropped her arms to her sides, squared her shoulders and came down the steps.

"Can I help you?" she called out in a loud voice.

As soon as Mr. Bryant and Chelsea went inside, he was going to make a report on this meeting.

MICHAEL TURNED AROUND and saw a woman coming down the steps. Petite, blond, with blue eyes and an upturned nose, she was immediately recognizable.

Chelsea Caldwell in the flesh.

"Can I help you?" she asked.

To his annoyance, he felt an instant zing of attraction. He hadn't come down here to start anything with her. He'd come to find out why she'd made up the ghost stories.

He shoved his hands into his pockets. "I'm Michael Bryant. I've booked a room here."

"Chelsea Caldwell," she answered. "I believe we spoke over the phone. I saw you looking around, and I wondered if you were thinking about staying here."

"I wanted to get an impression of the exterior before I came inside," he answered, thinking that the explanation sounded stuffy. And maybe defensive. That wasn't the way he wanted to start off, but now he was stuck with it.

"Well, I'll be waiting for you in the office. It's to the left of the front door."

"I'll come with you."

He followed her along a path made of some kind of white rocks that crunched under his feet. "This some kind of special gravel?"

"Oyster shells."

"Oh." Yeah, that made sense in an area where half the people made their living from the water.

When they came around to the front of the house, he reached for the handle of the suitcase at the same time Chelsea did, and their hands collided with a little jolt of electricity. They both drew back quickly and said "Sorry" at the same time.

"Electricity in the air," she murmured.

"Yes." Folding down the handle, he carried the bag up the steps to the front porch, then into a square front hall.

As soon as he stepped inside, delicious aromas wrapped themselves around him, and he took an appreciative breath.

Chelsea was watching him. "Aunt Sophie loves to bake. If you don't watch out, you'll gain weight while you're here."

"Warning taken."

Chelsea led the way past what looked like genuine antique furnishings to the office.

"I'm sure you'll like Jenkins Cove," she said. "What brings you here?"

"I just wanted to get away and enjoy the small-town holiday atmosphere," he answered, thinking that she wasn't what he'd expected at all. After reading the article, he'd wondered if she was involved in the murder. In person, he was having trouble picturing her in that role. Then he reminded himself sharply that he'd just met her, and that he had no basis to form an impression.

Moreover, the instant attraction he'd felt was dangerous.

He realized she was speaking again. "You're welcome to watch television or visit with the other guests in the living room. We also have a collection of DVDs that you can use with the television in your room."

"I should have asked, do the rooms have Internet access?"

"We've got a wireless network."

"Great," he said, meaning it. He'd be able to keep up his research while he was here.

"Breakfast is usually between eight and nine-thirty," she told him. "If you want to eat earlier, we can make special arrangements." She consulted a sheet of paper. "You said you didn't have any dietary restrictions."

"That's right."

"That makes it easy." She started toward the door and must

have seen that they were going to touch again if she tried to get past him.

Obediently, he stepped out of the way.

"The Preston Room is down here. You'll have a nice view of the water."

As they stepped into the living room, a plump woman wearing a dark skirt and blouse covered by a long white apron came bustling through a doorway. Her hair was pulled back in a bun, and her lined face was wreathed in smiles. It was obvious that she was related to Chelsea. The shape of her face was the same, and her gray hair still had some traces of gold.

"You must be Michael Bryant," she said.

"And you must be the woman who makes this house smell like a five-star bakery."

She flushed. "I'm Sophie Caldwell, and you've already met my niece, Chelsea."

"Yes."

"We serve tea and cookies and wine and cheese in the parlor in the afternoon at five. You're welcome to join us."

"Thank you."

"So, what do you do for a living?" she asked, taking him aback with the bluntness of the question.

"I'm a writer."

"Oh, that's so interesting. You know James Michener lived in the area when he was writing *Chesapeake*."

"Yes."

"And you'll find the books of a number of local writers in the shops on Main Street. Are you writing a novel?"

"Yes," he said. He had an idea for a novel that he was toying with. But that wasn't what he was working on now, of course.

"Does Jenkins Cove have a ghost tour?" he asked.

He saw Chelsea stiffen. But her aunt's expression turned

apologetic. "I'm sorry. The merchants' association has talked about it, but we never got around to doing anything about it."

"So are you saying there are ghosts in town?" he asked.

"There are ghosts in every town," Sophie answered serenely. "And, of course, Jenkins Cove has had its share of murders over the years." She lowered her voice as she said the last bit.

She seemed as though she was about to add something else, but her niece's narrow-eyed look made her close her mouth.

"I have some things to do in the kitchen," Chelsea said in a strained voice. "Aunt Sophie, would you mind showing Mr. Bryant to his room?"

"I'll be glad to. Come this way. You're on the first floor."

Chelsea hurried off, and the older woman led him down a hall to the Preston Room, which featured a bed with a blue and gold canopy that matched the drapes tied back over white-painted plantation shutters.

"Your niece seemed to get upset when I mentioned ghost tours," he commented.

"She had a bad experience recently."

"What happened?" he asked innocently.

She gave him a direct look, and he had the fleeting feeling that she'd seen through his ruse. But instead of calling him on his motivation, she said, "If she wants to tell you about it, she will."

She left him alone, and he sat in the comfortable chair by the window, flipping through the brochures Chelsea had given him.

He'd been in his room for about an hour when he heard voices down the hall. Glancing at his watch, he saw that it was about time for the wine and cheese hour.

When he walked into the front hall, he saw a thin, sallow-skinned woman standing by the stairs with Aunt Sophie, looking uncertain.

"There's nothing to be nervous about, dear," Aunt Sophie was saying.

"I've never done anything like this before," the woman said softly.

"Well, you're very brave to take this step. It's always a big decision to try and reach across the great divide to a loved one."

Michael stared from Sophie to the older woman. "Contacting the dead?" he said, hearing the rough quality of his own voice.

"Why, yes."

"You have people coming here for séances?" he asked, struggling not to make his voice sound accusing.

Aunt Sophie laughed. "Séances? No, no. They can be faked, of course. But I have built a psychomanteum in the attic."

"A psychomanteum?" he asked, as he rolled the pretentious-sounding word around in his mouth. "What's that?"

She smiled serenely. "You look alarmed. But it's nothing to worry about. It's just a room where the dead can contact the living—if they so choose."

Chapter Four

From the corner of his eye, Michael saw that Chelsea had stepped into the hall and gone stock-still when she realized that the subject had turned to ghosts—again.

Funny how they kept coming up.

"That sounds very interesting. I'd like to hear about this psychomanteum," he said, looking from niece to aunt.

Sophie gave him a bright smile. "I read about it on the Web. You can pick up so much information on the Web, don't you know? I started doing research on psychic phenomena after..." She glanced at Chelsea and stopped short.

"After what?" Michael prompted, pretty sure what she had stopped herself from saying. After Chelsea had said she'd seen a ghost. Of course the question was—which time? Fifteen years ago or last week?

Ignoring the question, the older woman went on. "I found a Web site that told all about it. It's a very ancient concept. Long ago, people might go into the forest, kneel down by a pool of water and peer into it as they asked the spirit of a dead relative to come to them. Today we're more likely to use a darkened room, hung with heavy curtains. My psychomanteum has a chair and a mirror, and candles for light. You sit in the chair, stare into the mirror and invite a spirit to come to you."

Michael wanted to tell her she was out of her mind. Either that or she'd found some way to make the psychomanteum pay big-time. Instead he settled for a noncommittal "I see," before turning toward Chelsea. "Have you ever tried it?"

"No!" she said sharply, then looked at her aunt. "And I don't intend to."

"It might help you," Sophie said softly, and Michael waited to see what Chelsea would say.

"I don't need that kind of help," she answered, and Michael gathered that he'd stepped into the middle of an old argument.

Chelsea looked from her aunt to Michael, then seemed to realize that there was a fourth person in the room.

"Mrs.…Albright?"

"Yes, dear," her aunt answered. "Mrs. Albright and I were talking in church about her dear departed husband, Norbert. She said she wished she could speak to him again, and I suggested she try the psychomanteum."

Chelsea answered with a tight nod.

"How much do you charge to use the psychomanteum?" Michael asked Sophie.

She looked startled. "Why, nothing. It's just…" She shrugged. "Just something I do for the community." Turning to Mrs. Albright, she said, "I'll take you up, dear, and get you settled." Then she asked her niece, "Can you get out the wine and cheese?"

"Yes."

"And don't forget those brownies and lemon bars I made this afternoon. I'll be down in a few minutes."

Sophie and her guest started up the stairs.

When the two women had reached the second floor and started down the hall, Michael leaned toward Chelsea. "Do you believe that? That people can contact the dead?"

"I don't know."

"Have you ever done it?"

"Have you?" she shot back.

"No."

"At least you're sure of what you believe."

"What's that supposed to mean?"

Instead of answering, she turned on her heel and headed for the dining room, where she exited through a door at the far end of the room.

Michael thought about waiting for her in the living room, since it might not be appropriate for the guests to go into the working part of the B & B.

The heck with it. He followed her through the doorway and found himself in the kitchen.

Chelsea was just setting wineglasses on a silver tray when the back door of the house opened, and a nattily dressed man in his midthirties walked in. He was of medium height with medium brown hair carefully combed to the side.

Chelsea's head jerked up. "Ned, what are you doing here?"

"Have you talked to your aunt about my offer?" He thrust his hands into the pockets of his gray slacks.

"No. And I'm not going to."

"The market could go down."

"That won't make any difference to Aunt Sophie. She's not interested in selling."

Michael cleared his throat. "Am I interrupting something? I was in a hurry to get here, so I didn't stop for lunch on the way down from D.C., and I was hoping for a head start on the wine and cheese."

"Of course," Chelsea answered, apparently glad that he was in the kitchen. She went to the refrigerator and took out a bottle of white Chablis, along with a tray that held crackers and small slices of cheese. "White or red wine?" she asked.

The brown-haired man gave Michael an annoyed look.

He could have cut the tension in Chelsea's voice with one of the knives in the rack under the window. "Red."

Picking up a glass she'd set on the tray, she poured from a bottle of Merlot. As she handed Michael the glass, she said, "Ned just stopped by for his weekly reminder that the House of the Seven Gables is sitting on prime town land and Aunt Sophie could make a fortune if she sold it to a developer."

The other man kept his expression neutral.

"But he's not going to get Aunt Sophie to sell," Chelsea finished.

"I'd like to talk to her," he said.

"She's busy."

He might have kept pressing his case. Instead he held up his hands, palms out. "Okay, another time," he answered with an edge in his voice. Then he exited the kitchen.

Michael watched him disappear down the walk. "He's pushy."

"Ned Perry never learned how to take no for an answer. With some people, it works. But Aunt Sophie loves this place. She'll never sell while she's still alive."

"If she sold, wouldn't she make enough to retire in luxury?"

Chelsea turned to him, her face set in firm lines. "She doesn't want to retire. That's why I came back to Jenkins Cove—to help her take care of this place." She blinked. "I'm sorry. You don't want to hear about our business."

"Actually, I do. I find that little drama very interesting."

"Well, the drama is over." She picked up the tray of cheese. "You can help me carry the wine and glasses."

"Sure."

When they returned to the living room, two more guests were seated on the sofa. Both gray-haired and slightly overweight, they were eating from the plate of cookies on the coffee table. Chelsea set down the tray of cheese, and Michael put the wine and glasses beside it. She took a straight chair by the door, leaving an easy chair for him.

"I'm Michael Bryant," he said.

"Ted Alexander."

"And Betty Alexander," the woman added. "We've been here for a few days. You'll love Jenkins Cove and the House of the Seven Gables."

Just as Michael sat down, Aunt Sophie joined them. "Well, it's nice to see you all."

"Where's Mrs. Albright?" Michael asked.

"She's still upstairs."

"She came to use the psychomanteum," Michael said helpfully.

Chelsea gave him a dark look, but Betty Alexander smiled broadly. "Oh yes. The ghost room upstairs. Ted won't have anything to do with it, but I tried it, hoping to have a little adventure. Unfortunately, nothing happened. I guess there were no spirits that wanted to contact me."

Ted gave his wife an indulgent smile. "It's a bunch of hooey, you know. But harmless."

"Now, now," Sophie answered. "Don't dismiss it out of hand. It might work for you—if you believed." She was about to say something else when the front door opened, and a tall, rangy man wearing dark slacks and a rumpled sports coat walked in.

Another guest? Come just in time for the afternoon snack.

"Sorry to interrupt," he said, looking around at the group seated in the living room.

"Oh, Detective McClellan," Aunt Sophie answered. "How nice to see you. Would you like a cookie or some wine and cheese?"

"No, thanks, ma'am. I came to talk to Ms. Caldwell," he said, glancing at the niece.

"Yes, right." She stood up and looked around at the faces turned in her direction. "Let's go into the den."

The cop nodded.

When he and Chelsea had left the room, Michael asked, "That was a police detective?"

Mrs. Alexander leaned forward. "She saw a murder in the swamp. Along the highway, you know."

"No!" Michael answered, feigning ignorance and surprise.

"Yes. And she saw a ghost, too."

"You don't know that," Mr. Alexander interjected. "I think she was just scared and overreacting, you know. Anyway, the local cops called in the state police."

Michael inclined his head toward the hallway. "Is that where he's from?"

"Yes," Sophie answered. She sighed. "Chelsea doesn't like to talk about what happened. It's too bad that ghost story got around town."

"You mean the ghost she saw when she was a little girl?" Betty Alexander asked.

"Both," her husband said. "The ghost she saw when she was a little girl and the one she saw on the road before she spotted the man and woman struggling in the swamp."

Michael sat back and listened. He hadn't picked up any new facts about the case. But he had found out something interesting. Apparently everyone in town knew about the two incidents. And they were willing to talk to tourists about it.

As he'd assumed, Chelsea had turned herself into a local celebrity.

DETECTIVE RAND MCCLELLAN of the state police waited while Chelsea Caldwell closed the door to the den, then turned toward him, a set look on her face.

He'd first interviewed her at the Jenkins Cove Police Station. The witness who discovered a body was always one of the murder suspects. And he'd investigated her pretty thoroughly. He was almost certain that she wasn't involved in the murder, although he still had to keep that option open.

He was here now to show her some pictures of known criminals. "Could you look at some photos and tell me if any of the men might be the man you saw attacking the woman?"

He laid a stack of photos on the table, and she paged through them, stopping several times.

When she finally looked up, she shook her head. "I don't think it's any of them. Who are they?"

"Men who were involved in crimes against women in various locations in Maryland."

"I'm sorry I can't help you. It was pretty dark that night. And the man was…too far away for me to get a good look at him."

"But you're sure it was none of these guys."

"I can't be absolutely sure. But I don't think so."

"We may have some more pictures later."

As he put the photos back into a folder, she cleared her throat.

"Yes?" he asked.

"You saw the newspaper story about the murder?"

"Yes."

"Do you happen to know who read my police report and gave the information to the newspapers?" she asked. Perhaps the question came out more sharply than she'd intended, because a flush came into her cheeks.

"Sorry. Yeah, I did notice that. But a lot of people had access to the report. I'd say it was from the Jenkins Cove PD, but I know that would sound self-serving."

She sighed. "I think it's more likely them than the state police. My guess is that one of the patrol officers wanted to make himself look like a big shot."

Rand made a disgusted sound. "Yeah. They were both young. I can talk to Chief Hammer about making sure his men maintain the confidentiality of police information."

He watched her work through the implications.

Apparently, her thoughts were running along the same track. "I hope you won't tell him you spoke to me about it."

"Of course not."

Changing the subject, she asked, "Are you making any progress in finding out who the dead woman is?"

He could tell her that he couldn't give out information about the investigation. Instead, he said, "We think she might be a runaway from Baltimore or some other part of the country."

As he spoke, he watched her closely. Maybe she wasn't involved in the murder, but she was certainly on edge.

"Because she matches the description of a missing person?" Chelsea asked.

"No, because we simply don't know *who* she is. One couple thought it might be their daughter and came down here to look at the body. But it wasn't her."

"I'm glad, for their sake," Chelsea answered softly. "You'll tell me if you find out her name?"

"Yes." He hesitated for a moment, then said, "I'd better be going."

"Was there something you wanted to tell me?"

"No," he denied, then opened the door of the den. "I can let myself out. You go back to your guests."

Rand walked out the front door, closing it behind him. He'd toyed with the idea of getting Ms. Caldwell's reaction to a piece of information from the autopsy. But he'd decided that there were enough leaks in the case.

The interview had given him another opportunity to observe her. She'd told a story about a ghost that would have most cops shaking their heads. Rand, however, had found out a couple of years ago that there could be more to a case than you could verify through your own senses or the usual police work. When he'd been investigating an explosion and multiple murders at the Cranebrook Labs in St. Stephens, some of the facts simply hadn't added up. In fact, he'd been sure the wrong guy—Gage Darnell—had murdered his partner, until Gage had convinced Rand that he was the fall guy, not the perp.

This case had some similar aspects. Was someone setting up Chelsea Caldwell? Or was she an innocent bystander who'd been at the wrong place at the wrong time?

TO CHELSEA'S DISGUST, when she returned to the living room, the group was still taking about ghosts. Aunt Sophie was telling a story that Chelsea had heard dozens of times before—about a boat that had come sailing into the Jenkins Cove Harbor and bumped up against the dock.

"People thought they saw a young man on the deck," Sophie whispered. "Working the sails and manning the tiller. But when they investigated, the only person they'd found on the boat was downstairs in the main cabin."

She looked around, making her audience wait for the punch line. "It was a very sick young woman who claimed that she and her husband had been out sailing. Both of them had gotten food poisoning, and he put her to bed, then came up to sail the boat into port. The woman was taken right to the hospital, where she recovered. Nobody ever found a trace of the man, and a lot of people think his ghost sailed the boat to Jenkins Cove as his last loving act before crossing over."

The Alexanders were listening wide-eyed. Michael Bryant was sitting back in his chair with a skeptical look plastered on his face. When he saw Chelsea standing in the doorway, he said, "What do you think?"

"I think he sailed the boat into the harbor and then tumbled overboard."

"Did they ever find his body?"

"Not that I know of."

"Because it wasn't there. It was somewhere out in the bay," Aunt Sophie said.

Chelsea shrugged. She looked as though she was about to say something, when a noise in the hall made her turn. It was Mrs. Albright.

Aunt Sophie jumped up. "Did you speak to your husband?" she asked.

Mrs. Albright's eyes brimmed. "No."

"I'm so sorry. But we can't always count on the spirits being available," Aunt Sophie said. She got up and the two women walked across the hall, talking in low tones. When they stepped outside, Michael lost sight of them.

"This is all so fascinating," Mrs. Alexander said.

"It's good party conversation," her husband answered.

Chelsea gestured stiffly toward the trays on the table. "Feel free to help yourselves. I'll be back later for the trays." She looked at Michael. "We lock the door in the evenings, so please take the key when you go out." Addressing the room in general, she added, "I'll see you all at breakfast. Can you give me some idea when you'd like to eat?"

"Eight-thirty," Mrs. Alexander said. "We'd like to get an early start in the morning."

"I'd like to sleep in. So nine would be good," Michael said, figuring he could avoid eating most of the meal with the couple, since he didn't particularly like them.

Mrs. Alexander looked disappointed. Her husband gave him a little shrug.

It was already getting dark as Michael turned and walked down the hall, thinking he should take another look at the list of area restaurants he'd gotten when he checked in.

But his mind was on Chelsea. Initially he'd thought she was a woman who wanted everyone to marvel at the fact that she had seen two ghosts. To the contrary, however, she seemed to want to avoid the subject.

That led him back to his theory that she was somehow

involved in the murder. And perhaps the ghost business was a smoke screen...

He'd like to talk to her about it some more. But he'd found out in the past few hours that she wouldn't welcome the topic.

Well, maybe he could start with something else and work his way back to the ghosts. That might be the right approach.

Or maybe he should give up the idea of including her in his book.

He blinked, wondering where that wayward thought had come from. He'd come all the way down here to corner her, and he wasn't going to let her put him off. He wanted to find out what made her tick. For professional *and* personal reasons.

He brought himself up short. Personal reasons had no place in his plans. At least not where Chelsea Caldwell was concerned.

CHELSEA COULD NOT STOP thinking of Michael Bryant. Not as a guest. As a man. A very handsome man.

Carrying the tray of glasses to the kitchen, she stopped short, nearly spilling the crystal, as a realization hit her with a jolt.

She was attracted to him. Strongly attracted.

And that was too bad, because she couldn't shake the feeling that he wasn't being entirely honest with her and Aunt Sophie.

Maybe the mistrust had started right at the beginning—when she'd seen him prowling around the outside of the house before stopping in the office to tell them he had arrived.

She filled the sink with soap and water, then began to wash the wineglasses, since she didn't trust stemware in the dishwasher.

As she worked, the light by the kitchen door gave a pop and went out.

"Damn," she muttered.

At this time in the evening, she needed all the light she could get if she was going to wash Mrs. Alexander's lipstick off the wineglass. So she got another bulb from the pantry, then carried over the kitchen stool that she kept under the edge of the island.

The stool seemed a little more shaky than usual, but she was in a hurry, so she climbed up and started to unscrew the shade.

MICHAEL TUCKED THE restaurant brochures into his back pocket and walked back toward the public areas of the house. He had a legitimate reason to talk to Chelsea now—if he could find her.

A couple of lamps burned in the living room, but the trays of cheese and wine had been cleared away.

"Chelsea?"

When she didn't answer, he listened for a moment and thought he heard a noise down the hall.

Hurrying through the dining room, he pushed open the swinging door into the kitchen and heard a scrabbling sound— and a gasp.

Chapter Five

Michael's heart leaped into his throat as he sprang through the door. He was in time to see a kitchen stool toppling over, and hear a crash as Chelsea hurtled toward the floor.

He caught her before she landed, pulling her body tightly against his. His heart was pounding like a tom-tom in his chest as he tightened his hold on her, struggling to keep them both from falling over.

Her hands flew over his back, then settled on his shoulders. As the two of them regained their balance, he waited for her to push him away, but she still clung to him.

He muttered a curse under his breath, then added, "I'm so sorry."

He'd come charging into the kitchen like a bull chasing a red flag, and apparently he'd knocked Chelsea off the stool when she was changing a lightbulb.

Now he was holding her in his arms. She felt warm and feminine in his embrace. And more fragile than he would have imagined.

"Are you all right?" he asked, the question coming out low and gritty.

"Yes."

Now was the time to turn her loose. His brain registered that fact, but his arms simply wouldn't drop away from her body.

He felt her move, but it was only to raise her face to his. There he saw her questioning look and a very appealing flush spread across her cheeks.

He focused on her lips, then raised his gaze to her eyes. Time stretched, long enough for an eternity of silent messages to pass between them. Somewhere in his mind, he knew none of this should be happening. He shouldn't be holding her—for so many reasons.

He had come here because…

At this moment, the reason didn't matter. The only thing his brain had room for was that she was standing in his embrace.

That was reality. Their reality.

His gaze switched to her mouth again. Her lips were parted now, her breath shallow. Slowly, giving her a chance to pull away, he lowered his head, and his mouth touched down on hers.

Had he meant to be gentle? Had he meant to comfort her?

Those were his intentions. And that was the way the kiss started. She was passive for a moment. Maybe she was even shocked. But then he felt her respond to him. The returned pressure of her lips against his fueled a hot, frantic jolt inside him—a jolt that reverberated between them and at the same time wrapped itself around them like a protective shield.

A cannon could have gone off beside the house, and the explosion wouldn't have made them move away from each other.

He heard a sound well up in her throat. Or perhaps it was from his throat. He couldn't be sure.

He felt her hands roving restlessly over his back, his shoulders, and he found he was doing the same thing to her.

They clung together, rocking slightly in the middle of the room as the kiss turned more urgent, more hungry.

The taste and feel of Chelsea Caldwell were the only reality in his universe. Well, that and the pounding arousal of his own body that swept away all thoughts but one.

He wanted her with an urgency that he had never felt before.

His mouth moved over hers, feasting on her. She kissed him with the same hunger. When she opened her lips, he accepted the invitation, his tongue sliding along the rigid line of her teeth, then beyond.

She met the invasion eagerly, fueling his need for more. With deliberate purpose, he eased far enough away to slide one hand between them so that he could gently cup her breast and stroke his fingers over the tip.

It had turned hard, abrading his fingers through her blouse. Thank the Lord she had taken off the sweater so that the bulky garment didn't get in his way.

The small sounds she made in her throat sent sparks along his nerve endings. Like the electric shock of the first time he'd touched her. That must have been a promise of things to come.

"Chelsea."

She answered with his name.

He took a step back, taking her with him, thinking that he would brace his hips against the kitchen counter so that he could equalize their heights and bring her center against his erection.

But as he moved his foot, something crunched under his heel. It sounded like broken glass.

She went rigid in his arms.

His eyes blinked open and he saw a look of panic bloom on her face.

"What are you doing?" she gasped.

"You mean what are *we* doing?" he heard himself correct her, maybe because he was feeling defensive about his own impulsive behavior.

He wanted to look away, but he kept his gaze steady. "Whatever it was, there were two people involved."

She had the grace not to challenge him on that. "Yes," she

whispered, and flushed again, only this time he knew it was from embarrassment, not passion.

His head was spinning as he scrambled to rearrange his thinking.

He'd come to Jenkins Cove to investigate the ghost stories Chelsea Caldwell was spreading around town to make herself important. Or to obscure something more sinister.

Since he'd arrived, she'd acted as if she wished all the fuss would die down. Then he'd burst through the kitchen door and knocked her down—and caught her in his arms. And she'd stayed there.

It had been an accident, for all the good that did him.

She was staring at him with a look of distress in her eyes—a look far different from her earlier expression.

"I'm sorry," he said. The words sounded lame, even to his own ears.

"This is crazy."

"I know."

"We can't do this."

"I know," he said again.

She backed away and crunched on glass again.

He looked down to make sure that she wasn't wearing sandals or something else dangerous. "Let me help you clean that up."

"I can do it."

He started to protest, but she cut him off. "Please leave."

He started to comply. Then he saw the stool lying on its side. One of the legs was bent at a strange angle. He walked over and picked it up. "This is broken."

"What?"

"The stool broke when it fell."

"But it only fell on its side." She inspected the leg, looking perplexed.

"You'd better get rid of it."

"I don't need your advice."

"Right. Sorry." He backed away. He could have argued that they needed to talk about what had happened. But he couldn't exactly imagine the conversation, and he had the good sense to step back through the door.

He walked to his room and grabbed his jacket, then left the B & B, heading for Main Street. He didn't care what restaurant he went to now; he just needed to get out of the house.

Now that the sun had set, the air had turned nippy, and the cold helped clear his head. But he still didn't know what had happened to him.

Chelsea Caldwell was a woman he didn't want to like. A woman he was investigating because he thought she was into some kind of scam. But doubts about his judgment kept cropping up in his mind. And as soon as he'd folded her into his arms, everything had changed.

He'd felt something simmering between them from the first moment they'd met. It had flashed into a rolling boil with alarming speed.

He considered going back to the B & B, grabbing his suitcase and leaving. For a whole lot of reasons. Did he really want to prove she was a fraud?

He swore under his breath. A few hours ago he'd been absolutely sure of his purpose. Now, however, he realized this research trip to Jenkins Cove wasn't exactly turning out the way he'd expected.

That was the way his profession worked, he reminded himself. You came in with certain assumptions, and you had to be prepared to change them if the facts warranted.

As he walked down Center Street, past an old warehouse that stood dark and hulking in the night, something strange happened. He came to a place where the atmosphere was suddenly colder than it had been just moments before. He raised his head and looked around, expecting to see that the wind had picked up and was blowing the branches of the trees around. But the air was still as a pond that was covered with a sheet of ice.

Then a prickling sensation at the back of his neck made him whirl around to find out who was watching him.

Every instinct told him that someone was there. When his eyes probed the shadows, he saw nothing. Yet the feeling of being watched only grew stronger. And the air seemed to darken or flicker.

"Who's there?" he called out, taking a step toward the spot where it seemed he might have seen some movement in the darkness.

"Come out and show yourself."

No one answered, and he stood on someone's lawn for several moments, frustration bubbling inside him.

He prided himself on being a rational man. But at this moment, he felt that something was happening totally outside his control. He didn't feel the wind blowing, but he heard something. A high-pitched whispering that grated on his ears and his nerve endings.

He tried to take a step forward, but he felt as if he'd hit an invisible barrier that held him in place.

He clenched his teeth, thinking this was the strangest experience he had ever had. It was getting weirder by the heartbeat.

Along with the strange sound, he thought he heard words, and strained to hear them. He couldn't bring the syllables into focus so that they made any sense.

It was as though someone was speaking to him over a radio frequency, but he wasn't equipped to bring in the signal.

Or, to put it another way, he might have said that a phantom from the invisible world had invaded this stretch of Center Street. A phantom that was here to give Michael Bryant a warning, or an urgent message that he wasn't able to capture.

A warning or a message from a phantom?

He shook his head, dismissing the outlandish notion, yet at the same time feeling the pounding of his own heart.

Apparently, he was so off balance from his encounter with Chelsea that he was seeing ghosts in the bushes and hearing their voices in the air.

"No."

As he spoke, reality twisted again. The air grew a few degrees warmer, and suddenly he found that nothing was holding him in place. He could walk forward.

No, nothing had been *holding* him in the first place. Nothing besides the inability to make his own muscles move.

Still, when he found out that he was free, he began walking rapidly toward the Christmas lights and the holiday crowds on Main Street. When he realized he was practically running, he made an effort to slow down, cursing under his breath.

Was he losing it? First that kiss in the kitchen, and now this.

Whatever this was.

CHELSEA SWEPT THE BROKEN lightbulb into a dustpan. Then she wet some paper towels and picked up the tiny pieces of glass that she couldn't see, working slowly and methodically.

She'd once gotten a piece of glass in her bare foot, and it had been painful—worse than a wooden splinter. She didn't want to repeat that experience.

The remembered pain wasn't the only reason she was concentrating so fiercely. She wanted to focus on the job at hand—not what had happened between herself and Michael Bryant.

He'd knocked her off the stool when he'd come into the kitchen. Then he'd caught her before she'd hit the floor.

So far, so good.

The rest of it was what she couldn't wrap her head around. She'd ended up in his arms, and she'd stayed there. The embrace had turned into a kiss.

He'd brought his hand up between them and cupped her breast, rubbed his fingers across her nipple. She should have stopped him. Truth to tell, she hadn't wanted him to stop.

It was only when his foot had crunched on the glass that she'd come to her senses.

What in the name of God was wrong with her? After the first ghost incident, she'd been careful not to let people know the real Chelsea Caldwell until she was sure it was safe. That had cut down on her social life because she came across as guarded in personal relationships. After that she'd withdrawn even further into her work.

That was one reason the B & B was good for her. It forced her to interact with people. She enjoyed it, maybe because she knew the guests would be leaving in a few days and she didn't have to keep up a relationship with them.

Was that what she'd done with Michael Bryant? Subconsciously decided he was "safe"?

Surely not because she trusted him.

Or had she responded on a more base, primal level? He was a handsome, sexy man, and she was a healthy young woman. Well, she'd have to be careful not to let it happen again. And not to be alone with him.

Really, she'd like to tell him to find another B & B in Jenkins Cove. She was even willing to help him do it. But she couldn't let her personal feelings get in the way of Aunt Sophie's business.

After finishing with the glass, she walked over to the stool and looked at the leg. Michael was right. She'd better get rid of it.

The stool had been fine the last time she'd used it, she recalled. What had happened? Had a ghost come into the B & B and broken it?

She tried to laugh, but the sound only grated in her ears.

MICHAEL THOUGHT ABOUT GOING into the first restaurant he came to, but he refused to acknowledge that he was uncomfortable out in the open. He kept walking down the main street of the town. The shops were closed, but all of them were decked out in their holiday best, many with waterman themes. He even saw some ornaments made out of oyster shells or fishermen's nets.

He walked for several blocks until the commercial establishments began to thin out. There was only one more place up ahead of him.

It was called the Duck Blind, and when he walked inside, he found it was an informal bar and restaurant with wood-paneled walls, a plank floor and tables lit by fake stained-glass chandeliers.

It seemed so familiar, so normal after his strange experience on Center Street. He'd started to question his own sanity there for a while. Somehow, though, this eatery helped restore his equilibrium.

He slid onto a stool at the bar and picked up the menu.

After a few moments, another guy came in and took the next stool.

The man was wearing scruffy jeans, work boots and a heavy beige sweater that had several pulls in the knit. His brown hair was a little straggly around the edges. He looked to be in his early thirties, but his hands were rough and weathered. His whole appearance gave the impression that he did some kind of manual labor.

He gave Michael an assessing look. "You're not from around here."

"Right," Michael acknowledged.

"The crab cakes here are good. And they do a good job with the fries."

"Thanks for the tip."

A sad-faced man with thinning salt-and-pepper hair and a short, scraggly matching beard came walking along behind the bar toward them. He was wearing a plaid shirt and a rumpled apron. "What'll you have?"

Michael ordered a cup of coffee, and then the crab cakes, coleslaw and fries.

The man on the next stool got the same thing, with beer instead of coffee. Apparently he wanted company because after the bartender poured a mug of coffee, he said, "Name's Phil Cardon. You here for long?"

"Michael Bryant. I'm taking a few days to visit the area."

"Vacation?"

Michael took a sip of his coffee before he answered. "I'm thinking about setting a novel here."

The man nodded. "Well, there's plenty you could write about."

"That sounds intriguing. Like what?"

The guy downed the rest of his beer and signaled the bartender for another one. Cardon lowered his voice and said, "Like Rufus there. Rufus Shea. His son died thirteen years ago, and he's never gotten over it."

"How did he die?"

"He was murdered. Out in the bog."

"You have a lot of murders around here?" he asked.

The man laughed. "Not so many."

Before Michael could ask another question, the guy launched into a monologue.

"This is a town of real contrasts. You've got your rich people who buy up the prime property. And they're likely to stay here only a few months out of the year. Well, not the Drakes. They live here all year round."

"Who are the Drakes?"

"Brandon Drake and his uncle Clifford. They have a lot of business interests. Shipping. The Drake Yacht Club. Stuff like that. They got offices in town and big houses on the creek. I just did some wallboard repairs for Clifford. A plum job."

"Uh-huh." Michael filed that away.

Rufus Shea came back with the crab cake platters. "Enjoy your meal," he said.

"Thanks."

Michael took a bite. "You're right. This is good."

"Told you," the other diner said. He took another swallow of beer. "People like the Drakes have the cash to pay you. But then there are the watermen who are having a hard time making ends meet now with the fishing industry going down the tubes."

"It is?"

"The crabbing and oyster businesses aren't so good anymore, because the bay's not getting any cleaner."

"Uh-huh."

Phil Cardon dipped a French fry in ketchup, bit off the end and chewed before continuing. "Guys like the Drakes can afford to pay what your work is worth. Not like the bed-and-breakfast owners. They haggle with you 'cause they watch every penny."

"They're not doing well?"

"The tourist industry is the main business in Jenkins Cove, and there's a lot of competition. Where are you staying?"

"The House of the Seven Gables."

He made a whistling sound. "Those two ladies are a little…" Instead of finishing the sentence, he held his hand flat and wiggled it.

"Yeah." Michael laughed. "You think they're just kooks? Or do they have some scam going?"

"The aunt's got some psycho…psycho something up in the attic."

"Psychomanteum," Michael said. "How do you know about it?"

"Everybody does. She showed it to you?"

"Not yet. A lady from town came to contact her dead husband." The handyman snorted.

"You don't believe in ghosts."

"Naw."

Michael considered asking if Cardon had ever felt cold spots in the air or felt as if someone invisible was watching him. He decided to keep that question to himself.

CHELSEA LISTENED FOR THE SOUND of the door. The couple from Baltimore had come in a half hour ago, but Michael Bryant was still out.

There was no reason she should be waiting for him. Especially in light of the scene in the kitchen earlier this evening. She should keep as far away from him as she could get. A little difficult, since he was staying in the same house with her.

She glanced at the clock. It was almost nine. His car was still in the parking lot across the street, which meant he'd walked into town. She wondered what was he doing till nine o'clock. Was he the kind of man who solved problems with drink?

Or had something happened to him? That was a ridiculous assumption, she told herself. Yet she couldn't turn off the nagging feeling of impending doom.

She snorted. Impending doom. That was a pretty strong phrase. Yet since the night of her trip to Tilghman Island, she had felt hypersensitive, tuned to fears and worries that hovered below the surface of her consciousness.

She couldn't turn the sensations off. They lingered with her, much like the feelings she felt in her dreams. Feelings that someone was whispering to her, only she couldn't quite decode the message.

Now, for some reason she couldn't identify, Michael Bryant was part of the equation.

That made no sense. She didn't even know him. Why should she care about him?

Unable to talk herself out of her worry, she kept listening for the sound of the key. After a while, she walked downstairs, intending to sit in the living room. Instead she walked to the front hall and stared out the sidelight, watching the street.

No, watching for Michael Bryant.

"WHAT DO YOU THINK about the niece? Chelsea," Michael asked his dinner companion.

"She's pretty."

"Yeah."

"I'd ask her out, only she keeps to herself."

"Oh?" That hadn't exactly been Michael's experience. She'd been more than willing in the kitchen a while ago. Not that he would share that experience with a casual dinner companion.

Instead he said, "The aunt says Chelsea saw a ghost."

"More than one, the way I hear it."

"Yeah," Michael answered again. "But you think it's a bunch of crap."

A strange expression crossed Phil's face. "I do," he said, but he didn't sound perfectly sure.

The guy looked around as if he wondered who had been listening to the conversation.

"I'm talking too much," Phil said.

"Of course not."

He climbed off the bar stool, reached in his pocket and got out some bills, which he left on the counter. Then he turned and walked to the door, weaving a little, and Michael wondered what Phil had really wanted to say.

Rufus Shea came back, presumably to clear the plate away. He stopped and rubbed a hand against his scraggly beard. "I guess Phil was giving you an earful about Jenkins Cove."

"Yeah."

"People around here tend to be opinionated."

"I'm finding that out."

He wondered how much of the conversation Shea had heard—like the part about his son dying.

"Phil was bragging about working for the Drakes," Shea said.

"Mmm-hmm."

"They're the big cheeses here in town. Of course, since Brandon's wife died, he's kept mostly to himself. He was hurt bad in the accident."

"She was killed in an accident?"

"Car accident."

Maybe Brandon Drake would show up at the House of the Seven Gables to try and contact his dead wife through the psychomanteum. Or maybe he already had.

In the short time he'd been here, it felt as if all roads in Jenkins Cove led back to death—murder or accidental.

Chapter Six

Michael walked back the way he'd come. The Christmas lights still gave the shops along Main Street and in the town square a festive air.

Maybe he was avoiding going back to the B & B, but he kept walking through the shopping area, past the turnoff that would take him directly back to the House of the Seven Gables.

Finally, when he was on his way out of town, he turned around and took Carpenter, heading toward the town dock.

Once he left the shopping area, he realized he had his ears tuned for any unusual sounds. Did he hear footsteps behind him? He stopped and listened intently. If anyone was there, they stopped, too.

Had someone followed him from the Duck Blind, or even from the House of the Seven Gables? That would make more sense than ghosts hiding in the bushes. Well, more sense if you were trying to fit this evening into the pattern of reality.

But who would have a reason to be checking up on him?

He didn't know.

Could it be someone with an interest in the B & B? Like that real-estate guy, Ned Perry, who had come into the kitchen?

But what would he want with one of the guests?

As Michael turned over the possibilities in his mind, he

found that he was walking faster than usual. When he realized what he was doing, he deliberately slowed his pace. No way was he going to let a ghost or anyone else chase him.

A ghost. Good Lord, was he really starting to think in those terms? Was the atmosphere of Jenkins Cove turning his mind to mush?

He gritted his teeth. If he was being honest with himself, he'd have to admit that somehow Jenkins Cove was affecting him in ways that he couldn't figure out. It was as if he'd crossed some invisible barrier into a world where the laws of the universe were different—and unpredictable.

Even as the thought surfaced in his mind, he scoffed at it. He'd been in some of the world's real hellholes. He wasn't going to let this small town on the Eastern Shore of Maryland get to him. More important, he was not going to leave until he'd accomplished his mission.

CHELSEA PUT ON HER COAT and stepped out the back door. She wasn't sure what she was doing out here. She just had the feeling that she should be outside.

Then, from where she stood on the back porch, she saw a figure walking along Carpenter Street. A man. As she stared at him, she was sure it was Michael Bryant.

Finally.

A little speech played through her mind. She wanted to tell him that she was worried about him. That he should have told her if he was going to come in so late. And he should be coming straight back to the House of the Seven Gables. He shouldn't be making a detour to the dock area.

Then she told herself those thoughts were so out of bounds that they shouldn't even have surfaced in her head.

She wasn't his wife.

Lord, where had that come from?

He didn't owe her any explanations. Just because she'd fallen into his arms and kissed him didn't mean that they had a relationship.

She was about to go back inside when she saw a little gust of wind hit him as he walked across the bridge toward the dock.

He lurched unsteadily. Then she saw headlights barreling up the street in back of him, the car moving much too fast as it approached the bridge.

It looked as though Michael didn't know the car was there, maybe because the wind had picked up.

But the vehicle was heading right for him.

She found herself running and shouting at the same time, "Michael. Watch out! Michael."

He glanced up and must have caught the twin beams streaming past him.

Luckily his reflexes were good. The speeding car was only inches from him when he jumped out of the way. But he was already so close to the edge of the little creek that when he jumped, there was nowhere to go but into the brackish water.

"Michael!" she shouted again, hurtling down the path toward the creek that separated the B & B from the dock. From the corner of her eye she saw the car careen along the lane, then turn and head back toward Main Street. But she wasn't focused on that.

The man in the water was her main concern. The creek probably wasn't deep. But it was lined with rocks to keep the banks from eroding, and if he'd hit his head when he went over the side, he could be in trouble.

"Michael, are you all right?" She couldn't see him, and she wished she had a flashlight.

When he didn't answer, her heart leaped into her throat. Then she heard a splash followed by a scrambling noise. As she climbed down the rocks, she saw a figure climbing up.

She waved, then reached out her hand. "Michael. Over here, Michael. Thank God."

Grasping a large rock with one hand, she leaned over and reached down with the other.

His fingers fumbled for hers. Then they locked on, and he hauled himself up.

In soaking-wet clothes, he weighed a ton, but in the light from the dock area, she saw that he'd managed to keep his head out of the water.

When he reached the edge of the pavement, he wavered on unsteady legs.

Chelsea grabbed his arm. "Are you all right?"

"Yeah," Michael answered. "If you don't count wet and cold." He looked in the direction where the car had vanished. "Is that a street?"

"Not one that's used very often."

"I don't suppose you got the license number?"

"Sorry. I was looking at you—not the car."

Michael's teeth started to chatter.

"You have to get inside," Chelsea said.

He looked at her, registering the fact that she'd been outside. "What were you doing out here?"

"I go for walks."

The explanation sounded lame, but he wasn't going to call her on it—not when she'd probably saved his life with her warning. "Lucky for me that you saw the car."

"Come on inside." She tugged on his arm, leading him toward the house, and he didn't resist. He needed to get out of the elements.

"Do people around here usually drive like that?" he asked.

"Not usually. Maybe it was a tourist."

"From my point of view, it looked like someone was deliberately trying to run me over."

She winced, craning her neck back toward the turnoff where the car had disappeared.

"Why would someone try to run you down? Do you have enemies?" she asked.

"Not that I know of. And certainly not in Jenkins Cove. I just got here." He tipped his head to the side. "Is this a dangerous town?"

"I didn't think so. Until the murder," she clipped out as she marched steadily toward the house.

She stepped onto the screened porch, and he followed her into the kitchen, dripping on the tile floor.

She eyed him critically. "You need to take off your clothes."

He managed to laugh. "Is that an invitation?"

"Very funny." She gave him an annoyed look. "I have some of those white bathrobes we give guests."

She walked into a laundry room off the kitchen, then emerged with a robe. "Get undressed in there. And leave the clothes. I'll wash them."

"The jacket's got to go to the cleaner's, I think."

He stepped into the laundry room, closed the door behind him and took everything off—except his wet briefs because he didn't want to leave her his underwear. Then he put on the robe and got his damp wallet, keys and change out of his pockets.

He was feeling awkward when he came back to the kitchen, but she was very matter-of-fact as she handed him a steaming mug. "Hot chocolate."

"Thanks." He took a sip. "This is good."

"And it will warm you up." As she said that, she looked away, and he knew she was sharing the awkward feeling.

"I hate to put you to any trouble," he mumbled.

"I have to do a load of wash anyway."

"I left my shoes over by the door."

"That's fine."

"You should get into bed. Get warm."

"Yeah," he answered, thinking that every word that came out of her mouth seemed to have a double meaning, although she probably didn't intend it that way. "Thanks for being there. I'll see you at breakfast."

"Maybe not."

"Oh?"

"We have a woman from town who helps us. I'm probably going to be in my studio." She walked toward the front of the house; he followed, the mug warming his hands.

She hurried toward the stairs, leaving before he could think of anything else to say to keep her there.

They still hadn't resolved the kiss in the kitchen. Now it looked as if they weren't going to get a chance to talk in the morning, either.

He set down the mug on a hall table and let himself into his room. He'd been going to check his e-mail. Instead he took everything out of his wallet and set the damp leather on the shelf above the radiator. Then he washed off the creek water in the shower before climbing under the covers.

Taking a sip of the hot chocolate, he replayed the incident with the car. Had someone really tried to kill him? Or had it been an accident? Maybe a drunken tourist driving along the dock.

He went over it again and again in his mind. But the only conclusion he could come to was that he'd been damn lucky Chelsea had been outside.

He was tired, but he had trouble getting to sleep. He tossed and turned most of the night, then finally fell asleep just before dawn.

He slept until nine, barely giving him time to make the breakfast hours at the B & B.

True to her word, Chelsea wasn't there. But her helper, who introduced herself as Barbara, had apparently been waiting for him. She handed him his shirt and pants, freshly washed.

"Thank you. Thank Chelsea for me."

"Certainly. We put your shoes on the radiator. They're dry, too."

"Yeah. I did the same with my wallet." He took the clothing back to his room. When he returned, he poured himself a cup of coffee from the sideboard, then ate a piece of quiche along with a blueberry muffin.

Neither of the Caldwells showed up while he was there, so he put on a heavy sweater and walked to the dry cleaner's, where he left his jacket. They had an expensive four-hour service, so he'd be able to get the jacket before the evening chill.

Next he went back to the dock. With a small digital camera, he snapped some pictures where he'd gone into the water. Then he took more pictures along Center Street and Main Street, which was bustling with tourists.

In some of the shops, he pretended he was interested in local souvenirs like duck decoys, little lighthouses and books on the waterman's way of life. He also managed to start conversations about the woman who had seen the ghost.

He didn't find anyone who hadn't read the story in the paper or heard about it.

"So, what do you think?" he asked a gray-haired woman who ran a candy shop.

She gave him a narrow-eyed look. "I think it's bad for business. There are fewer tourists here than in the past couple of years."

"But she had to report the murder," he argued, finding himself suddenly defending Chelsea.

The woman shuddered. "Yes, but she should have kept ghosts out of it. Murder is bad enough. Ghosts just make it worse."

Michael left with a bag of hard candies, wondering about his motives. Was he being objective or merely looking to bolster his case against Chelsea?

As he stepped onto the street again, the back of his neck tingled. Apparently that was going to be a regular occurrence as long as he was in town. Casually, he stopped to look in the window of a real-estate company. Using the reflection of the glass, he tried to see if someone was following him. But the street was crowded, and he couldn't pick out anyone in particular, even when he walked all the way down the block, pausing frequently to surreptitiously look behind him.

After crossing the street, he wandered into the Chesapeake Gallery, where he stopped short when he saw a painting he recognized. He'd seen it on Chelsea's Web site. It was a landscape scene that he assumed was near Jenkins Cove. He saw a marsh with cattails and a mist rising from the ground. In the background was a grand house with balconies and multiple chimneys.

A small woman with dyed black hair noticed his interest. "That's by Chelsea Caldwell, one of our local artists."

"It's very evocative," he allowed. "Is that a real house?"

"The Drake mansion."

"Um."

The Drakes again. He'd heard about them last night from that guy in the Duck Blind—Phil Cardon. Maybe they were like the local nobility.

He wondered if the house was really in back of a marsh, or if she'd moved elements around to create the effect she wanted.

When the woman asked if he was interested in buying the painting, he disappointed her by saying that he wasn't going to purchase anything until the end of his stay in town.

He walked around the gallery and saw several more paintings by Chelsea. New works, he assumed, since they hadn't been on the Web site. She was good. He could see why she'd done well in Baltimore. He hoped she sold as well in Jenkins Cove.

That thought brought him up short. He kept letting his feelings interfere with business.

It happened again when he returned to the B & B, hoping to

see Chelsea. When she wasn't anywhere around, he fought a stab of disappointment.

He could have made himself comfortable in the living room. Instead he got in his car and drove to the approximate location of the murder. Pulling onto the shoulder, he climbed out and snapped some more pictures.

Keeping busy, he returned to town and found the owner of a fishing boat who was willing to take him for a ride and point out local landmarks. Some creek, he thought. It was almost a hundred yards wide.

He snapped pictures of the Drake estates, both of which were on the bay, separated by a spit of land. One of them was definitely the house he'd seen in the painting.

From the fisherman, he found out that it was Brandon's house in the painting. So, was Chelsea friends with the local nobility?

Chelsea. He kept coming back to her. Even when he wasn't asking questions about the lady who'd seen the ghost.

Thinking that he was acting like a teenager with a crush, he deliberately walked in the other direction. After picking up his jacket at the dry cleaner's, he had an early dinner that kept him away from the B & B during the wine and cheese hour.

It was dark by the time he came back, and nobody was on the first floor. He returned to his room, got out his laptop and uploaded the pictures he'd taken, then settled back to look at a slide show.

The first two images seemed normal, but he got a jolt when he clicked on the third one, a view along Center Street. While the previous scenes had looked bright and sunny, in this one, mist seemed to hang over the area. The same mist that he hadn't seen when he'd been out for his walk.

A chill skittered along his nerve endings. It was as if he'd captured something strange in the atmosphere of Jenkins Cove.

He paged rapidly through the rest of the innocuous pictures

he'd taken until he got to the one taken in the swampy area where Chelsea had seen the murder. There again he found the same kind of foggy patches that he'd encountered on the Center Street image.

What was he seeing? Some trick of the light? An atmospheric disturbance that was only apparent on a digital image?

Or was there something wrong with his camera? Would he get the same kinds of distortions with a camera that used film?

He spent a long time studying the images, feeling stranger and stranger as he did so.

Finally he turned off the computer and spent another restless night. His dreams were filled with foggy images and Chelsea.

Chapter Seven

When Michael got up the next morning, he felt fairly certain that Chelsea was avoiding him. He had to change that. Because he wanted to get her to tell him ghost stories…or because he just wanted to see her?

In the dining room Sophie greeted him warmly. "How are you enjoying your stay in Jenkins Cove?"

"Fine." He poured himself a cup of coffee from the sideboard, then brought it to the table that had been set for him with silver, china and a basket of freshly baked muffins.

"Where's Chelsea?" he asked as he unfolded his napkin.

Aunt Sophie answered in a chipper voice. "She's been anxious to get a painting finished. She's up in her studio."

She bustled out of the room and returned with a slice of cheese frittata, bacon and cubes of cantaloupe.

As soon as he'd finished eating, Sophie came back into the dining room, and he wondered if she had been waiting for him to leave so she could clean up.

Instead she said, "I can take you up to see her studio, if you'd like."

He thought about that for a moment. Chelsea probably wouldn't appreciate his barging in. If her aunt were with him, however, she couldn't complain.

"I'd like that," he answered.

Sophie led him to the third floor of the B & B. Several closed doors lined the hallway.

A sudden thought struck him, and he asked, "Is the psychomanteum up here?"

"Why, yes. Would you like to see it?" She sounded delighted that he'd mentioned her pet project, and he was suddenly on the alert, wondering if she was going to try and sell him shares or something.

"Okay," he answered guardedly.

She gave him an encouraging smile. "I won't leave you in there."

"You think I'm afraid to stay by myself?" he snapped, then was sorry he'd let his tension get the better of him.

"Some people are."

"Well, I'm not," he said firmly, sounding to his own ears like a little kid proclaiming he wasn't afraid to enter a haunted house.

"Jenkins Cove is noted for psychic phenomena," she said.

"Why?"

"Because we have such a long history. This was one of the first places settled in Maryland, due to our many rivers and creeks. In colonial times, water was the easiest way to get around."

"The town didn't grow much," he said.

"That's because we're isolated from the mainland by the Chesapeake Bay. The water that was an advantage in the early days turned out to be just the opposite as people moved farther west."

Sophie opened a door and switched on a light, then stepped into a room that was bathed in black. It emitted an eerie feel. The ceiling was painted black, the walls were hung with black curtains and a dark carpet covered the floor. In the middle of the room sat a chair facing an enormous rectangular mirror framed in ornate gold. It leaned against one of the side walls. Various antique chests and small tables decorated the room, all of them decked out with pillar candles and slender tapers in elaborate candelabra.

Aunt Sophie saw him eyeing them. "You have no idea how hard it is to get unscented candles," she said. "I don't want this place smelling like vanilla or cinnamon or something like that. So I started making them myself. Then I did get into the scented ones for downstairs."

"Right," he murmured. His gaze flicked to the heavy mirror and the curtains. "Who set this up?"

"I did. Well, it's all my idea, but I hired Phil Cardon to paint the ceiling, hang the curtain rods and carry the mirror up here. I sewed the curtains myself," she added proudly.

Suddenly, the fixture in the ceiling dimmed. With the black curtains and paint, the room became much darker—and spookier. He jerked around to see Sophie working a dimmer switch.

"People who use the room adjust the light the way it's most comfortable for them," she said.

"Uh-huh. Do people really communicate with ghosts in here?"

"Yes."

"How do they know?"

"The spirits speak to them."

"How do they know it's not their imaginations working overtime?"

"They have faith." She dragged in a breath and let it out. "I've spoken to my sister in here. She died fifty years ago."

"How do you know it was her?"

"She told me things that only the two of us would remember."

He could have argued that the conversation was coming from Sophie's imagination, but he didn't want to challenge her. If it made her happy to think she had spoken to her sister, that was okay by him. Just so she didn't have a microphone in here where she pretended to be speaking for the dead. Yeah, he'd better check on that.

"If you want to have a session, just let me know."

"I don't know any of the ghosts around here."

"Well, the spirit world has no physical boundaries."

It would be a cold day in hell before he took her up on the offer to contact the dead.

When they stepped back into the hall, he immediately felt some of the tightness go out of his throat. "Chelsea's studio is down the hall," she said.

Instantly the tightness was back, but for a different reason. He was going to see Chelsea again for the first time since he'd stood in the kitchen in a borrowed bathrobe.

Sophie led the way to the opposite end of the house where the hall turned a corner.

As they stepped to their right, light flooded in through a huge window with a half transom addition above the rectangular section.

It took a moment for his eyes to adjust to the brightness. When they did, he could see Chelsea in a room right in front of them. She was standing at an easel, dabbing paint on a canvas. An artist's pallet sat on a tall narrow table beside her.

When she looked up and registered their presence, her eyes widened in shock. Was she thinking she could avoid him? Or was it unusual for her aunt to bring a guest into her private space?

"What…what are you doing here?" she asked, her gaze accusing him of stepping over an invisible boundary.

He kept his tone neutral. "Your aunt offered to show me your studio, and I took her up on it."

She regarded him for several heartbeats, then gave Sophie an annoyed look. "I'm supposed to be working. You know I like my private time."

"Of course. But Mr. Bryant seemed so interested," Sophie said with enthusiasm.

"Can I see what you're painting?" he asked.

Her mouth tightened.

"I'd like to see it, too," Sophie said.

When Chelsea gave a little shrug and stepped back, Michael and Sophie took up positions in front of the painting.

The canvas showed downtown Jenkins Cove on a winter evening, with all the shops decked out for the holidays. It was very much like the way the street had looked when he'd walked down to the Duck Blind, only in the painting, snow was lightly falling, dusting the road and shops.

"It's very good. Charming," he said, meaning it. "I love the way you've done the lights. They seem to glow."

She looked at him as if to determine whether he was sincere.

"Chelsea is donating it to a charity auction," Sophie said. "That's why she's in a hurry—so it can dry in time for the big Christmas party."

"I'm about finished," Chelsea said.

"Mmm-hum." What was it about these women that reduced him to such replies? Casting around for something else to say, he asked, "Where do you get your ideas for paintings?"

She gave him a strange look. "People ask me that all the time. But I wouldn't expect the question from you."

"Why not?"

"Because you're a writer. Where do you get *your* ideas?"

He flushed. "Right. But ideas for books are different."

"Why?"

He fumbled for an answer. "You're working in a visual medium. I'm not. Each painting you do is like a snapshot. You don't get to show any progression."

"Sometimes I do, like when I paint the same scene at different times of the day or different seasons."

"True."

Sophie leaped into the conversation. "I showed Mr. Bryant the psychomanteum."

Chelsea's head snapped toward her aunt. "And he thought it was a waste of time," she guessed.

"I think he sees it as artificial," the aunt answered before Michael could give his own opinion. Changing the subject completely, she said, "I think you should take advantage of the nice weather. Take him to the old warehouse down by Smugglers Bend where he can experience something real."

Chelsea blinked. "Why?"

"Because it's supposed to be haunted. It's something real, not a room that an old lady set up. He can see if he picks up any vibrations."

"Is that a challenge?" Michael asked.

"Yes," Sophie answered.

"Why don't *you* take him?" Chelsea suggested.

"I have some baking to do. And, of course, I'm not as spry as I used to be. It's a trip best undertaken by young people."

"I can go on my own," Michael said, glancing at Chelsea and then away.

"You'll never find it," she was quick to answer, and then her face contorted as she probably realized that she'd basically offered to take him.

"Let's go," Michael said, before she figured out an excuse to change her mind.

She looked as though she wanted to protest, but apparently she wasn't going to be rude to a guest in front of her aunt. With a little sigh, she took off the smock she was wearing over her shirt and jeans, then went to the sink in the corner and washed her hands.

As they all started downstairs, she asked, "You really want to go to the warehouse?"

"Aunt Sophie thinks it will be good for me."

"You catch on real quick, young man," the woman in question answered.

When they descended to the first floor, Michael went to get

his jacket and his camera. Chelsea was waiting for him when he came back to the front hall.

She eyed the jacket, which looked a lot better than it had after his dunk in the creek. "You stopped at the dry cleaner's?" she asked.

"Uh-huh. The coat's as good as new."

She gave him a long look, the first halfway friendly gesture of the morning. "And you're okay?" she asked softly.

"Yes."

"Good."

They climbed into her small car. "I never did actually thank you for saving my life."

"No problem."

"Maybe not for you. But it made a great deal of difference to me."

He saw that she couldn't quite suppress a grin.

As THE WATCHER SAW THE PAIR exit the House of the Seven Gables, he pressed back into the shadows of the storage shed.

Michael Bryant and Chelsea Caldwell together.

Very interesting.

What were they up to now?

He'd thought he could simplify his job by running down Bryant on his way back from the Duck Blind the other night. But Chelsea had saved him.

Since Bryant had come to town, the guy had been asking a lot of questions. Mainly about ghosts. But that might not be his main interest.

Was he really an investigative reporter…or was he an under-cover cop or a private eye?

The sooner Bryant left Jenkins Cove, the better—either under his own power, or on a stretcher headed for the medical examiner. Either way was absolutely fine.

But right now the two of them were up to something.

When Chelsea pulled out of her parking spot, the watcher walked back to his own vehicle, which was over at the other side of the town parking lot. He didn't need to keep them in sight. He'd already put a transponder on Chelsea's car. And on Bryant's, too.

So all he had to do was turn on his GPS, and he could follow at a discreet distance.

MICHAEL MIGHT have gotten Chelsea to grin, but now that they were in her car, he could have cut the silence with a knife. As they turned onto Main Street, he heard himself say, "You've been avoiding me."

"Don't you think that's the best policy?" she snapped.

"I don't know."

"I don't usually end up in clinches with men I barely know," she said.

Keeping his voice light, he answered, "I thought that getting me to move out of the path of a speeding car showed you cared."

"That was just common courtesy."

"Okay." After another few minutes of silence he said, "I'm only going to be here for a few more days."

"Are you suggesting that we have a fling while you're in town?" she asked, her voice tight.

"Come on. That's not what I said at all. I just think we should try to get along with each other."

She nodded.

"So, have you lived in Jenkins Cove all your life?" he asked.

She glanced at him, then turned back to the road. "I grew up in Baltimore."

"How did you start painting?"

"I always liked to do it. My parents left me some money— enough to live on for a few years while I established my career."

"Your parents are dead? I'm sorry."

"Losing them was hard. But it made me self-sufficient."

"Yeah. My dad died when I was little. My mom wasn't so great at coping."

"I'm sorry." She paused, then commented, "So I take it you didn't have a happy childhood."

"No. We didn't have a lot of money. And my mom didn't spend it wisely." He heard the tightness in his voice. "What about your childhood?"

She shrugged. "It was pretty typical."

Except for seeing a ghost, he thought.

"So why did you agree to take me to the old warehouse?" he asked.

"The place has always had a bad reputation. I want to find out why. And I don't want to go alone."

"You're trying to prove something to yourself?"

"Maybe. Are you?"

"Maybe," he admitted.

"Were you trying to prove something by going into the psychomanteum?"

"I was curious."

"Uh-huh."

"People really think they've communicated with loved ones?" he asked.

"Yes."

"Do you think it's true?"

"I don't know."

He didn't press his luck by asking about her personal experiences with ghosts. He'd come to Jenkins Cove prepared to interrogate her. Since arriving, he'd been having a lot of second thoughts.

She wasn't what he'd expected at all, and he was struggling to adjust his thinking.

They drove along the highway toward Tilghman Island. A few miles outside town, Chelsea slowed, then turned right onto a one-lane gravel road.

It was an isolated location. Trees grew close on either side, and he saw there were places where the ends of branches had been hit. "The warehouse is not used?"

"That's right."

"But someone has been down here."

"How do you know?"

"A vehicle lopped off the ends of some branches."

"Maybe it was teenagers looking for a deserted place to have—" She stopped before she said the word *sex*. "You know what I mean."

She clamped her hands on the wheel, and he had the feeling she wished she hadn't brought up the topic.

"I thought that this place had a bad reputation," he said.

"Kids would ignore it."

He wasn't so sure, but he wasn't going to argue with her. The road took a bend, and when they emerged from the foliage, he saw the blue gleam of water in the sunlight and a building ahead of them. It was constructed of weathered wood, with some of the boards missing on the sides. From what he could see, it was partly on land and partly sticking into the cattails that lined the shore.

She drove up to a weed-strewn parking area and cut the engine.

They were facing a wide doorway, covered by a sliding door.

Michael eyed the building. "This place is pretty run-down. What was it used for?"

"Fifty years ago, it was a shipping depot and a warehouse. But there's not much direct shipping to Jenkins Cove anymore."

They climbed out, and he slipped his hands into his pockets as they stood facing the building, bracing against the wind that had sprung up.

This was just a run-down warehouse, he told himself, yet he couldn't shake the feeling that there was something more here. When he glanced at Chelsea, he saw that she had her arms wrapped around her shoulders. So either she, too, was reacting to the place, or she was reacting to being alone with him.

"I want to see what's inside," he said.

She gave him a startled look, and he saw her swallow. "Okay."

The sun had gone behind a cloud, and wind buffeted them as they walked toward the double doors.

"Is it safe to go in there?" he asked.

"I guess we'll find out." She marched up to the door and gave it a tug. Nothing happened.

"It's probably rusty." He stepped to the barrier and pulled on the handle. The door gave a little, and when he kept up the pressure, it rolled to the side.

The interior was mostly in shadow, although there were patches of weak sunlight shining through.

For long seconds, neither of them moved, and he felt his nerves jumping.

"There's something in there," Chelsea whispered.

"What?"

"I don't know."

"Let's find out."

"No." She grabbed his arm, but he pulled away and took a step forward, then another.

He didn't turn, but he heard Chelsea following him.

The floor of the old building was made of cracked cement, with a few hardy weeds growing up through the cracks.

Something on the floor glinted in the sunlight, and he walked forward to see what it was.

As he reached the center of the room, a white and gray cloud of whirring, flapping ghosts came rushing toward them.

Chelsea gasped. Michael caught her in his arms, covering her head with one of his hands as a flock of seabirds flapped around the interior, then found their way out through the holes in the roof.

The large room was suddenly silent again. But everything had changed in the space of a heartbeat. Once again, he was holding Chelsea in his arms. And once again, he marveled at how good that felt.

He murmured her name, and she raised her head. Their eyes met, and he silently asked her the question.

"Don't," she whispered. "Don't kiss me."

He ached to cover her mouth with his, but he wouldn't go against her wishes. Still, he kept his arms around her. "Why not?" Male arrogance had him adding, "We both want to."

"Yes," she acknowledged. "But not here. They're watching."

He looked around. "There's nobody here."

"Can't you sense it?" she asked in a hushed voice.

He stood very still, feeling the beating of his own heart and imagining he could feel hers, too. Above that rhythm of life, he detected something else.

The air in this place was thick. Not with dust or any kind of man-made particles. It was thick with a kind of energy that seemed to swirl around him and press in against him, making it hard to breathe.

Like the night he'd walked along Center Street, he felt a coldness in the air.

He could explain that part, though. In here, the roof of the building was keeping out the sun, so naturally it was colder.

"The air," Chelsea whispered. "It's cold and thick. And there are voices."

"Voices?"

"Don't you hear them?"

He went very still, listening. He thought he heard the whispering of the wind, but that was all.

"What are they saying?" he asked.

"I don't know. Not for sure. But it's important."

The sounds around him had taken on an urgency. Then, once again, he tried to put down the uneasy feelings to his overactive imagination.

He dragged in a breath and caught a faint odor wafting toward him. The odor of unwashed bodies. Or was his imagination working overtime again?

Chelsea had turned into him, burying her face against his chest.

He stroked his hands over her back and shoulders, comforting her and drawing comfort in return.

When he felt her shiver, he clasped her more tightly.

"It's okay," he said, not actually sure what he meant. All right to hear the whispering voices? Or all right to dismiss them?

"I can't stay in here any longer."

He nodded, unwilling to voice his agreement. "Give me a second."

"What?"

He stepped away from her, then strode to the place where he'd seen something on the floor. Stooping, he picked up a shiny piece of metal. A woman's earring.

"Someone was here," he said.

"Kids," she said again, but she didn't sound perfectly sure.

He'd brought his camera. Pulling it out of his pocket, he snapped several pictures, wondering if they'd come out like the strange ones from his trip around town.

He didn't tell Chelsea about those, as he slung his arm around her again and led her back toward the door.

They stepped into the open air, and he took a deep breath. A dark cloud had slid across the sun, so that the adjustment from the gloom wasn't as sharp as it would have been.

That was probably why Michael saw a flash of movement in the bushes. And then a figure was running away from the warehouse.

"Stay here," he shouted, calling the order over his shoulder as he took off after the fleeing figure.

"Come back!"

"I'll be okay." As he ran, he tried to see where the watcher had gone.

It had looked like a man, but he couldn't be sure. Michael headed for the spot where the guy had disappeared into a screen of vegetation. No one was there, but the weeds at the side of a pine tree were crushed down, as though someone had been standing there.

He thought he detected a path someone had made through the underbrush. He followed it, trying to catch up with whoever had been watching them.

Then he stepped on a patch of ground that gave way under his feet—and he was falling into blackness.

Chapter Eight

Chelsea heard Michael call out. It sounded as though he was in trouble.

With her heart blocking her windpipe, she went dashing into the woods, heading for the place where he'd disappeared into the underbrush.

She heard him shouting at her, but she couldn't see him.

"Chelsea. Stay back."

She stopped in her tracks, her heart pounding. "Michael, where are you?"

"I fell into a trap. Watch out."

She sucked in a sharp breath. "Where?"

"Over here. Be careful. There could be more of them."

"I can't see you. Keep talking to me. Are you all right?"

He hesitated for a moment. "Yes."

"You're not sure."

"Nothing major."

Her stomach knotted. Was he lying to her? She wasn't going to find out until she got to him.

"Keep talking."

"I'm below ground level. So be careful not to fall into a trap—" His breath caught.

"What?"

"That guy. He could still be here."

She stopped short, wanting to protest. But he was right. "What should I do?" she called in a harsh whisper.

"Get out of here."

"No."

She scanned the woods. Someone could leap out of the bushes at any time, yet she couldn't leave Michael. It sounded as though he was hurt. And if the guy came back, he'd be a sitting duck.

She waited for several moments. It seemed as though they were alone. Of course, the man could simply be waiting to grab her. But if so, why hadn't he already done it?

She'd figured out Michael's approximate location. Following a narrow trail, she kept walking until she came to a place where she saw a mat of leaves on the ground and a ragged hole at one side.

Creeping closer, she went down on her hands and knees and peered into the pit. Michael was at the bottom, looking up at her.

"Are you all right?" she asked.

"I whacked my knee on the way down. No big deal."

"Can you climb out?"

"Not on my own. The wall crumbles when I grab it."

"What do you want me to do?"

"I don't suppose you carry rope in your car."

"No."

He sighed. "See if you can find a fallen branch. Something I can use to pull myself up."

She stepped away, surveying the area, and saw that the covering of the pit was partially made of pine boughs. "Maybe we can use these," she said. As she spoke she reached out to grasp one of the branches and almost lost her balance.

"Watch out," Michael shouted.

"I am." This time she was more cautious, tugging on the end

of a branch and pulling it toward her. It slid forward, and she maneuvered it over the hole where he could see it.

"Will that work?" she asked.

"I hope so. Can you turn it the other way, so the branches are facing upward?"

"Yes." She eased it down into the pit, then tugged at another branch, which she lowered to Michael.

He arranged the two branches, propping them against the wall of earth. Then he looked up at her. "Better stand back. I'm going to do this fast."

She took a step back, watching as he tested the horizontal branches sticking out from the main bough. Then he began to scramble upward, using the two sets of limbs as a ladder.

He had almost made it to the top when she heard a crack and saw him drop back down. Leaping forward, she reached over the edge and grabbed his jacket, pulling upward.

She wouldn't have been able to hold him up by herself. But he must have still had one foot on a branch, and her grip was enough to keep him from falling back into the pit. He plowed ahead, practically leaping the last few feet so that they tumbled together onto the ground.

Michael landed atop her, panting and wincing.

"Are you okay?"

"The damn knee. Did I hurt you?"

"No."

He rolled to his side and looked into her eyes. "That's the second time you saved me. I mean, if you hadn't been here, I would have been stuck in that trap until whoever dug it and covered the pine boughs with brush came back to see what he caught."

She winced, alarm written on her features as she stared at him. Lifting her hand, she touched his cheek.

That touch, and the look in her eyes, undid him.

Without giving her time to protest, he leaned forward,

finding her mouth with his. The kiss was a celebration. Celebration that he'd made it out of the pit, and that she was here in his arms.

He turned his head first one way and then the other, devouring her with an urgency that no longer surprised him.

No matter why he had come to Jenkins Cove, no matter what he had started out thinking about her, everything had changed.

He had assumed she was running some kind of scam. Or at the very least, trying to make herself seem important. But nothing could be further from the truth. She was so totally open and honest that the knowledge made his guts ache.

She could have walked away from him a few minutes ago. Instead she'd almost tumbled into the trap as she tried to help him get out.

That was the kind of person she was. If she thought she'd seen a ghost, then that was what she truly thought. He still didn't know if he believed in phantoms, but he understood that strange things had been happening to him since he'd arrived in Jenkins Cove. Things that he couldn't explain in any of the rational terms that he'd used all his life.

Falling for her was no exception. He'd never let a woman sweep him off his feet. But it had happened with Chelsea Caldwell. And it had happened totally against his will.

He kissed her with an urgency that might have surprised him, except that he had given up fighting what he was feeling. He hadn't known her long, and maybe the realization that he had been unfair to her fueled his need. He wanted to apologize. But there was nothing he could say without getting himself into deep trouble. He could only show her what he was feeling.

So he devoured her mouth, using his lips and teeth and tongue. He slipped his hands under her coat, moving them restlessly over her as he drank in her sweetness.

He felt her breathing accelerate. Felt her move her body restlessly against his, wordlessly telling him that they were in perfect harmony.

Flames leaped inside him. Flames that threatened to consume him. He wanted her with an urgency that took his breath away. With an unsteady hand, he pushed her coat out of the way, so that he could cup her breast through her shirt and slide his hand back and forth across the hardened tip while he nibbled at her jaw, then the slender column of her neck and her collarbone.

She tasted wonderful. Felt wonderful. He knew he had been aching to do this since he'd kissed her in the kitchen.

"Michael," she murmured, her hands just as restless as she ran her fingers through his hair, then under his coat and shirt so that she could stroke his ribs, his back. Her intimate touch almost sent him over the edge.

Though they were racing rapidly toward the point of no return, he allowed himself to revel in the heat of their passion for a only few moments longer. Then he lifted his mouth and forced himself to put a few inches of air between them.

Her eyes had been closed. They blinked open, and she stared at him, looking dazed and confused. That look tore at him.

"Michael?"

"I'm taking advantage of you," he said, hearing the raw sound of his own voice.

"No."

"We've only known each other for a few days. This is going too fast—for you." Her wounded look made him gather her close. "I want you," he whispered. "More than I've ever wanted any other woman. But I'm not going to make love to you out here in the woods. Certainly not when someone could be out there watching or coming back."

Her sudden look of alarm made his insides twist.

"You're right. What was I thinking?" She sat up and glanced around as though she expected someone to leap out of the bushes.

He sat up, as well, then stood, testing his knee and wincing. "Michael!"

"I just need some ice to keep it from swelling up."

"Which we won't get here. We'd better go home."

"Yeah. But first…" He pulled her into his arms again, sliding his hands down her body, cupping her bottom so that he could press her against his erection. He needed to feel her there. And he needed her to feel what she had done to him.

"I'm going to make love to you," he said in a gritty voice. "That's a promise. But not until you know me better. I'm not going to sweep you along on a tide of passion. I want you to make a conscious decision about what we're doing."

She tipped her head back, staring up at him. "Did I have the misfortune to get tangled up with a gentleman?"

"I hope so," he muttered, feeling the weight of the confession he should make to her. But not yet. Not until he had time to think about what he was going to say.

She reached to stroke back the lock of hair that had fallen across his forehead. "I think I can cope with that."

"Good." He knitted his fingers with hers and started back the way they'd come, trying not to limp.

And as he walked, he scanned the ground and woods around them, watching for sudden movement and for more traps. There were none on the way back to the parking area.

As they stood beside the car, she gave him a critical inspection. "Your jacket's dirty."

"Back to the cleaner's."

The comment made her frown. "What's happening? I mean— first the murder, then someone tried to run you over and now this."

He felt his face harden. "I don't know. I saw someone watching us, and I'm going to find out who it is."

"Not a ghost," she whispered.

He looked back over his shoulder. "A ghost didn't dig a hole in the ground and cover it with brush. A ghost didn't lead me right to it, so I'd fall in."

"Should we call Chief Hammer?"

"Let's stop by the police station."

"You want to see him in person?" she asked.

He caught the tone of her voice. "You don't think that's a good idea?"

"I don't feel comfortable around him."

"Why not?"

She raised her head and gave him a direct look, then stared off into the distance as she began to speak again. "Something happened when I was a kid." She huffed in a breath and let it out. "You just mentioned ghosts. When I was ten, I thought I saw the ghost of a woman when I was at a friend's house."

He felt a shiver go over his skin. He knew all about that. But now she was telling him. Should he admit that he'd investigated her? "Did you?" he managed to say.

"I don't know," she said in a low voice. "I saw a woman. I'm sure of that much. Maybe she ran away," she said uncertainly. Her voice hardened when she added, "But my friend told people and before I knew it, everybody in town was talking about it. Hammer was on the police force then. He wasn't the chief, but he was an officer.

"Before that summer, I used to come to Jenkins Cove all the time. After that, I begged to stay home. I would have stayed away permanently, except that Aunt Sophie needed me to help her run the House of the Seven Gables." She dragged in a breath and let it out. "So don't be surprised if Hammer blows us off."

"If he comes out here, he'll see the pit. To my way of thinking, it looks like it's a security measure."

"And he'll probably tell you it's for hunting deer."

Michael laughed, then sobered again. "We should tell the

chief. And I don't want to do it at the house, because I don't want to worry your aunt."

"You're right. If we make a report at the station, she doesn't have to know about your falling into the trap." She gave his coat another critical look, then began brushing it off with her hand, getting off the worst of the dirt.

He reached to fish a piece of grass out of her hair, then picked more off her coat. "I guess we look presentable enough."

They climbed into the car, and she sat for a moment without turning the key. "This is totally outside my experience," she finally said. "I mean us."

"Yeah."

"What would you call it?"

He laughed. "Strong attraction." Then he sobered. "But it's more on my part. I was attracted to you right away. The more I get to know you, the more I like you."

She flushed, then said in a low voice, "You don't know me very well."

"I mean to change that. What's your favorite food?" he asked in a teasing voice.

"Chocolate-chip brownies."

"Good choice. And what's your favorite color?"

"Blue. What's yours?"

"Blue."

"Honestly?"

"Yeah. See, we have something important in common."

"What's the best thing you remember from your childhood?"

He didn't even have to think about that. "Discovering Robert Heinlein. I loved reading his books. What about you?"

"The acrylic paint set my parents gave me when I was twelve."

"What about brothers and sisters?" he asked. That was something he hadn't checked on.

"I was an only child."

"Me, too. Was that good or bad for you?"

"Good. I got a lot of attention from my parents. What about you?"

"My mom was busy supporting us, so I spent a lot of time alone. But that was okay," he said quickly. "I'd lose myself in a book."

"Where did you grow up? City or country?"

"In Chicago. They have a great transportation system so I could go to the Field Museum, the planetarium or the movies anytime I wanted. And I'd go down to Navy Pier, along the lake-front. It's so big it feels like an ocean. What about you?"

"We lived in Ellicott City, outside Baltimore. I was in the suburbs so I couldn't go anywhere on my own. If I wanted to go to the mall or the movies, my mom had to drive me." She dragged in a breath and let it out in a rush. "It's getting easy to talk to you. I'm usually cautious with men."

"Why?"

"That ghost incident years ago made me realize how easily people can turn on you."

"You felt attacked?"

"I felt like people didn't want to believe it, so they turned it around on me."

"Then I'm honored that you let me get close."

"Honored?"

"Does that sound too stiff?"

She grinned. "It sounds old-fashioned."

He grinned back at her, letting his happiness bloom in the confines of the car. He wished he could totally relax, but he couldn't banish a nagging worry that his original purpose for coming to Jenkins Cove was going to blow up in his face.

Sometime very soon, he was going to have to fess up. But not yet.

Instead, he asked, "Did you sense something strange in the warehouse?"

"Did you?" she shot back.

He felt his jaw clenching, but he managed to say, "Yes."

"What?"

"I can't describe it. The feeling of the air being thick with menace. The feeling of a presence there that I couldn't define."

"Yes," she answered. "It was something like that. But not exactly menace. I felt like there were spirits in the building, and they wanted my help."

"I guess that's the difference between you and me. They think they can reach you."

"So you believe?"

"I didn't before I came to Jenkins Cove."

"Of course, my aunt does. That's why she has the psychomanteum. To help people. That's how she is. She's generous."

"So are you. Do you think she was a big influence on you?"

"I always admired her." She turned toward him. "What influenced you?"

He struggled for an answer. "I learned early that you have to be responsible for yourself. I think that made me goal-oriented. And maybe rigid."

"Do you wish you were different?"

She was giving him an opportunity to come clean with her. But he couldn't take it. Not yet. "Sometimes. What about you?"

She swallowed. "I'd like to be more open with people. I'm working on it."

Perhaps neither one of them wanted to reveal any more. They rode in silence for a few minutes. Then Michael said, "I guess we'd better agree on what we're going to tell Chief Hammer."

"What do you have in mind?"

"We stick as closely as possible to the truth. Your aunt suggested that we go look at the warehouse because I was interested in local history. Someone was watching us. When I ran after him, I fell into a covered pit."

"Local history," she said in a low voice. "Okay."

He reached over and placed his hand over hers. "It's not exactly a fib."

"But it's not what she really said. I've always felt better about sticking to the truth."

"Yeah," he answered, inwardly wincing. He'd feel better about it, too. But he'd trapped himself.

He sat in silence beside her as they drove to the police station, knowing her tension was increasing as they approached.

"One more thing before we get there. I've been thinking about who might have a reason to—" He stopped and then started again. "Harm you."

She sucked in a sharp breath. "Why would anyone want to harm me?"

"Well, there's the obvious—the murder. If the guy thinks you can identify him, he might come after you."

"I can't!"

"Maybe he doesn't know that."

She took her lower lip between her teeth. "I guess it won't do any good to take out an ad in the paper."

"Unfortunately, no." He turned to her. "Let's talk about that real-estate guy—Ned Perry."

"Ned? What about him?"

"Well, he's trying to convince your aunt to sell a piece of prime property right on the harbor. But your aunt still wants to run the B & B—which she can't do without you."

Chelsea made a strangled sound. "Do you think he'd really go after me?"

"You're in his way. But I don't know how far he'd go to remove an obstacle."

She gave him a worried look. "You're not planning to say anything to Chief Hammer about it, are you? I mean, it's just a suspicion."

"No. But I'll keep an eye on Ned. And maybe I can find out where he was this afternoon."

He heard her swallow.

"You know," she said in a strangled voice, "a couple of times I thought maybe someone was lurking around the house."

"Yeah?"

She shrugged. "I never saw anyone. It was just a feeling that I was being watched. So I don't want to say that to the chief, either."

"You're sure?"

"Yes."

"How well do you know Phil Cardon?" he asked.

"Why?"

"He came into the Duck Blind right after I did the other night. He sat next to me at the counter and wanted to get into a big conversation. He could have followed me back and tried to run me down."

"I always thought he was harmless."

"Okay," he answered, but he'd keep the guy on his suspect list.

Ten minutes later, they arrived at the police station. Chief Hammer was at his desk. Michael could understand Chelsea's concerns as soon as he met the smug, overconfident man. Toward Chelsea, he was highly condescending.

Apparently he was the kind of bozo who responded better to other men, so Michael took over the interview, telling about how he'd tried to follow the guy watching them.

"You didn't have to go after him," the chief said.

"I wanted to know what he was doing there."

"That could have been dangerous."

"It turned out to be," Michael answered. "Somebody dug a hole in the ground and covered it up. I fell in."

The chief inspected him. "You get hurt?"

"Not much."

"Well, it was probably kids fooling around," Hammer answered.

"Maybe," Michael allowed. "But we'd be remiss if we didn't report it to you."

"Thanks for stopping by," the chief answered.

Michael clenched his fists at his sides. Was Hammer going to investigate? He stopped himself from asking the question.

When they stepped into the sunshine again, he muttered, "It's good to get a breath of fresh air."

Chelsea gave him a sidewise glance. "So it's not just me being paranoid about the chief."

"No. Now let's go back and tell your aunt it was an interesting experience."

"Okay," she answered in a small voice.

Once again, he could feel her tension growing as they rode back to the House of the Seven Gables.

When they got out of the car, he came around to her side and slung his arm around her. She turned toward him, and he pulled her against him.

"I'm not used to depending on anyone else," she whispered.

"Neither am I."

"Guys aren't expected to depend on people," she answered.

Aunt Sophie chose that moment to come outside.

Chelsea took a quick step away from Michael, her gaze fixed on the boats in the harbor.

"I see it was a successful trip," her aunt said.

Michael swallowed. "Yes."

"So, what did you think about the warehouse?" Sophie asked.

"It was atmospheric," he answered.

"Long ago, indentured servants were brought to the Colonies. Some of them came through Jenkins Cove. They came here under horrible conditions. Not much better than the way slaves from Africa were transported."

Chelsea gasped. "I never knew that." Her gaze shot to her aunt. "You're not saying that warehouse is over two hundred years old, are you?"

"No. That building is newer. But it's constructed on the location of one of the old docks." Sophie put a hand on her niece's arm. "Some of those people died soon after they arrived. You're sensitive. I think you sense their agony."

Michael felt a shiver go up his spine.

Chelsea stared at her aunt. "How do you know about the slaves and the indentured servants?"

"I did some research at the historical society."

Chelsea's gaze turned inquisitive. "Why didn't you tell me any of that?"

"Years ago, when you saw that ghost, you were too young. But that's why I sent you to the warehouse. And sent you with Michael, in case you had any problems."

He shifted his weight from one foot to the other and winced.

Chelsea's gaze flew to him. "Your knee. You've been standing here all this time."

"What about his knee?" Sophie asked.

Chelsea looked as though she was searching for an explanation.

Michael did it for her. "I tripped when I was out there by the warehouse."

"Yes. I told him he should put some ice on it."

"A good idea."

They all went into the house.

"You sit down," Chelsea ordered, gesturing toward the living room.

He sat, and so did Sophie.

Quickly Chelsea returned with a freezer pack wrapped in a dish towel. He put it on his knee and leaned back.

Chelsea stood regarding him for a minute. "There are more ice packs in the freezer if you need another one."

"Thanks."

She reached out her hand and let it drop back. "You took some pictures. Can I see them?"

"Sure." He pulled out the camera, then tried to turn it on. Nothing happened. "Damn."

"What?"

"I must have broken it when I fell."

She nodded. "That's too bad."

"Yeah," he agreed. He'd wanted to see what kind of effects he got in the warehouse. Now that wasn't going to happen.

Chelsea looked toward the hall, then back again. "I have things to do."

"Sure."

When Chelsea had left, Sophie murmured, "She's sensitive. Don't hurt her."

Maybe the older woman didn't want to hear his answer, because she got up and walked into the kitchen, leaving Michael sitting in the living room, feeling a sudden chill as if a cloud had slid across the sun.

Chapter Nine

"You don't have any other guests?" Michael asked Sophie the next day, when he was the only one who showed up for breakfast.

"We turned down some bookings because we're getting ready for the town Christmas party. It's going to be here this year. And you're invited."

"You're sure I'm not in the way?"

"Of course not. We've got a lot of jobs for a man—if you're game."

"Of course."

"Come help me rearrange some furniture in the living room so we'll be ready for the Christmas tree."

He dutifully moved the sofa and one of the chairs.

"We're hoping that Brandon and Clifford Drake can come to the party," Aunt Sophie said as she stood back to see how the arrangement looked.

"You mean the local squires?" he teased her.

"Something like that." She handed him a feather duster. "You're tall. Can you make sure the top of the wall molding is free of cobwebs?"

His mother had made him do a lot of household chores, and he'd sworn that he would never do them again. At home in

D.C., he had a maid who came once a week. But he did as Sophie asked; he liked her and he wanted to help.

Over the next few days, he saw that the party gave Chelsea the perfect excuse to avoid him. She was helping her aunt get ready for one of the premier Jenkins Cove events of the holiday season. But he needed to speak to her, and when he saw the opportunity to corner her in the kitchen, he took it.

The kitchen. That room had connotations he'd like to avoid. But she was there, and he wasn't going to miss the chance to talk to her.

She was standing at the stove, stirring a large pot of something that smelled wonderful and listening to Christmas music on a CD player. She looked wonderful, too, even if she appeared a bit frazzled.

When she looked up and saw him, her hand froze.

"How have you been?" he asked.

"Okay."

"I've been worried about you."

"I'm fine!" She gave him a critical look. "How's your knee?"

"Much better."

He wanted to close the distance between them, turn her around and pull her into his arms. Instead, he kept his hands at his sides.

"You told me you'd seen someone lurking around the house. Then there was that guy out at the warehouse. Have you seen anything else suspicious?"

"No."

"You'd tell me if anything worried you."

"Yes."

The way she said it held the sound of dismissal, but he stayed where he was. "You and I need to talk."

"I know. But I'm so focused on the party now. It's going to have to wait until after that."

In response, he walked across the room and turned off the burner, then lifted the spoon out of her hand.

She stared at him, wide-eyed. "What are you doing?"

"This." He pulled her into his arms.

"Michael, don't."

He kept saying things—doing things—that surprised him. This was no exception. "Just for a minute. I need to hold you for a minute."

He'd tried to stay away from her, but now, when he lowered his mouth to hers, the familiar heat flared between them.

She didn't resist him. As soon as their lips touched, she was kissing him back with all the passion he remembered.

"Thank God," he murmured against her mouth. "I thought you were avoiding me."

"I was," she answered, still kissing him.

He sipped from her, nibbled at her, pushed them both to a level of arousal that he knew was a mistake. There was nothing they could do about it now. He couldn't carry her away from the stove and into his bedroom. Or—

He laughed softly.

"What?" she murmured.

He lifted his mouth from hers and said, "I was picturing myself dragging you into the pantry and making love to you against the shelves."

"Oh!"

"But when I make love to you for the first time, it's going to be in a nice comfortable bed," he added, then pressed his mouth more firmly to hers again, stroking his hands over her back and shoulders, then lower so that he could pull her hips against him.

He was so far gone that his brain had stopped functioning. He wanted her and he couldn't get the bed image out of his mind. What if he really did take her back to his room and do what they both wanted so much?

Then he heard the doorbell ring. Moments later, footsteps sounded in the hall.

Chelsea sprang away from him, smoothing her hair, then turning on the burner again with a jerky motion and starting to stir with such vigor that spicy sauce slopped out onto the stove.

Twenty seconds later, the door opened, and Sophie bustled in with a large, flat box in her hand.

"Cookies for the party," she said, then saw that Chelsea wasn't alone.

"Why, Michael," she said, "what are you doing here?"

"I was just leaving."

"Have one of Mildred's blond brownies. They're famous in Jenkins Cove."

"They can't be more famous than your own," he managed.

Aunt Sophie flushed with pleasure.

Michael grabbed a brownie and made a hasty exit from the kitchen, thinking that in another minute he would have had Chelsea's blouse off. And then what would Sophie have thought?

Well, it would only be confirmation of what she already suspected. At least the fooling around part. The question was, did she suspect why he'd come to the House of the Seven Gables?

No, she couldn't. If she had, she wouldn't have been so hospitable.

He ate the brownie as he hurried back to his room. Grabbing his coat, he exited the B & B. The day before, he'd spent a lot of time at the Maritime Museum, poking into the history of the town, and he'd bought some books about the area at the museum's gift shop and at some of the other shops in town.

Now he climbed in his car and headed for the warehouse where he and Chelsea had gone two days ago.

THE WATCHER STAYED IN THE shadows of the shed down by the dock. Maybe this was the opportunity he'd been waiting for.

Bryant was leaving. Which left the two women in the house alone—since they hadn't booked any other guests for the rest of the week.

From where he stood, he had a good view of the kitchen through two big windows. He could see Chelsea standing at the counter beside the sink—working on party preparations, he assumed.

The aunt marched in, pulled a sheet off the magnetized notepad stuck to the refrigerator and started taking notes. It looked as though she was going to the grocery store—for a ton of stuff, judging from the amount she was writing.

Perfect!

Now all he had to do was wait for Chelsea to leave the kitchen for a few minutes and he could have some fun with her. Well, more than fun, he hoped. Maybe he could get rid of her this morning.

THIS TIME MICHAEL HAD NO problem finding the access road to the warehouse on his own.

He drove up the narrow lane, keeping his eyes peeled for trouble. Once again, there appeared to be no one around, but this time he wished he was carrying a gun.

Though he didn't have a permit for one, he hated feeling exposed.

After getting out of the car, he rolled back the warehouse doors on their rusty hinges and stepped into the cavernous space, feeling the familiar twinge of uneasiness.

As they had the last time, a flock of seabirds took flight, getting out of his way as he strode to his left and stood against the wall. The birds were gone, but it still felt as if the place was occupied.

He might have said the building was haunted. By the ghosts of indentured servants who had died in Jenkins Cove?

He didn't want to put it in those terms. He'd settle for saying that the warehouse gave him the willies.

Gritting his teeth, he ignored the prickling at the back of his neck as he looked around and realized something was different from the day before.

Last time he and Chelsea had been here, debris had littered the floor. Now it looked as though someone had swept the place clean, except for the bird droppings that had collected along the walls.

Had the police been here? Surely they wouldn't have swept up.

So who had felt compelled to clean the floor? And why? Those were interesting questions.

Maybe the guy who'd been here was using the building for something illegal. Smuggling, perhaps. Would Hammer blow that theory off, too?

In any case, the building gave off bad vibes, and he wanted to step outside into the sunshine again. He forced himself to stay inside, listening.

He could hear the wind whistling through the cracks in the walls. As he strained his ears, it seemed to change in tone—to a sound more like people screaming.

Screaming?

He shuddered and heard himself say, "Stop."

There was no reason for the wind to obey him, but the sound changed again. This time it was like voices whispering Chelsea's name.

He pressed his hands over his face, fighting to keep his equilibrium. If he stayed here much longer, he would go insane.

Teeth clenched, he walked to the door. Still, he knew it was dangerous to simply walk outside again. Last time someone else had been here. Forcing himself to hang back in the shadows, he scanned the parking area and the woods.

Apparently, nobody had followed him from town. Suddenly that was not reassuring.

If the person who was lurking around wasn't watching him, then he was watching Chelsea.

That was why the voices had called her name.

He shook his head. The analysis didn't make perfect sense. Still, he couldn't fight the urgent feeling that he had to get back to the House of the Seven Gables.

He raced back to his car, jumped in and headed toward Jenkins Cove, blowing the speed limit to hell.

When he pulled into the lot across from the B & B, he saw that Aunt Sophie's car was missing. She must be out. As he started toward the house, he thought he saw someone dart behind the side of a shed down by the harbor.

Was that the person Chelsea had seen watching the house?

He took off at a run toward the shed, but by the time he reached the area, he saw no one.

Then a roaring sound made him whirl.

A boat starting up.

Charging onto the dock, he saw a small motorboat with a low canopy top rapidly pulling into the harbor. The driver was hidden by the canopy.

He cursed under his breath. He'd come back to town because he was worried about Chelsea—and he'd let himself be lured away to the dock.

Turning, he trotted back to the house.

He'd covered about half the distance when he heard Chelsea scream.

Fear leaped inside him, and he started running flat out.

In seconds he was at the back door. Throwing it open, he bolted into the kitchen, which was where the scream had come from.

Chelsea was standing by the sink, looking dazed.

"What happened?" he shouted as he ran toward her, almost slipping on the wet floor. Regaining his balance, he took her in his arms.

Her lips moved, but instead of answering, she gave him a confused look.

Being careful not to slip again, he scooped her up, then carried her to one of the kitchen chairs, where he sat down and cradled her in his lap. She had started to shake.

"What happened?" he asked again. "Take a breath and tell me."

She gulped in air and let it out again. "I turned on the blender and I got a bad shock," she whispered.

His curse rang through the kitchen.

"The blender," she said again, in a strangled voice. He stared at the machine, which sat on the counter, the glass bowl full of lumpy pink and white ingredients. Then his gaze shot to the water on the floor again. "You could have gotten killed!"

Her lips trembled, and he wrapped his arms around her, rocking her gently, silently thanking God that the shock hadn't been worse.

Her right hand was curled into a loose fist. He uncurled it and pressed it to his lips.

It could have been an accident. But the way things were going, he wouldn't bet on it.

"Were you out of the kitchen before it happened?" he asked.

"Why is that important?"

"Just answer the question."

"Yes. I went up to the bathroom."

"And then you came back and turned on the blender?"

She nodded. "I was going to make a salmon spread for the party."

"Was the floor wet when you left the kitchen?"

"The floor?" Her gaze shot to the puddle of water on the tile. "Where did that come from?"

"I'd like to know."

He turned so he could look at the door—which he'd left open. "The door was unlocked?"

"It usually is during the day."

"So someone could have come in here and put the water on

the floor. I guess you were damn lucky that the ground fault interrupter tripped."

Her breath caught. "Who would do that?"

"Good question."

"Maybe there was a leak from the sink," she murmured.

"I don't see the puddle getting bigger," he pointed out.

He stroked his hands over her back and shoulders. "Have you had trouble with the blender before?"

"It was okay the last time I used it."

"Which was when?"

"Yesterday."

He might have gotten up, strode to the blender and emptied the contents into the sink, but he couldn't turn Chelsea loose yet.

As he winnowed his fingers through her hair, she lowered her head to his shoulder and clasped her arms around him.

"You think someone came in here while I was out of the room?" she whispered.

"I don't know. I saw someone outside."

She gasped. "Where?"

"Over by the dock."

"That's not exactly in our yard. It could have been anyone."

"They took off in a boat when I went over there."

"Still…"

"From now on, I'm going to stay around the house."

Her head jerked up. "I don't need a babysitter!"

"I wasn't suggesting you did."

"Then what?"

"I want to make sure you're safe."

She answered with a small nod, then cleared her throat. "And are we going to call Chief Hammer?" Her voice turned edgy as she asked the question.

"Do you want to tell him about this?"

"No! We can't prove anything."

"There could be fingerprints."

"You don't think someone who would come in here to…do mischief would be careful about something like that?"

"You're probably right," he conceded.

THE MAN WHO HAD TAKEN OFF in the boat slowed the craft and lifted a pair of binoculars to his eyes. This little scenario wasn't working the way he'd expected.

There was Chelsea in the kitchen, sitting on Bryant's lap. He'd expected her to drop to the floor, electricity coursing through her body because he'd crossed the wires in the old metal blender. But the circuit breaker had tripped or something and turned off the damn power. Saving her life.

Too bad, because she was still a problem that needed to be solved. Of course, the guy who'd hired him was getting a little worried about how things were going. But the watcher was on top of it. If the boss wasn't going to take drastic measures, somebody needed to do it for him.

His thoughts were interrupted by a car pulling up in the parking area near the B & B. Aunt Sophie returning from the grocery store. Well, maybe it was time to head across the harbor before one of them spotted him.

A NOISE AT THE BACK DOOR made both Michael and Chelsea start.

"Who left this door wide open?"

Aunt Sophie walked into the room, holding two bags of groceries. Her gaze shot to the couple sitting on the kitchen chair.

"Well!" she said. "Pardon me for barging in."

Chelsea leaped up, then started to speak rapidly. "I had an accident. Michael heard me scream, and he came in to find out what happened."

"And what did happen?" Sophie asked.

"The blender gave Chelsea a bad shock."

Her aunt gasped. "Are you all right?"

"Yes."

Michael cleared his throat. "Have you ever had anyone coming into the house making trouble for you?"

She stared at him as if he'd asked her if she'd recently taken a rocket ship to Mars. "Of course not. Why are you asking?"

"Because there was water on the kitchen floor and Chelsea didn't spill any."

As he spoke, Chelsea knelt down, opened the cabinet below the sink and felt inside.

"It's dry," she murmured.

"You haven't seen anyone lurking around here?" Michael pressed.

The older woman's face wrinkled. "Sometimes we get kids making mischief. Once I had some boys throw eggs at the front door."

Chelsea winced. "You never told me about that."

"It only happened once—a few years ago."

"But nobody's come in and done anything in the house?"

"Not that I know about," she said.

"Well, I think it might be a good idea to keep the doors locked," Michael said.

"Young man, I operate a bed-and-breakfast. How can I possibly keep the doors locked?"

"You give your guests keys," he said. "Like you do when they come back after hours."

"You give out a bunch of keys, and someone's going to lose one," Sophie objected. "And if I do it, people will think we've got security problems in town."

"Possibly. But I hope you'll consider taking that precaution."

"I will. But you're the only guest here now," she pointed out.

"I can take a key to a locksmith and get some made for you," Michael offered.

Sophie's expression changed. "You're serious about this."

"Very serious."

Chelsea sighed, then walked to a drawer and took out a key and handed it to him. "I'll go to the locksmith with you."

He'd been hoping she'd say that, but he hadn't wanted to be the one to suggest it.

"Let's clean up first," she said. She started sopping up the water with paper towels.

Michael pulled the plug on the blender cord in one quick motion. Then he turned the blender over and examined the bottom. It looked as though someone might have fooled with the casing, but he couldn't be sure because he didn't know the condition of the appliance.

When Chelsea walked back to the counter and reached for the blender, he saw her hand was shaking. But she lifted off the glass container and emptied the contents into a mixing bowl, which she put into the refrigerator.

Then she grabbed her coat. "We'll bring in the groceries," she told her aunt.

When they'd transferred the groceries to the house, they stepped outside again.

"I'm not used to being stalked," she said.

"That makes two of us."

"But it looks like they're after me."

"I'm the one who almost got hit by a car."

"Yes. But it still could have been an accident."

"You believe that?"

"I don't know!" She kept her face turned toward the harbor, but she gave him a sidewise look. "Show me where the guy was standing and where his boat was moored."

Chapter Ten

Chelsea felt her throat tighten as they walked toward the harbor area. When Michael reached for her hand, she jumped. "Don't."

"Why not?"

"People will know there's something between us."

His voice took on an intimate warmth. "I want them to know."

Chelsea could not manage a reply.

They walked the rest of the way, holding hands. She wasn't used to anything like that, but she told herself to relax. He was putting his mark on her. It was a strange sensation, yet she couldn't deny that she liked it.

Still, she warned herself not to like it too much. What would happen when he left Jenkins Cove? She shoved that thought to the side and let him lead her to the place where he'd seen someone watching the house.

"This is the shed," he said, pointing to the small wooden building. "Who owns it?"

"The company that takes tourists on little cruises up and down Jenkins Creek. They own a boat that's in dry dock now. They use the shed for storage. But this is the off-season, and it's not running."

"So anybody could have been around here." He walked to the shed and rattled the door. It was unlocked. Stepping inside, he looked around. He saw some folding chairs, some life preservers and some packages of plastic cups. In the middle of the floor was a crumpled brochure. He stooped to pick it up, then stepped outside into the sunlight and smoothed it out.

Chelsea looked over his shoulder. "It's one of those maps that the chamber of commerce gives out. They distribute thousands of them every year."

"But look at this." He tapped his finger on the map. "Some of the landmarks are circled. Like your house, for example." He slipped the map into his pocket.

He walked around the building, looking at the ground. Along one side was a bald spot in the grass, where someone could have been standing. Or maybe the spot had been there since the summer, and nobody had gotten around to putting in a patch of sod.

"Where's the boat slip?" she asked. "Where you saw him take off?"

He led her onto the dock, then a few yards farther along. "You know who this belongs to?"

"It's one of the slips tourists can use. But most people don't come here by boat at this time of year."

"So we still don't know anything."

"Sorry."

He cleared his throat. "You didn't have any problems in town—until you ran across that man assaulting a woman in the swamp?"

"Well, there was the old ghost story."

"Yeah."

"I should get back to work," she said, changing the subject.

"We were going to get keys made. And you could take a lunch break."

"I already grabbed some leftovers."

"I can get some takeout and bring it back to the house."

"There's still some quiche. Unless you think real men don't eat quiche."

"I ate it for breakfast," he pointed out. "Where's the locksmith?"

"Just across Main Street."

"Okay, I'll take you up on the lunch offer, if you walk there with me."

She nodded.

They walked down to the locksmith, where she ordered six keys. Then he stopped at the coffee shop that was right on the corner of Center Street. Although he looked casual as he stood in line to order, she was getting to know him, and she saw that he was watching the people.

"You're wondering who did it?" she murmured.

"Yeah."

"If they left in a boat, they probably aren't still here."

"Unless they came back."

She gave him a quick glance. "I just can't think of Jenkins Cove like that."

He lowered his voice. "We have to go back to the main event. The murder was real."

"Yes."

Neither one of them mentioned the ghost on the road. Was that real, too? She had wanted to dismiss ghosts from her life. It seemed she wasn't allowed to do that.

After he bought his coffee, they walked back to the House of the Seven Gables, where she heated a slice of quiche in the microwave and set out a basket of muffins.

Probably they should be continuing the discussion about the blender and whether someone had come into the house, but she was distracted. The party was a big deal, and she wanted it to come off well, not only because of Aunt Sophie but because she had something to prove to the town—that she could fit in here.

MICHAEL NOTED that the activity at the House of the Seven Gables got more frantic as the day and hour of the party drew near. Not only were Chelsea and Sophie cooking and cleaning, but they were decorating the house for the holiday.

A curvy brunette with gray eyes delivered boxes of garlands for the fireplace mantels. Chelsea introduced her as Lexie Thornton, a local landscape designer who was selling Christmas greenery for the holiday season.

But the garlands were far from the major decorations in the public areas of the B & B. Crystal bowls of shiny glass balls, teddy bears wearing holiday outfits and ornamental nutcracker soldiers were set around on tables.

Chelsea's painting of Main Street occupied a place of honor over the living room mantel. On a nearby table was a dual roll of tickets and a box where people could pay ten dollars a chance to win the painting. The proceeds were earmarked for town improvements.

Michael managed to get out of the house to take the blender to a repairman who operated out of his home a few miles from town. But he had a lot of backlog, and he said he couldn't check out the appliance until later in the week.

The night before the party, Phil Cardon delivered a huge fir tree, which he set up in the living room. Michael watched him closely, but Cardon seemed only interested in doing his job, getting paid and leaving.

Michael, Chelsea and Aunt Sophie stayed up until well after midnight decorating the tree with strings of miniature white lights and antique ornaments.

The next day, when Chelsea sent Michael out for an emergency carton of sour cream and eight ounces of cream cheese, he was glad to escape from the frantic preparations.

After all that work, he expected Chelsea to look frazzled. But when she came downstairs just before five on Thursday in a floor-length green satin dress that hugged her curves and set off her pale skin and blond hair, he almost forgot to breathe.

"You look spectacular," he told her.

She slid her gaze over his black slacks, blue shirt and tweed sports jacket. "So do you."

"Should I put on a tie? I didn't know it was such a fancy affair."

Aunt Sophie came bustling in from the kitchen with a tray of cookies, which she set on the lace-covered table in the dining room. She was wearing a bright red skirt and a creamy blouse with frills down the front. Studded through the folds of lace were tiny lights that blinked on and off. It put her in competition with the Christmas tree.

"Some people dress up more than others," she said to Michael. "Dr. Janecek and some of the other men will probably come in tuxedos. And Phil will wear a work shirt and jeans."

"Who's Dr. Janecek?"

"A physician in town."

"Clifford Drake usually wears a tuxedo, too."

The guests started arriving around five. Or rather, the suspects, as Michael thought of them. He wanted a chance to meet these people and see how they interacted with the two Caldwell women.

In the next twenty-five minutes, the B & B filled up with guests. As advertised, a man came in wearing a tuxedo. He was slim and had dark brown hair with silver wings. His eyes were also dark.

"Clifford Drake or Dr. Janecek?" Michael asked Chelsea.

"Clifford."

A few moments later, another tuxedoed man joined the crowd. He was slender and balding, which he had tried to disguise by combing long strands of hair to the side. His lips were thin, and his dark eyes were deep set.

"The doctor?" Michael asked.

"Yes."

One of the women immediately cornered him, and Michael

supposed from his expression that he was being asked for free medical advice.

Another man came in wearing a three-piece suit with a watch hanging from a chain. He looked a little nervous, and Michael was immediately on the alert.

He leaned toward Chelsea. "Who's that?"

"Edwin Leonard, the butler at Brandon Drake's house."

"Is he upset about something?"

"He does look a little on edge," Chelsea whispered.

When Leonard spotted Sophie, his eyes lit up, and he crossed the room toward her.

"He's been here before," Chelsea said. "I think he's sweet on Aunt Sophie. And the feeling is mutual."

They went over, and Chelsea made the introductions.

"Is Brandon coming?" Sophie asked eagerly. "It's been such a long time since we've seen him in town."

"I'm afraid he decided to stay home once again," Edwin answered. "But he practically ordered me to come to the party and have a good time."

"It's too bad he wouldn't come himself."

The butler shook his head. "He's still grieving for Charlotte. I suggested that he might talk to her through the psychomanteum, but he doesn't want to try it."

Michael listened, nonplussed. It was strange to be hearing a perfectly normal conversation, then hear mention of the psychomanteum.

Sensing spirits in the old warehouse was one thing. Going into a darkened room and inviting them to communicate with you was quite another.

"Poor man. Maybe you can change his mind," Sophie murmured.

"There are some other people I'd like you to meet," Chelsea said.

Michael took the hint. Chelsea was giving her aunt and Edwin Leonard a chance to be together.

As she led him through the crowd, he heard someone clear his throat. Turning, Michael saw the doctor.

"We haven't met."

"Dr. Janecek, this is Michael Bryant," Chelsea said.

In answer to the doctor's inquiring look, she added, "Michael is spending some time with us at the House of the Seven Gables."

"Did he come down here to use the psychomanteum?" the doctor asked.

"No," Michael answered. "I'm just taking a few days to enjoy Jenkins Cove."

"I'm glad you don't believe in that claptrap," Janecek said.

Michael saw Chelsea's jaw tighten, but she didn't come back with a denial. When he saw her glance across the room, he spotted Chief Hammer talking to some of the Main Street merchants, while he ate from a paper plate of cookies and other goodies that he'd gotten off the buffet table.

The chief spotted Chelsea and nodded. She nodded back but stayed on her own side of the room.

Michael watched Ned Perry sidle up to her.

"Have you talked some sense into your aunt?" he asked.

"If you mean about selling the House of the Seven Gables, I have no intention of doing that."

"You're making a mistake," he said in a tight voice.

"I don't think so."

Michael watched the exchange with interest. He hadn't liked Perry on their first meeting, and the man was making himself even more unpleasant. Could he have been the one who'd been following them around? Or what if he'd hired someone to do it?

And what if Ned was willing to go even further? What if

he'd hired someone to come into the house and spread that water on the floor?

Michael moved Ned Perry to the top of his suspect list, then wondered if he was jumping to convenient conclusions. He wanted a solution, so he was manufacturing one.

Once again, he checked to see what Chelsea was doing and found her talking to one of the Main Street merchants.

At the beginning of the party, she'd seemed to be having a good time. Now she looked a little distracted, as though she were listening to voices other people couldn't hear. That thought set his nerves tingling.

He wanted to ask her what was wrong, but he couldn't really do it now.

He saw other people he recognized. The garden center owner, Lexie Thornton, had come in and was talking with Rufus Shea. There seemed to be something between them.

"They know each other pretty well," Michael commented to Aunt Sophie.

"Lexie used to date Rufus's son, Simon."

"The guy who died."

"We presume he's dead. He disappeared thirteen years ago."

Michael watched the parade of guests. People from all strata of Jenkins Cove society seemed to be mixing and mingling. On the surface, they appeared to get along, although Michael suspected that there were probably some truces that had been called for the holidays.

Still, the party was a success. It was close to midnight by the time the house was finally cleared—except for Edwin Leonard, the butler from Drake House.

Sophie went to a box on a table near the fireplace and looked through the cash and tickets there.

"We collected almost five hundred dollars for the town fund," she announced.

"That's fantastic," Edwin said. He added, "Let me help you clean up."

"I don't want to put you to any trouble," Sophie answered.

"No trouble. I'm an expert at it."

"Of course."

True to his word, Edwin was excellent at cleaning up. He organized the four of them into teams. Michael and Chelsea carried food into the kitchen. Sophie and Edwin put it away.

Then they all tackled the plates and cups that guests had left around the house. Sophie and Leonard went out onto the back porch.

Chelsea turned to Michael. "You were a big help, too. Thank you."

As they walked into the hall, he thought this might be his chance to ask her what had happened at the party to disturb her. She looked so worn-out that he only said, "You go to bed. I know you've got to be exhausted."

She nodded and started toward the steps. But something about the set of her shoulders told him that she wasn't headed for bed.

So what was she up to?

He hung back, then followed her to the second floor, where he was pretty sure her bedroom was located. Instead of stopping, she climbed the steps to the third floor.

She couldn't be going to work in her studio, could she? Not after such an exhausting day. And not in her party dress.

He caught his breath as he saw her turn the other way down the hall from her studio. When she opened the door to the psychomanteum, his heart started to pound.

CHELSEA TURNED ON THE DIM overhead lights and closed the door behind her. She'd always resisted coming into this room.

But after Edwin had mentioned it during the party, her thoughts had kept coming back here.

Edwin was a levelheaded man. If he thought that Brandon Drake could contact his dead wife, then maybe there was something to it. But it wasn't just Edwin's suggestion that had sent her up here.

She shuddered. In the warehouse, she'd had the sensation that a spirit was trying to speak to her. She'd told herself then she was just letting her imagination run away with her.

Tonight, however, the feeling was even stronger, and she knew she was just going to lie in her bed, tossing and turning, until she came here and tried to make contact.

She shuddered again.

She didn't *want* to make contact. She just wanted to be left alone. Apparently that wasn't an option.

She picked up the lighter on one of the tables and walked around the room, lighting the candles. Then she turned off the overhead lamp and sat down.

She wasn't even sure what to do besides stare at her own reflection in the mirror. She appeared ghostly in the flickering light.

Maybe she should have changed out of her party dress. But she'd wanted to get this over with and had rushed up here. Now she was stuck.

If you were uncomfortable, she wondered, did that make it harder or easier to communicate with the dead?

Whichever it was, she was going to sit here and wait—even if she spent the night in this room.

What a thought!

She had been dead tired. Now she was wide-awake because all her senses tingled with anticipation.

She wasn't sure how long she sat staring into the mirror. She wanted to look at her watch, but that seemed like too much of a modern intrusion when the room harked back to ancient times.

After a while, the flickering candlelight and the late hour made her want to close her eyes. But if she did that, she wouldn't be able to see the mirror, and that was part of the process, wasn't it? Too bad she hadn't paid more attention to how this place worked.

Realizing her hands were clenched in her lap, she tried to relax them. But she needed someone to hold on to, and she was the only one here.

Or was she? Goose bumps suddenly covered her bare arms as she stared into the mirror. She was the only person who had walked into the room, and yet she thought she saw another figure—a woman—standing in back of her.

Her breath caught as the figure became more real, more solid. No, maybe *solid* was the wrong word. Though she could see the woman standing there, she could still see right through her.

As the back of her neck prickled, the urge to turn around assaulted her. She fought it.

"Did you come to talk to me?" she whispered, hardly expecting an answer.

"Yes," a voice answered, so close that she imagined she could feel the woman's breath on her neck.

Not warm breath. Cold.

She gasped, and it took every ounce of willpower she possessed to keep herself from jumping up and dashing out the door. But she stayed where she was.

"Chelsea Caldwell," the woman said in a high, strained voice that seemed to come from everywhere and nowhere.

"Yes." Chelsea kept her gaze fixed on the mirror, watching the ghostly shape beside her. The figure looked like a woman wearing a translucent veil that covered her from head to toe.

"You must help me." The woman spoke in a thick accent that made it hard to understand her.

"How can I do that?"

"You must bring us justice."

Chelsea raised her hand pleadingly, gesturing toward her own reflection. "But...I don't know how."

"You must go back to that place where you saw the murder! Near it. Near the pine tree that has half its branches burned away on one side."

"What do you mean?"

"You will know when you see it. Go to the place where you saw me murdered."

Chelsea gasped. "You? That was you?"

"Yes."

Gathering her courage, Chelsea asked the question that had been deviling her since the incident on the road. "I saw you lying on the road. Then I saw someone murder you. How is that possible?"

"The first woman was not me. It was another one who died here. Long ago. She came from the same country as I did."

"What country is that?"

"It is far away. It had a different name when she lived there. That is not the important part. She and I are not the only ones. Many people have come to this charming little town as we did. Some with hope in their hearts and some with despair. But they had one thing in common. They died. They are buried in a mass grave. You must help the police find them."

Chelsea's throat had gone so tight that she could barely drag in enough air to speak. "Why…are you asking this of me?" she managed to ask.

"Because you are sensitive to us."

"No."

"My name is Lavinia. Remember my name."

The way the woman spoke and the directness of her contact sent a shiver up Chelsea's spine. Still, she protested. "I have no idea where to look for this grave."

"I told you. Near the spot where you saw me murdered. Look for the tree. And do not deny your abilities. You have powers you have never wanted to recognize. That is why I can reach out to you. No one else. It happened when you were a girl, didn't it? But you weren't ready."

Chelsea gasped. "Who was that first woman?"

"Another one of us."

As the woman spoke, she raised a ghostly hand, a hand still shrouded by the veil.

When she came closer, Chelsea huddled away from the advancing form. "Don't," she whispered.

Ignoring her, the woman touched Chelsea's cheek, sending a dart of icy cold onto her skin and through her body.

Unable to help herself, she cried out.

Chapter Eleven

Michael threw the door open and sprinted into the psycho-manteum.

He felt a whoosh, as though a vacuum had suddenly opened in the enclosed space, pulling air out of the room and into some other place.

Last time he'd been here, the ceiling light had illuminated the room. Now it was lit by dozens of flickering candles. Chelsea sat on the chair in the center of the floor, facing the ornate mirror.

When the door opened, she leaped up and whirled toward him, wavering on her feet.

"Michael?" she gasped.

He rushed around the chair and caught her in his arms the way he had after the blender had shocked her. In the dim light, she looked much as she had then.

Shocked. But this time it wasn't because of electricity.

"You have to get out of here," he said, recognizing the urgency as he spoke the words.

When she opened her mouth, no sound came out. Scooping her into his arms, he cradled her against his chest as he strode out of the room.

"The candles," she murmured. "You can't leave the candles burning."

"Damn." He turned back toward the room, and his breath caught in his throat. The candles had gone out, as though someone had walked through the room, extinguishing them the moment they had left.

That was impossible. Yet he had seen it with his own eyes.

He might have puzzled on that longer, if not for Chelsea. She hooked her arm around his neck and pressed her cheek to his chest.

"I'll take care of you," he murmured as he carried her downstairs to the second floor. "Which is your bedroom?"

Without hesitation, she answered, "At the end of the hall. In the right-hand wing. The family wing."

He strode past the guest area, to a doorway that closed off the end of the hall.

Once he had turned to shut that door, she murmured, "First room on the right."

She leaned over, turning the knob, and he carried her into a bedroom that was furnished much like the guest rooms in the house—with lovingly restored antiques. Only, this room was filled with personality.

Her possessions were arranged on the tables and dresser. Little ornaments like a Japanese good luck cat. Family photos. A bookcase along one wall was brimming with art books and paperbacks.

He laid her on the bed, and when he tried to straighten, she kept her arms around his neck.

"Don't go. Hold me," she whispered.

He wasn't sure that was such a good idea, but he understood that she needed him at that moment. In truth, he couldn't resist the invitation. He kicked off his loafers and eased onto the bed beside her.

She sighed. "Thank you."

She turned her head, staring at something, and he followed her gaze to find she was looking out the window into the darkness.

"You see something?"

"No. That's the trouble," she said, as though she were totally confounded by the lack of light outside. "So I can't do it now."

"Do what?"

"Find the mass grave."

He winced, feeling as though he'd come in in the middle of the conversation. "What are you talking about?"

She gave him a quizzical look, apparently realizing that she'd left out a few details.

"Something happened to you in that room. What was it?" he demanded.

She kept her gaze fixed on his face as she swallowed hard. "A ghost came to me."

He swore under his breath, then apologized. "Are you sure?"

"Yes. I felt someone calling me during the party, and I knew that I had to go up there. I knew that something was going to happen in that room."

"Is that why you got that strange look on your face?"

"Yes. After Edwin started talking about the psychomanteum, I knew I had to go in there." She gulped. "It was like a…force tugging at me. It turned out to be a ghost. She said her name was Lavinia."

"She gave you her name?"

"Yes." She raised her head so she could give him a direct look. "You don't believe me."

"You believe it. That's good enough for me," he said. "But I wasn't there, so I don't know what happened."

"She wanted me to know about a mass grave. But it's too dark to find it now."

"Yeah."

She kept her gaze fixed on him. "I have to do it first thing in the morning. Will you come with me?"

"Of course."

"Thank you." She tightened her grip on him, and he shifted her body so that she was cradled against him.

He'd fantasized about lying with her in a bed. He'd even talked to her about it. And he wanted her now.

When she nuzzled her lips against his neck, he was pretty sure she was thinking the same thing.

Before she could tell him she wanted to make love, he raised his head. "We're both dead tired."

"Yes."

He stroked his lips against her cheek, then said, "Which makes the timing pretty bad right now."

She heaved in a breath and let it out. "Are you making excuses?"

"No. I'm being realistic. But there's the other side of the equation, too. The idea of leaving you when you've had a frightening experience makes my stomach knot. I want to hold you for a little while. Will you let me stay?"

The warmth in her eyes almost broke his resolve not to do more than hold her.

"Yes." She turned off the light on the bedside table.

He settled down beside her, gathering her close, staring down at her breasts, wanting to cup them through the silk of her dress. He knew that if he went that far, though, he would throw good intentions out the window. Instead he contented himself with stroking her arms and shoulders, soothing her with his hands and words. He felt the tension in her, yet his touch seemed to help her relax. It worked for him, too.

He closed his eyes, letting himself drift, feeling the mattress below him and Chelsea in his arms. With his eyes closed, he could focus on the wonderful scent of her and the soft sound of her breathing.

When he opened his eyes again, he was shocked to see that it was no longer dark. Faint light was coming in through the window.

When he shifted slightly, her eyes blinked open. For a moment he guessed that she didn't know why he was in bed with her.

Then comprehension dawned.

"Last night, I talked to Lavinia in the psychomanteum. Now I have to go out to the bog to look for the grave," she whispered.

"Now?"

"Yes."

"Aren't you going to help your aunt finish cleaning up?"

She shook her head. "There's someone coming in from town to help. That was part of the deal when we agreed to have the party here."

"Okay." He got out of bed and scuffed his feet into his loafers. It had been a while since he'd slept in his clothes, and he wanted to take a shower and change, but he wasn't going to insist on it.

She also got up. When she looked down at the green party dress she was still wearing, she made a face. "I can't go out to the swamp like this. And if I'm going to change, then I might as well shower."

"Okay. I'll meet you downstairs in half an hour."

He left her room and tiptoed down the stairs. Before he reached the bottom, Aunt Sophie walked across the front hall, carrying a tray full of paper plates and napkins that were left over from the party.

She stopped and looked at him.

"It's not what you think," he said.

"Oh?" She kept her gaze fixed on him. "Come down the rest of the way, so you don't tower over me."

Obediently, he descended to the first floor.

"Chelsea went into the psychomanteum last night. A—" He stopped short and started again. "A spirit contacted her, and she was upset. I stayed with her, in her room, and we both fell asleep."

"Uh-huh."

Speaking quickly, he went on. "The spirit wanted her to do

something. To go look for a mass grave. She wants to do it as soon as possible, so we're both changing our clothes and going out."

"Search for a mass grave," Sophie repeated in a soft voice. "A spirit asked Chelsea to do that?"

"Yes."

She gave him a long look. "You think you'll find it?"

"I don't know," he answered honestly. "But I'm not letting Chelsea go out there by herself."

"Thank you."

"I need to take a quick shower and change first."

"And I'll fix you something to eat."

"I don't think Chelsea wants to take the time."

"We'll see about that," Sophie answered, heading off toward the kitchen.

Michael hurried down the hall to his room, thinking that some mighty strange things had happened to him since coming to Jenkins Cove. And the conversation he'd just had with Aunt Sophie was one of the strangest. She'd taken it for granted that Chelsea's encounter with the ghost had been real. Now she was making sure her niece had a good breakfast before going off to follow the spirit's instructions.

He took a shower in record time, then dragged a razor over his face and brushed his teeth before putting on clothes and the waterproof hiking boots he'd bought at one of the shops in town.

By the time he returned to the kitchen, Chelsea and Sophie were both there, speaking in low voices. They both looked toward the door as he walked in.

Her aunt spoke up in a firm voice. "I've persuaded Chelsea that the grave's not going away. There's no point in skipping breakfast."

Chelsea answered with a little nod, then accepted a cup of steaming coffee from her aunt.

"I'll make you bacon and eggs," she said as she brought Michael coffee.

"I don't want that much," Chelsea objected. "Besides, we have all those cookies and quick breads from last night."

Sophie gave her a disapproving look. "That's not a very nourishing breakfast."

"In this case, it's going to have to do."

Chelsea retrieved the plate of pumpkin bread and a tin of cookies.

"My kind of breakfast," Michael said as he helped himself to a spice cookie. But he could tell Chelsea was in a hurry, so he didn't allow himself to linger.

They were out of the house a few minutes later.

"I'll drive," Chelsea said.

"I'm not used to being driven around," he shot back. "What's your excuse this time?"

"The same as last time. I know where we're going, and you don't."

He watched her expression turn grim as they climbed into the car. He wanted to tell her that she didn't have to do this—just because a ghost had given her an assignment. He knew it wasn't strictly true, though. Chelsea had to do it.

They turned right on Main Street and drove toward Tilghman Island. A few miles outside town, she slowed, and he saw her looking for something.

"This is the same location where they found the body?" he asked.

"Near here. The body was a little farther up that way." She gestured. "I use that sign as a marker."

He wanted to point out that he could have headed for the sign, but he saw the tension on her face as she pulled onto the shoulder.

"You have some other landmark?" he asked.

"Yes." She peered around, apparently searching for something, and pointed to a tall, misshapen pine that looked as though it had been struck by lightning. "The ghost told me to look for a tree that had its branches burned off on one side. That must be it."

"Okay."

A car drove slowly past. The driver looked at them, but didn't stop.

"Was that Phil Cardon?" Michael asked.

"Yes."

"I wonder what he's doing out here."

"He probably had a job."

Or he followed us, Michael thought.

Chelsea opened her purse and took out a small revolver. Michael gaped at her. "You have a gun?"

"Yes. For protection."

"And you have a permit to carry?"

She made a face. "No. But I'm going to do it anyway."

They both climbed out of the car and stood on the gravel shoulder, where she slung the strap of her purse over her shoulder.

She looked around. "I haven't been back here since…that night. But now that I see it in the daylight, I remember this place. A friend used to have a fishing cabin about a half mile from here. Her father would take us out there."

"Where do you want to start looking?"

"Let's head toward the tree."

"All right." Michael reached for her free hand and clasped her fingers tightly as they started walking into the swampy area. There were cattails and scrubby bushes and low trees that he didn't recognize. Though most of them were leafless in the winter, some still had foliage—either broad-leaved or pine.

Mud sucked at their boots, making it hard to walk as they tramped farther from the road. Michael kept his gaze on the ground, unsure of what he was looking for. Probably not a white cross sticking out of the muck.

When they came out onto slightly higher ground, he breathed out a little sigh. With the mud no longer trying to pull his boots off, the walking was easier, yet he felt a coldness in the air, like the first night when he'd walked from the House of the Seven Gables to Main Street.

Beside him, Chelsea raised her head, looked around and made a small sound, and he wondered if she was feeling the same thing.

"This place is spooky. I think I'd go home if I were alone."

"Safety in numbers."

She swung toward him. "Not just anyone would do," she said in a low voice.

He felt his heart leap. Instead of speaking, he slung his arm around her shoulder.

She turned in a small circle. "I wish the ghost had been more specific. I don't know where to start looking."

He wanted to be supportive, even though he had little faith in a ghost's orders. "Follow your instincts."

She sighed. "Maybe I had a hallucination last night."

"Do you mean you wish you did?"

"Yes," she whispered, and once again, her honesty tore at him. She wasn't making up stories about ghosts. Something had happened, and she obviously didn't know how to handle it.

She started walking again, and he stayed close beside her.

After about five minutes, he spotted something that wasn't natural to the landscape. Something grayish-white, half buried in the ground.

He pointed. "Over there."

When they came closer, he stifled a spurt of disappointment. It was only a tennis shoe.

"Anybody could have lost that," she murmured, echoing his thoughts. "Maybe that's its mate over there."

She pointed to another object about the same color. But when they came closer, he caught his breath. The shape wasn't much like a shoe.

"I think this is something a little more significant." He found a stick he could use to dig. Squatting down beside the grayish-white lump on the ground, he began to carefully scrape the dirt away.

As the shape emerged, Chelsea gasped. "It's a skull," she whispered. "A human skull, not some animal who died out here."

"Yes, it is."

"So this *could* be a mass grave. What should we do?"

"I think we'd better leave the skull here and see if we can find anything else."

"Okay."

They kept tramping across the ground, both of them looking down. When Chelsea made a small sound and pointed to her right, Michael hurried over. This time they saw a long bone— like part of an arm.

"Either this is a graveyard, or animals scattered some bones," Michael muttered.

He had just started off to search some more when he was stopped by the sound of a small explosion and something whizzing past his head.

Lunging back, he caught Chelsea's hand and tugged her toward the ground.

Chapter Twelve

Chelsea gasped as Michael pulled her down.

Turning her head, she stared at him. "Someone took a shot at us?"

"Yeah."

She made a strangled sound, trying to wrap her head around what was happening. "Who would do that?"

He brought his mouth close to her ear. "Keep your voice down. It's someone who doesn't want us to get out of here and report what we've found."

As he spoke, it happened again. The small explosion and then the sound of something whizzing past them.

Chelsea's heart skipped a beat, then started up again in double time, and she had to clench her jaw to keep from crying out. Somehow when she'd bought her gun and practiced at a firing range, she hadn't imagined someone shooting back at her.

"They didn't even warn us," she whispered.

"I think that's the idea."

His words made her picture two more bodies in the swamp—Michael's and hers—and she shuddered.

He clasped her shoulder.

"It's going to be okay," he whispered.

Was it?

"Give me the gun."

She handed it over. Michael moved along the ground, so that his body was covering hers, shielding her.

"Stay down," he whispered.

They huddled in the bushes, and no more shots sounded.

"Where are they?" Chelsea whispered. "And what are they going to do?"

"I'd like to know. If we're lucky, we can get back to the car and get out of here. Can you follow me?"

"Yes," she answered, because she didn't see any alternative. They couldn't stay out here like sitting ducks. And what good did a gun do them if they couldn't see who was shooting at them?

Hysterical laughter threatened to break through her terror. Or maybe it was because of the terror. Sitting ducks. A lot of people shot at ducks in this part of the country. She'd never thought she would be like the water fowl.

Michael began crawling across the ground, using a clump of bushes as a screen. As he moved, he circled around, heading back toward the road. They had covered about thirty feet when she heard four more shots, rapid-fire.

"It's not near us," Michael whispered as he reached back to put a hand on her arm. "Quiet."

She did as he said, and she heard a whooshing sound. "What is it?"

"I think that's air escaping from your tires."

She struggled not to gasp.

"So we can't drive away," he clarified. "We've got to go the other way. Come on."

Michael started moving farther into the underbrush, staying low to the ground. Chelsea followed as fast as she could. It was a hard way to travel, and she wasn't sure how long she could keep it up.

But she had to. If she didn't, whoever was out there would find them.

She wanted to look behind her, but she knew that would only slow her down and expose her face. Instead, she kept crawling.

They traveled through the underbrush, stopping every few yards to listen. They were heading toward the bay. She knew that much. Beyond that, she didn't have a clue.

What would they do if they came to the creek? Plunge into the frigid water or turn along the bank? Neither seemed like a good alternative.

As she kept moving, it felt as if the air was thickening around her, the way it had in the psychomanteum.

Something made her look up. Ahead of her, she saw the air waver. Then, to her astonishment, she saw the figure of a woman.

When she made a strangled sound, Michael turned. "What?"

"Up there."

He looked where she was pointing, then shook his head. "What?" he said again.

"You don't see her?"

"I don't see anything."

"It's the ghost. Lavinia."

He closed his eyes for a moment, then opened them again, and she wondered if he thought the stress had driven her around the bend.

The ghost gestured, then spoke in a low whisper. "This way. Hurry."

Chelsea caught the urgency in her voice. She crawled past Michael, following the ghost because that seemed to be her only option.

As she moved, her hand and then her knee hit something solid, something different from the springy vegetation that they had been crawling over. A series of wooden boards.

She stopped short, and Michael came up beside her.

"What?"

"There's something here." She gestured urgently toward the boards.

He moved to the side and pulled the solid surface. Like a door, it opened to reveal a hole in the ground.

"It's like the pit at the warehouse," he muttered. "Only it's designed to keep someone out—not make them fall in."

He pushed the door up just enough so that he could slip inside, then reached his hand up. "Come on."

She didn't like going into a hole in the ground. If the person stalking them found them down there, they were trapped. But if they stayed out here in the open, the gunman would likely gain on them, because they couldn't make much headway crawling.

Michael seemed to think it was the best alternative, which gave her the guts to climb down into the hole.

She slipped under the cover, squeezing through, scraping the top of her hand before dropping a few feet to the ground below.

She winced.

"What happened?"

"My hand. It's just a scrape."

He cursed. "Sorry."

"I'm fine," she said, even though her hand was throbbing.

"What is this place?" he whispered.

"Maybe smugglers used it. Or it could be from the underground railroad."

"That was over a hundred and fifty years ago." After a second he added, "We'd better not talk."

"Okay."

It was almost pitch-black inside the hole. She wouldn't use the small flashlight in her purse; it might shine out through the cracks in the boards. Then, to her astonishment, an eerie blue glow rose in one corner of the space.

She gasped and jumped back. If there wasn't someone

outside with a gun, she would have scrambled back out of the hole in a heartbeat.

"What the hell?" Michael muttered, taking a step back, his whole body poised to fight some unknown enemy.

"You see it?" she whispered.

"Yes."

As she stared at the blue light, a strange sensation stole over her. The light had startled her initially, but now she felt a kind of friendly feeling emanating from it.

Michael tried to shove her behind him, but she put a hand on his arm. "It's okay. I think the ghost is lighting this place for us."

Even to her own ears, that sounded ridiculous. At the moment, though, that was the only explanation she could come up with.

"Yeah, well, the ghost is going to get us caught," he muttered.

The light flickered for a moment, then steadied.

"We'd better use it," she whispered as she began to inspect their refuge.

It was a pit about six feet deep and five feet square. In the blue light, she could see a wooden wall at one side. Crossing the dirt floor, she pulled at the wall, and it swung aside, revealing another, smaller space.

"We need to get in there," she whispered.

Michael looked doubtfully at the tiny crevice.

His hesitation made her stomach knot. "Please. Just do it. And hurry."

He turned to stare at her, then did as she asked, climbing in, then reaching for her.

She squeezed into the narrow passage after him, pulling the wall back into place. There was hardly any room, so that they had to huddle together.

As they did, she heard a sound—footsteps walking through the underbrush above them.

She felt Michael's body stiffen and knew he had raised the gun. In the darkness, she clung to him.

Was the blue light still shining in the main chamber? Would it give them away?

And would her breathing? It seemed to ring in her ears, to fill the whole enclosure with sound.

She kept repeating a silent prayer. *Keep walking. Just go on by us. You don't know we're here.*

Whoever was searching the area above them didn't seem to get the message. He stopped walking, and she waited for him to pull the door back.

Instead, from above, she heard another volley of gunshots, coming in rapid succession, this time blasting through the wooden planks and into the hole. Four, five, six shots.

She cringed.

Then there was a scraping sound, and she realized the gunman was pulling the boards aside.

Would he figure out where they'd gone? That they were in the hole, hidden from view by the door at the side of the pit?

Breath frozen in her lungs, she waited and she felt Michael tense, ready to shoot.

Long seconds passed, and her body grew stiff from holding the same position. But she dared not move.

Finally, whoever was up there muttered a curse—presumably because he thought the hole was empty and he didn't know where they had gone.

After what felt like an eternity, he dropped the wooden cover back into place with a bang. Again, centuries ticked by before she heard his footsteps recede.

Michael brought his mouth to her ear again and spoke in a barely audible voice. "We have to stay here for a while."

"How long?"

"I don't know. Until he gives up looking for us and leaves."

She nodded against his shoulder. "Can we get out into the main pit?"

"Better not. He could come back and decide we doubled back and hid in here."

"Okay." She shifted a little, trying to get more comfortable.

He reached up to touch the ceiling above them, then the walls. Keeping his voice low, he said, "I think we can stretch out our legs. If we hear him coming back, we'll pull our legs in and move the door back into place."

"Okay."

He moved the door aside, then slid his legs forward, making a sound of satisfaction as he shifted out of the cramped position. She did the same. "What a relief."

He gripped her arm. "Keep your voice low. If he hears us, we're dead."

"We have a gun."

"A revolver. And he's got an automatic weapon. Unless we can set up some kind of ambush, he's got too much of an advantage."

She dragged in a breath that sounded more like a moan.

"Sorry."

"No. You're right," she answered in a barely audible voice. "And he's probably still out there looking for us."

As they both contemplated that unhappy truth, Michael asked, "I don't suppose you have a cell phone?"

"Sorry. I left it in the car. What about you?"

"I'm not getting enough bars in the area, so I left it in my room." He sighed. "That was a serious miscalculation."

"Neither one of us thought we were going to get shot at."

"So why did you bring a gun?"

"I guess I've been…worried."

"Since I came here?"

"Before that." She swallowed. "I kept feeling like someone

was watching me." Raising her head, she looked upward. "So, who do you think it was up there?"

"I wish I knew. We have to assume it's somebody involved in the murder. He followed us out here."

"We saw Phil Cardon drive past."

"Do you have any reason to believe he might be a killer?"

Chelsea thought about it. "I can't say I like him a lot, but I also can't picture him killing that woman. Lavinia."

The mention of the ghost brought her back to the way they'd found this hole in the ground.

"She helped us find this place." She turned her head toward Michael, although she couldn't see him in the dark. "Do you believe that's true?"

She heard him drag in a breath and let it out. "I guess I have to. I can't come up with any other explanation for your finding the hole or for that weird blue light."

"Yes."

He gripped her hand. "There's something I should say to you."

The way his voice sounded in the darkness made her stomach knot. "What?"

"When I came here, I thought the whole ghost business was…" His voice trailed off.

"A bunch of crap?" she asked, unable to keep an edge out of her own voice.

He sighed. "You could put it that way."

"Everybody was talking about me."

"Yeah."

She wanted to ask him more questions, but a sound from above made them both go rigid.

Footsteps? Was the guy coming back, looking for them?

Quietly, Michael drew his feet back into the hole. Chelsea did the same, then reached for the wooden wall and pulled it back against the opening to the little tunnel. Michael shifted again so that he was cradling her and yet still holding the gun in firing position. He pressed his lips to her cheek, and she closed her eyes, huddling with him in the dark, wishing she could pretend they were in bed together and not a hideyhole in the ground.

The footsteps passed by, not right beside the hole but a few feet away. Either the guy wasn't going to look in the hole again or he'd forgotten the location. Neither meant he was giving up.

Michael shifted so that he could look at his watch. It was after nine. If they planned to wait until cover of darkness, they had a long wait.

Above them, thunder sounded, shaking the ground nearby. Then rain began to pour down.

She could hear it pattering on the wooden boards that covered the top of the hole.

It pounded steadily, and when the ground underneath them grew wet, Chelsea grimaced. Pushing the wooden wall aside, she saw rain pouring into the hole.

"Maybe this was a safe hiding place when we first came down here," Michael muttered. "But it's not safe now. We've got to get out of here."

She felt her throat tighten. "What if the guy is still up there?"

"Maybe he thinks the storm will do us in."

It could, she thought, but she didn't say it aloud.

"I'll go up and have a look," Michael said.

She grabbed his arm. "No!"

"If we stay down here, we're going to drown in mud," he said. "So unless you have a better suggestion, I'm going topside."

Chapter Thirteen

While Chelsea waited in the dark, wet hole, Michael stretched up and eased the cover aside. As weak daylight and rain flooded in, she braced for the sound of shots. Luckily all she heard was the rain pounding down and splashing into the water at the bottom of the pit.

Michael heaved himself up and flopped onto the ground. Again, she waited for shots. Again there was only the rain—and another clap of thunder.

Long seconds ticked by until Michael finally reached down for her. Clasping his fingers around her forearm, he tugged her up, and she slithered onto the ground.

"Stay low," he warned as he started crawling through the underbrush.

She followed him, moving awkwardly, praying that they got out of the area without being spotted.

They were fifty yards from the pit when he stopped behind a clump of scrubby trees.

Chelsea pulled up beside him. Her coat and pants were soaking by now, and she knew they had to find shelter.

"Did you say there was a hunting cabin around here?" he asked.

"Yes."

"Do you remember where?"

"No. But maybe I can find it." She looked around, trying to orient herself. She hadn't been to the cabin in years, but she remembered it was closer to town than where they'd stopped the car.

"Can we stand up?" she asked Michael.

"I hope so," he answered, getting to his feet and looking around.

Cold rain pelted down, and now it was mixed with sleet. If they didn't get inside soon, they were going to be in big trouble.

She pulled up the hood of her coat, grateful for the shelter it gave her. Glancing at Michael, she saw water running through his hair and dripping down his face.

When he saw her expression, he pulled her close and gave her a quick, hard kiss.

"More later," he promised, then wrapped his arm around her waist as they made their way through the scrubby landscape, both of them stepping into water-filled holes from time to time as they floundered onward.

Chelsea's teeth chattered. Her hands had started to feel like blocks of ice, and she could barely put one leg in front of the other. With the part of her brain that was still functioning, she fought panic, because she was pretty sure that she had missed the cabin.

"I have to stop," she whispered.

"No. You have to keep going," Michael answered, holding her up as they staggered onward.

When she was about to drop in her tracks, she did a double take. A building loomed ahead of them in the gloom—a building she hadn't even seen until she was almost on top of it. At first she thought she had made it up, as she took several wavery steps forward, but it stayed real and solid. It wasn't the hunting cabin. It was someone's summer home.

"There." She gestured with as much strength as she could muster.

They approached the door and climbed wide front steps. Reaching out a hand that looked half-frozen, Michael rang the doorbell. When no one answered, he tried to turn the knob. She almost sobbed when it didn't open.

Plopping down on the steps, she sat with her teeth chattering, looking out at the rain and sleet falling around them.

They were so close to shelter, yet it might as well be a million miles away.

Michael began searching along the edge of the steps. Several flowerpots had been grouped in an arrangement near the door. He picked them up, then held up his hand triumphantly, showing her a key.

When he'd opened the door, he hauled her up and into a foyer.

There she sat down on a bench, waiting while Michael walked down the hall, her brain too numb to take in much—other than the reality that they were finally sheltered from the storm.

Leaning her head against the wall, she closed her eyes for a moment. She wasn't sure how long she sat there. But she opened her eyes abruptly when Michael laid a hand on her shoulder.

"Come on."

"Where?"

"To the bathroom."

He led her down the hall to a white marble bathroom. She looked down at their muddy footprints. "We're making a mess."

"We'll clean up later."

He tugged off her wet coat, then started working on her wet pants. Next he sat her down on the closed toilet seat and helped her out of her boots.

When she was wearing only her damp underwear, he helped her into the bathtub, where he dipped a cloth in a small pot of warm water and washed off her hands and face.

"Where did that come from?" she asked in confusion.

"The hot water is turned off, but there's a propane tank for the stove. I heated a little water."

When she was cleaned up, he led her down the hall to a

bedroom, then pulled aside the covers. It was cold in the bed, but her body heat and the wool blankets he'd piled on began to warm the sheets.

A few minutes later, Michael came back and slipped in beside her.

She sighed as he rubbed his hands up and down her arms and over her back and shoulders.

"That feels good," Chelsea murmured.

"I'm glad."

"I wish we could turn on the heat."

"That's not working. Neither is the phone, unfortunately. We're lucky there's propane in the tank."

"Can he find us here?" she whispered.

"I think he gave up the hunt when the rain started."

"But you don't know for sure."

"He'd have to plunge into the bush to find us. This house is an unlikely spot to take refuge. And if he tries to get in, we've got a better chance here than in that hole. So your job is to get some rest. Then we'll find our way back to town."

She moved closer to him.

A little while ago she'd been so cold that she could barely think. Now she was warming up. As her body returned to normal, she couldn't help noticing Michael's muscular leg against her. His broad shoulders. His narrow hips. And the erection pressed to her middle. She ducked her head away from him and grinned.

He'd told her more than once that it wasn't the right time to make love. Now, though, she had him trapped in a bed—and she meant to make the most of the opportunity.

"Are you feeling better?" he asked.

"Yes. And I think you are, too." She raised her face to look at him as she slid her hand down his body and cupped the bulge at the front of his shorts.

His exclamation sounded like a mixture of surprise and need. "Don't."

"Why not? Are you going to tell me this is the wrong time and the wrong place? Again?"

"I should."

"I have a better suggestion. Give in to what we both want."

She rocked her hand against him, marveling at her own audacity but loving the wonderful feel of him.

She'd never been the aggressor in lovemaking. But now she was going to get what she wanted.

When Michael's mouth came down on hers for a hot, hungry kiss, she knew that she had wiped away his doubts.

At least for now.

She'd settle for that—and figure out the rest later.

The storm still raged outside. Inside the vacation house, another kind of storm seethed.

When he covered her mouth with his, she opened for him, telling him with her lips and body and hands how much she wanted him.

His kiss was greedy. The greed itself gave her as much pleasure as the physical sensation of his mouth moving over hers.

Heat coursed through her as he strung small kisses over her cheeks, her jaw, her neck and then lower, to the tops of her breasts.

Reaching around her, he unhooked her bra, pulling it off and out of the way as he ducked under the covers so that he could nuzzle his face against her breasts, kissing first one inner curve and then the other.

"So good," he whispered.

"Yes," she answered, cupping the back of his head and holding him to her as he took one hardened nipple into his mouth and sucked.

The pleasure was exquisite. It doubled as he took its mate between his thumb and finger, imitating the action of his mouth.

He rolled to his side, taking her with him so that they were facing each other on the bed.

His gaze locked with hers as he slid his hands over her back and shoulders, pressing her breasts to his hair-roughened chest, then slipping lower to cup her bottom and seal her more tightly to his erection as he rocked her in his arms, creating an exquisite friction between them.

She played her fingers over his shoulders, down his back, loving the feel of his body. Boldly, she slipped her hands into the back of his shorts, cupping his buttocks, massaging him there.

"I love the way you feel," she whispered.

"Likewise."

He slid his hand between them, into her panties, dipping into her most intimate flesh, stroking her in a way that raised the level of her arousal to fever pitch.

"You're so hot and wet for me," he growled.

"Yes." She pulled down her panties and kicked them down her legs before tugging at his shorts. He helped her get rid of his underwear, then angled her body so that he could stroke her cleft with his erection.

She caught her breath as he bent his head, sucking at her nipple again.

The pleasure was exquisite, and she couldn't hold back a sobbing sound.

"I want you inside me," she gasped. "Now."

She rolled to her back and opened her legs. He followed her over, covering her body with his, and she guided him to her.

As he entered her, he brought his mouth back to hers, his kiss hot and tender at the same time.

Then he raised his head, looking down at her.

She met his gaze, marveling that this was finally happening.

He held still for several long seconds; then, when she was about to beg him to move, he did, setting up a steady rhythm.

He built her tension, holding back his own need for release until she was poised on the brink of climax.

Only then did he increase the tempo, sliding his hand between them to press against her core as he pushed her up and over the final rise.

She soared to the top of a high peak, then toppled over the edge, sobbing his name as rapture took her. As incredible pleasure rolled over her, she felt him follow her.

Spent, he collapsed on top of her, and they both lay breathing hard and fast.

When he tried to move off her, she clasped him to her. "Stay here."

"I'm too heavy."

"No. I like the feel of you on top of me."

She turned her head to slide her lips against his neck.

Circling her shoulders with his arms, he pulled her against himself and rolled to his side, still joined to her.

She snuggled against him, trying to absorb the reality of this moment. She had known him only a few days, yet nothing else in her life had ever felt so right.

"You should sleep," he murmured.

"You, too."

"Someone has to keep guard."

She winced. He'd transported her from the real world into a place where only the two of them existed. But that was only an illusion. Someone had tried to kill them, and he was still out there somewhere.

She hitched in a breath. "We have to get back to town."

"Not in this storm."

"Maybe there's a car in the garage."

"Maybe. But we don't have the keys. Starting cars without them isn't one of my talents."

"Too bad."

MICHAEL STROKED his hands over Chelsea's hair and shoulders, then pressed a light kiss to her cheek.

"Sleep," he said again, willing her to relax. It was heavenly to lie next to her, to hold her in his arms. Heavenly to have made love with her. Yet at the same time, so many worries swirled in his head that it was impossible for him to relax.

Someone was still stalking them. He didn't know who it was or if he was going to come crashing in the door. But Michael vowed to keep Chelsea safe.

He lay there holding her for another few minutes, listening to the sound of her even breathing. Then he eased away from her, careful not to wake her up.

Outside the warm bed, he shivered. Picking up the gun from where he'd left it on the bedside table, he went exploring through the house. It was small. There was only one bedroom, with a large closet. Obviously, a married couple with no kids came down here in the summer months. Maybe for long weekends.

In the closet he found both men's and women's clothing. He pulled on jeans that were two inches too short and a sweatshirt.

He couldn't find jeans that looked as though they'd fit Chelsea, but he figured men's sweatpants would do. And another sweatshirt. He laid them on the end of the bed, then went to the bathroom and found their wet hiking boots, which he put into the oven on low heat. Hopefully, they'd dry out in a few hours.

The refrigerator was off, and open, but he found some food in the pantry. A box of crackers. Some canned soup, which he could heat on the stove.

He looked out the window. It had stopped raining, and that worried him. With the weather cleared up, the guy who had tried to kill them could resume his search. Hopefully this was an unlikely place for him to look. Michael could now see that the house was part of a small community of summer houses.

He pictured himself going out and knocking on the doors of

the other houses. Then he changed his mind. From this vantage point, it looked as though nobody was home.

He stepped out, inspecting the walkway leading to the front door. The rain had washed away their muddy footprints, so that didn't give them away.

Hopefully, they were safe here for a few hours, but he wanted to get back to town soon and report the shooting incident to Chief Hammer. There was no way the chief could ignore the bullet holes in the boards. Or could he?

He'd just stepped back into the hall when a noise in back of him made him draw the gun and whirl.

When he saw Chelsea standing a few feet away with a shocked expression on her face, he shoved the gun into the waistband of his jeans. "Sorry. I guess I'm a little jumpy."

She nodded. "We both are."

He saw that she'd dressed in the clothing he'd laid out for her. "Where are my shoes?"

"In the oven. I couldn't find any in the closet that fit you. What are you doing up?"

"I guess I couldn't sleep."

"Then we should eat something and get out of here. I found soup and crackers."

"We're already making a mess of these people's house."

"We can leave them a note—telling them where to get in touch with us. And we can clean up later. Maybe they'd like a free couple of nights at the House of the Seven Gables."

"Right."

They went into the kitchen. While he fixed some chicken noodle soup, she wrote a note. Then they sat down and quickly ate the simple meal.

When Chelsea started to rinse the bowls under cold water, she winced.

"What's wrong?"

"My hand." She held it up, and he could see that the place where she'd scraped herself had reddened.

He crossed to her and held the wound up to the light coming in the window. "It looks like it's getting infected. You'd better have the doctor look at it."

She answered with a tight nod.

He returned to the bathroom and picked up their coats.

Chelsea followed him. "They're still wet."

"We'll leave them here and borrow some."

"I don't like to do that."

"I know. But it's safer. If we're dressed in clothing he doesn't recognize, that may make the difference between getting back to town safely and not."

She made a disgusted sound. "You keep thinking of things I don't."

"You're not used to evading killers."

"Are you?"

"No. But my devious mind comes up with unpleasant scenarios and offers solutions."

"What about my car?"

"We'll get a tow truck to haul it back later."

"My registration is in there."

"Yeah. But whoever was shooting at us already knows who we are."

"Thanks for reminding me."

They hung the wet coats in the attached garage and wiped the mud off the hall floor. Then they ripped off the sheets and put them in the laundry room.

Back in the closet he found two light rain jackets. Neither was very warm, but they each put on another sweatshirt underneath. The jackets had hoods, which would help disguise their appearance.

And he found a woman's scarf, which Chelsea used to partially hide her face.

By the time they were ready to leave the house, it was almost three in the afternoon.

He was praying it was safe to head back to town. Still, he felt a shiver go through him as they stepped outside and closed the door behind them.

He replaced the key that he'd found under the flowerpot. "Do you know where we are in relationship to the highway?" he asked.

She looked around, then pointed to an access road. "I think we'll find it if we go that way."

"Okay."

As they started off down the long drive, he kept checking their surroundings, alert for anyone suspicious.

They reached the highway, just as a police car with flashing lights came speeding toward them.

It screeched to a halt, and a young officer jumped out. "Police. Freeze. Hands in the air."

Chapter Fourteen

Michael cursed under his breath, but he raised his hands. Beside him he could see Chelsea do the same thing.

At the same time, she called out, "Officer Draper. It's Chelsea Caldwell and Michael Bryant. Why are you holding a gun on us?"

"Chelsea?" the cop asked. "Okay, take off that hood. But don't make any funny moves."

Chelsea shoved the hood back, then unwound the scarf, revealing her face.

"It's you, all right," the officer muttered. "What are you doing breaking into a house?"

"You know about that?" she gasped.

"Yeah." He looked from her to Michael. "One of the neighbors saw you come outside a while ago."

"I thought nobody was home," Michael told him, "or I would have asked for help."

"Explain what's going on."

He nodded, then asked, "Can I put my hands down?"

"Keep them where I can see them."

Michael did as instructed, hoping the guy wasn't going to pat him down and find the gun.

"We were out near the site where Chelsea saw that woman killed, and somebody started shooting at us," he said.

Officer Draper stared at him. "Uh-huh."

"Well, we can show you the fresh bullet holes in the boards above the hole where we hid."

"Okay."

"We left a note in the house where we were inside," Chelsea said. "I left my name and number so the people could get in touch with us. We can show you that, too."

Draper nodded.

Michael cleared his throat. "We were out at the site of the shooting, because…" He stopped, wondering how he was going to put the next part.

"Because what?" Draper demanded.

"Because we had information that there was a mass grave out there."

Draper's eyes narrowed. "Information from where?"

Beside him, he could hear Chelsea drag in a sharp breath.

"From an old diary," Michael said, lying through his teeth.

"Oh yeah?"

"Chief Hammer will want to have a look around there. We found a human skull. There are probably other bones. We think that's why whoever it was shot at us. He didn't want anyone poking around the grave."

Draper's stance had changed. "Let's go back there and have a look," he said, watching them carefully.

"Sure," Michael said. After the initial shock of almost getting arrested, he had started to realize this was the best thing that could have happened to them. If someone was trying to kill them, he was unlikely to do it in the presence of a cop.

"First, I want to see that note you said you left in the house," Draper said.

Michael wanted to yell at him that the graves and the bullet holes were a lot more important than the interior of the house, but he forced himself not to object. Instead, he waited while the patrolman made a call to his chief. Then they went along quietly, Michael holding his tongue as the cop inspected the condition of the house. From this vantage point, he was glad that Chelsea had left that very apologetic note.

After Draper had wasted enough time at the house, they headed for the highway.

When they reached the location of their ordeal, they found Chief Hammer waiting for them. He was looking at Chelsea's tires.

"You see the bullet holes?" Michael asked.

"Yeah. Who shot at you?"

"I'd like to know."

"Show me the pit where you hid."

Michael glanced at Chelsea. "You want to stay here?"

"I want to come with you."

They all tramped back into the swampy area, and for a while, Michael's stomach clenched when they had trouble locating the pit.

Too bad Lavinia didn't appear to guide them again.

No, scratch that.

Finally they found it by themselves.

He stood with his arm around Chelsea as Hammer inspected the bullet holes. "It looks like you were damn lucky. How did you find this place?"

Chelsea cleared her throat. "I used to play around here when I was a kid," she said.

Apparently she had decided that if Michael could lie, she could, too. No, he silently amended. She *had* played around here; she just wasn't prepared to tell him how she'd actually discovered the pit.

"We found the skull over there," Chelsea said, pointing to the approximate location. But when they led the cops back there, the evidence was missing.

"My guess is that the killer took it away," Michael was quick to add. "If you keep looking, you'll probably find more bones."

Hammer made a noncommittal sound.

So, what was wrong with this guy? Michael wondered. For a cop, he didn't seem much interested in evidence of murder. Was he lazy? Incompetent? Or did he have something to hide?

"Can you recommend a company to tow my car?" Chelsea asked.

Hammer gave her the name of a local garage.

"And there's the question of who shot at us," Michael said.

"There's that."

"Are you going to report it to the state police? It sounds like it's part of the murder case."

"Mmm-hmm," Hammer said, without really answering the question.

"Chelsea could be in danger," Michael added. "The killer may think she knows something. But we're actually both clueless."

The chief turned to her. "Maybe you want to get out of town for a few days."

Michael wanted to ask what good that would do if the chief wasn't going to solve the crime, but again he held his tongue.

As they started back toward the road, Michael reached for Chelsea's hand, and she winced.

His gaze shot to her.

She held up the hand. "That scrape."

Michael turned to Draper. "Can you drop us at the doctor's house on the way back to town?"

"Sure."

They rode back to town in the backseat of the cruiser, and the young officer stopped at Dr. Janecek's office. The doctor was finishing up with a patient, but his receptionist thought he could fit Chelsea in.

As they sat in the waiting area, Michael leaned toward Chelsea. "The fewer people who know what really happened, the better."

"What do you want me to say?"

"That we were out for a walk, and you slipped and hurt your hand."

"Okay."

A few minutes later, the receptionist called Chelsea's name. When she stood, Michael also got up and walked back with her.

The doctor looked surprised to see him, but he didn't make any comment as he gestured for Chelsea to sit down on the examination table. "What happened?"

"We were out for a walk, and I slipped."

Janecek inspected the hand. "This didn't just happen. It's starting to get infected."

"It was this morning. I thought it was okay at first."

"You didn't clean it properly," he said.

She glanced at Michael, then away. "I guess I was careless."

The doctor turned to him. "You should take better care of her, young man."

"Sorry," he said.

The doctor returned his attention to Chelsea. "I'm going to take a blood sample, just to make sure you haven't given yourself blood poisoning. Then I'll give you some antibiotics."

"Okay."

Michael looked at the diplomas on the wall. "You went to medical school in Prague?" he asked.

Janecek gave him a startled look. "Why, yes. I was born in the U.S., but I went back to my parents' country for medical school."

"How did you end up in Jenkins Cove?"

"The town needed a doctor, and I liked the pace of life here."

Deliberately, Janecek turned back to Chelsea.

Michael nodded, watching as the physician swabbed alcohol on Chelsea's arm and took the sample. Then he gave her an antibiotic shot and some pills for a follow-up. When they were finished, Michael excused himself to use the bathroom, then took a quick look around. Janecek seemed as if he was being evasive. Was he hiding something? Like maybe he'd faked his medical degree?

Or maybe he just wasn't used to anyone asking questions about his background. Still, it might be worth checking him out.

They were out of the office in less than half an hour.

"Was the doctor here when you were a little girl?" Michael asked.

"I think so. Why?"

"I'm just curious."

"I hope Aunt Sophie isn't worried," she said, changing the subject.

"Incredible as it may seem, we haven't been away all that long."

She nodded. "I guess it only seems like days since we started out this morning." She gave him a questioning look. "What happened to the gun?"

"I've still got it."

"Good. Because we might need protection."

"I'm glad you're taking this seriously."

"That's why I bought it in the first place."

"Yeah."

"Maybe we should call the state police and make sure they know about the grave site." She swallowed hard. "Thanks for not mentioning the ghost."

"I didn't think Draper or Hammer would deal with that too well."

When they stepped back into the House of the Seven Gables, Aunt Sophie gave them a questioning look. "What happened to the two of you? Chelsea, where's your coat?"

"It's a long story."

Her aunt's eyes narrowed. "I think you had better level with me. Something's been happening and you've been keeping me out of the loop, haven't you?"

"Yes," Chelsea admitted in a low voice.

"Come into the kitchen. I want both of you to tell me what's going on." She made a little sound. "Well, not *everything*. There are some things I don't need to know."

Chelsea flushed, and Michael felt his face heat. Apparently Aunt Sophie didn't miss much.

In the kitchen they told her about the shooting incident and their escape.

"This is getting serious," Sophie murmured.

"I'm afraid so."

"It's lucky we're not having a lot of guests this week."

"Is that unusual?" Michael asked.

"Well, we wanted to relax after the party," Sophie allowed.

They talked for a while longer, and then Chelsea excused herself to call the garage.

After he'd showered and put his own clothes back on, he went up to her room. When he knocked, she called out, "Come in."

She was standing in the middle of the room, with wet hair and wearing one of the B & B's robes. She looked so sweet and vulnerable that his heart turned over.

"How are you?" he asked, crossing the room and taking her in his arms.

"Fine."

"You can't be, after what you've been through."

"I'm fine when you're holding me." She tipped her head up, and he brought his lips to hers for a kiss that quickly turned greedy.

"So, what are we going to do?" she asked when the kiss broke. "Do I sneak down to your room tonight, or do you sneak up here?"

"Do you think either one of those is a good idea?" he asked.

"You're right. It will be harder to explain your being up here. I'll come down to your room."

"Chelsea!"

"You don't want me?"

"Of course I want you."

She grinned and pulled the edge of the robe open a little, then guided his hand inside.

He made a low sound when he encountered her naked breast, and felt her nipple tighten under his touch.

"We can't do this now," he muttered, hearing his voice turn rough.

"I just want you to know what you'll be missing if you lock your door. It won't do you any good, anyway. I've got the key."

"Yeah. So I might as well surrender."

"Good decision."

He knew that if he didn't take his hand away, they were headed for the nearby bed. He pulled back and asked, "Can you do me a favor?"

"What?"

"Get Phil Cardon in here to do some work. I'd like to have a look in his tool kit. And his car. We might even find out something from the way he acts."

She thought for a moment. "There are several repairs we need done, and some painting. With the house almost empty, doing the work now would make sense."

"Do you mind having him do those things? I could pay for it, if that's a problem."

"No. We need to have the work done anyway. I'll call him after I get dressed."

Before Michael could get into trouble, he left the room.

CHELSEA DRESSED and walked downstairs to the office, where she called Phil.

"I was hoping you could do some repair work for us," she said. Quickly she outlined the projects. "When could you come?" she asked.

"I had a cancellation for tomorrow," he said.

"Perfect."

"Around nine?"

"Yes."

After transacting the business, she hung up, then stood looking out the window, suddenly overcome by everything that had happened since last night.

It had been quite a lot—starting with the ghost and ending with almost getting arrested. In between, she and Michael had made love. And she was getting ready to do it again tonight.

Things were moving very quickly with Michael. More quickly than they ever had in her life.

Well, she'd worry about that later, she told herself as she climbed the stairs to her room. Right now she was dead tired.

She lay down, intending to relax for a few minutes. Instead, she was instantly asleep.

MICHAEL EXPECTED TO SEE Chelsea that evening. But when he heard a knock at his door, he opened it and found Aunt Sophie standing there.

"In case you were planning on meeting Chelsea later, I thought I'd better warn you that she's sleeping. And she looks like she's down for the count."

He tried to keep his voice cool. "I appreciate your telling me."

"Things have changed between you," Aunt Sophie said.

He shifted his weight from one foot to the other but didn't answer.

Sophie gave him a long look, but mercifully, she said nothing else before turning on her heel and leaving.

In truth, Michael was also zonked by the day's ordeal. He went to bed early and woke up to the sound of pounding somewhere in the house.

Quickly he got up and dressed, then went into the dining room, where he found Chelsea waiting for him.

"Sorry," she murmured.

"About what?"

She lowered her voice. "Not coming to your room."

He stepped closer and cupped his hand over her shoulder. "We both needed to sleep."

"Still…"

He looked toward the kitchen and leaned forward so he could give her a quick kiss.

She stepped closer, leaning into him. They stood close together for several moments, and he drank in her familiar scent.

A noise in the kitchen made them both jump and move a few feet apart.

"Is that Phil working?" he asked.

"Yes."

"Keep him in the kitchen. I'm going to go out and look at his truck. If it looks like he's coming out, warn me."

She nodded and disappeared into the kitchen.

Quickly he exited through the front door and walked around to where the handyman had left his truck—the same one they'd seen him in the day before.

The door was unlocked, and Michael leaned inside. He found what he was looking for in the glove compartment—a handgun.

Before he could check to see if it had been fired, a sharp rap on the window made him slam the compartment closed and leap out of the truck.

He'd barely closed the door when Phil appeared.

The handyman gave him a long look. "Something I can do for you?"

"No. I was just catching a little air."

"Without your coat?"

"Yeah," he said, his eyes fixed on the man. "Like you."

"I'm only out here to get my paintbrushes and tray."

"I'm only out here for a few minutes," Michael countered.

Phil brushed past him and headed toward the tool locker in the truck bed.

Michael ducked back into the house, where Chelsea was waiting for him. "Thanks for the warning."

"I wonder if he thinks we're up to something."

"Don't know."

"You have a lot of experience with this cloak-and-dagger stuff?" she asked.

He shrugged. "A little."

"Where did you pick it up?"

He shrugged again. "Here and there."

He could have told her that it was a skill an investigative reporter needed, but he ducked the question by asking, "What's for breakfast?"

"French toast."

"Sounds wonderful."

In the dining room, he picked up a copy of the *Washington Post,* folded it to the editorial section and read some of the commentaries as he waited for his breakfast.

Phil exited the kitchen and walked through the dining room, carrying his painting equipment. He gave Michael a sharp look as he passed.

Michael just kept reading the newspaper.

Aunt Sophie delivered his breakfast, and he began to eat. He was still sitting at the table when he heard voices in the kitchen.

Was that Phil talking to Aunt Sophie?

No, Phil had gone to some other part of the house. He could have come back in, though, through the kitchen door.

And he could be up to no good.

Quietly, Michael stood up and walked to the door. When he pushed it open a crack, he saw a man he didn't immediately recognize. Then he remembered the guy's name. Edwin Leonard.

He and Aunt Sophie were talking earnestly, both with their backs to him.

Taking the opportunity to find out what they were concerned about, he stayed where he was, eavesdropping.

"I don't like to be disloyal to Mr. Brandon," Leonard was saying as he hunched his shoulders and leaned closer to Sophie.

"Just because he's hiding papers, that's no reason to get upset," Aunt Sophie said gently.

"But I've been with him for years, and it's not like him to be so secretive."

"Well, if you're worried, you should go to the police," Aunt Sophie murmured.

"I've never trusted the cops," Leonard answered.

"Yes, well, I can understand why you don't think much of Chief Hammer."

"There's something about that man that sets my teeth on edge," Edwin muttered.

"I agree entirely."

A noise from behind him made Michael go rigid. Quietly he closed the door and turned—to find Chelsea staring at him.

"Can I help you?" she said, an edge in her voice.

Chapter Fifteen

Michael took several steps away from the door and turned to face her. "Edwin Leonard is upset about something. Something to do with Brandon Drake."

"It makes me uncomfortable when you listen in on Aunt Sophie."

"Well, it was actually Edwin. Maybe we've been looking in the wrong direction."

"Maybe," she conceded.

"It's got to do with Brandon Drake hiding some papers. Maybe you can find out more about it."

"If I can find a graceful way to do it."

Michael could see that Chelsea was on edge. He didn't blame her. He was on edge, too. He was just handling it differently.

He cleared his throat. "What's the name of that detective who was here from the state police?"

"Rand McClellan."

"I think I'm going to tell him what's been happening to us." She answered with a tight nod.

"You don't approve?"

"I do. But I'm starting to wonder about my judgment."

He gave her a long look. He wanted to ask exactly what she

meant. But he didn't want to push her into saying something he didn't want to hear.

"I wonder if Chief Hammer will think we're pulling rank on him," she whispered.

"The heck with Hammer. I want to make sure nothing happens to you."

He wanted to reach for her and hold on to her—to reassure himself that everything was okay between them. But the look in her eyes made him back away.

In his room he debated whether to call the barracks or just show up. He liked the idea of taking the detective by surprise, but he could be wasting a trip out there if the guy wasn't available. So he called.

Rand McClellan wasn't at his desk when Michael arrived at the barracks. He was outside on a basketball court behind the building, wearing sweatpants and a sweat jacket and dribbling a ball.

"Kind of informal, aren't we?" Michael asked as the detective passed the ball to him. He dribbled it a couple of times, then aimed for the basket, made the shot and passed the ball back.

Was this guy putting him on?

The cop dribbled the ball a few times and took a shot.

"You must have played in college," Michael commented.

"High school—like you."

Michael watched the ball hit the rim and circle before dropping into the basket. "You had to do some digging to find about my high school basketball days."

"But your article about the clients at that investment firm was pretty easy to find. Did ghosts bring you to Jenkins Cove?"

To hide his surprise, Michael bounced the ball, then shot again—and missed. "Okay, yeah."

"So, what do you want to know—if I think Chelsea Caldwell really did see a ghost?"

"No, I've changed my mind about the supernatural."

"Oh yeah? What happened?"

"Some weird stuff that you probably wouldn't believe."

"Try me."

"Let's just keep this on the factual level. I want to tell you that Chelsea's in danger." As he gave an account of the incidents of the past few days, the cop stopped dribbling and studied him. "Hammer share any of that with you?" Michael asked.

"Actually, no."

"Why do you think that is?"

McClellan shrugged. "It could be because I'm invading his territory."

"You think he doesn't want to find out who killed that girl?"

"Maybe."

"But you're not sure about his motives," Michael pressed.

"I try not to jump to conclusions."

"That's refreshing."

"I appreciate your stopping by," McClellan said. "And if you can keep me in the loop, I appreciate that, too." He handed Michael a card with a phone number. "That's my direct line."

"You have any leads on the case?" he asked McClellan. "Did you identify the woman who was murdered?"

"Nobody reported missing." The cop gave him a direct look. "It might be safer for you if you got out of town."

"Funny, that was the advice Hammer gave Chelsea. But she's not going anywhere, and neither am I. That would leave her unprotected."

"You aim to protect her?"

"I do." His gaze bored into the detective. "Have you taken her off your suspect list?"

"What makes you think she's on it?"

"She found the body."

McClellan sighed. "That's the only connection I can find."

"Good."

The detective turned toward the station, then spun back. He gave Michael a long, hard look. "A piece of advice, Mr. Bryant. Watch your back."

As Chelsea entered the office she remembered the unsettling feeling from earlier that day when she'd stepped into the kitchen. Edwin and her aunt had been talking but had gone quiet as soon as she stepped in.

Had they been talking about Brandon Drake? Or had the conversation turned personal?

She hadn't found out because almost as soon as she'd entered the room, Edwin excused himself, saying he needed to get back to Drake House.

Aunt Sophie had offered no insight when Chelsea had questioned her.

"The conversation was nothing you have to worry about," she'd said.

Since then, Chelsea had other things on her mind. Serious things. Like Michael. She'd rushed into an intimate relationship with a man she hardly knew, and now she was wondering if she'd moved too fast.

Michael kept surprising her with his expertise in what she'd called cloak-and-dagger skills. And when she'd asked him about it, he'd been evasive.

He reminded her more of a private investigator than a writer. Was he here in Jenkins Cove on some covert assignment he couldn't talk about?

An unsettling memory rattled her, and she went still. She remembered a handsome, smooth-talking art dealer she'd dated a year ago. Carl Whitman. He'd claimed he was interested in a relationship but she'd found out that what he really wanted was to get her paintings for a good price.

She winced. Was Michael doing something similar? Well, not with her work. With something else.

She clenched her hands into fists. Perhaps she was getting cold feet and was looking for reasons to put some distance between them.

Well, maybe she should do what she should have done in the first place—see what she could find out about him.

Pulling the chair up to the desk, she switched on the computer and opened a connection to the Internet.

Then she went to Google and typed in *Michael Bryant.* It was a common name, but since he was a writer, she could sort out which one he was.

Only, the citations weren't what she'd expected.

He'd written several books—one on the civil war in Rwanda, another on New Jersey mobsters and another on the rapid changes in technology.

And he had a whole slew of articles in prestigious national magazines.

She'd thought he was working on a novel. But all of his books were nonfiction.

So he'd come down here and misrepresented himself. At least, he'd let her and Aunt Sophie come to the wrong conclusions about him.

As she scanned more notations about his career, she quickly gathered that the topics he picked were generally something he wanted to debunk or expose.

So what did that mean for Jenkins Cove? What was he really doing down here?

With a tight feeling in her chest, she began searching for more evidence.

One of his recent articles had been about a Chicago investment broker whose clients were getting bilked by a medium. Michael had exposed the woman as a fraud.

The summary of the article set her teeth on edge. He'd certainly gone after the medium with a vengeance.

As Chelsea looked for more references, she found several instances where he'd participated in chat rooms or done guest blogs. One of the blogs was by a man who was writing snide comments about the current interest in psychic phenomena.

"I have to agree with you," Michael had written. "There's no scientific basis for belief in ghosts. People who claim to have seen them are obviously making a bid for attention. Take the case of a woman in Jenkins Cove, Maryland, who claimed to have seen a ghost when she was a little girl. Recently, she's come up with another story that can't be verified by any known facts."

Chelsea's heart started to pound as she stared at the entry. It was written the week before he'd come down here.

Michael was talking about her.

He hadn't come here to write something unfavorable about Jenkins Cove.

He had come here to write something unfavorable about *Chelsea Caldwell!*

No wonder he'd been abashed when she'd asked where he got his ideas. It was from his own nasty prejudices.

Just as she finished scrolling through the snide comments he'd written on the blog, the door to the office opened, and the man himself stepped in.

"Oh, there you are," he said. "I thought we could…"

She wanted to run and hide from this poseur who thought so little of her. Instead, she pushed back the chair and stood up, facing him squarely.

MICHAEL FELT his blood run cold as he looked wildly around the room. Unable to identify the problem, he rushed toward Chelsea.

"What is it? What's happened?" he asked as he stepped in front of her and grasped her shoulders.

He felt her go rigid. "Take your hands off me," she said in a voice he hardly recognized.

"What's wrong?" Even as he asked the question, he had a horrible suspicion of what she was going to say.

She stepped aside and pointed to the computer screen.

"Did you write this?" she asked in a voice as cold as ice.

He looked at the reply he'd made to the blog entry and repressed a groan. Detective Rand McClellan wasn't the only one who had looked him up. Apparently Chelsea had decided to do it, too.

"That was before I knew you," he said.

"Yes, well, you should have kept it that way."

"That was my stupid uninformed opinion."

"You came to Jenkins Cove to write about me. To prove that I'd made up ghost stories to get attention—or maybe something worse."

He felt as if the floor had dropped out from under his feet. Still, he kept talking. "I can't deny that. But you know that's not what I think anymore."

She didn't seem to be listening. Either that or she didn't care what he had to say. "You've been using me," she spat out.

"No!"

"What would you call it?"

"I've fallen in love with you."

She answered with a mirthless laugh. "Oh, please. You saw an opportunity to get into my pants and you took it."

He could have argued that he'd kept himself from making love to her as long as humanly possible—given how much he wanted her. He could have told her that cold fear had gathered in his gut when he'd thought about her finding out his original motivation.

"Why did you pick on me?" she asked in a strangely quiet voice.

"A friend got me interested in the subject. He's an investment broker, and he found out a number of his clients were consulting a medium and losing money every time they followed her hot tips. Some of them got bilked out of their life savings. It made me remember something I'd repressed from my own childhood, when my mom consulted a medium after my father died. The woman got a lot of money out of her before she decided she wasn't really communicating with my dead father. I knew the woman was lying to her, and I had to stand there and watch it happen, because I was a kid and she wouldn't listen to me. I can't stand liars. And I thought you were one. That article in the *Gazette* said you'd been talking about ghosts."

"That was a damn lie. I never talked about it. The story got around, and the reporter assumed I had said something."

"Yes. As soon as I talked to you, I started doubting my assumptions."

"Yeah, right."

Ignoring the interjection, he plowed on. "And the better I got to know you, the more I realized you were absolutely honest. It only took a few days for me to realize you have a genuine gift."

"Thanks for the ringing endorsement. Now get out of here," she said. "I mean, pack up your things and get the hell out of my house."

"You can hate me," he said between clenched teeth, "but I'm going to stay here to protect you until we find out who's trying to kill you."

"Did you make that up to get close to me?"

"Now you've really gone off the deep end," he muttered. "You think I made up someone shooting at us?"

"Maybe you were working with him. You insisted on taking the gun away from me. Then you never did shoot back at him."

"Because I couldn't see him! And then I would have announced that we were in that hole."

She snorted.

Seeing that nothing he said would make any difference at the moment, he turned and left the room.

"Pack your things and get out of here," she called after him. "I'll call Chief Hammer if you're not gone in an hour."

Ignoring her, he walked to his room and grabbed his jacket, then walked out of the house, where he stood breathing in the crisp December air. It made his chest hurt, although he suspected that simply breathing would be agony.

She'd ordered him out with vehemence and conviction. No way was he leaving, not when he'd lose his access to her. He had to change her mind about him. How, he wondered, when Chelsea wasn't going to give him a chance to get close to her again? And he wouldn't even blame her.

He should have confessed days ago. He'd tried to do it yesterday but he'd only said half of what he needed to say to come clean.

Too bad he'd been a coward then.

As he stared across the harbor, he heard another door in the house open.

Quickly he charged around to the side yard in time to see Chelsea slam the door behind her and head toward the road—where the car had tried to run him over the first night in Jenkins Cove.

As he watched her stride away from the house, a car swerved around the corner. It stopped, and he saw someone inside roll down the window, although he couldn't tell who it was from where he was standing. Yet he sensed danger.

"Stay away from the car," he shouted. But either she was too far away to hear him, or she was too angry to pay attention to anything he said.

Briskly, she walked toward the vehicle and got in as Michael's warning died on the breeze. The car drove away.

Chapter Sixteen

Michael's heart leaped into his throat.

He had no proof that anything bad was happening—except for the telltale knot in his gut.

With only one goal in mind, he bolted toward the vehicle.

With a lurch, the car roared away. It was a silver Honda, one of the most common cars on the road.

His gaze dropped to the license plate, but it was obscured by mud. So he couldn't tell the cops what car to look for. And what would they do, anyway? He had no evidence of any crime.

He felt numb and cold as the car disappeared. He didn't have his car keys, and by the time he got them, the vehicle could be anywhere.

Frustration and agony bubbled over in a string of curses. He had no idea what he was going to do. Then an image leaped into his mind.

The psychomanteum. It was his only hope to find out who was in that car and why Chelsea had gotten inside.

The idea that he'd turn to the psychomanteum blew his mind. Yet he dashed into the house, then up to the third floor.

Inside the blackened room, he flipped on the light and looked around, seeing the chair, the black curtains and the mirror.

What should he do now?

He remembered the scene when he'd rushed in here and found Chelsea just after she'd been talking to Lavinia.

Lavinia. The ghost who had revealed the location of the grave-yard. And the ghost who had shown them the hole in the ground where they could hide, and then illuminated it so they could see the tunnel. He hadn't seen the ghost but he'd seen that eerie glow.

He looked around and saw a box of matches on the table to the left of the door.

Quietly he walked around, lighting the candles; then he turned off the ceiling fixture. In the flickering light, he sat down and stared at his own reflection in the mirror.

Now came the hard part.

Tension tightened his chest. He would have felt like a fool doing this, except that he was desperate.

He sat there, staring at the mirror. But nothing seemed to happen. He shifted in his seat, feeling as if the walls of the room were closing in around him.

Finally, he spoke. "Lavinia, I need your help. Please, come to me."

Still, nothing happened, and Michael felt a lump of fear expand inside his chest.

CHELSEA STRUGGLED not to give away her terror. There were two men in the car—one driving and one holding a gun. The driver was the man she'd seen hanging around down by the dock. He wasn't anyone she knew. Not Ned Perry or Phil Cardon. But the gunman…

She knew *him*. It was Dr. Janecek. He'd been at the Christmas party. And yesterday he'd treated the wound on her hand. Now he was taking her away.

He'd called her over to the car before by saying he wanted to discuss her lab results. She hadn't even noticed the strange driver until she was in the backseat with a gun aimed at her head.

A few blocks from the House of the Seven Gables, the driver pulled into an empty garage and closed the door.

"Get out," the doctor ordered.

"What do you want with me?"

"Quiet," he snarled.

She got out of the car, trying and failing to keep from shaking.

"Hands behind your back."

She took her lower lip between her teeth as the driver pressed her hands behind her. Roughly, he wound duct tape around her wrists and then her ankles. When he came at her with another piece of tape for her mouth, she couldn't hold back a moan. For all the good it did her.

After they had finished, he carried her to another car and dumped her in the backseat like a sack of horse feed.

The door was open, and she could hear the men conferring a few yards away.

She didn't know the driver's name. But now she wished she'd paid more attention to him. He must also have been the man Michael had seen—the man who had escaped by boat.

"Listen, Franz, I'm tired of your acting on your own without waiting for my say-so," Janecek said.

"I was taking initiative."

"You're working for me, not the other way around. I need you to follow orders instead of making up jobs on your own. Go back and pick up Bryant so we can take care of both of them."

Chelsea tried to scream, "No." But the sound was muffled by the tape.

She'd been angry and hurt by Michael's betrayal when she ran out of the house. She was still angry. But now fear for him made her go cold all over.

And fear for herself. What were they planning to do with *her?*

The doctor got behind the wheel and pulled out of the garage.

Panic flooded through her system, making her feel as though her breath was choking off.

In the backseat, she tried to wrench her wrists apart, but it was no good. The tape was too tight and too firm. Terror threatened to sweep away all rational thought, but she struggled to rise above it, to make her mind function logically.

She remembered coming outside and how, just before she'd gotten into the car, she'd spotted Michael.

He'd seen her.

Either he'd seen that the doctor had a gun, or he'd sensed she was in danger, because he came running to save her. Only it was already too late.

Now he had no idea where to look for her.

From the front seat, the doctor spoke to her. "You couldn't leave well enough alone," he said, his voice regretful.

Her only thought was of Michael. He'd said he loved her, and like a fool she'd ignored him. Now she'd never get the chance to see him again.

BACK AT THE House of the Seven Gables, Michael struggled against his fear and frustration. Again, his pleas were met only by silence.

Unable to stay in the chair, he stood up and paced from one end of the psychomanteum to the other. When his agony bubbled over, he shouted, "You have to help me. Chelsea is in danger. I'll do anything it takes to save her."

"Will you?"

He hadn't really expected an answer, which was why the voice in his ear was so startling. When he whirled around, he saw nothing. Or maybe he did. Maybe he detected a small wavering in the air.

"Lavinia?"

"Yes," the voice answered. He couldn't be sure if she'd

spoken aloud or in his head. But he knew she had a thick accent. Russian or somewhere else in that part of the world.

"You have to help me," he gasped out.

"Why should I?"

FROM WHERE SHE LAY on the backseat, Chelsea could see the upper stories of buildings and the tops of trees passing by. When the view switched to only trees, she knew they were heading out of town. After what she judged was a few miles, they turned onto a bumpy road.

Branches pressed in on either side of the car, and she felt shocked when she recognized where they were headed.

This was the road to the old warehouse where she and Michael had gone a few days ago.

Silently, she called out to her only hope.

Michael, please, I need you. I'm at the old warehouse. The place where we went the other day. The place where you fell into that trap.

Please. Please come find me here.

She felt she was sending the message out into a black hole, where it would never emerge into the sunlight again.

Michael wasn't going to find her here. She was on her own, and she had to save herself.

The car stopped abruptly.

Dr. Janecek got out and walked away from the car. Then she heard a scraping sound. Moments later he was back and driving into the warehouse through the open doors.

He got out again and she could see him walking around to the trunk. He got something out, something she couldn't see because it was below the level of the windows. Then he walked back to the trunk again. Finally, he opened the back door of the car, sat her up and hauled her out. Picking her up, he carried her a few yards away and laid her on a flat surface. A padded table.

Next he secured the lower half of her body to the table with straps. Then he cut the tape on her hands.

When she tried to lunge at him, he leveled a blow to her face. Stars flashed in front of her eyes.

Too stunned to move, she could only lie there as he secured her hands to straps at the side of the table. Then he cut the tape on her ankles and strapped her feet the way he had her hands.

When he stepped back, staring at her, the look on his face made her stomach churn.

"What…what are you going to do?" she asked.

"Solve two problems at once. Too bad you were poking your nose in where it didn't belong. If you'd just driven by a little later, we would have had that woman buried. And you never would have gotten a chance to interfere."

"Please. Let me go," she begged.

He laughed, and it wasn't a pleasant sound. "So you can go straight to the cops? Of course not. But you're going to help me out. I have a buyer for a heart. And you're a match. I established that when I took that blood sample from you the other day."

MICHAEL STRUGGLED TO SPEAK around the constriction in his throat. He'd come to Jenkins Cove thinking that ghosts were total nonsense. Now here he was in the psychomanteum throwing himself on the mercy of a spirit.

From skeptic to true believer in a heartbeat.

In answer to the ghost's question, the truth came shooting out of his mouth with the force of a volcano breaking through the surface of the earth.

"You have to help me find Chelsea because I love her. And it's my fault she's in trouble. She went storming out of the house because she was mad at me. If anything happens to her, I'll never forgive myself."

Lavinia said nothing, and he felt his heart pounding as agonizing seconds ticked by.

When she spoke, it wasn't what he wanted so desperately to hear. "Why was she mad at you?"

He gulped. "Because before I came to Jenkins Cove, I was mouthing off about how she must be a fraud."

"A fraud because she claimed she'd seen me?"

"Yes," he answered. "And now, if I have to get down on my knees and beg you to help me find her, I'll do it." He dragged in a breath and let it out. "I'll do it *now*."

He climbed out of the chair and sank to his knees beside it.

"Help me," he said again. "Please help me."

When he had finished pleading, he held his breath, waiting for an answer. And for long moments, he thought Lavinia was going to leave him in agony.

Then, to his profound relief, her voice whispered next to his ear, "Dr. Janecek is holding her at the old warehouse."

The words were so unexpected that he blinked. Was she putting him on? "Dr. Janecek? Why would he do that?"

Her ghostly voice turned flinty. "He's been bringing people into Jenkins Cove for years. Illegal aliens. From Eastern Europe. He speaks those languages, so he can communicate with them."

Michael's brain was on overload. They'd been to see the doctor after Chelsea hurt her hand. If Janecek was behind the killings, then they'd played right into his hands.

"What…what does he bring them in for?" he managed to ask in a cracked voice.

"Some are sex slaves. Some paid a lot of money to get into the country. Or they might pay for their passage with a kidney. Like me. Only I didn't plan to do that. I saved my money so I could pay up front, but then the doctor said I had to donate a kidney anyway."

The ghost was silent for several moments; then she made a strangled sound.

"What?"

"You must hurry. Chelsea is in grave danger. The doctor is going to take her heart for a transplant patient."

Michael scrambled to his feet. When he almost lost his balance, he grabbed the back of the chair to steady himself. "Her heart," he gasped. "Oh God, not her heart."

He dashed out of the room and pounded down the steps to the ground floor. First he ran to the living room and picked up the phone. Fumbling in his pocket, he pulled out the paper where he'd written down Rand McClellan's number.

Centuries passed while the phone rang at the other end of the line. When McClellan answered, Michael started to shout at him. Then he realized it was a recorded message. The detective wasn't there.

All Michael could do was spit out his message and pray the guy got it. "Chelsea is being held at the old warehouse on the edge of town where I told you I fell into that hole. Janecek is going to kill her."

Slamming down the receiver, he charged out of the room and onto the porch.

Then he thought maybe he should tell Sophie to alert Chief Hammer. He'd just called out to her when a voice spoke behind him.

"Hold it right there."

He whirled around again. Instead of Aunt Sophie, he saw a man step out of the bushes beside the house and onto the oyster-shell path. He was of medium height and weight. There was nothing much distinctive about him except that he was holding an automatic pistol.

"Hands up."

Michael stared at him. "Who the hell are you?" But even as

the question tumbled out of him, he was pretty sure he knew the answer. It was the man who had been watching the house. The man who had tried to run him over. The man who had tried to kill Chelsea in the kitchen with the blender and the water on the floor, before escaping in a boat from the dock. And probably the man who had hunted them out in the bog.

"It don't matter who I am. You're coming with me."

"Where?"

"You'll find out soon enough."

THE DOCTOR TURNED AWAY from Chelsea, and she saw him set up another table a few feet from where she lay. When he had it in place, he walked back to the car and retrieved a black bag he'd brought. His back to her, he laid out a white towel, then began taking out shiny, frightening instruments.

Once more he returned to the car trunk, and this time he took out a carrying case. She recognized it from television programs she'd seen. It was the kind of container they used to transport human organs.

She wanted to scream, "No. Let me go. I haven't done anything to hurt you."

But she knew that was a lie. She'd done something to hurt him the moment she'd driven to the police station. She'd gotten in the way of his illegal operation, and he wasn't going to allow her to trip him up that way.

She pulled at the straps that secured her to the table, but she was held firmly in place. She wasn't going anywhere. This was it.

In a few moments she would be dead. Did the doctor plan to give her anesthetic when he cut her open? The question was too horrible to contemplate.

She squeezed her eyes shut for a moment because that was the only way she could be alone. She'd been a fool. She understood that now. But it was too late. All her hopes and dreams would end right here, in this warehouse.

She'd rushed out of the house because she'd been so hurt when she'd read Michael's comments on that blog. But she knew he had changed his mind since coming to Jenkins Cove. She knew he'd tried to tell her about it before he'd made love to her. But he'd lost his nerve, and she understood why. He'd known she'd be angry and hurt. He'd told her part of it and he'd probably been hoping to find the right time to tell her the rest. Only she'd gotten ahead of him and found it out herself.

Oh Lord. If she'd only let him explain, she wouldn't be in this mess now.

But his words on that blog had felt like the worst kind of betrayal—because she'd fallen in love with him.

Now she was in this old warehouse, strapped to a table, about to die. And she wouldn't get a chance to tell Michael what she felt for him.

"Michael, I forgive you," she whispered in a voice too low for the doctor to hear. "I wish I could tell you that. I wish I could tell you I love you."

A whisper of sound answered her. Not Michael. Someone else.

Chelsea looked around her. The air seemed to stir.

"Lavinia?"

The ghost didn't answer, but Dr. Janecek spun around, his eyes fixed on her. "What did you say?"

"Lavinia," she said in as strong a voice as she could muster. "She's here."

"She can't be. She's dead."

"But she came back. She spoke to me in the psychomanteum."

"That's just a bunch of hooey."

"Is it? Then how do I know her name?"

"You found the list of people coming in that shipment," he shot back.

"Shipment! That's a wonderful way to put it. And where do you think I would have seen it?"

"You came to my office. That Michael Bryant guy wasn't with you every moment. He must have gone snooping around."

"Is that where you keep your lists?"

"You know I do!"

She struggled to hold her voice steady, to sound logical. "You're clutching at straws."

The doctor's eyes narrowed. "Don't try to turn this around. You're the one in trouble. You've been snooping into my business, and now you're just trying to stall me, to keep yourself alive for a few more minutes."

"Go on thinking that," Chelsea said in a firm voice. "Until the cops come to get you."

"I know you didn't call the cops," he shot back.

Ignoring the comment, Chelsea said, "That wasn't you the other day out in the marsh shooting at us."

"Hardly. I don't go in for tramping around in the mud unless I have to. That was my assistant, Franz Kreeger—the man who was with me in the car. But you're not going to get a chance to tell that to anyone."

"He killed Lavinia?"

When Janecek didn't answer, she asked another question. "Why are you doing this? I mean all of it—not just the part about me."

"For money."

"You don't need it!"

He turned to glare at her. "How would you know what I need? I grew up in a family where there was never enough of anything to go around. I decided I wasn't going to live that way ever again."

"So you took advantage of helpless people?"

"Stop asking questions," he said with a snarl in his voice.

Instead, she changed the subject again. "I understand why

you went after me. But why did Franz Kreeger try to run over Michael when he first arrived in town?"

"Did he?"

"You know he did."

"We were keeping tabs on you and everybody who came to the House of the Seven Gables, in case they were there to help you make trouble for us. We knew that Michael Bryant was a journalist. But I didn't tell Franz to run him down. If he tried it, that was his idea."

So the doctor had been smart enough to look Michael up, long before she'd thought of it. Score one for him.

More than one. Because she was the person strapped to the table and he was the one with the surgical instruments.

As her thoughts whirled, the air behind the doctor shivered, then changed and thickened. Chelsea felt a sudden surge of hope. She saw a figure standing behind the doctor. A woman she could see right through.

"Lavinia?" she called out again as something unseen rushed at Janecek. He must have felt it, because his face took on a look of horror as the phantom flew past him.

Chapter Seventeen

Michael stood facing the man with the gun, his mind churning as it sought a way out.

Then from the corner of his eye, he saw someone else. Aunt Sophie. She had come around the side of the house and gotten behind the man. In her hands she held a pot of something steaming.

He could guess her plan. But he could see that she was putting herself in terrible danger.

He wanted to shout at Sophie to get out of there. Duck for cover. Call the cops. But trying to communicate with her now was out of the question. The best he could do was keep the gunman's attention focused squarely on him so that Sophie wouldn't get hurt.

He cleared his throat and raised his head slightly. "Put down the gun."

The man laughed. "You must be kidding. You're coming with me."

"And if I don't?"

"I shoot you right here."

Michael tipped his head to one side. "Don't you think that will attract a lot of attention?"

"Not before I get the hell out of here."

"This time you didn't bring a boat, did you? You'll have to leave by car. That'll be more dangerous for you."

Behind the man, Aunt Sophie raised the pot and hurled the steaming contents at the gunman's neck.

The man screamed as hot liquid hit him, and the smell of cinnamon filled the air.

The gun fired. But Michael was already out of the way.

The man dropped the weapon and began scrabbling at his burning skin, but the hot liquid seared him like napalm.

Michael kicked the pistol aside, then leaped at the gunman, throwing him to the ground, pummeling him with his fists.

"You bastard," he shouted. "Chelsea better be all right, or I'll kill you."

"Michael, no," Aunt Sophie shouted. "Get away from him. I have him covered."

He looked up to see that Chelsea's aunt had grabbed the gun and was holding it in a two-handed grip like a lady detective in a cop show. Apparently Chelsea wasn't the only woman in the family who knew how to handle a firearm.

As he stepped away from the man on the ground, a noise filtered into his consciousness. It was a police siren heading this way.

"I called the cops before I came out," Aunt Sophie said.

Two squad cars screeched to a halt in the parking area beside the house. Chief Hammer leaped out of one. The deputy named Sam Draper leaped out of the other.

"What's going on?" the chief demanded.

"This man tried to kill Michael Bryant," Sophie said, the gun never wavering from the suspect. "I was making Christmas candles, and I threw hot wax on him."

"He's working with Dr. Janecek," Michael added. "The doctor has Chelsea out at the old warehouse. He's going to kill her. We've got to get out there."

"That's a lie," the guy on the ground shouted. "These people attacked me. The old lady pulled a gun."

Michael answered with a curse. If they all ended up at the

police station sorting through truth and lies, it would be too late for Chelsea.

Lord, what was he going to do, steal a police cruiser and go roaring out of town?

The tactic had a certain amount of appeal. The trouble was, there were two cop cars here. The officers would chase him, maybe shoot at him. And if he ended up wrecking the car, he was no closer to helping Chelsea than he was standing here.

FROM HER POSITION on the table, Chelsea watched the doctor turn back to his instruments. He sorted through the tools he'd laid out, then picked up a scalpel and examined it.

Apparently satisfied, he advanced on Chelsea. As she saw light gleaming off the blade, she tried to squirm away, but the straps held her fast.

The doctor had taken two steps forward when something whooshed at him again. This time it wasn't just one phantom. The air in the warehouse shimmered with shapes Chelsea could barely see. Suddenly the shapes took form. The room seemed to be filled with a whole host of people. Men, women and children crowded into this one enclosure. She knew they had come to help her. These must be the victims Dr. Janecek had killed. Yet he didn't seem to know they were there.

Or did he?

A low buzz filled the air, like the buzzing of a thousand bees. The doctor raised his head, looking around, his gaze darting from one corner of the warehouse to the other.

THOUGH MICHAEL WANTED TO SHOUT at Hammer or, better yet, rush the cop, he spoke slowly and clearly. "Let's try again. Dr. Janecek is holding Chelsea out at the abandoned warehouse southwest of town. The one at the site of the old dock on Jenkins Creek. He's been using it to bring in illegal aliens. This guy was helping him. He's the man who murdered that woman out along the road. He's the one who shot at us out in the marsh. He and Janecek have been stalking Chelsea ever since she saw the murder. If you keep standing here, questioning me, Chelsea is going to end up dead and you are going to be responsible. Do you want that on your conscience?"

The chief looked uncertain.

Aunt Sophie stood with her hands on her hips. When she spoke, her voice had taken on a hard edge. "Charlie Hammer, you know me. Would I throw a pot of hot wax on an innocent man?"

The chief looked from her to the man on the ground.

"Well, consider this," she continued, her face as stern as a teacher who has caught one of her students carving her initials on his desk, "if you let my niece die, I will never forgive you. And I will make sure the whole town knows what happened. Jenkins Cove is a small place. Is that how you want to be remembered?"

Without answering her, Hammer turned to his deputy. "Take the guy to the station."

"I'll sue you," the man shouted as Draper escorted him to one of the cruisers and ducked his head as he pushed him inside.

"I doubt it," Hammer muttered, then turned to Michael. "How do you know Chelsea is at the warehouse?"

Michael's throat clogged. What would happen if he told Hammer the truth?

Once again, Aunt Sophie came to the rescue. Gesturing toward the other police cruiser, she said, "That man you're taking away told us."

The audacity of the lie made Michael blink. Neither one of them had heard the guy say anything of the kind. He had to believe, then, that Aunt Sophie had known he was in the psychomanteum and knew where he'd gotten the information.

His gaze shot to her, and she answered with a tiny nod.

In the middle of the silent exchange, Hammer spoke. "Okay, but was he telling the truth?"

"It's our only lead," Michael argued. "And if we don't get there in time, we'll all be sorry."

To Michael's profound relief, Hammer nodded. "Let's go."

Michael climbed into the police car with the chief, and they sped off.

"You know the turnoff to that old warehouse down by the water? The place where I fell into a trap."

"I know where you mean."

Siren blaring, they raced through town, and sped up when they reached the highway. Still, Michael's heart was in his throat. If he was going to get to Chelsea in time, every second counted.

He had another worry, as well, one that twisted his gut. He couldn't be perfectly sure that the police chief and the doctor weren't working together.

THE DOCTOR ADVANCED on Chelsea, still clutching the scalpel in his hand. He raised his arm, and she wanted to close her eyes as the arm came down in a slashing motion. But, to her astonishment, instead of slicing into her chest, the blade slashed through the strap that held her right hand to the side of the table.

"What the hell?" he cried out as he saw what he had done. Obviously it hadn't been what he'd intended, but somehow the mass of ghosts in the room had influenced his actions.

She saw his features firm, and she knew that he was fighting their power over him.

"No!" he shouted as he raised the instrument again, but this time Chelsea wasn't helplessly strapped down. She was able to crash the fist of her free hand into his mouth. Howling in pain, he toppled backward, landing against the table of instruments and scattering them across the floor.

While he was trying to sort himself out, Chelsea rolled to the side, so that she could reach the other strap. Desperately she fumbled with the leather.

Janecek was on his feet, advancing toward her again.

Teeth gritted, she pulled at the buckle on the strap, trying to loosen her other hand. But her fingers were clumsy, and she couldn't pull the end of the leather through the buckle.

"You won't get away," he swore. "Even if I can't get your heart, you won't get out of here alive."

The doctor had almost reached her when the air around him seemed to thicken again. In a surge of translucent shapes, the ghosts were coming after him, trying to keep him from getting to her.

But she saw the determination in his eyes. He was going to finish her off so she couldn't talk—then get the hell out of here.

As she was still fastened down by one hand and her two feet, the best she could do was roll away from the doctor, turning over the table and crashing to the floor.

For a moment she was stunned. Then Janecek leaped around the table, coming at her again. With a growl of anger, he slashed at her, the blade slicing through the fabric of her shirt and into her flesh.

She cried out in pain, but she wouldn't give up. One of her legs had come free of its strap in the fall, and she kicked out at him, landing a blow to his gut.

He howled again, then dived for her.

Before he could inflict another slash into her flesh, she saw something in back of him. This time it was not a ghost. It was a man—running at full speed across the floor.

It was Michael.

She screamed his name. "Watch out. He's got a scalpel."

As Michael closed in on the doctor, Janecek whirled around and swung his arm. Michael ducked under the knife, landing a blow on the man's chin.

Behind Michael, another figure entered the warehouse. Chief Hammer.

He ran forward, his service weapon in his hand.

"Stop or I'll shoot," he shouted.

Both Michael and the doctor ignored him. With the men struggling, there was no way Hammer could get a clear shot at the doctor—if that was his intended target. She couldn't be absolutely sure which man he wanted to shoot.

Michael grabbed the arm with the scalpel, bending it back so that the doctor screamed in pain.

"Drop it," Michael shouted, "or I'll break your damn arm."

The doctor screamed again as the pressure increased. Finally he dropped the blade and lay breathing hard.

"Cuff him," Michael panted.

As he heard the words, the doctor made a desperate lunge for safety. Michael tackled him again and held him in place. "Do it now!"

For a heartbeat the chief hesitated. Then he rushed forward and slapped handcuffs on the doctor. Michael ran to Chelsea. When he saw that she was cut, he gasped. "You're bleeding."

"It's not bad."

"It better not be."

He knelt beside her, freeing her other hand and her leg, then pulling a strip of cloth from the table and pressing it to her wounded shoulder.

Chief Hammer was starting back toward them when something happened, something that made her eyes bug out.

From out of nowhere came a shriek that sounded like the protest—or the triumph—of a long-dead spirit finally evening the score with the living.

Then others took up the cry, and the air around them was filled with what sounded like a thousand unseen voices.

"What the hell is that?" Chief Hammer cried out, running

toward Michael and Chelsea. He crouched beside her as something flew over their heads. Something they could barely see.

"Keep your head down," Michael called as he bent over Chelsea, gathering her close, sheltering her body against the overturned table.

The air inside the warehouse churned and boiled. Darts of light sailed over and around them as the sound rose, like some kind of indoor windstorm. And above the wailing of the wind, they heard Janecek screaming.

Chapter Eighteen

Suddenly, it all stopped. The wind, the churning of the air, the noise.

In the utter silence, Hammer asked, "What was that?"

"Ghosts," Michael said. He wasn't looking at the chief. He was looking at Chelsea.

"What do you mean, ghosts?" the chief snapped.

"Couldn't you feel them, hear them?" Michael asked, his gaze still on her.

"I don't know what all that was." Hammer stumbled to his feet and crossed the floor, where he knelt beside the handcuffed man.

"He's not breathing." Bending lower, he began administering artificial respiration.

"I think you're wasting your time," Michael muttered.

Another voice spoke from the door. Michael's head jerked up, and he saw Rand McClellan and a state patrolman standing in the doorway. "I got your message. It looks like I got here for the mop-up."

"Chelsea's hurt," Michael answered. "The doctor was going to take out her heart, but he only cut her shoulder."

McClellan winced. Reaching into his pocket, he pulled out his cell phone and called 911, reporting on Chelsea and the doctor.

While the detective was talking to the dispatcher, Michael stood and stripped the rest of the padding off the table, then lifted Chelsea and laid her on it, so that she was no longer sprawled on the cold floor. "How are you?"

"I'm fine now," Chelsea answered. "Thanks to you—and the ghosts." She kept her gaze on Michael as she spoke.

"Yeah, the ghosts," he answered.

"Where did they go?" she murmured.

"I think they went to their rest."

Chelsea nodded and closed her eyes. She was still feeling dazed and still unable to completely come to grips with everything that had happened. Now that the emergency was over, she struggled to hold herself together.

"I'm so sorry," Michael said in a gritty voice.

Her eyes blinked open again, and she shook her head. "No, I was stupid to run out of the house. You warned me to stay inside. But I was too angry to think."

"It's not your fault. I…hurt you."

The sound of a siren in the distance made him glance around.

Minutes later, paramedics rushed into the room. One headed for the doctor, the other ripped the top of her shirt and began examining her wound.

As he worked on her, she heard his partner call out. "The doctor's gone."

"What killed him?" Chief Hammer demanded.

"I can't determine that. You'll have to wait for the report from the medical examiner."

"You need your shoulder stitched," the medic told Chelsea.

"I want to talk to the chief first," she answered.

He heard her. Looking uncomfortable, he crossed back to her.

"Dr. Janecek told me he was bringing illegal aliens into the country," she said. "Some of the women were being sold into sexual slavery. Some of them had to pay for their passage with a kidney or other organ."

The chief winced.

Rand McClellan, who had been listening to the exchange, walked over and addressed the chief. "What do you know about that?"

"Nothing," Hammer answered, but the look in his eyes made her skeptical. Perhaps, she told herself, he was just too shell-shocked by his experience with the ghosts.

"He told me he was going to take my heart for a transplant," Chelsea told him.

The chief swore and strode out of the building.

"He knows more than he's saying." Michael muttered as the other medic bent over Chelsea.

She nodded.

So did McClellan. His mouth firmed. "I should have suspected the doctor. That woman whom you saw murdered— she'd had a kidney removed."

Chelsea gasped. "Why didn't you tell me?"

"That was information confidential to the investigation. I checked at a bunch of hospitals, and I couldn't find where the operation had been done. I should have started checking local doctors."

"That doesn't mean you would have found anything," Chelsea murmured. "He'd been getting away with it for years."

She stopped speaking as the EMTs wheeled in a stretcher.

"We'll take you to the hospital, Ms. Caldwell."

She looked at Michael. "Can he ride with me?"

"Yes."

McClellan and his patrol officer were conferring as the EMTs wheeled her past. Michael climbed into the ambulance beside her, but there was no chance to talk privately.

Then, when they arrived at the hospital, the doctor asked him to leave while he cleaned and stitched her cut.

"Draper's waiting to take your statement," Michael said when he came back into the room.

"What should I tell him?"

"The truth."

She gave Michael a long look. "About the ghosts attacking the doctor?"

Michael sighed. "Maybe you want to leave that part out."

"Why?" she pressed.

"Because it just makes people think you're a nut."

"But that's no longer your personal opinion?"

"You know it's not. Or if you're a nut, then I am, too. Because I went into the psychomanteum and begged Lavinia to tell me where to find you."

Her eyes widened. "You did?"

"Yeah. How do you think I figured out where you were?"

"I didn't know."

A knock on the door interrupted the conversation. It was Draper, who asked if she'd mind reporting what happened. She gave him an account of her kidnapping. Then she said, "And there's another guy who was working with the doctor."

"Franz Kreeger," Draper answered. "He tried to kill Mr. Bryant and your aunt."

Chelsea sucked in a sharp breath as her gaze shot to Michael. "I didn't know about that."

"We haven't had much time to talk."

Michael turned to the deputy. "So you believe us and not Kreeger?"

"There was evidence in his car linking him to the doctor. We also found a woman's purse with bloodstains. We think it will match the blood of the woman you saw murdered," he said to Chelsea. "I've already talked to Detective McClellan. He'll be over in the morning to collect the evidence and take Kreeger into custody."

"Glad to hear it," Michael murmured.

The officer shifted his weight from one foot to the other, then cleared his throat. "There's something I want to say."

Both Michael and Chelsea instantly tensed.

"I want to apologize," Draper said. "That report you turned in about the murder… I told my wife about it and she told her friends. That's how the story about the ghost got around town. I'm hoping you'll forgive me."

"She had everybody whispering about me," Chelsea said.

Michael slung a protective arm over her shoulder.

"And now they're going to be talking about how you broke up a very nasty human smuggling operation and an organ transplant ring," Michael said.

"I'd rather they didn't."

"They won't get it from me," Draper vowed. "But it's news. It'll be in the *Gazette*."

"Yes," she answered.

The young officer cleared his throat. "Do you need me for anything else?"

Michael figured this was a good time to get some concessions out of the guy. "Actually, we could use a ride back to the House of the Seven Gables." He turned toward Chelsea, who was wearing a hospital gown instead of her blood-soaked blouse. "And if there's a shirt and coat she could wear, we'd appreciate it."

"I think the nurses can lend her some scrubs," Draper said. "I'll see what I can round up."

When the guy had left, Chelsea sighed. "He caused me a lot of trouble, but he didn't mean to do it. That murder was big news in Jenkins Cove and a big deal for the local cops."

"You don't hold a grudge."

"I'd like to put it behind me."

He nodded, marveling that she could let it go. When a nurse brought back scrubs, Michael stepped out while the woman helped Chelsea dress.

Fifteen minutes later, they were met at the door of the B & B by an anxious Aunt Sophie.

"Oh, Chelsea," she exclaimed, eyeing the hospital outfit her niece was wearing. "Are you all right? I was so worried before the detective called."

Chelsea looked questioningly at Michael.

"McClellan called her from the warehouse. Then I gave her an update while you were getting stitched up," he answered.

"Come into the living room and sit down. I was so nervous after you left that I went into the kitchen and started baking. We have apricot nut bread, spice cookies and cinnamon buns."

Chelsea laughed, then sank onto the sofa. Michael stood awkwardly in the middle of the room. He was bursting to speak to her about the two of them. But it didn't look as though that was going to happen anytime soon.

"Sit next to me," Chelsea murmured.

Sophie bustled off, and Michael sat.

"We have to talk about us," he said, hearing the gritty sound of his own voice.

"As soon as we can get away. But right now you're going to tell me about what happened with that man—Franz Kreeger."

"He was holding a gun on me. I assume he was planning to take me out to the warehouse and finish me off, but your aunt threw a pot of hot wax at him."

Chelsea winced, just as Aunt Sophie came back into the room with a plate of goodies.

As she set them down, she said, "I knew there was something sinister going on in Jenkins Cove."

"You did?" Chelsea asked.

"Yes. But I couldn't prove it. Anyway, who'd listen to a nutty old woman?"

"You're not nutty," Chelsea said quickly.

"Of course I am. I have that psychomanteum upstairs. Don't

think I don't know some people talk about me like I'm cracked. But I knew there were ghosts here and I knew that they could tell you—" She stopped and swallowed, then looked directly at Chelsea. "They could tell you what was wrong. That's why I asked you to come back and help me here."

Chelsea drew in a sharp breath. "You what?"

"But you weren't ready to deal with the ghosts," Sophie finished. She looked down at her hands. "It made sense when I thought of it. I didn't know I was going to put you in danger. I'm sorry."

"You didn't! It was seeing the ghost out on the road that started it."

Michael slid over and put his arm around her, drawing her close.

"No. It started with your seeing that other ghost—fifteen years ago," Sophie said. "I kept praying that you'd finish what you began."

Chelsea nodded. "I tried so hard to forget about that."

"And it came back to haunt you," her aunt said. "Let's stop talking about it now. Eat some of the cookies I made."

For the next twenty minutes, they ate cookies and drank mulled cider while they told Sophie about what had happened in the warehouse. Finally Sophie gave her niece a critical inspection. "You look done in. You should get some rest."

Michael scuffed his foot against the carpet, wondering if he was going to have to let Chelsea go up, then follow her when the coast was clear.

Sophie waved her hand. "Both of you might as well go on up to her bedroom. I can see you want to be alone with her, Michael. I just had some things I needed to get off my chest."

Grateful to escape, Michael helped Chelsea up the stairs. At the entrance to her room, he hesitated. But she pulled him inside, closed the door and wrapped her arms around him.

"I'm sorry," they both said at once.

"Let me get this off my chest," he begged. "I'm sorry I didn't tell you why I'd come to Jenkins Cove. And I'm sorry I didn't believe you from the beginning." He cleared his throat. "There's something else I should say. From the moment I got here, the ghosts tried to tell me I was wrong. When I left the house that first night, Lavinia or another one followed me down the street."

"She did?"

"Yeah. She gave me this really spooky feeling, but I didn't want to believe anything weird was happening so I convinced myself I was imagining things." He sighed. "Now what are you apologizing for?"

"For storming out of the house so Janecek could scoop me up."

"You didn't know he was out there."

"But you'd warned me to be careful. I should have paid attention to that. I could have gotten us both killed."

"If you hadn't gone out, Kreeger would probably have broken in and killed your aunt before going after us."

She winced.

When he pulled her close, she gasped.

"Your shoulder. I'm sorry."

"It's not that bad. Especially with the painkillers they gave me."

While he was holding her, he said what he'd been bursting to tell her since the warehouse. "I love you, Chelsea. I hope you can forgive me."

She tipped her head up so that she could meet his eyes. "I love you, too. That's why I was so upset."

He gathered her to him, lowering his head and covering her mouth with his. His kiss conveyed all the passion he'd kept bottled up inside as he'd waited to be alone with her. When the kiss broke, she began to speak.

"When I was strapped to that table in the warehouse, all I kept thinking of was how I wouldn't get a chance to tell you I love you."

"Thank God you did. Because of Lavinia."

"And you. Janecek was still trying his damnedest to kill me when you got there. He thought that if I was dead, he could still keep his secret. He didn't know the cops had already arrested Kreeger."

Michael held on to her, vowing he would never let her go. "So is it too soon to ask you to marry me?" he asked softly.

She raised her head and looked into his eyes. "It's pretty fast. But I don't need to think about the answer." She smiled. "It's yes."

"Oh, Chelsea, you've made me so happy." Then an inconvenient truth struck him.

"What is it?" she whispered. "You're having second thoughts?"

"No. I'm thinking about supporting a wife. I mean, I'm going to have to give up the current book, which means I have to scrounge around for another topic, and it may be a few months before I get anything started."

She kept her gaze fixed on him. "You can do the same book. Well, partly the same book."

"How?"

"Why don't you make it an investigation of which supernatural claims are real? You can start with the Jenkins Cove ghosts."

"That's a fantastic idea. But would you really want me to write about what happened here?"

"Wouldn't that give the book more authenticity?"

"Yes. But I don't want to do anything that would upset you."

She grinned. "I'm the one who suggested it, remember?" Before he could raise any more objections, she brought his mouth back to hers for a long, drugging kiss.

When he finally raised his head, he looked down at her and smiled.

She looked a bit unsure.

"What is it?"

"I know Aunt Sophie said she asked me back to Jenkins

Cove to contact the ghosts, but she really does need help. Is it going to be a problem living here? I mean, no matter how you spin it, my aunt is a little nutty."

"I'm adjusting. To the psychomanteum—and the cookies. Besides, this would be a perfect place to write. Maybe I can even start that novel I told you about." He grinned. "Which gives me another idea. If I sell my house in D.C., where the prices are sky-high, we'll be rolling in cash."

"Hold off on that until you're sure."

"I'm sure. The luckiest day of my life was the day I called to get a room here."

"Lucky for both of us. We just had to work our way through some problems," she answered.

He nodded and folded her close. "Is your aunt going to get worried if we don't emerge from your room for the next two days?" he teased.

Chelsea laughed. "She'll be okay with it. And I can send you out for food."

"You're kidding."

"I'm not sure. I'll let you know in the morning," she promised, then brought his mouth back to hers for a kiss full of passion and promises.

* * * * *

CHRISTMAS
AWAKENING

BY
ANN VOSS PETERSON

Ever since she was a little girl making her own books out of construction paper, **Ann Voss Peterson** wanted to write. So when it came time to choose a major at the University of Wisconsin, creative writing was her only choice. Of course, writing wasn't a *practical* choice—one needs to earn a living. So Ann found jobs ranging from proofreading legal transcripts to working with quarter horses to washing windows. But no matter how she earned her paycheque, she continued to write the type of stories that captured her heart and imagination—romantic suspense. Ann lives near Madison, Wisconsin, with her husband, her two young sons, her border collie and her quarter horse mare. Ann loves to hear from readers. E-mail her at ann@annvosspeterson.com or visit her website at www.annvosspeterson.com.

To Rebecca, Norman and Patricia and our wonderful
time exploring Maryland's eastern shore.

Prologue

Edwin Leonard's heart beat hard enough to break a rib. He adjusted his reading glasses and studied the sketch's deft lines. So much detail. So much planning.

This was proof. Proof of murder.

He slipped his glasses into his pocket. He'd been butler at Drake House since he was a young man, yet he never would have guessed such hatred pulsed within the borders of his beloved estate. Such a malicious, *murderous* force. The paper rattled in his shaking hand, fear adding to the tremor he'd acquired with age.

He needed to hide the sketch. Stash it away until he could get it to the police. If the killer found it and destroyed it, the only evidence of murder would be Edwin's word.

And that of a ghost.

He circled Drake House's south wing and followed the freshly laid oyster shell path through the south garden. The soles of his shoes crunched with each step. Too loud.

He paused, scanning the area, making sure no one had heard. The old mansion's grounds were quiet; only the lap of waves on rock along the shoreline reached

him. He was alone. Even so, he found himself holding
his breath.

Stepping along the edge of the path, he continued.
He had to stash the sketch and get back into the house
before anyone noticed his absence. He knew just the
hiding place. A spot where no one would think to look.

He quickened his pace, following the white shells
into the redesigned east garden. He stopped at a bench
nestled among holly bushes and grasped the seat.
Grunting with effort, he shifted the seat to the side,
exposing a hollow space in the concrete base.

A space just the right size.

He rolled the sketch in trembling hands and slipped
it into the crevice. He shifted the seat back into place.

It would be safe there. Safe until morning when he
could turn it over to Police Chief Hammer. Still, something didn't feel right. Maybe it was nerves. Maybe it was
some sort of sixth sense. Maybe it was related to what
he'd experienced in the candlelit room in Sophie's attic.
Whatever caused the feeling, it bore down on him, thicker
and more invasive than the humid, late autumn night.

Anger. Evil.

He had to get a hold of himself. Straightening, he
combed his hair into place with his fingers. He brushed
off his suit, pulled a linen handkerchief from his pocket
and dried his palms. Extracting his timepiece from his
pocket, he tilted the face to catch the light of the moon.

Mr. Brandon would wonder what had happened to
him if his bed wasn't turned down when he chose to
retire. That certainly wouldn't do.

Edwin slipped the watch back into his vest pocket.
It clinked against the skeleton key he'd stolen along
with the sketch.

The key. He'd forgotten to stash the key. Turning back toward the bench, he reached into his pocket.

The blow hit him before he could react. The force shuddered through his skull and down his spine. He dropped to his knees on the sharp shells.

Another blow brought darkness. He couldn't move. He couldn't think. He felt his legs being lifted, his body being dragged down the path. Out of the garden. Over the lawn. To the pier jutting out into the bay.

No. Not the water.

He tried to move, to fight, but his body wouldn't obey. Rough hands pushed him. He rolled into the water. Salt filled his mouth. Cold lapped at his body. His head went under.

Then he felt nothing.

Chapter One

"When a loved one dies, it's normal to want answers, Miss Leonard," the police chief drawled. He stopped near the break in the boxwood hedge that opened to the Jenkins Cove Chapel's redbrick walkway, as if he couldn't wait to get out of the graveyard…or maybe just away from Marie. "But sometimes you got to accept that accidents happen."

Accept? Marie gripped a damp tissue in her fist. Maybe she could accept, *if* her father's death really *was* an accident.

She focused on the arrangement of holly and poinsettia draping Edwin Leonard's casket. It was all wrong. The sunny day and cheery Christmas greenery. The sparsity of the black-clad crowd that wandered away from the graveside now that they'd offered their condolences. And most of all, the words coming from the chief's mouth. "I know you've ruled my father's death an accident, Chief Hammer. I'd like to know what led you to that conclusion."

"What led me?" The police chief drew up to his full height, what little there was of it.

A squat, bulldog of a man, Charles Hammer had

struck Marie as lazy, ever since he'd poo-pooed her report of boys smoking marijuana back when she was a sophomore at Jenkins Cove High. His quickness to dismiss her father's death as an accident before he knew all the circumstances just underscored that impression. Obviously nothing had changed in the ten years since she'd left Maryland's Eastern Shore. "Why do you think it was an accident?"

His mouth curved into a patronizing smile. "The evidence of accidental death is pretty clear in your father's case. In fact, nothing suggests it was anything *but* an accident. He was walking on the dock at night. He slipped and hit his head on the rocks along the shoreline. Accidental drowning. Pure and simple."

"It couldn't have happened that way."

"I know." He shook his head slowly, his bald scalp catching the sun's rays. "It seems so random."

Tension radiated up Marie's neck, fueling the headache that throbbed behind her eyes. "No, that's not it. It couldn't have happened the way you said. It's not possible."

He peered down his pudgy nose. "That's what our evidence indicates."

"The evidence is wrong."

"Evidence is never wrong."

"Then the way you're looking at it is wrong."

He drew in his chin, making himself look like an offended old lady. Or a turtle. "What do you do for a living, Miss Leonard?"

"I'm a philosophy professor."

He grinned as if that explained everything. "Well, I'm a police chief. I deal in hard evidence, not silly theories. I've investigated deaths before. Have you?"

She let out a frustrated breath. Her father had always warned her about her lack of tact. She should have tiptoed around the chief's ego. Flattered him. Buttered him up. Then he would probably be more open to her ideas. Instead, she'd turned him into an enemy.

She stared up at the spire of the gray stone church she'd attended as a kid. "I'm sorry. There's just something you don't understand."

"I understand the evidence. And in your father's case, that evidence clearly says accidental drowning."

She leveled her gaze back on the chief. "That's what I'm trying to tell you. My father never would have accidentally drowned."

"Your father hit his head. Even Olympic champions can't swim when they're unconscious."

"My father couldn't swim. Not a stroke."

"Then how can you find accidental drowning impossible?"

She tried to swallow the thickness in her throat.

"Because he was deathly afraid of the water. He never would have gone near it."

The chief looked unimpressed. He edged closer to the redbrick path between the boxwood. "I'm sorry, Miss Leonard. Facts are facts. Your father did go near the water that night. The case is closed. I'm sorry for your loss."

The finality of his words struck her like a kick to the sternum. She watched him amble down the path and join the last of the funeral-goers milling along Main Street.

The man from the funeral parlor eyed her from beside her father's casket, waiting for her to leave so he could lower Edwin Leonard to his final resting place beside her mother.

Marie pulled the collar of her black wool coat tighter around her shoulders. She didn't know if murder victims truly rested or not, but she sure wouldn't. Not until she knew what had happened to her father.

Not until she made his killer pay.

MARIE FORCED HER FEET to move up the loose gravel walk to the kitchen entrance of the sprawling white antebellum mansion. Drake House. An uneasy feeling pinched the back of her neck. The feeling she was being watched.

She spun around, searching the grounds. Waves danced on Chesapeake Bay and the mouth of Jenkins Creek, a body of water ironically broader and deeper than many lakes. Evening shadow cloaked the mansion's facade, transforming it to a dark hulk against the gleam of sunset on water. It looked austere, empty. The Christmas decorations that blanketed every house and shop in town were nowhere to be found here. No evergreen swags draping the balconies. No wreaths adorning the doors. Dark windows stared down at her like probing eyes.

She was home.

A bitter laugh died in her throat. She might have grown up in this house, but it wasn't home. Not without her father.

A gust of wind blew off the water, tangling her funeral-black skirt around her legs. Even though it was early December, the wind felt warm to Marie. And the shiver that ran over her skin had nothing to do with temperature.

Was someone watching her from the house? Brandon?

A flutter moved through her stomach. She gritted her

teeth against the sensation. The last time she'd seen Brandon Drake, she'd been a teenager with delusions of true love. She'd changed a lot since then. Grown stronger. Wiser. Her heart had shattered and mended. Still, she'd been relieved when Brandon Drake hadn't attended her father's service. She didn't want to see him. Not when she was aching from her father's loss. Not when her emotions were so raw. Not when she was feeling less than strong.

Unfortunately, if she wanted to find the truth about her father's murder, she had to start at the place he'd lived…and died. Drake House.

She tore her gaze from the mansion's upper floors and the balcony that ran the length of the private wing. Setting her chin, she increased her pace. The quicker she could get into her father's quarters, look through his things and get out, the better. It was all over town that Brandon had become a recluse since his wife died. He didn't take visitors. If she entered through the kitchen and dealt with the servants, maybe she could find enough to convince Chief Hammer to reopen her father's case as a homicide without ever having to face Brandon Drake.

At least she could hope.

Unease tickled over her again, raising the hair on her arms. She looked up at the house, beyond to the boat-house, then turned toward the carriage house. A man with the flat and misshapen nose of a prizefighter stared at her from the other side of a long black car. He nodded a greeting, then resumed rubbing the hood with a chamois.

The chauffeur. She recognized him from her father's funeral. At least someone from Drake House had come.

She gave the chauffeur a little wave, circled a gray

stone wall surrounding the pool and clomped up the wooden steps. Pressing the doorbell, she peered through wavy glass and into the kitchen where she'd once had milk and cookies after school.

It looked so much the same. Too much the same. A dull ache throbbed in her chest.

A woman with the thin, strong look of steel wire bustled across the kitchen and opened the door. Penciled eyebrows tilted over curious eyes. "Yes?"

"I'm Marie Leonard."

"Of course. Miss Leonard. I'm so sorry about your father." She opened the door with one hand, using the other to usher Marie inside. "I'm Shelley. Shelley Zachary. We talked on the phone."

Marie nodded. The cook, now housekeeper. The woman Brandon Drake had promoted to take over her father's job before he was even in the ground.

"It's nice to finally meet you. I worked side by side with Edwin for the past eight years, and a day didn't go by that he didn't mention you. I'm so sorry I wasn't able to make it to his funeral. Running a house like this in addition to cooking is very demanding."

Marie forced a smile she didn't feel. "I'm here to go through my father's things."

"Of course. Isabella can help you, if you need it."

Marie followed the housekeeper's gaze to the corner of the kitchen where a young woman with huge blue eyes and luxurious, auburn hair polished a silver tea service. She wore a uniform of black slacks and blouse with a white apron, more covered than the stereotypical French maid, yet because of her bombshell body, nearly as sexy.

"Isabella? This is Edwin's daughter."

Isabella continued with her work as if she couldn't care less.

At one time, the servants at Drake House were Marie's family, and a caring and tightly knit one at that. Not just her father, but everyone who'd worked at the house back then, from the maid to the cook to the chauffeur, liked to read her stories and bring her treats. They watched out for her, and she never questioned that each cared about her and about each other.

Clearly that family atmosphere had deserted Drake House in the past ten years.

That was fine. Marie didn't need a surrogate family. She needed answers. She focused on Shelley Zachary. "Do you have my father's keys?"

"Of course. I'm running the house now."

"May I have them? Or at least the keys to his quarters?"

"You don't need keys. Isabella can assist you."

Marie pressed her lips together. She didn't want someone looking over her shoulder. "I can handle it myself."

"You'll need help. Your father lived here a long time. Cleaning out his quarters is going to be a big job."

She was sure it would be. Especially since she intended to do a little snooping while she was here. "Really, I'd rather be alone. You understand."

Shelley Zachary didn't look as though she understood at all, but she nodded all the same. "Fine. But before I give you keys, I'll have to clear it with Mr. Brandon."

The name zapped along Marie's nerves like an electric charge. "No, that's not necessary."

Shelley frowned. "Excuse me? He's the master of the

house. He certainly has a say in who can and cannot have keys to his property."

There she went again, speaking without thinking, making enemies where a little tact might have made her an ally. Marie held up her hands, palms out. "That's not what I meant. It's just that I know he's busy. And I hear he's not taking many visitors lately."

The severe line to Shelley's mouth softened slightly. "No, he's not. Not since he lost his Charlotte."

A pang registered in Marie's chest at the sound of Brandon's wife's name…even after all these years.

"He never minds a visit from me." Isabella tossed Marie a smug smile. "I'll ask him."

"Ask me what?"

Marie's heart stuttered. She looked to the dark doorway leading to the dining room for the source of the deep voice.

Brandon Drake emerged from the dining room shadow. His shoulders filled the doorway. The dying rays of the sun streamed sideways from the kitchen windows and fell on his face.

Marie gasped.

A scar ran from his temple to the corner of his mouth, slick, red skin slashing across his cheek. He stepped forward, leaning on a brass and teak cane. "Hello, Marie."

Chapter Two

Brandon could see Marie stifle a gasp as she took in his face, his limp. The thought of her seeing his weakness hurt more than the burns themselves. He tore his eyes from her, not wanting to witness more, and focused on Isabella. "What were you going to ask me?"

The little vixen didn't answer. Instead, Shelley piped up. "Miss Leonard is here to clear out her father's things. She asked for keys to the butler's quarters."

"Give her the keys."

"You're hurt." Marie's voice was almost a whisper, as if she was murmuring her thoughts aloud, not intending for the rest of them to hear.

He kept his gaze on Shelley, careful not to look in Marie's direction. Her hair was a little shorter than it had been ten years ago, only jaw length now, and her face had lost its teenage roundness. But she was still Marie. He couldn't take seeing horror on her face as she scrutinized his injuries. Or worse, pity. "Where are those keys, Shelley?"

"I'll get them, sir." Shelley bustled off into the pantry.

Marie stepped toward him. She raised her hand.

Brandon wasn't sure what she intended to do. Touch

him? Soothe him? Heal him? He stepped back, removing himself from her reach. "It's nothing, Marie. I'm fine. Charlotte was the one who was hurt."

Pink suffused Marie's cheeks. She dropped her hand to her side and clutched a fistful of her black skirt. "I know. I mean, I'm sorry about your wife's death."

Guilt dug into his gut. He was such an ass. Sure he had to keep his distance from Marie. He owed Edwin that much. Just as he owed Charlotte. And when it came right down to it, he owed Marie. But he could have kept away from her without slapping her down. Just one more bit of proof that he didn't belong anywhere near someone as decent as Marie Leonard.

"My father didn't tell me you were hurt as well."

"Like I said, it's nothing." He glanced at the pantry. Where was Shelley with those keys?

"It's not nothing. If I'd known, I would have come…I would have—" She let her words hang as if she suddenly recognized the inappropriateness of what she was saying. She dipped her chin, looking down at his hand gripping the cane, at the wedding ring still on his finger. "Anyway, I'm sorry."

He nodded, hoping she was finished. "You don't have to put yourself through all this, Marie. Isabella can pack up Edwin's things and send them to you."

"No. I want to do it myself. It will…it will make me feel closer to him."

Brandon gripped the head of his cane until his fingers ached. The thought of Marie spending time in Drake House threatened to unhinge him. Even two floors up and in another wing, he'd be aware of every move she made. But what could he say? That she couldn't pack her father's things? That he refused to let her into the house where she'd grown up? That would make him more of an SOB than he already was. He forced his head to bob in a nod. "Take all the time you need."

"Thanks. You won't even know I'm here."

Fat chance of that.

Silence stretched between them, each second feeling like a minute. From outside he heard waves slap the shore and a yacht hum on Jenkins Creek, probably his uncle taking advantage of the unusually warm December.

Weather. That would get his mind off Marie. Sure. Where in the hell was Shelley?

Brandon cleared his throat. "I'm sorry about Edwin. He was a good man. I don't know what I'm going to do without him."

Tears glistened in Marie's eyes, but they didn't fall. "Thank you."

A car door slammed outside.

Isabella looked up from the tea service she was buffing.

Brandon held up a hand. "I'll get it." He headed for the kitchen door, trying not to lean too heavily on his cane. He was sure the maid was wondering what was going on. Since Charlotte died, he'd refused visitors whenever possible. But right now he had to get out of the cramped kitchen. He had to get away from Marie.

How on earth was he going to handle having her in his house the next few days?

IN THE PAST TEN YEARS, Marie had imagined countless times what it might be like to see Brandon again. But even in her worst nightmares, she'd never pictured things going so badly.

"All right. Here you go." Shelley Zachary emerged from the pantry with a set of keys jangling in her hand. "There's a key for this kitchen door and one for the butler suite. That should be all you need."

Marie nodded. She was hoping for her father's set, which held keys for everything on the estate, just in case she needed to follow up on anything she found. But she didn't see how she could ask for that without raising more than a few eyebrows. She'd just have to figure out another way to snoop. "Thank you."

"Where is Mr. Brandon?"

"Talking to Doug Heller." A tray with the tea service in her hands, Isabella nodded in the direction of the kitchen door, then disappeared through the arched hall to the dining room.

Marie peered through the windows to the porch. His back to her, Brandon was talking to a man dressed in jeans, work boots and a rough canvas coat. The name sounded familiar to her, as if her father might have mentioned it at some point. "Who is Doug Heller?"

As if sensing her scrutiny, the man talking to Brandon raised his weather-beaten face and stared at her through watery blue eyes.

A chill raced over her skin.

Shelley crossed the kitchen. "He works for Drake Enterprises. Operations manager."

"I thought Brandon was running the foundation. Is he back working for the company?"

Shelley plopped the keys into Marie's hand. "No, no. Brandon's uncle is still running Drake Enterprises. Mr. Brandon has his hands full with the foundation."

"Then why is the operations manager here?"

"Oh, I'm betting he's not here about Drake Enterprises. It's probably about that developer again. Ned Perry. He's trying to buy up waterfront property. More tenacious than a terrier."

"Developer? Brandon isn't thinking of…" She couldn't finish. The thought was too abhorrent.

"Selling Drake House? Turning it into condos?" Shelley laughed. "Mr. Brandon would rather die."

A morbid thought, but one that inspired relief. At least he still loved the historic old mansion. And though it might not feel like home without her father here, Marie had to admit being inside these walls made her feel grounded for the first time since Chief Hammer had called to break the news of her father's death. "I'm glad to hear he's not selling. It's just when I saw no Christmas decorations and then you mentioned a developer…"

"Mr. Brandon has canceled the Christmas Ball, I'm afraid."

Marie frowned. The annual Christmas Ball and charity auction was an institution in Jenkins Cove. "That's too bad."

"He said there's no point without Charlotte here. Oh, and your father. He doesn't even feel like celebrating Christmas."

"I'm sorry to hear that." Marie was. Brandon had always embraced Christmas, especially since the annual ball and auction brought in a lot of money the foundation could distribute to people in need. Brandon had always believed in spreading his good fortune to others. It was the reason he'd devoted his life to the foundation instead of taking his spot at the head of his family's company. It was one of the many things she'd admired about him.

Marie shook her head. She couldn't afford to nurse good feelings about Brandon and Drake House. Not unless she wanted to forget herself the way she had when she'd first seen his scarred face. She had to remember things were different than they were the summer before she'd gone to college. And even then, things between her and Brandon weren't really the way she'd imagined them to be.

Marie let out a heavy sigh. Her father had always said the old-money Drakes were different from working people. That even though she grew up in Drake House, she didn't belong in their world. That summer after high school graduation, when Brandon had given his mother's diamond ring to Charlotte instead of her, she'd finally realized her father was right.

"…to Sophie Caldwell."

Marie snapped her attention back to Shelley. "I'm sorry. What did you say?"

The woman blew a derisive breath through her nose. "I said, you should talk to Sophie Caldwell."

It took a second for her to process the name. "The woman who runs the bed-and-breakfast down by the harbor?"

Shelley nodded. "The House of the Seven Gables. Word was Sophie and Edwin were quite the item."

Her father? Seeing a woman? "He never said anything to me."

"That might not be something a father tells a daughter."

Marie didn't appreciate the woman's gossipy tone, but this time she managed to hold her tongue. As unlikable as she found Shelley Zachary, the woman was the best source of information she had when it came to her father and the goings-on at Drake House. "I wish he'd told me. I always worried he'd been lonely."

"He didn't have time to be lonely. Just ask Josef."

"Josef?"

"Our chauffeur. Josef Novak. Poor Josef. Another man who lost his love. She died in the hospital. An illness, just like the way your mother went. He used to drive Edwin to the Seven Gables several times a week. He doesn't talk much, but he probably understood your father better than anyone, except Sophie, of course."

Of course. Marie pictured the man who'd been buffing the car outside, the man who'd waved to her and had attended her father's funeral. Josef. She couldn't imagine her father having many heart-to-hearts with the quiet chauffeur, no matter how much they had in common. Better to go straight to the source, Sophie Caldwell.

She glanced at Brandon through the kitchen windows. The manager, Doug Heller, was still stealing glances at her that gave her the creeps, but judging from the men's body language, their conversation was drawing to a close.

And that meant Brandon would be returning to the kitchen.

"I think I'll run over to talk to Sophie Caldwell right now. Will you pass my thanks to Brandon for the keys? I'm parked out front, so I'll just scurry out through the foyer."

"Fine." Shelley looked pleased to be rid of her. Maybe that was her intent all along.

"I'll be back later tonight to start on my father's things."

"Fine. Don't park near the kitchen. This is a busy house."

Late at night? Marie doubted it, but miraculously held her tongue. The decision to leave and come back later was looking better all the time. Later, after the servants were gone. And after Brandon had retired to his third-floor suite.

When she could be alone.

Chapter Three

It didn't take long for Marie to drive into the town of Jenkins Cove and wind her way through its quaint little streets. She parked in a lot off Royal Oak Street and walked the rest of the way to the bed-and-breakfast.

Connected to the harbor area by a narrow, concrete bridge, the House of the Seven Gables perched on the edge of the water. Masts of sailboats jutted into the twilight sky. A few yachts docked at a seafood restaurant nearby, and the scent of crab cakes teased the air. Christmas music mixed with the lap of the waves.

Unlike Drake House, the bed-and-breakfast was already decked out for the season. Wreaths adorned every door. Ropes of holly wrapped the porch posts and draped the balcony above. Marie climbed the steps to the front and rang the bell.

Footfalls approached, creaking across a wood floor. The door swung inward and a pleasantly plump, gray-haired woman peered out. A broad smile stretched across her Cupid's bow lips and crinkled the corners of her eyes. "Merry Christmas. Please, come in." She wiped her hands on her apron and gestured Marie inside with a sweep of her arm.

Marie couldn't help but return the woman's smile. She looked familiar, and Marie was fairly certain she'd seen her at the funeral.

"Are you interested in a room? We have one left overlooking the harbor."

"No, thanks." Was this the woman her father had been seeing? She hoped so. The woman seemed so gregarious and kind. Marie would like to think her father had someone like this caring about him and sharing his life in his final months. "I'm Marie Leonard."

"Of course. Edwin's daughter. I'm sorry I didn't recognize you right away." She opened her arms and engulfed Marie in a soft hug. When she finally released her grip, the woman had tears in her eyes. "I'm so happy to meet you, dear. I wanted to talk to you at your father's funeral today, but I…" She fanned her face, unable to go on.

A stinging sensation burned the back of Marie's eyes. She blinked. Getting her emotions under control, she met the woman's blue gaze. "I need to ask you some questions about my father, Ms…"

"Sophie. Please, call me Sophie." She took Marie's coat and led her into a parlor with windows gazing out onto the garden and the water beyond. She gestured to the corner of the room where an easel propped up an artist's canvas. The scent of paint thinner tinged the air. "And this is my niece, Chelsea."

Marie started. She hadn't even noticed someone else was in the room. She looked beyond the canvas and into the beautifully haunting face of a blue-eyed blonde. "Nice to meet you."

The young woman nodded. Quietly, she set down her paintbrush and glanced out the window as if her thoughts were far away.

Marie couldn't put her finger on it, but there was something about her...something disconcerting. As if when Chelsea looked out over the water, she could see things Marie couldn't even imagine.

Sophie ushered her to a grouping of white wicker near the canvas. "Please, sit down and feel free to ask me whatever is on your mind, honey."

Marie lowered herself into a chair across from Sophie. Staring at the cameo necklace around Sophie's neck, Marie searched for the right words to lead into her questions. "About my father...you two were close?"

The woman nodded her gray head. "Your father was a light in my life." Again, her eyes filled with tears.

Marie fought her own surge of emotion. Silence filled the room, making her feel the need to break it. She wanted to ask if Sophie knew who would murder her father, but how was she supposed to do that? The woman was obviously as grief-stricken as she herself. Throwing around suspicions of murder might send Sophie over the edge. Tact. Marie needed to use some sort of tact. To tread carefully for once in her life. "How did the two of you meet?"

Sophie smiled. "We met through your mother, in a way."

Marie looked askance at the woman. "My mother? My mother died of cancer when I was eight."

Sophie nodded as if she was perfectly aware of that fact. "And your father missed her horribly."

"She was the world to him. Well, along with me and Drake House. I was worried about him being lonely after I left for college." She'd mostly been worried about him devoting every waking moment to the Drakes, exactly what he hadn't wanted for her. She wished he would have told her he'd met a woman. It would have made her feel so much more at ease. "But I still don't understand how the two of you met through my mother."

Sophie and Chelsea exchanged looks.

"What is it?"

Chelsea shrugged to her aunt and let out a resigned sigh. "You might as well tell her."

"Your father came to me because he believed I could help him communicate with your mother."

"Communicate?" The ground seemed to shift under Marie's feet. "What are you? Some kind of medium?"

"No. Not me. Chelsea has more talent in that area than I have."

Chelsea shot her a warning look. "We don't need to go into that. She's here to learn about her father."

"Yes, your father. He wanted to use a room I have upstairs."

"For what?"

"As a portal to reach your mother."

"A séance?" Marie wasn't buying any of this. Not one word. She couldn't imagine her father holding some sort of séance. If Chelsea wasn't here, looking so serious and grim, she'd chalk up Sophie as a bit of a kook.

"Not exactly a séance. A portal to communicate."

"A room upstairs?"

She nodded. "A special room I've constructed. A room that acts as a door to the spiritual world."

A laugh bubbled through Marie's lips. She covered her mouth with a hand.

"This isn't a joke." Chelsea crossed her arms over her chest. "And my aunt isn't off her rocker, or whatever it is you're thinking."

"I wasn't…" Marie's cheeks heated. Fact was, she'd been thinking exactly that. She focused on the older woman. "I'm sorry. Please explain. I need to understand my father. I know you can help me do that."

Sophie's smile didn't change, as if Marie's disbelief didn't bother or surprise her in the least. "Have you ever heard of a psychomanteum?"

"A what?"

"It's based on a phenomenon we first see in Greek mythology. A psychomanteum or oracle of the dead."

Marie had studied Homer as an undergraduate. "The pool of blood in Odysseus."

Sophie's face brightened with the glow of a teacher who had just broken through to a lagging student. "Exactly. Odysseus dug a pit and filled it with animal blood. Through the reflection in the blood, he could communicate with spirits."

Marie suppressed a shiver. What kind of strange things had her father gotten involved in? "Your attic is filled with blood?"

Now it was Chelsea's turn to cover a smile.

"Oh, heavens, no." Sophie laughed. "You must really think I'm a nut."

Marie's cheeks burned. Her face must be glowing red. "I'm sorry. I didn't mean…I'm just trying to understand."

Sophie laid a comforting hand on Marie's arm. "Of course you are, sweetheart."

"My aunt uses mirrors, not blood," Chelsea explained. "Communicating through a psychomanteum really has quite a long tradition, and it crosses cultures. Africans, Siberians, Native Americans…they all used different forms, whether they were gazing into water or blood. There's even a story about Abraham Lincoln seeing his future reflected in a mirror."

Marie had heard of some of these traditions. It had never occurred to her that they were anything but superstition and myth. "And my father believed he could look into mirrors and contact my mother?"

Sophie's smile widened. "He didn't just believe it. He did it."

"He did it? He contacted my mother?" Marie shook her head. This was impossible. Ridiculous. "What did my mother say?"

"She didn't *say* anything. The psychomanteum experience isn't like some séance you see in a movie, dear. A ghost doesn't just appear and recite his or her life story. Not usually, anyway. It's a bit more subtle than that."

"How does it work?"

"It's more like meditation, opening yourself to stimuli we don't pick up normally."

"So my father meditated by staring into a mirror, and he spoke with my mother?"

"He sensed your mother. He could feel she was there. He could feel her happiness that he'd met me."

So that's what this was about? Sophie was worried Marie wouldn't approve of her relationship with her father and she thought some spiritual mumbo jumbo would help her cause? "I don't know about any psychowhatever, but I'm glad he met you. I really am. I was worried about him after I left for school. Worried he'd be lonely. And he was. For years."

"That means a lot to me, honey." Sophie's expression shifted. "But your mother's acceptance wasn't all he experienced in the psychomanteum. There were other things. Not-so-pleasant things."

"About my mother?" A shiver raced along Marie's nerves. Weird. She didn't believe any of this, yet Sophie's comment and tone of voice left her cold.

"Aunt Sophie…" Chelsea's voice held a warning ring.

Her aunt splayed her hands out in front of her. "She needs to know what Edwin experienced. She's here to look into his murder."

Marie's chill turned to shock. "How did you know that? Did the police chief—"

"Police Chief Hammer?" Chelsea rolled her eyes. "All that man cares about is making his job as easy as possible. A murder might mean that he has to do some actual work."

That certainly jibed with Marie's assessment of the man. "Then how did you know why I'm here?"

Sophie leaned forward and placed her fingers on Marie's arm. "You know your father. He wasn't one to enjoy walking the shoreline."

"Exactly." At least Marie wasn't the only one to recognize something very wrong with the police's accident theory.

Sophie nodded her head, her gray bun bobbing. "Contacting your mother was a good experience. A peaceful experience. The unpleasantness didn't have anything to do with your mother. It had something to do with Drake House."

"Drake House?" Marie's head spun. She held out her hands palms out, trying to physically push back all these bizarre claims and confusing twists of logic.

"Your father learned things in the psychomanteum. Things that upset him."

"What?"

"He wouldn't tell me. He said he didn't want to endanger me, especially after all I went through with Chelsea and her fiancé, Michael."

"Aunt Sophie…" Another warning from Chelsea.

Sophie gave Marie a conspiratorial look. "I'll fill you in on that story sometime." She glanced at Chelsea.

"When I'm not around to stop you?" Chelsea shook her head. "My experiences don't have anything to do with your father, Marie. My aunt just likes telling stories."

Sophie harrumphed at her niece, then returned her focus to Marie. "I wish I could tell you more about what your father experienced, sweetie. All I know is that it upset him greatly. And he said it led him to a dangerous secret."

"A dangerous secret?" The secret that got him killed?

Chelsea nodded as if reading her thoughts. "Your father was murdered to keep him quiet about what he learned."

"How do you know that?"

Chelsea shifted in her seat and glanced at her aunt.

Sophie smiled. "You mean are we basing that theory on fact or on some sort of vision in a mirror?"

"Well…yes."

"*I'm* basing it on what he told me before he died. Edwin was scared for me. He was also scared for his own life."

Sophie's words wound into a hard ball in Marie's chest. She couldn't picture her father frightened. He'd always been so strong, so in control. The only times she'd known him to be truly worried were when her mother was sick…and after he'd witnessed the way she looked at Brandon the summer before she'd left for college.

"I can't reach him in the psychomanteum. I've tried every day since he died, but it's no good. Maybe he's still trying to protect me. Or maybe I'm not the one he needs to communicate with."

The older woman stared at Marie so hard, Marie couldn't fight the urge to shift in her chair. She didn't want to ask what Sophie was getting at. She had a feeling she didn't want to know. "It's getting late. I'd better get back."

"He always talked about how he hadn't seen you in so long, how he had so much he wanted to tell you, so much he needed to say…."

"Aunt Sophie, if she doesn't want to—"

"If your father will communicate with anyone, it will be you, Marie. He loved you so."

Marie shook her head. "I can't possibly. I don't even believe."

"It won't hurt to try."

Marie grabbed the handles of her bag in one fist and thrust herself out of her chair. "I really have to go." She picked up her coat from the sofa arm where Sophie had draped it.

"It's not ghostly, Marie. Forget about all those movies you've seen. That was horror. This is real life."

"I'm sorry. I don't mean any disrespect, Sophie, really I don't. Talking to ghosts might be your real life, but it's not mine." She pulled on her coat and hurried out the front door and down the steps, nearly tripping over her own feet in her rush to get away.

THE MAIN FLOOR of Drake House was dark by the time Marie drove back through the gate, down the winding drive and parked in the empty servants' lot next to the carriage house. Dinner having been served, the servants had no doubt returned to their own homes. She looked up at the light in the private eastern wing of the house. The master suite, among other rooms. Brandon was home. She couldn't help but wonder what he was doing.

Thinking of her?

Pushing away that idea, she started through the east garden to the kitchen entrance. After recovering from her experience at Sophie's and grabbing a dinner of crab cakes at one of the harbor restaurants, she'd debated skipping Drake House and heading straight for the bed-and-breakfast off Main Street where she'd reserved a room. In the end, she'd decided she wouldn't be able to sleep, anyway, not after her conversation with Sophie and her niece. If she did slip into sleep, she'd spend the night hashing out their strange ideas in her dreams.

Better to get to work on her father's suite and keep her mind off both ghosts *and* Brandon Drake.

Marie followed the curvy path made of loose white shells. The night was dark, but she didn't need light to see where she was going. Even after ten years, she knew Drake House the way she knew her own heart. Even though some details had changed, there was something about this house and its grounds she recognized deep inside. Something that would be with her forever. Like the tune her mother always hummed. Like the almost imperceptible twinkle in her father's dry smile.

She swallowed into a tight throat. She missed him so much. Her father was so much a part of Drake House, she could still feel him, even outside on the grounds. The next few days, being in his rooms, sorting through his things, weren't going to be easy. But at least she'd feel closer to him. Just being back on the estate made her feel closer.

The night was warm for December, yet pockets of cold, still air dotted the path, raising goose bumps on her skin. She rubbed her arms and quickened her pace. She probably could have parked in the lot near the grand entrance and cut through the inside of the house to the butler's quarters. But somehow that felt presumptuous, as if she thought she belonged at Drake House or was some sort of honored guest. Here in Jenkins Cove, she was the butler's daughter, pure and simple. In the past ten years, she had learned her place.

She circled the corner of the east wing and approached the back entrance. A light glowed from a set of windows off the kitchen. Her father's quarters.

Her steps faltered.

The light dimmed and shifted. Not lamplight. More like a flashlight beam.

Was someone searching through her father's rooms?

A flutter of nerves made her feel sick to her stomach. Who would gain from searching her father's quarters? A murderer trying to cover his tracks?

The light flicked off. Darkness draped the house.

Marie pressed her lips into a hard line and covered her mouth with her hand. Whoever it was, the last thing she wanted was for the intruder to know he'd been spotted. She stepped off the path and slipped behind a holly bush. Reaching into her purse, she grasped the keys Shelley had given her, threading them between her fingers so they protruded like spikes from her fist.

The kitchen door closed with a click. Marie peered through spined leaves. A figure wearing a boxy rain slicker crossed the porch and descended the steps to the path. The hood covered the intruder's face, and the size of the slicker made it impossible to discern the size or shape of the person beneath. The figure turned in her direction.

Marie pressed back behind the bush, hoping the night was dark enough, the evergreen bush thick enough to hide her. The rhythmic crunch of footsteps on oyster shells approached…slowed…stopped.

She drew in a breath and held it.

Suddenly darkness rushed at her. Hands grabbed her shoulders. A fist slammed into her jaw. Leaves clawed at her like frantic fingers.

A scream tore from her throat.

Chapter Four

Brandon relived it almost every night. Fighting his way into the blazing car. Choking on smoke and gasoline. Charlotte's scream ringing in his ears. Helpless to save her.

He jolted up from the window seat, surprised he was in his room, no fire around him. No choking smoke. No Charlotte.

The scream came again.

Not Charlotte. Not a dream.

"Oh my God. Marie."

He thrust to his feet. His leg faltered, folding under him, and he grabbed the window molding for balance. He snatched his cane. Willing the damn limb to function, he bolted for the door. Clutching the carved railing with his free hand, he thundered down the back stairs and sprang into the parlor. He moved through the dining room, half hopping, half galloping. He had to move faster.

He raced through the kitchen and burst out the door. The night was dark, no moon, no light. He couldn't see a thing. Couldn't hear a thing but the rasp of his own breath. He held the cane out in front of him like a weapon. "Marie? Who's out here? Marie?"

A quiet groan emanated from a tall hedge of holly near the path leading into the east garden. "I'm here. I'm okay."

Pressure bore down on his chest. Her voice sounded small, shaken. Not at all okay. He followed the sound. He couldn't see her at first, but he could feel her. He could smell the scent of her shampoo. Something both spicy and sweet. Something that reminded him of a warm summer and good times. "Where are you?"

"Here." Holly leaves rustled. She sat at the bush's base, struggling to free herself from sharp leaves.

As he reached for her hand, his heart felt as if it would burst from his chest. "Can you get up?"

"I think so…yes."

She grasped his fingers, and he pulled her to her feet. "What happened?"

She focused on him, round caramel-colored eyes in a pale face. "Someone was sneaking around in the house. An intruder. He saw me."

"He attacked you?"

She lifted her fingers to her jaw. "He hit me…I think."

Brandon tried to discern the discoloration of a bruise, but it was too dark.

"I saw a light in my father's quarters. When I heard the kitchen door close, I hid."

"In a holly bush?" He could see something dark on her cheek, feel something slightly sticky on the hand he clutched in his, probably blood. No doubt the sharp edges of the leaves had scratched her up pretty good.

"I hid behind the bush, not inside the bush. When he hit me, I fell."

"Let's get you inside." Still gripping her hand, he led her toward the open kitchen door.

"What are you going to do?"

"Call the police."

"What are you going to tell them? I didn't see his face. I don't even know if it was a him."

"I'll take care of it." He hurried Marie up the steps and into the house. Closing the door, he locked it behind them. He didn't know what the police could do, but he wanted them there. If nothing else, they could check out the grounds and make sure the bastard who attacked Marie was gone.

He turned to look at her. In the light of the kitchen, he could see the pink shadow of a bruise bloom along her jaw. The holly had scratched one cheek as it had her hands. Beads of blood dotted the slashes. Snags and runs spoiled her black tights. "You're hurt."

"You should have seen the other guy." She tried for a smile, but it turned into a flinch of pain.

"Let me see." He brushed her hair back from her cheek with his fingertips. Her skin was soft. Her hair smelled like…cinnamon. That's what it was. Like the cinnamon gum she'd chewed as a teen. He took a deep breath. In the back of his mind he recognized the clatter of his cane falling to the floor.

"Does it look bad?"

He forced himself to focus on her injuries. "Not too bad. I'll get some ice for that bruise. And there's a first aid kit here somewhere. I'll get those scrapes cleaned."

"I can do it."

He met her eyes and swallowed into a dry throat. What was he thinking? He was having a hard enough time touching her skin and smelling her hair without doing or saying something he'd regret. Playing nurse-maid would send him over the edge. "Of course. I'll find the kit for you."

Her lips trembled. "I can get it. My father always kept it in the same place."

"Yes, all right." Come to think of it, he had no idea where Edwin kept the first aid supplies. He had even less of an idea what he thought he was doing hovering over Marie. He needed to step away from her, to focus on something other than the way her hair smelled and the warmth of her body and the tremble in her lips. But right this minute, she was all he could see.

He bent down and picked up his cane. Pulling in a measured breath, he stepped to the burglar alarm and punched in the activation code.

"Do you usually have the alarm on at night?"

He nodded, but didn't allow himself to look at her. He'd only be back to hovering if he did, noticing things he couldn't let himself notice. "I told Shelley to leave it off for you."

"So Shelley knew it was off. Who else?"

"Isabella. Maybe Josef. Anyone who knew you were planning to come back tonight, I guess. I doubt any of them would be looking to break in. They're in and out of here all day."

"The man you were talking to when I was here earlier? Did he know the alarm would be off?"

"Doug Heller? Maybe. Yeah, he was probably still here when I talked to Shelley." Something was going on. Something Marie didn't want to tell him. Despite his better judgment, he turned around and eyed her. "What are you getting at, Marie?"

"Do you think it's just a coincidence someone broke in the one night the alarm was off?"

"Good point. I'll mention it to the police. But I can't

see the staff involved in some kind of break-in. Or Heller, for that matter."

She shrugged a shoulder, the gesture a little too stiff. She was working on some sort of theory about the break-in. A theory she obviously didn't want to share with him.

Not that he could blame her. She'd trusted him with more than a theory before, and he'd thrown her to the dogs. She'd be smart to never trust him again.

"I've got to make that call. Whoever attacked you could still be out there." He made his way to the household office and plucked the cordless phone from its charger. He stared at the receiver in his hand. He didn't want the hoopla of calling 9-1-1. But he didn't even know where Edwin kept the phone book. Without Edwin, it seemed he couldn't handle a damn thing.

Glancing back to the kitchen, he let the idea of asking Marie sit in his mind for less than a second. The feeling he'd gotten when near her still vibrated deep in his bones. When she was close, she was all he could focus on. When he was touching her, the sensations were so strong they were painful.

After Charlotte's death, he'd wished he could no longer feel. Not the torment of his injuries, not the guilt in his heart, not the emptiness that hadn't been filled in far too long. Now that Marie was back, now that she was here in Drake House, he couldn't do anything *but* feel.

He had to keep control of himself. And if that meant staying away from her, he'd find a way.

He called up the directory feature on the phone. Sure enough, Edwin had programed the police department's nonemergency number. His butler had saved him yet again. If he wasn't so shaken by everything that had happened tonight, he'd find that ironic.

"Jenkins Cove Police Department," an official-sounding woman answered. "What is the nature of your call?"

"I'd like to report a possible burglary at Drake House."

"Mr. Drake?"

"Yes."

"Will you hold, Mr. Drake? The chief is here right now. He'd like to talk to you himself."

"Sure." Brandon frowned into the phone. It wasn't unusual for the chief to personally handle anything having to do with Brandon or his uncle Cliff. He supposed that was what happened when your family had nearly single handedly established and nurtured a small town like Jenkins Cove. Parks were named after you. Statues of your father and grandfather and generations back graced the town square. And the chief of police personally handled your crime reports. Still, it was awfully late for the chief to be in. It must have something to do with the state police's investigation of the mass grave that had been found just down the road.

"Brandon," Chief Hammer's voice boomed over the phone. "I hear you had a break-in. I hope no damage was done."

Damage. Brandon had been so absorbed with Marie he hadn't even looked for damage. He stepped out into the kitchen and swept it with his gaze. "None that I've noticed."

"Glad to hear that. We've had problems with some teens in the area. Vandalism. You might have read about it in the *Gazette*."

Brandon had read about a lot of wild things in the *Gazette* lately, with the coverage of the mass grave, the doctor who was rumored to be responsible and his lackey the state police had hauled off into custody. A lot more excitement than usual in Jenkins Cove. The teen delinquent stories must have been buried on a later page. "I know my uncle Cliff has had some problems with vandals. Let me look around to be sure there's nothing damaged."

Getting a grip on himself, he made his way to Edwin's suite. The door was open and Marie stood in the sitting room, her back to him. He forced himself to notice the room's condition and that of the two bedrooms beyond, not the curve of her hips in the skirt and sweater, now that she'd taken off her coat. "Notice anything missing or damaged?"

Marie shook her head. "No. I don't think so, anyway."

He nodded and forced his attention back to the phone. "The rooms we think the burglar entered don't seem disturbed."

"We?" Hammer repeated over the phone.

"Edwin Leonard's daughter, Marie, is packing up his things."

"I see."

"She saw the light on in the butler's quarters. The burglar attacked her trying to get away."

"Is she all right?"

"Just a bruise and a few scratches."

"This is going to seem like an odd question, Brandon, but are you sure someone was in the house?"

Brandon paused. "Of course I'm sure."

"Did you see anything yourself? Hear anything?"

"What are you getting at, Chief?"

"Nothing. I'm just a little concerned about Marie

Leonard. I had a talk with her today at the funeral, and she seemed to be having a bad time of it."

Brandon cupped a hand over the phone and stepped out of the room. He wasn't sure what Hammer was getting at, but he knew he didn't want Marie to overhear. "Her father died. Of course she's upset. You think it's more than that?"

"I'd call her paranoid."

"Paranoid?" Not a word he would associate with Marie. If anything she'd seemed too calm, too in control. But then, he'd been so turned inside out since he'd first seen her this afternoon, maybe she was just controlled in comparison. "What is she paranoid about?"

"She seems to think someone killed her father."

His words probably should have surprised Brandon, but they didn't. They explained a lot. "Why does she think that?"

"You'll have to ask her. I'm afraid it isn't based in reality. I've found no evidence that Edwin Leonard was murdered."

Of course, knowing Hammer, he hadn't expended much effort looking. "Thanks for the heads-up, Chief. But no matter what is going on with Marie, I don't think she imagined this attack."

"I'm not saying she did. I'm concerned about her. That's all."

"Well, if you could send someone out here, I can guarantee Ms. Leonard would feel a whole lot better. And so would I."

"Soon as I can, Brandon. I only have two officers on tonight, and one is securing the state police's dig site. It might be the state's investigation, but you wouldn't believe the monkey wrench it's thrown into our day-to-day operations."

Brandon grimaced. Apparently the chief hadn't had a good few days, either. "Send someone out as soon as you can. I want to make sure whoever it was is gone."

"In the meantime, stay inside, make sure your doors are locked and turn on that fancy alarm system of yours just to be on the safe side."

"Already done." He turned off the phone. The only problem with the chief's advice was the idea of locking himself in with Marie. Still, he couldn't see how he was going to find it within himself to let her leave, not when whoever had attacked her might still be outside.

"Is an officer on the way?"

Something jumped in his chest at the sound of her voice. He looked up to see her standing in the doorway to Edwin's quarters. "It might take a while. You have a place to stay?"

"A B&B in Jenkins Cove."

"How long are you planning to hang around yet tonight?" Edwin Leonard was an impeccably neat and organized man. Still, he'd been the butler of Drake House since before Brandon was born. Cleaning out his rooms was going to be a big job.

"I'll be here a few hours at least. I don't think I can sleep after all this."

He was sure he wouldn't be sleeping, either. But at least he had the sense not to offer to help. "Why don't you stay?"

She raised her brows.

"In your old room. Edwin would have insisted. And I would feel better if you didn't go back outside. Not until the police have a chance to check out the grounds."

He had to be crazy, inviting her to stay under his roof. Drake House was big, but not big enough to keep him from listening for her all night long and noting her every movement.

At least that way he could keep her safe. Edwin would have insisted on that as well.

"Thanks."

"Chief Hammer is concerned about you."

She twisted her lips to one side. "I'll bet he is."

"Why?"

She waved her hand in front of her face as if trying to erase the words between them. "Nothing. Never mind. It's just been a long day, that's all."

"He said you believe your father was murdered."

She held his gaze but said nothing, as if waiting for some kind of prompt.

"I take it you do. Why?"

"My father never walked near the water. You know that. He was deathly afraid of water."

"So he couldn't have accidently fallen in."

He wasn't sure if she'd nodded or not. She just watched him as if waiting for him to discount her theory.

"Hammer says there's no evidence."

"Because he's too lazy to find it."

That was the Charles Hammer he knew. If the answer wasn't easy, Hammer wasn't interested. "So that's why you're here."

"I'm here to pack up my father's things."

"And look for evidence he was murdered. And that's what you think our burglar tonight was doing, too, don't you? Looking for something incriminating. Something that ties him to Edwin's murder."

Again she didn't react. She just seemed to be sizing him up, watching, waiting. For what? Did she think he was going to tell her she was wrong? Hell, it should have occurred to him earlier how unlikely it was for Edwin to venture close to the water. He should have been looking for explanations himself. "Talk to me, Marie. Maybe I can help."

She didn't look convinced.

"Well, there's no reason for you to tie up a room at the B&B during Christmas shopping season. You can stay here as long as you need. Shelley gave you keys?"

"Just to the kitchen entrance and my father's quarters."

Leave it to Shelley. The day he'd promoted her to fill Edwin's job, she'd collected keys from all employees, doling them out only when she deemed necessary. The woman wielded her new power with a closed fist. "I'll get you a complete set."

"Thanks." Her lips softened. Not quite a smile, but an acknowledgment. Something.

"It's the least I can do. Your father meant a lot to me." *And so do you.* The words stuck in his throat. Not that he would ever say them out loud. He'd hurt too many people the last time he'd given in to that indulgence. Himself, Marie, and Charlotte most of all. He deserved the pain. But Charlotte… He couldn't erase what he'd done to her. Nor would he risk hurting Marie again. No matter what happened, he had to protect her. He owed Edwin. And he definitely owed her. "I'll go wait for the police. Good night, Marie."

MARIE LAUNCHED into the fifth drawer of her father's personal desk. So far she'd found nothing. No questionable photos or letters or anything that even hinted why someone might want him dead. But she had gone through almost a half box of tissues wiping the tears that continuously leaked from her eyes.

What she wouldn't give to have him back.

She closed her eyes, her lids swollen and hot. She didn't know what she'd do without him. Ten years ago, he'd helped her put her life in perspective. He'd hugged away her tears in that stiff-backed way he had. He'd encouraged her to get away from Drake House and make the life she deserved.

She hadn't lived with him for over ten years, but she knew whenever she had a question, whenever she needed to know if she was making the right decision, he was only a phone call away. Without him, she felt lost.

If only she could talk to him about her stirred-up feelings for Brandon.

She rubbed her eyes. She knew what her father would say. He would tell her to go home. To get away from Brandon, from Drake House. The same thing he'd told her ten years ago.

Too bad she couldn't follow his advice this time. Not until she found out who killed him. Not until she brought his murderer to justice.

She reached to the top of the desk and snapped on the ancient transistor radio she remembered her father using to listen to his beloved Orioles on summer nights. She turned her attention to the last desk drawer. "I'll Be Home for Christmas" drifted over the airwaves.

Great.

Here she was. Home for Christmas. Except the only person she had to come home to was gone. Taken away forever.

She turned the dial. Static took over.

Fabulous.

She twisted the knob. Now she couldn't get a signal at all. She rubbed a hand over her eyes. She was too tired for this. Maybe she should get some sleep and finish going through the desk tomorrow. She reached up to switch the radio off. Shadows of a voice rustled among the white noise. "Murder."

Marie jerked her hand back.

"Murder."

There it was again. A whisper rising from the static.

Marie frowned at the radio. It had to be a news report. Maybe something about the mass grave the state police were investigating, the one the waitress in the crab shack had been buzzing about last night. Marie gave the dial a twist, moving the needle back and forth, trying to get better reception. The static fuzzed on.

"Marie."

The whisper again. Saying her name?

She snapped the radio off. Sophie Caldwell's theories about communicating with ghosts flitting through her mind, she thrust herself to her feet and walked into the bathroom. She was tired and she was imagining things. That was all it was. All it could be.

Turning on the water to warm, she fished a hair band from her bag and pulled her bob back from her face. She looked into the mirror.

Sophie and Chelsea believed mirrors were like oracles. A way to see into the spiritual world. A way to communicate with loved ones lost.

The only image in her mirror was herself with her hair in a hair band. Not her best look.

She thrust cupped hands into the warm water and

lifted it to splash her face. She froze before the water reached her skin.

That scent.

Marie took a long breath. She knew the smell. The fragrance was faint, but she recognized the exotic notes, a blend dominated by jasmine.

She let the water drain between her fingers.

Pressure lodged under her rib cage, hard as a balled fist. Glancing around the bathroom, she dried her hands on a towel and turned off the tap.

The scent had to be caused by soap or air freshener. But look as she might, she didn't see a source. As she searched, the scent grew stronger. She could swear it was coming from the other side of the bathroom door.

A tremor moved through her chest. Her pulse thrummed in her ears.

She'd remember that scent all her life. And the woman who wore it. So exotic, so sophisticated. And so much more than little Marie Leonard. More beautiful, more accomplished. In every way, more.

No wonder Brandon had made her his wife.

But Charlotte had died six months ago. Why was Marie smelling her scent now? Here in the butler's quarters?

Sophie and Chelsea had talked about spirits communicating through images in mirrors, not voices carried on radio static, not scents. She was freaking herself out over nothing…wasn't she?

Pulse thrumming in her ears, she stepped out into her father's sitting room. The room was as vacant as before. She tested the air again. The scent was stronger, but it didn't seem to be coming from this room, either.

She followed her nose to the door leading to the estate office and kitchen area. The cloud cover had cleared outside, and stainless steel and stone counter-tops stretched long and cold in ribbons of feeble moonlight shining through window blinds. The scent was even stronger out here. It teased the air as if Charlotte had just walked through the room.

Ridiculous.

More likely Brandon had the furnace filters treated with the scent to remind him of Charlotte. Or Shelley used jasmine air fresheners to memorialize the mistress she adored, à la Mrs. Danvers from Daphne du Maurier's *Rebecca*. A giggle bubbled up in Marie's throat. She was being absurd, letting her imagination run away with her—first to ghosts and now to characters from novels. Silly or not, she followed the scent.

Marie wove her way through the kitchen and veered through the hall and into the dining room. She circled the grand table and stepped quietly across the parquet floor and oriental rugs in the first-floor sitting room. A hint of moonlight filtered through draperies, creating misty images on leaded mirrors. Images that almost looked like ghosts.

"Marie?" Brandon's voice boomed from the shadows. "What is it?"

Marie started. She whirled around to see him jolt up from a sofa in the sitting room.

His eyelids looked heavy, as if he'd just awakened. He reached for his cane and walked toward her. He stopped just inches away. Close enough for her to trail her fingertips over his stubbled chin and the slick, scarred skin of his cheek.

Marie's nerves jangled. For a moment she couldn't think.

His dark eyebrows dipped with concern. "Is something wrong?"

Something? *Everything* was wrong. Him standing so close. Her need to touch him, to hold him, to pretend the past ten years had never happened. She shook her head. "Don't you smell that scent?"

"What is it? Something burning?"

"No. It's like perfume. Jasmine." Maybe Brandon was used to it. Maybe he didn't even detect it anymore. Marie took another deep draw. The fragrance had faded, but the whisper of it was still there. "I noticed it in my father's room and followed it out here. Don't you smell it?"

"Jasmine?"

"It was the scent Charlotte used to wear."

His mouth flattened in a hard line. She could see him moving away from her, withdrawing, even though he hadn't physically moved an inch. "Why are you saying this?"

Realization hit her with the force of a slap across the face. She'd blurted out what was in her mind without any thought about who she was talking to, how bringing up his dead wife would make him feel. Her lack of tact knew no bounds.

She took a step backward as heat crept over her cheeks. "I'm sorry. I got carried away."

"Carried away by what?"

"My imagination, I guess. The house. The conversation I had with Sophie Caldwell."

"You talked about Charlotte?"

She shook her head. "We talked about ghosts."

If she'd thought he had given her a cold look before, she was mistaken. The temperature in the room dropped twenty degrees.

She'd better at least try to explain. "They wanted me to try to contact my father."

"That crazy psychomanteum of theirs?"

"I guess." She wished she could crawl under a rock. "I'm sorry for bringing up Charlotte. I just heard a voice and smelled that scent and my imagination went a little wild, I think."

"A voice?"

She shook her head again. She didn't want him to get the wrong impression. "On the radio. It was nothing. Like I said, just my imagination."

His lips softened. "You've been through a lot. Don't worry about it."

His kindness did more to rattle her than even his anger. "I didn't mean to… I'm going to go to bed now."

He leaned toward her, as if he wanted to touch her but didn't quite dare. "Let me help you."

Help her go to bed? She knew that wasn't what he meant, but another giggle bubbled up inside her, anyway. Fatigue. Hysteria. She choked it back.

Brandon didn't seem to realize her struggle. He looked at her with that same concerned look. A look that made her want to curl up in his arms and cry.

Finally he let out a heavy breath. "There's no reason you have to look into Edwin's death alone. I know people. I can help."

All she could manage was a nod.

"Has Hammer given you a copy of the accident report?"

"Yes." She forced a word out. A miracle.

"How about the autopsy?"

"No."

"What do you say tomorrow we go to Baltimore and have a talk with the medical examiner?"

"You can do that? I called, and his secretary or assistant or whatever gave me the runaround."

"I'll give him a call. He'll make time."

"Of course." The world worked differently for Brandon than it did for her. There were perks to being a Drake.

"Like I said before, Edwin was important to me, too. Very important." He gave her a controlled nod. "Tomorrow morning, then?"

Marie took a deep breath. The scent was gone. Even though the desire to touch Brandon still pulsed through her veins, she felt focused once again. Focused on her father, on finding his killer, on bringing his murderer to justice. As long as she could remember why she was here, she could handle the rest.

Even being around Brandon Drake. "See you tomorrow."

Chapter Five

By the time Marie ate Shelley's wonderful breakfast of crab benedict and rode to Baltimore in the quiet comfort of Brandon's chauffeured car, she was beginning to understand just how different Brandon's life was from her own. And when the Maryland medical examiner was actually waiting to talk to them, she knew accepting Brandon's help had been the right thing to do.

Or at least she hoped.

She concentrated on the harsh disinfectant and repulsive fleshy smells of the morgue. Staff bustled through the halls clad in baggy scrubs, some wearing stiff long-sleeved aprons over top. The distraction didn't work. She didn't have to look at Brandon to feel him next to her. She didn't have to smell the leather of his jacket to be aware of every move he made.

His almost black hair glistened in the fluorescent light. His black leather car coat accentuated his broad shoulders as if it were made for him alone. Of course, it probably was. Even his cane only played up the aristocratic air about him.

No wonder she'd fallen so hard when she was a

teenager. Good thing she knew better than to trust the emotions he brought out in her now.

The medical examiner was waiting for them when they entered his office. An older man with skin that resembled a wrinkled brown paper bag, he motioned for them to take off their coats and sit in a pair of chairs facing the desk. Brandon made introductions, and Marie shook the man's hand.

After the formalities were finished, Dr. Tracy started flipping through a pile of file folders lying on his bland, government-issue desk. "I'm sorry I haven't had time to pull your father's records from the recent cases. This will just take a second. Your town has been keeping us awfully busy lately, what with the state police excavation site."

After reading the first few articles back in Michigan, Marie had avoided the story of the mass grave, even though it was in papers and on news channels all over the country. The whole thing was too upsetting. Too depressing. The thought that all those people were victimized just because they wanted a better life. The thought that a doctor who'd sworn to do no harm had forced them to give up organs in return for their passage into the country. The thought that many had given their lives through no choice of their own, their hollow shells dumped into mass graves.

She shuddered. "They caught the men responsible for that, didn't they?"

"One is dead and now the other…" Dr. Tracy peered over his reading glasses at Marie, his hands still shuffling through a stack of reports. "You haven't heard."

"Heard what?"

"Franz Kreeger, the one who was jailed. They found him dead this morning."

Brandon's eyebrows dipped low. "Suicide?"

"I don't know. But I guess I'll find out."

Marie nodded, realizing that what the doctor said was literally true. He would find out, personally. Or at least he would with the help of his staff. Just as his staff would examine each of the bodies buried outside Jenkins Cove. "Have they recovered all the bodies from the mass grave?"

He shook his head. "They're bringing in new ones every day. Very old ones. Fresh ones. It seems like they'd need more than two men to do all that damage. Not that I'm speculating." He pulled a file from the pack and set the others aside. Adjusting his glasses, he flipped open the folder. "Now, how can I help?"

She paused, waiting for Brandon to speak. Instead, he gave her an encouraging nod.

She cleared her throat. "The police told me my father's death was an accident."

"And you want to know if it really was?"

"Yes."

"I can't tell you that."

"Can't tell me?" Marie slumped against the back of her chair. How could that be? "Don't you determine cause of death?"

"Yes. That's exactly what I try to do. And your father's cause of death was drowning."

Marie's throat tightened. Her father had always hated water. He'd always been scared to death of it. The fact that he'd drowned was unspeakably cruel.

"The police believe Edwin hit his head and fell in the water," Brandon said. "Is that possible?"

Marie pressed her lips into a grateful half smile. At this moment, she wasn't sure she could talk. Not unless she wanted to start bawling.

"Yes. He had an injury to the back of his head that could be considered consistent with that theory."

Marie tilted her head to the side. It sounded as though the medical examiner wasn't quite sure the police were on the right track.

Of course, that could just be what she wanted to hear. She forced her voice to remain steady. "Could it have happened differently?"

"Yes. When I say something is consistent with the police's theory, that doesn't mean their story of the death is the only one possible." The doctor glanced down at the report and then pointed to his own bald head. His finger stopped near the top. "The bruising occurred right about here."

"Did he have other bruising that suggested he fell on the rocks? Like on his back or shoulders?"

"No. He had some scrapes on his legs, but that could have been caused by the rocks after he was in the water."

Marie swallowed into an aching throat. She knew the doctor was trained to look at her father's death—any death—in an objective and emotionless way. But it was impossible for her to listen to these details with the same detachment. She was just glad, once again, that Brandon was with her.

Brandon narrowed his eyes on the doctor's head as if trying to visualize what had happened to her father that night. "So he would have had to fall nearly upside down. As if he went off the pier in a somersault and didn't make it all the way over."

The doctor nodded. "That could explain it."

Marie shook her head. That wasn't how she imagined it happening. That wasn't it at all. "He was hit from behind."

The doctor looked down at the report, then back to Marie. His expression was matter-of-fact, as if her statement didn't surprise him at all. "The bruising is such that he could have been hit from behind."

A trill vibrated up Marie's backbone. This was what she had come to find. Something that would prove he was murdered. Some kind of evidence Chief Hammer would have to acknowledge. "Will you tell the Jenkins Cove police chief that?"

Dr. Tracy's forehead furrowed. His lips took on a sympathetic slant. "Just because it's possible doesn't mean it happened that way."

"But it's more likely than my father walking along the water and doing a somersault onto the rocks."

The medical examiner waved his hands in the air between them, as if clearing out the words they'd spoken. "What I'm saying, Ms. Leonard, is I can't tell exactly how your father hit his head before he drowned. It could have happened exactly the way the police said. If you're looking for evidence he was murdered, this is not going to do it."

Marie lifted her eyes from the document in the doctor's hands and stared at the overhead lights. She couldn't let herself cry. She knew her father was murdered. The ambiguity of the autopsy results didn't change that. She'd just have to find better evidence. She'd have to dig harder.

But where to look next?

"Thank you for your time, Doctor." Brandon thrust out a hand. The men shook.

Marie stretched her hand out as well. Swallowing the emotion welling inside, she forced her voice to remain steady. "I appreciate your candor."

The doctor enfolded her hand in his. His graying brow furrowed in concern, as if he could sense how close she was to losing control. "If you have any further questions, you know how to reach me."

"Yes." She turned away and made for the door, needing to escape the smells, the emotion, the doctor's concern more than she remembered needing anything. Brandon slipped a gentle arm around her waist, and at his tender touch, her tears started to flow.

BRANDON HANDED Marie the pressed handkerchief Edwin always insisted he carry and guided her out of the morgue. He'd been amazed she'd been able to hold back her grief this long. While he hated to see her cry, he knew it would be better for her to let it out.

He spotted Josef waiting on a side street and flagged him to bring the town car over. The car sidled up to the curb, and Brandon helped Marie inside.

They were humming down the interstate skirting Annapolis by the time Marie composed herself enough to talk. "I'm sorry."

"Don't apologize. If Edwin was my father, I wouldn't be holding it together half as well as you are."

"That's not true. I'm a mess."

He wiped a tear from her cheek with his fingers. Despite his better judgment, he let his fingers linger, soaking up the satin feel of her skin, the warmth. Both he and Marie had lost their mothers when they were young. Ten years ago they'd connected through their shared experience. Even then he'd been impressed how strong and accepting she'd been of her mother's passing. And he knew how much she loved her father. "You're a lot of things, Marie. A mess isn't one of them."

"I don't know about that. I feel like I can't think straight."

That's how he felt, too, at least when he was this close to Marie. And he knew it had nothing to do with grief.

"I can't stand to think of him as just some case in a... It's just so hard."

He moved his fingertips over her cheek to her chin.

She tilted her face up to him. Her eyes glistened. Tears clumped her lashes. Her lips parted.

He leaned toward her. Kissing her right now felt like the most natural thing in the world. As though it was meant to be. Yet that didn't make it any less impossible.

Especially now.

He dropped his hand from her chin and stared straight ahead through the windshield. The Bay Bridge stretched in front of them, twin ribbons of steel curving high above the wide blue of the Chesapeake.

"Can you do me a favor?" Marie's voice sounded pinched.

"Anything."

"When we get back to Jenkins Cove, will you drop me at Thornton Garden Center? It's over—"

"I know where it is." She must want to see Lexie Thornton. Lexie had decorated Drake House for the annual Christmas Ball every year since she'd started working in her parents' business. And just this fall, Edwin had hired her to redesign the east garden. Brandon had forgotten she was Marie's childhood friend. He was relieved Marie still had a friend in the area. No doubt she needed a shoulder to cry on. He only wished it could be his. "Josef?"

The chauffeur nodded. "Thornton Garden Center. Yes, sir."

Chapter Six

Located on the edge of town in a redbrick building off Main Street, Thornton Garden Center was decked out like a Christmas wonderland. Pine bough swags and wreaths were draped dark and fragrant behind clusters of red, white, pink and blue poinsettias. Gold and silver ornaments filled baskets and decorated sample trees. And a variety of holiday-themed and other sun catchers filled wide windows, sparkling like curtains of colored and sculpted ice.

Marie pushed back memories of past Christmases amidst the grand decor of Drake House and entered the center. More decorations cluttered the inside, competing with flower pots, garden orbs and birdbaths waiting for spring. "Carol of the Bells" tinkled in the pine-scented air.

A man in jeans and a heavy sweater looked up from a stack of boxes he was unpacking. Ornate sleighs made of gold wire scattered the countertop in front of him. He held a price gun in one work-roughened hand. "Can I help you?"

"Is Lexie around?"

"She's in the back room working. If you wait just a second, I'll get her for you."

"You look busy. I'll just peek in myself, if you don't mind. I'm Marie Leonard. We're old friends."

His rough brow furrowed. "Any relation to Edwin Leonard?"

"My father."

"I'm sorry. I did some work for him at Drake House. He was a good man."

Marie gave him what she hoped was a grateful smile and nod. After the emotional upheaval she'd gone through in the morgue and in the car with Brandon, she didn't trust herself to talk. The last thing she needed was more tears. "I'll just go back." She turned away before he had the chance to say anything more. Reaching the small workroom, she peeked her head inside.

Lexie stood at a table strewn with pine boughs and ribbon. She attached a luxurious gold bow to a Christmas wreath.

Only a day had passed since Marie had seen Lexie at her father's service, but after all that had happened, she was so relieved to see her friend, it felt as if it had been weeks. "You told me to stop in. I hope my timing is okay."

"Marie. Your timing is perfect. I'm just finishing these up to bring to a client." Lexie set the wreath down, circled the table and took Marie's hands in hers. "Are you okay?"

Marie tried her best to smile. After her latest bout of crying, her nose was sore and her eyelids felt like over-filled sausage casings. She must look horrible. "I'm fine."

Lexie looked doubtful. "I'm not buying it."

The hazards of having a best friend. Even after all this time, Lexie could see right through her. Once again, tears threatened to break free. She shook her head. "How much can one person cry?"

Lexie surrounded her in a hug. "You lost your dad, Marie. Grieving is normal."

Marie nodded, her cheek snug to Lexie's shoulder. If anyone knew about grief, it was Lexie. Marie and Brandon could never be together, but at least she knew he was living his life, albeit without her.

And that was precisely why she'd needed to see Lexie this afternoon.

She pulled out of her friend's embrace and looked her straight in the eye. "You might think I've lost it, but I have a favor to ask you."

"I would never think you'd lost anything."

"Wait until you hear the favor."

"Okay, shoot."

"Do you know anything about the woman who owns House of the Seven Gables?"

"The bed-and-breakfast? Sure. Sophie Caldwell. She comes into the shop. I helped with some of the decorating for their big holiday open house. What about her?"

"She has a way to communicate with people who have died." She told Lexie about the psychomanteum.

Marie waited to see the skeptical look sweep over Lexie's features. It didn't. Instead, she nodded. "You want to try to speak to your father."

Marie teared up, this time with relief. "You don't think that's weird?"

Lexie shrugged. "Weird? No. I'm not convinced it will work, but I think it's natural for you to want to talk to your dad, to say goodbye."

"That's not all I want to say."

"You want to ask him how to handle Brandon Drake?"

Marie choked back a bitter laugh. She could still feel the heat of Brandon's fingertips on her cheek, her chin. And her chest still ached from the way he'd pulled back. She didn't know if she wanted to talk about Brandon. Not even with Lexie. "My father would tell me to handle him by staying far, far away. And he would be right."

Lexie nodded to a nearby window. "I saw his car drop you off. And I heard you were staying at Drake House. It doesn't seem like you're staying very far away."

So much for avoiding the subject of Brandon. She'd forgotten how quickly news could travel in a small town like Jenkins Cove. "Where did you hear I'm staying at Drake House?"

"Shelley Zachary. You gave her something to gossip about, something besides Brandon's reasons for canceling the Christmas Ball." Lexie shook her head. "You didn't tell me he was hurt when Charlotte died."

"I'm sorry, Marie. Your father asked me not to. He was afraid you'd come back. And I have to admit I agreed with him. The last time you were around Brandon, things didn't turn out so well. Be careful, won't you?"

Marie nodded, but she could tell by Lexie's expression that her friend wasn't convinced. "I'm just staying there to see if I can find some kind of evidence my father was murdered."

"That's another reason you're thinking about going to this psychomanteum thing at Sophie Caldwell's, aren't you? You want to ask about his death."

Marie nodded. She'd told Lexie her suspicions the morning before her father's funeral. Now after hearing what the medical examiner had to say, she felt she was on the right track. If she could learn something from the psychomanteum, anything at all, it would be worth it. "What do you think of the idea?"

Lexie shrugged. "Try it. What's to lose?"

"Will you come with me?"

Lexie shifted her work boots on the floor. "To hold your hand?" It was meant as a quip, but judging from Lexie's discomfort, she knew what Marie was about to say next.

"To contact Simon."

Lexie started shaking her head before the words were out of Marie's mouth. "Simon died thirteen years ago, Marie. There's no use trying to relive the past."

"Why not? Like you said, it might not work, but there's nothing to lose."

"There's nothing to gain, either. Simon's dead. Let's just leave it that way."

Marie nodded. She didn't want to press her friend. Lexie had gone through enough after Simon had died on that Christmas Eve they had planned to run away together. She'd raised his daughter alone. She'd thrown herself into her family's business. She'd pulled her life together. The last thing Marie wanted to do was make her feel as though she had to revisit those dark times. "You're right. You've moved on. You've done an amazing job with Katie."

Lexie pressed her lips into a smile. "Thanks. Although you might not agree when you meet her. She's got a pretty good preteen snit going on these days."

"I hear her mother and her mother's friend were pretty good at that preteen snit in their day."

Lexie smiled. "My mom always told me she hoped I had a daughter like me. Now she reminds me of that regularly."

At the mention of Lexie's mom, the tears misted Marie's eyes. She was all alone now. Now she didn't even have her dad. "I want to see your parents before I go back to Michigan."

"They would have your hide if you didn't." Lexie laid a hand on Marie's shoulder. "But now why don't you go ahead and try to contact your father? I have to deliver these wreaths to a client who lives near the harbor. I'll drive you to Sophie Caldwell's place."

MARIE FOLLOWED SOPHIE up the staircase to the third floor of the old bed-and-breakfast. She'd been chattering nonstop since Marie and Lexie had shown up at the door. Fine with Marie. The more Sophie talked, the less Marie had to. And right now she was so nervous, she doubted she could string three words together that made sense.

"The best way to do this is to spend a day meditating and centering yourself, honey. But nowadays, I know people just don't seem to have the time."

Unease fluttered in Marie's chest. "No. No time."

"I know you think I'm a little crazy with all this stuff, but you don't have to believe in ghosts, if you don't want to. Think of this as meditating. Just relax and open yourself to your deepest thoughts. That's all you need to do."

All? Right now she felt as though relaxing was the

toughest thing in the world, and she was trying to avoid her deepest thoughts.

"I use breathing exercises. In through the nose, out through the mouth. Count slowly while you're doing it. It calms me." Sophie reached the hallway at the top of the steps and spun to face Marie. She breathed in and out, moving her arms with each breath as if conducting an orchestra. She kept it up until Marie joined in. "That's it, sweetheart. In and out. In and out. Starting to feel better?"

"Strangely enough, I am."

"Good. Now follow me." Sophie pushed through a door and led Marie into a darkened room. She flicked a light switch.

Even with the overhead light blazing, the room still felt dark. Black-curtained walls, black ceiling and dark carpet made the space feel smaller than it probably was. Marie eyed the single chair positioned in the room's center. It faced a large gold-framed mirror. "That's the oracle."

"That's right."

Even though she knew the mirror was merely silvered glass, it felt deeper, as if it were calling to her, drawing her in.

She pulled her gaze away and scanned the rest of the items in the space. Antique chests and small tables dotted the carpet, the surface of each one covered with equally antique candelabra holding tapers and other holders cradling fat column candles.

"You built this place?"

"With the help of my handyman, Phil. Phil Cardon. I'm determined, but not exactly strong. Not physically strong, anyway." She pulled a long lighter from one of the tables and bustling around the room, she lit the candles. Once she'd finished, she snapped off the overhead switch. A gentle, flickering light filled the room. "I made my own candles, too. Sometimes scent is part of the experience we get from the other side. Perfumed candles can mask that. So all these are one hundred percent fragrance free."

Marie thought of the jasmine she'd smelled in Drake House. Maybe she was right to think of ghosts when she'd experienced that scent. Not that Brandon would agree.

Pressure assaulted her chest at the thought of him.

She pressed her hand against her breastbone and looked into the mirror. Her emotions were so jumbled where Brandon was concerned. That was part of why she was here. The part Lexie had guessed.

Her father loved Brandon like a son, yet he'd warned Marie about him ten years ago. About his need to be in control of his emotions. About his choice to marry Charlotte. Marie's father had helped her break her ties with Brandon and start a new life. She needed him to help her sort through her feelings now. "I sit in the chair, right?"

"That's right, dear. Look into the mirror and relax. Use those breathing exercises."

"How long will it take?"

"There's no telling. Sometimes communication happens right away. Sometimes it can take hours to open yourself up enough."

Marie lowered herself into the chair. Hours. She couldn't see herself staring into a mirror for hours. She didn't even like looking at her face for the five minutes it took to put on makeup in the morning. "I hope it's faster than that."

"You have to be patient." She could hear Sophie rustle toward the door behind her. "Concentrate on your father. How much you love him. How much you miss him." The woman's voice faltered. Clearly she was talking about her own feelings as much as Marie's.

Before Marie could turn around, the door closed, and she could hear Sophie's footsteps receding down the stairs.

Marie turned back to the mirror and looked into her own eyes. Tears sparkled at their corners in the candle-light. She did love her father. She did miss him. She ached at the prospect that she'd never again see his smile.

She scrutinized her own smile in the mirror. She wasn't ugly, but she was a far cry from the glamorous Charlotte. She didn't need a picture to remember Char-lotte's wavy blond hair and flawless skin, her vibrant laugh, her sparkling, intelligent eyes. That was the woman Brandon had chosen. And that was the image she should keep in her mind, especially after what had happened today.

Or *almost* happened.

She let her eyes stare and become unfocused. Relax. That was what Sophie had said. Drift. Her image blurred, obscured by clouds of light and dark. This was better. At least now she didn't have to stare at herself, compare herself to Charlotte. She could just drift…open herself…love her father….

At first she didn't identify the scent. Exotic. Slightly spicy. Pleasant.

She pulled in a deep breath. It was that jasmine blend, all right. The same scent she had followed through the halls of Drake House. Charlotte's scent. She breathed in again, but the scent was gone.

She shifted in the chair.

"Marie." The voice was light as air.

Had Sophie returned? Marie twisted to look behind her.

The door was closed, the room empty.

"Murder." The voice again. The same one she'd heard in the radio static. Or was it?

A tremor seized Marie's chest.

"Murder."

There it was again, faint, indistinct. Marie could swear the sound was coming from the mirror, yet it was all over the room at the same time. "Daddy?" Even as she called out, she knew the whisper wasn't his. She stared at the center of the gold frame, waiting to see something, anything. But only her own reflection stared back. Candlelight danced behind her. "Who's there?"

The scent tickled her senses again. Jasmine.

"Charlotte? Is that you?"

The scent grew stronger.

This was crazy. It couldn't be happening. She must have fallen asleep in her chair. She must be dreaming.

Cold moved over her. Penetrating deep like the first cut of a blade. She gripped her legs and dug fingertips into the muscles of her thighs. "Charlotte? If it's you, answer."

"Marie." The voice hissed like a steam radiator. The scent grew overpowering.

Marie forced herself to stay in the chair, though every cell in her body clamored to run. "Charlotte? What is it? Why are you communicating with me?"

"Love." The hiss trailed off, but the word was clear.

Charlotte loved her? She found that impossible to believe. "You love Brandon. That's why you're speaking to me?"

"Love."

"Are you trying to warn me away from Brandon? Is that it? Are you staking your claim to him even from the grave?" Marie's inside shook. With fear, with anger, she wasn't sure which. She was getting tired of playing this guessing game. She wanted answers, and she wanted them now. "Out with it, Charlotte. What are you trying to say?"

The cold deepened. The tremor inside her grew until her whole body shook.

The hiss came again, barely loud enough to hear. "All Brandon loves will die."

Chapter Seven

Marie was still shaking when she arrived at the Jenkins Cove Police Station, only a few blocks from the B&B. After she heard the voice, she'd panicked, bolting out of the attic room. She'd escaped from the House of the Seven Gables without explaining to Sophie anything of what she'd experienced. What was she going to say? That Charlotte's ghost had spoken to her? That Charlotte said she was murdered? That the entity had suggested Brandon was responsible?

All Brandon loves will die.

Charlotte's ghost hadn't come out and said Brandon was responsible, only that those he loved would die. But what did that mean? That Charlotte's ghost would kill anyone Brandon loved? Was she warning Marie away?

Marie gathered her wool coat tight at the neck with one hand and clutched her bag against her side with the other. She didn't know what to believe. Heck, she didn't even know what she'd just experienced. But one thing was clear. She needed to know more about Charlotte's death. And save asking Brandon, the only place she could think to get that kind of information was the Jenkins Cove Police Station.

She set her jaw and mounted the steps of the remodeled old house that served as home to the police department. She wasn't sure how she was going to explain her questions to Chief Hammer. He'd probably think she was some kind of paranoid conspiracy nut, seeing a murder behind every accident.

She'd be happy if paranoia was all it was.

She stepped into the entry. Still sporting its original hardwood floors, the station looked very little like a house on the inside. Instead of a foyer, a high desk squatted about ten feet from the door, making it impossible to get into the rest of the station without being seen. A heavy woman wearing a trim polo shirt emblazoned with the Jenkins Cove PD seal looked up from the bank of three computer screens surrounding her. "Can I help you?"

"I was wondering if I could talk to someone about an accident investigation."

"Miss Leonard." Chief Hammer's voice vibrated off the hardwood floors. He poked his head around a corner and gave her an insincere smile. "Are you still *investigating* your father's death?"

She couldn't help note his patronizing tone. "Yes, I'm still looking for answers. But that's not why I'm here this afternoon. I was wondering if you could answer some questions I have about another matter."

Chief Hammer looked relieved. He actually gave her a friendly smile. "Come on in, then. We're pretty short-handed around here, but I'll see what I can do."

He led her into a surprisingly large office just around the corner from the dispatcher. "Have a seat."

Marie sat, though she'd rather stand. At least she remembered her manners this time. No reason to get the chief defensive about her refusing his offer of a chair before their chat even began. "I was wondering if you could fill me in on another accident that took place at Drake House in the past year."

His relieved look melted like an early snow. "Charlotte Drake."

"Yes."

He groaned and shook his head. "A horrible, tragic accident. But I'm not sure what you expect from me. If you want to know more about Mrs. Drake's accident, why don't you ask Brandon Drake himself? I hear you're staying out at Drake House."

It seemed the entire town knew she was staying at Drake House. Of course, Chief Hammer had learned of it from last night's break-in, not Shelley's gossip. "Brandon is still grieving. I don't want to upset him if I can help it." At least that was the truth.

"Of course." The chief leaned back in his desk chair and tented his fingers. "I'll do my best to answer, within reason. What do you want to know?"

"What happened that night?"

"Charlotte, er, Mrs. Drake was drinking. Late in the evening she got into her car. She lost control, and her car collided with a stone wall on the property. The gas tank ruptured, and the fuel ignited."

"And Brandon?"

"Oh yes. Brandon was badly burned trying to pull her out of the fire."

Marie loosened her grip on her coat. She set her bag in the chair beside her. Brandon had risked his life to save Charlotte. So he couldn't have been responsible, could he?

Murder.

The word popped into Marie's mind, carried on a whisper as it had been in the psychomanteum and on the radio. If not Brandon, could someone else have killed Charlotte? "Was there any evidence of foul play?"

There was the expression she knew was coming. The expression that said Chief Hammer thought she was out of her ever-loving mind. "You're kidding, right?" He glanced around his office as if Marie were setting him up, and he was searching for the camera that must be recording the joke.

"No. I'm not kidding. I'm asking. Was there any chance Charlotte's death wasn't completely accidental?"

His gaze finally landed back on her. "It was an accident, Miss Leonard. Just like your father's death was an accident. Neither of them was murdered."

"I can understand why it seems far-fetched for Drake House to see two unrelated murders in the span of six months, Chief. But two accidents in that time span seems odd, too." She paused, weighing her words, careful not to offend Chief Hammer. "What if my father found out something about Charlotte's death? What if he was murdered to keep him quiet?"

A bushy brow crooked toward his nonexistent hairline. "Are you sure you're not some kind of murder-mystery writer?"

"I'm serious, Chief."

"I'm serious, too, Miss Leonard. I don't know what you're after here, but this is ridiculous. And it's starting to get on my nerves. We're very busy around here with real life. I don't need to spend any more of my time on your silly theories."

Obviously she had no talent for diplomacy. "Really, if you hear me—"

"I'm done here, Miss Leonard." Hammer rose to his full modest height. "If there's anything rational that we can do for you here at the police department, let us know."

"Would it be possible for me to see Charlotte Drake's accident report?"

"Why would you want to do that?"

"I need to understand what happened."

Hammer puffed out his bulldog cheeks. He didn't move.

"Accident reports are public record, aren't they?"

With a grunt, he thrust himself from his chair and stalked to the office door. "I'll get them for you. It might take a while. Half my staff is assisting the state police." He closed the door behind him, leaving her alone in the office.

Time ticked by, and Hammer didn't return. Finally Marie left the office to find out what had happened to the chief and his promise. Rounding the corner, she stepped into the dispatch area.

The last person she expected to see was Brandon. But there he was, powerfully sexy in his black leather coat, taking a sheaf of papers from the chief himself. "Hello, Marie."

"CHIEF HAMMER CALLED you, didn't he?" Marie stopped stock-still on the police station's front porch and stared a hole through Brandon.

Brandon's gut ached. "What does it matter? You needed a ride back to Drake House, anyway." He looked out across the street where his car idled, Josef waiting patiently for them. Clouds hung low and ominous in the sky. The air smelled like coming rain.

"You could have waited until I called. You could have sent the car. Why did he call you? Because I was asking too many questions?"

"Because you were forcing him to work too hard, I think."

Marie and he had found common ground when he'd mentioned Hammer's laziness last night. Now her expression darkened and she clamped her jaw tight. "What did he say to you? Be honest."

Brandon should have known Marie wouldn't let him get away with ducking the subject. He used to like that about her. Her directness. Her doggedness. Now he wasn't so sure. "He said you were asking a lot of questions about Charlotte. Questions he thought I could do a better job of answering."

"Or a better job of avoiding?"

She was right. The last thing he wanted to do was stand here in the rain and talk about Charlotte. Especially with her.

"You rushed over here to get me to back off, didn't you?"

"Yes."

"You don't want to talk about Charlotte."

"No."

Her lips tightened. She clutched the top of her coat, pulling it protectively around her throat.

"What do you expect me to do? Lie? I don't want to relive Charlotte's death, especially not with you." He gripped the head of his cane until his fingers ached. His wedding band dug into his flesh. Having Marie around had been a struggle from the first moment. Between his old feelings for her coming to life and his need to keep from hurting her again, he'd tied himself in knots. But he really couldn't stomach dredging up his past with Charlotte. His failure. His guilt. Scars so much deeper than the ones on his face and leg. "Why are you asking about Charlotte? What could you possibly need to know?"

"I think she was murdered."

He took a step backward, his heel hitting the base of the porch railing. He'd been ready for her to say a lot of things, but not that. "Why on earth would you think she was murdered?"

She rolled her lower lip inward and grasped it in her teeth. "Something Sophie Caldwell said."

"What?"

"She said my father discovered something right before he died. Something he told her was dangerous."

"Why do you think whatever it was he found has anything to do with Charlotte's death?"

She searched his eyes, her gaze moving back and forth as if she wasn't finding what she was looking for. "Doesn't it seem strange to you? I mean, two fatal accidents at Drake House in a six month time period?"

"I already told you I agree your father's death seems suspicious."

"Then an accident and a murder."

"Coincidences can happen."

She stiffened and shook her head. "You're not listening."

"No, you're not listening, Marie. I *know* Charlotte wasn't murdered. I know why she died. I was there, remember?"

She released her coat and balled her fists at her sides, her chest rising and falling with shaky breaths. "No, I don't remember. You haven't told me anything about

Charlotte's death. Neither did Chief Hammer. Neither did my father or Lexie. Everyone seems to be trying to protect me. Well, I don't need protection. And I don't want it. I want the truth. I want some answers."

"Charlotte wasn't murdered."

She held up a hand as if shielding herself from his words. "*I* have reason to believe she was. Not just what Sophie said, but reasons I don't want to talk about. *And* I have reason to believe my father was murdered after he found out who killed her. Probably by the same person."

He drew in a breath to speak.

Marie gestured again with her hand. Her fingers were trembling. "I don't want to hear your pronouncements. If you can't enlighten me, stay out of my way."

God, he hated to see her so upset. And he had no one to blame but himself. He had been avoiding the subject of Charlotte since her death. It was the reason he avoided venturing out into public wherever possible. It was the reason he canceled the Christmas Ball. It was the reason he discouraged the few servants he tolerated around him from even mentioning her name. He even tried to prevent himself from thinking about her, although he failed regularly at that. And since Marie had come back to Drake House…

He waved an arm, directing Josef to swing the car around to this side of the street. Brandon knew that he'd made a royal mess of everything, and that he needed to set things straight. To come clean. At least with Marie. The rest of the damage he'd done could never be repaired. "Marie? Get in the car and I'll tell you everything."

As Josef pulled to the curb, Brandon stepped off the

porch. Drizzle misted the car's windows and felt cool on his cheeks. He opened the back door and gestured Marie inside.

She held his eyes for a second, as if deciding whether he was sincere about his promise. Then she slid into the seat. He followed, settling in beside her. For a moment all he could think about was kissing her, actually going through with it this time and pressing his lips to hers. Tasting her mouth. Feeling her body yield to his, soft and accepting.

He nodded for Josef to drive and focused straight ahead. As they drove through town, he watched the windshield wipers sweep the glass periodically and searched for words that would make this easier.

Nothing would make it easier.

Finally he just spoke. "Charlotte lost control of her car. As she was leaving Drake House, she veered off the drive just before the gate and hit the rock wall. Her car caught fire. I heard the impact. I saw the fire. I tried to pull her out, but she was trapped in the wreckage. She died right in front of me. I heard her last screams." He kept his voice flat, unemotional, but his stomach seized involuntarily at the memory. Charlotte's screams were always in his nightmares. Always lurking in the back of his mind.

Marie shook her head. "A woman doesn't just race her car into a stone wall. A car doesn't just burst into flame."

"I was there. It did."

"Did you see her before it happened?"

The tension in his stomach turned to nausea. And he'd thought this couldn't get worse.

"You said you'd explain. You said you'd tell me everything."

He blew air through tight lips. "Yes, I did."

"So?"

"Yes, I saw her."

"Was she upset about anything? How did she seem? Chief Hammer said she was drinking."

"She was."

"Why?"

For a one word question, that one was about as complicated as a question could get. "She just did. She collected fine wine. I still have the wine cellar to prove it."

"So she always drank?"

"She liked her wine."

"Chief Hammer said there was a vodka bottle."

"Yes. The police found it in the car. He told me that after the accident."

"Did Charlotte drink a lot?"

He couldn't stand this. "I don't think this has anything to do with anything. Sure, she was drunk. Sure, she shouldn't have been behind the wheel."

"Then why was she? Josef could have driven her, couldn't he? Was he working for you then?"

"She could have had him drive her. Back then we used him more as a handyman than a driver. We usually drove ourselves." He looked down at his leg. Those days were over. Now he was lucky to be able to walk, albeit with a cane. His doctor doubted his reflexes would ever be sharp enough again to drive safely.

Marie shook her head. "Charlotte didn't strike me as the type of woman who would—"

"We had a fight, all right? She was upset with me. That's why she was drinking. That's why she got behind the wheel. That's why she crashed."

The click of the turn signal and the swoosh of the wipers were the only sounds as they approached the long, winding drive. The gray stone wall stretched along the highway, opening only for the classic white pillar entrance of Drake House and the ostentatious redbrick and cast iron of his uncle's neighboring estate, The Manor at Drake Acres. Josef slowed the car to make the turn.

Brandon stared straight out the window. He didn't want to witness Marie's reaction to his confession. Getting the words out had been hard enough. Nor could he bear to look out the side window and see the stone wall as they passed.

The wall that still held a shadow of fire.

"It's not your fault, Brandon." Her voice sounded calm, soothing, forgiving.

He shook his head. He couldn't let himself listen. It was enough to undo him. "You still don't understand. It *is* my fault. It's all my fault. Charlotte was a good wife. She was kind and beautiful and so damn smart. She was any man's dream. And what did I do to repay her?" He lowered his head and pinched the bridge of his nose between thumb and forefinger. He couldn't explain. Not to Marie. Never to Marie.

"You had an affair?"

"No!"

"What, then? What did you fight about?"

He promised he'd tell her everything. He promised he'd be honest with her. But how could he be honest about this?

"What did you fight about, Brandon? What was so bad?"

He clutched the head of his cane in both hands.

Avoiding the platinum gleam of the ring around his finger, he raised his eyes to meet hers.

Most men probably wouldn't find Marie as beautiful as Charlotte. But most men were fools. To him, one look into Marie's eyes was more addictive than any drug. It had always been that way. Ever since the summer when he'd come home with his MBA from Harvard and found her all grown up. And try as he might, he hadn't been able to change his response. He couldn't change his response to her even now. "Charlotte and I fought about you."

Chapter Eight

"Me?" The word caught in Marie's throat, almost choking her. She couldn't have heard Brandon right. How could they have fought about her? At the time of Charlotte's death, she hadn't seen either of them for ten years. "I don't understand."

"Of course you don't. You're strong, resilient. After that summer, you moved on."

"After that summer?" Marie's stomach tightened into a knot. There was no question what summer he meant. The summer she'd given him everything she was, and he'd tossed it away. "You make it seem as if moving on was my choice. As if I had a choice at all. After that summer, you got married."

The car's tires popped over loose gravel. Drake House loomed at the end of the winding drive, bright white columns glowing in the dreary weather, gray slate roof glistening with rain. The crunch of the tires slowed. The car stopped in front of the main entrance.

"You were so young, just out of high school. I already had my MBA. I was ready to settle down in Jenkins Cove and run the Drake Foundation. I couldn't tie you down when you hadn't even had a chance to see the world."

"That's what my father told you."

"And he was right. You deserved the chance to live your own life. To see the world beyond Jenkins Cove. To discover who you wanted to be." He lifted his hand. For a moment, he let it hover in the air, as if he wanted to touch her, before returning it to his cane. "It wasn't just that. I had already promised Charlotte. She was a good woman. My age. Already accomplished. Ready to settle down. I thought she was the perfect wife for me. I had no misgivings about marrying her. Not until…that summer with you. That summer made me rethink everything I thought I knew, everything I thought I felt. I didn't know what to trust—feelings that had swept me up in one summer or plans that were years in the making."

So he went with the plans.

Marie stared at the grand house. She didn't want to hear this. Any of it. She'd tried so hard to overcome her feelings for Brandon. She'd tried so hard to forget him and stand on her own. "Why are you telling me this?"

"You asked."

"I asked about Charlotte's death. Not about you and me."

"But it's all linked. It's all tangled into one giant mess."

She focused on Brandon. "How?"

He tore his eyes from hers. "Josef?"

The chauffeur glanced over his shoulder. "Yes, sir?"

"We would like some privacy. Just turn off the engine and leave the car here."

"Very good, sir." The chauffeur switched off the engine and left the keys dangling in the ignition. He climbed from the driver's seat and closed the door behind him, the sound followed by an abrupt and deep silence.

Marie watched him cut across the lawn to the carriage house. With each step he took away from the car, the more panicked she felt. She wanted to call the chauffeur back, ask him to stay, use him to shield her from whatever was coming. She didn't know what Brandon was going to say, but she had the feeling that whatever it was, it would be better for her not to hear.

"Charlotte deserved someone who loved her."

Marie let his words settle into her brain. She felt Brandon's pain in them, his regret. But the shift inside her was more insidious, more dangerous. It was the shift from numbness to hope.

And that scared her more than anything.

She clutched the bag in her lap and held on. She had to get a grip on herself. She was no longer eighteen. She had to remember all she'd learned.

Her father had warned her about Brandon that summer. He'd told her of Brandon's childhood. Of the heartbreak Brandon suffered when he'd lost his mother and the tightrope he'd had to walk to please his demanding father and grandfather. Her father feared Brandon had been damaged. He feared all the trauma he'd suffered as a boy had combined to make him afraid to open himself to love. To vulnerability.

Even with a woman as amazing as Charlotte.

And that's what she had to keep foremost in her mind. Her father's warning. Her father's fears. Not the way Brandon had looked at her that summer as if she were beautiful. Not his tenderness when they'd made love, when she'd given him her virginity. And certainly not the kiss he'd almost given her this morning, the kiss she still longed to claim.

"That night…" Brandon's voice cracked. He drew a

deep breath. "The night Charlotte died, she asked me for one thing. Something I couldn't give."

Marie wrapped her arms around her middle and held on. She needed to stay in control of her feelings, her fantasies. She didn't want to go back to that raw, painful place. The place it had taken her years to escape.

Brandon reached into his pocket and pulled out a leather wallet. He flipped it open and slipped something free. He handed Marie a small photograph.

She tilted it toward the car's window. Her high school graduation picture stared back at her, long hair, freckles, goofy smile and all. "My senior picture?"

"Charlotte found it the night she died. She asked me to get rid of it. I couldn't."

Marie looked up at him. She didn't want to know...she didn't want to ask...but she couldn't help it. "Why?"

"I don't know."

She closed her eyes. She'd dreamed for years that someday Brandon would tell her he loved her. That he'd made a mistake. That he wanted her instead of Charlotte. Now even though he'd admitted to arguing with his wife about her picture, he still wouldn't say those special words.

And the worst part of it all, the part that made her feel sick inside, was that she still wanted to hear them. "That's what you fought over? My picture?"

"Yes." He shook his head, the movement slow and sad. "I never should have asked Charlotte to marry me. It wasn't fair to her. But I didn't know that. Not until after I'd proposed. Not until that summer."

That summer. Their summer. Marie watched the drizzle bead up and slide down the window like tears.

Now that he'd put his regrets out there, she had to know the rest. "Why did you go through with the wedding?"

"I didn't know how to break it off. There were so many reasons not to. My promise to her. Our families. And she suited me. At least I thought she should. My feelings for you were so new. So overwhelming. I'd never experienced feelings like that before. I didn't trust them. And because I was weak and indecisive…" He pinched the bridge of his nose once more, as if he thought doing so would push back the tears. "And because I was weak and indecisive, Charlotte paid the price."

Marie wrapped her arms tighter. She felt cold. Colder even than the Michigan winter. Suddenly what he'd been trying to say about Charlotte's death dawned on her, what he'd been trying to tell her all along. "You think she committed suicide."

He looked past her, past Drake House. Pain etched his face. His eyes looked more flat and hopeless than the overcast sky.

She had to go on. She had to know. For so long she'd kept a glimmer of hope alive…the wish that she and Brandon would find a way to be together. She'd tended it like a flicker of fire in the hearth, but with his confession, Brandon had doused the flame. "You think she killed herself because of you. Because you couldn't love her the way she needed. Because of the feelings you had for me. That's why you feel so guilty. You blame yourself for her death."

He looked down at his hands, knuckles white, clutching the carved head of his cane. He didn't speak. He didn't nod. He didn't answer at all.

He didn't have to.

MARIE STOOD in the darkened foyer of Drake House and stared up at the majestic twin staircase. For the first time she could remember, she felt truly relieved to be away from Brandon. After disabling the alarm and instructing her to lock the door behind him, he'd said something about wanting to check the boathouse. Promising to be back soon, he'd left her in the house alone.

Understandable that he wanted to be alone with his thoughts. With his regrets. She wanted to be alone, too, but not to think. She would be just fine if she never had to think of this evening again.

She mounted the steps. When she reached the first landing where the staircase split, each branch leading into opposite wings of the mansion, she paused. To the right, the stairs climbed into the house's grand ballroom and outer sitting rooms. Usually this time of year, the wing would be humming with activity as servants and outside contractors like Lexie readied it for the annual Drake House Christmas Ball. It would smell of pine boughs and cinnamon and jingle with music. Instead the space felt vacant and dead. No festive decor. No bustling energy. Just a forlorn sadness that made Marie miss her childhood Christmases even more.

But she wasn't here to relive Christmas memories and mourn the demise of Drake House tradition.

She turned away from the public west wing and started up the stairs that led east. She wasn't sure how Brandon would feel about her snooping in the house's private wing. Especially after what he'd just confessed. But just in case he didn't like the idea, she wasn't going to wait to ask permission. Better to ask forgiveness, as the saying went. Better still to find some evidence of murder—either Charlotte's or her father's. Then she wouldn't have to ask for anything.

Climbing the steps, Marie moved out of the light of the foyer and into the dark, enclosed portion of the staircase that led up to the rooms on the third floor. She groped along the wall. She had no idea where the light switches for the stairs and halls were located in this wing. She had only been in this area of the house a few times when she was young. The last time she'd ventured this way, she'd been exploring the house with Lexie. When her father had discovered them in the private wing unaccompanied and without permission, he'd grounded her for a week and called Lexie's parents. After that, they'd confined their exploring to the ballroom, parlors and guest quarters of the public wing.

She gripped the banister, feeling jittery in the dark, as if her father were going to jump out at any moment and demand to know why she was there. She smiled at the thought. She wouldn't mind being grounded for a week if she could see his face once more. She wouldn't mind at all.

Reaching the third floor, she stopped and tried to get her bearings. The rain sounded as if it was coming down harder now, its patter a constant din on the roof a full floor above her head. Located on a jut of land, Drake House offered views of the water on three sides. She peered through an open door facing the forest side of the house. The nursery. Big enough to house half a dozen children, it stood empty now, the whimsical carving of animals along the ceiling molding merely a reminder of the next generation of Drake children who would never occupy this space. She passed several locked doors she remembered were the nanny's quarters and various other rooms before reaching the back staircase that led to the third floor.

If she remembered correctly, Charlotte's study overlooked the east garden, which would put it at the end of the wing. When her father was first working up plans with Lexie for redesigning the garden's landscaping, he'd mentioned how enthusiastic Charlotte had been, since her rooms overlooked that part of the property.

Unfortunately, she'd died before work on the garden began.

Marie forced her feet to move down the dark hall. A door facing the water side of the house stood open. Despite a shimmer of unease at the back of her neck, she stopped in front of an open door and peered inside.

The wet glisten of rain and water shone through windows unencumbered by draperies. Heavy, masculine chairs clustered in the sitting area. The scent of leather hung rich in the air. She stepped farther into the room, to the next open door and the chamber beyond. A bed big enough for five people faced a window overlooking Chesapeake Bay.

The master bedroom suite.

Marie's pulse pounded in her ears. It didn't take much imagination to see Brandon in that bed, leaning back against the pillows, his bare chest gleaming in the first glow of the morning sun.

She shook her head. Blocking the image in her mind's eye, she returned to the hall. She felt like that girl again, exploring places she shouldn't, indulging in feelings she had no business feeling. She needed to forget what she and Brandon had together all those years ago. Forget the hurt. Forget it all.

Hearing Charlotte's voice and smelling her scent in the psychomanteum might or might not qualify her as insane, but going through the same thing over and over with Brandon and expecting a different outcome was the *definition* of insanity. She needed to wipe Brandon from her mind…and her heart.

Swallowing into a dry throat, she walked farther down the hall. She passed the open entrance to Brandon's study and skipped the door she knew led up to the widow's walk on the roof. At the eastern-most end of the wing, she stopped at a locked door and pulled the ring of keys from her bag. Trying each, she finally found the one that fit. She let herself in and flicked on the light.

Lamps artfully positioned around the room gave off a soft glow. The room was as feminine as the master suite was masculine. Dainty antique chairs covered with silk damask gathered around a fireplace. Built-in bookshelves flanked an ornate antique desk. Pillows decorated a floral sofa. And the scent…jasmine.

She drew in a deep, slow breath. Sure enough. The same scent she'd noticed last night. The same one she'd smelled in the psychomanteum. This wasn't her imagination. She wasn't crazy. This was real.

Like last night, she let the scent lead her across the study, toward the windows and the desk positioned underneath.

If Charlotte's spirit was responsible for the scent of jasmine and the voice she'd heard in the psychomanteum, maybe she was trying to tell Marie something now. "Charlotte? Are you here?"

There was no reply.

"Is there something to find here?"

Again, silence answered.

Great. Now she was talking to herself. At least there was no one home to hear. She could just imagine how Brandon would feel about her wandering through the house calling out his dead wife's name. "Charlotte, if that's you, did you commit suicide?"

A sharp thud came from somewhere in the house.

Marie jumped. Was that an answer? Or was the wind kicking up outside? "If that was you, Charlotte, it wasn't clear enough. You talked to me in the psychomanteum. Why not talk to me now?"

No sound. Just the scent.

Marie eyed the antique desk under the window. "Is it the desk? Is there something inside?" She didn't wait for a response this time. She pulled open the top drawer.

Empty. The second was empty as well, and the third. She moved to the closet, then on to the built-in wall units. There was nothing to be found. Brandon might have left the furniture in the room, but he'd cleaned out all Charlotte's personal things. Marie wondered what he'd done with them.

A creak sounded from the hallway. The soft, slow beat of footsteps.

Brandon.

Marie turned away from the empty wall units and walked to the door, her skin prickling with nerves. She told herself she was being ridiculous. There was no reason to sneak around, no reason to hide what she'd been doing. If Brandon didn't want her looking through the house, he wouldn't have given her the full set of keys. Still, the thought of facing him again after what he'd revealed in the car left her a little shaky.

No matter. She wasn't going to hide from him the rest of her time in Jenkins Cove. She needed answers, starting with what had happened to Charlotte's personal papers and possessions. She was going to get to the bottom of Charlotte's and her father's deaths, and she wasn't going to let anything get in the way. Especially not the past.

She crossed the room and opened the door. The hall was dark, and for a moment all she could see was a shadow.

A shadow without a cane. A shadow too short to be Brandon.

Suddenly the shadow rushed toward her and an arm clamped around her throat.

Chapter Nine

Rain spattered cold on Marie's cheeks. She could feel hands gripping her under her arms, pulling her. Her feet dragged over something rough.

She must have passed out.

She remembered the shadow, remembered the arm across her throat, bearing down. Her head throbbed. Her stomach swirled. Her throat burned like fire.

But she could breathe.

She scooped in breath after breath of cold, moist air and tried to fight her way to consciousness. She tensed her muscles. She forced her eyes open.

Color exploded in her head. Her vision swirled, dark and light. The night closed in around her. She saw the water far below, and white lines stretching on either side of her. They were the rails encircling the widow's walk.

She was on the roof.

She gritted her teeth and tried to clear her head, tried to think. Hell, she didn't have time to think. She had to move. She thrust her arms up, lashing out at the hands dragging her. She bared her fingernails like claws, trying to dig her stubby nails into flesh.

A blow rained down on her head, and rough hands pushed her into the railing. The top rail hit low on her thighs, but her upper body kept moving, flipping, carrying her over.

She hit the sloped roof. Air exploded from her lungs. She coughed, gasped, tried to breathe. Her body started to slide.

She scrambled to find a handhold, a foothold, but wet with rain, the shingles felt slick as ice. Her fingers slipped. Her feet thrashed.

And still she kept sliding. Closer to the edge. Closer to the three-story drop to the ground.

Her hand hit something. A roof vent. She grabbed on, the steel cutting into her fingers. Her legs jutted out over the roof's edge.

She stopped.

She clung to the vent, afraid to move. Rain pattered on her back. Water sluiced around her, beneath her and emptied into the gutter that ran under her legs. Her heart pounded against the wet slate. She slowly, carefully scooped in a breath. Then another. Her lungs screamed for more.

She peered down, past her dangling legs. She could see the gentle lighting of the east garden through the misty rain below. The concrete bench glowed pale against dark leaves of holly. So far down…so far…

She grew dizzy and closed her eyes. The edge of metal cut into her fingers. Her muscles trembled and ached. Her fingers started slipping.

Oh God. She was going to fall.

Pressure closed around her wrist and held her fast. Not cold like the rain, like the slate and steel she clung to, but warm as a human hand.

She looked up into the night. Through the rain the widow's walk railing gleamed white against a black sky. She was alone. Totally alone. And yet she could feel a hand on her wrist, a hand that kept her from falling, a hand that kept her safe.

"Marie?" a woman's voice screamed. Not from the roof, but from below. "Oh God, Marie! Hold on! We'll be right up."

Marie didn't know how long she clung there, the unseen hand binding her wrist, before she heard a clatter on the roof.

"Over here. This is where I saw her." A thump came from above. "We're here, Marie. We're coming for you."

The same woman's voice. A voice Marie recognized. "Chelsea?" What was Sophie Caldwell's niece doing here?

"Hold on, Marie."

Something scraped against the slate shingles above her head. A large hand encircled her wrist, replacing the pressure that had stopped her fall. "I've got you."

She looked up into a man's eyes. Rain sparkled in his dark hair. He gave her a reassuring smile. "It's okay. You can let go now."

She forced her fingers to obey.

He pulled her up, slowly, gently, until the two of them reached Chelsea on the widow's walk.

"Thank God," Chelsea said. "It's a miracle you held on. It took a few minutes to rig a rope. We were afraid you'd fall before Michael could reach you."

And she might have.

Marie looked out over the wet slate. Her whole body trembled. Her legs felt like loose sand. "Something held me. A hand. It kept me from going over the edge, but I couldn't see anything there. It was like…" She searched for the word, but her mind balked. Even after the experiences she'd had lately, she didn't want to say it out loud.

Michael gave a knowing nod. "A spirit?"

"Yes."

Chelsea and Michael exchanged looks. "Let's go inside," Chelsea said. "We have a lot to talk about."

WHEN BRANDON MOUNTED the steps to the kitchen entrance of Drake House he was surprised to see the lights still on in Edwin's quarters. He'd sat in the boat-house for hours and listened to the rain patter on the roof, trying to process what had happened with Marie, trying to get his head straight. And even though he didn't feel any better than he had when he'd left, he thought by now it would be safe to return to the house. He thought she would be asleep.

He unlocked the kitchen door and stepped inside. The door to the butler's quarters stood open. "Let me check your eyes again, just to be sure." A woman's voice. Not Marie.

He crossed the kitchen and peered through the open door.

A blond woman leaned over Marie's chair. She directed a flashlight to the side of Marie's cheek and peered into Marie's eyes, one after another. "Looks good. I think you're going to survive."

Alarm prickled along Brandon's nerves. He stepped forward into Edwin's sitting room. "Survive? Survive what?"

"You must be Brandon." A man nearly as tall as

Brandon with the build of an athlete pushed himself up from a chair. He stepped across the room and offered his hand. "Michael Bryant. This is Chelsea Caldwell."

Brandon made the connections in his mind while shaking the man's hand. He nodded to the blonde. "You're related to Sophie Caldwell?"

"My aunt."

So they'd made their introductions, but no one had answered his initial question. He focused on Marie. "What happened, Marie? Are you hurt?"

Marie wrapped her arms around herself as if she was cold. She looked so small sitting on the love seat. Small and fragile.

"Marie had an accident," the blonde supplied.

Something inside him seized. He struggled to keep himself steady, to stay calm and wait for the details instead of racing to Marie and gathering her into his arms. "What kind of accident?"

Marie glanced from Chelsea to Michael. "Thanks so much for everything you've done. And everything you told me. I think it's better if I talk to Brandon alone, if you don't mind."

"Yes. That's a good idea." Chelsea exchanged looks with Michael. Brandon led them to the front entrance of Drake House. "Thank you," he said as they plunged out into the rain and ran to their vehicle. Brandon locked the door and set the alarm behind them.

When he walked back into Edwin's sitting room, Marie was still huddled on the love seat. She looked as if she hadn't moved a muscle. A welt rose on her scalp, just above her right ear.

"You're hurt."

"Just a bump and a headache. I don't have a concussion. Believe me, Chelsea has been checking me every hour. I guess I just have a hard head."

His gaze moved down to her neck. Although she had a throw blanket wrapped around her shoulders, he could see a bruise starting to purple on the pale skin of her throat. He swayed a little on his feet. "And that?"

"I'll tell you about all of it. But first, you'd better sit down."

Brandon didn't move. "Who did this? Have you called the police?"

"They were already here."

"And a doctor? You need to see a doctor. We need to get you to a hospital. I'll call Josef."

"A paramedic was here, too. I'm just bruised. I'm going to be fine. Now sit down."

He couldn't. He needed to do something. Sitting felt too passive. Besides, the only place he wanted to sit was in the love seat beside her. More than anything he wanted to take her in his arms and keep her safe. "I'll stand."

"Fine." She explained how she'd been looking through Charlotte's study, how she'd thought she'd heard him return from the boathouse, how she'd been attacked. When she got to the part about being thrown off the roof, he started pacing, a habit he'd broken since he'd injured his leg. A habit that saved him now. "Why didn't I hear any of this? I should have heard something. I should have known. You could have died." Damn him. Marie had already been attacked once since she came to Drake House. Why in the hell had he left her alone? What had he been thinking?

"Chelsea found me. She and Michael saved me."

He managed a nod. What he wanted to do was smack himself in the head…or worse.

He ran a hand through his hair before walking back the length of the room. He hadn't been thinking. Not about anyone but himself, anyway. He'd simply wanted to get away. Far away. Where he didn't have to see the pain and disappointment in Marie's eyes. Where he wouldn't be tempted to take her in his arms and make promises he feared he could never keep.

At least Chelsea Caldwell and this Michael had been here. Brandon eyed Marie. "Why *were* Chelsea and Michael here? And how did they find you on the roof?"

"Chelsea sensed I was in trouble."

"She *sensed* it?"

"She sees things other people don't see."

"Like what? The future?"

Marie watched him. A little too closely for his comfort. "She sees ghosts. They communicate with her."

His stomach felt as if he were cresting in a roller coaster and hanging in midair. "You're joking."

"You know the mass grave we've been hearing so much about? Do you know how the police discovered it?"

She'd lost him. "What does the mass grave have to do with what happened tonight?"

"A spirit named Lavinia appeared to Chelsea. Michael saw her, too. The spirit led them to the graves. She helped them figure out the truth."

"Let me guess, Lavinia was one of the people buried in the mass grave."

"Yes."

He massaged his forehead with his fingertips. What kinds of stories had Chelsea and Michael been telling? "You don't believe all this stuff, do you?"

Marie watched him a long time. Rain and wind beat against the windows and whistled over the chimneys of the old house. He was about to ask again when Marie finally spoke. "Yes. I do."

"You're kidding."

She narrowed her eyes to caramel-colored slits. "You don't believe there are things in this world that we don't understand?"

"Things like ghosts?" He couldn't even believe they were having this conversation, and he still had no clue where it was leading. "I've never really thought about it."

"Would you believe if you saw one? Or heard one?"

"I don't know. I suppose I might."

"Would you believe if I told you that a ghost has contacted me?"

An uneasy feeling knotted deep in his gut. "How did this go from a story Chelsea told you to this? What are you trying to say, Marie?"

"Just that. I've been contacted by a spirit. I didn't want to believe it myself at first. But it's real."

He shook his head.

Marie slumped back in the love seat. "You don't believe me. You haven't even heard what I have to say, and you don't believe me."

"I'm just trying to get this straight." He didn't have a clue what to think. This whole conversation was so unlike Marie. She had a romantic streak, yes. But she always seemed to have her feet firmly planted in reality. She was like her father in that way. "The ghost you saw. It was your father?"

"I didn't *see* a ghost. I heard a voice. I smelled a scent."

He went cold inside. Memories of their argument at the police station popped into his mind. The way Marie had insisted Charlotte had been murdered. She couldn't be leading where he feared she was. She wouldn't. "It was your father, right?" *Please let it be Edwin.*

"I tried to contact my father. I couldn't reach him."

"Then…" He couldn't ask. He didn't want to know.

"Brandon, it was Charlotte."

"The jasmine."

"Exactly."

"It was a scent, Marie. Just a scent. Charlotte lived here for ten years. It isn't unheard of that the house would still smell like her."

"I didn't just smell it here. I smelled it in Sophie's psychomanteum."

"How do you know the scent was Charlotte? How do you know it wasn't from some other source? Jasmine isn't common, but it's not rare, either."

"I heard her voice, Brandon."

His heart stuttered. "You're sure?"

"Yes."

Even though he had an idea of what Marie's answer would be, he forced the question from his lips. "What did she say?"

"She said she was murdered. She said, 'All Brandon loves will die.'"

He stared at the wall, the moldings on the ceiling, anything but Marie. The part about Charlotte saying she was murdered, he'd guessed. The other part…*All Brandon loves will die.* What did that mean?

"You still don't believe." Marie's voice trembled.

Something inside him broke at the sound. He met her eyes. "It's not that I don't want to, Marie. I just…"

"You can't."

"I don't know. I'm trying to absorb it. That's all." He turned away from her and strode the length of the room, the extra beat of his cane on the parquet making his footfalls sound as unbalanced as all of this felt.

Murder. Charlotte murdered. As much as he wanted to believe Marie, as much as he wanted to believe Charlotte hadn't killed herself, that he wasn't responsible for his wife's death, he didn't know if he could. "Who would murder Charlotte?"

"You tell me. Did anyone stand to gain from her death?"

"You mean financially?"

"Sure. Or other ways."

He walked back to where Marie sat. The answer to her question was obvious and inevitable. "Me."

Marie shook her head. "Who else?"

"No one else." He thought for a moment. This whole exercise was so foreign to him. Murder? Motives? For crying out loud, *ghosts?* It was as if he'd fallen down some surreal rabbit hole. "Her mother is still alive. But she isn't in need of money. And she adored her daughter. She was crushed when Charlotte died."

Marie stared into the empty fireplace, deep in thought. "What if you died without having children? Who would inherit?"

"My uncle. He's not in need of money, either." Brandon took several steps and stopped. The words Marie had repeated, the ones she said had come from the ghost, whispered through his mind.

All Brandon loves will die.

His fingers tightened on his cane. Charlotte had died, only he hadn't loved Charlotte. Not the way a man should love his wife. But… "What about this attack tonight?"

She met his eyes, unflinching. "I'm pretty sure my father was killed because he found something, something that proved Charlotte was murdered. Maybe the killer thinks I've found whatever that is. Or maybe he or she is afraid I will."

There was one other possibility. One Brandon didn't want to entertain. That a ghost's warning was real. The ghost of his dead wife.

He finished his trek back to the love seat.

Arms wrapped around herself, Marie peered up at him, so pale, so fragile. Even though he knew she was strong as steel inside, he still had the urge to sweep her into his arms and take her far away. Somewhere she would be safe.

He wasn't sure he could believe any of this. But maybe he didn't have to. Maybe his role was simpler than that. "I don't know what's real and what's not, Marie. But I know one thing. Whoever attacked you tonight, I won't let him hurt you again. I promise you that."

Chapter Ten

Marie had heard all about the ostentatious redbrick mansion Clifford Drake had built on the jut of Drake family land right across the small inlet from Drake House. She'd even seen it across the water. But none of that was the same as having it looming before her now, up close and personal.

Josef held the car door. Brandon climbed out and joined Marie on the sidewalk. "Here it is. The Manor at Drake Acres. Uncle Cliff's answer to the fact that my father inherited Drake House."

"It sure is big." And red. The rich color of the brick glowed in the morning sun. His tall white pillars and three and a half stories' worth of windows stretched up to the gabled roof.

"Big. Yes. I think that's what he was going for. Bigger than Drake House, at any rate."

Marie had to turn her head first fully to one side, then to the other just to take in the length of the place. Not easy with a sore neck. And she wasn't even counting the garages and guest house and cabana. If she turned far enough, she could see stables, too, a few hundred yards beyond. The gardens surrounding the house were equally opulent. Last night's rain and the humidity still hanging in the air made even the late autumn garden smell alive and lush.

"It might be big and fancy and new," Marie said, "but it doesn't have the beauty of Drake House. Nor the class."

A smile flickered over his lips.

A corresponding flutter seized her chest, despite her efforts to clamp it down.

"What?"

She shook her head. "Nothing, really. I just…I think that's the first time I've seen you smile since I came back."

The smile faded.

She wished she hadn't pointed it out. But it was probably better this way. His smile only reminded her of better times. Times she couldn't afford to think about now. She focused on the sprawling house. "Maybe you're right. Maybe Cliff has all the money he needs."

"I was thinking about that. Maybe it's not about money. Maybe it's about the one thing I've got that he doesn't. Drake House."

Chills trickled down Marie's spine. Could that be it? It seemed to make sense. "If you and Charlotte had children, Drake House would pass to them. But if you died without heirs, Cliff would finally get what he feels should have been his inheritance all along."

Brandon nodded. "It's hard for me to believe Cliff would take things that far, but I suppose it's possible. He and my father defined the term *sibling rivalry*. Maybe it's more about that than anything else."

Unfortunately Cliff wasn't home. After a brief exchange with the servant who answered the door, they followed his instructions and circled to the boathouse and long pier that reached into Chesapeake Bay. A lethal-looking speedboat bobbed in the water. A lethal-looking redhead lounged inside the craft.

"Brandon!" Isabella shouted from the yacht's deck. She flipped her hair over one shoulder and sat up in the boat, giving her employer the benefit of her full attention and her electric blue eyes. She artfully ignored Marie. "What a wonderful surprise. Are you coming out with us?"

Marie did her best to ignore the twinge of jealousy. Even in jeans and a leather bomber jacket, Isabella had the pin-up potential of a swimsuit model.

"*We* are here to have a word with Cliff."

"You can chat with Cliff on the boat. Really, Brandon, it's not an imposition to have one more. Cliff won't mind, I'm sure. I feel like I haven't seen you very much in the past few days." She leaned forward in her seat. Her unzipped jacket parted to reveal a low-cut top framing ample cleavage.

Marie tried her best not to let Isabella get to her. It was obvious she had the hots for Brandon. And likely his uncle Cliff, or she wouldn't be here on her day off. But whatever games she was playing with the Drake men, it wasn't any of Marie's business. She had to remember that.

Cliff emerged from the redbrick boathouse, a miniature mansion in itself. Dressed in a Burberry windbreaker, a cashmere sweater and perfectly tailored slacks, he looked every inch the wealthy playboy he was. His thick hair had gained some gray since the last time Marie saw him, but the new look only served to add sophistication to his list of charms.

He nodded to his nephew. "Brandon." Judging from his tone of voice, he wasn't as excited to see his nephew as Isabella was. He eyed Marie. "And...Marie Leonard, right?"

Marie nodded. Cliff had always intimidated her growing up. He'd seemed so confident, carefree and in control of his life. A man who lived big and wasn't ashamed to let the world envy him for it. He was the opposite of everything her humble, decorous father had instilled in her, and more than once she'd been totally bowled over by his presence. She could only hope now that she was an adult, she'd be able to handle him better. "Hello, Mr. Drake."

"Call me Cliff, please." He managed to look her up and down in a manner that was more flattering than intrusive. "You've grown up since the last time I saw you."

Marie held his gaze. She wasn't sure if Cliff's once-over was meant to bother Brandon or Isabella or both. But whatever was going on, she wanted no part of it. "I have a few things I'd like to ask you."

He raised his brows. "Sure. I'm glad you stopped by. I heard you were visiting Drake House."

"Visiting? My father died."

"Yes. A great loss. I'm so sorry."

Surprisingly, his tone sounded sincere. Maybe there was more to Clifford Drake than she'd ever guessed. Or maybe he was just trying to throw her off balance. "Thank you."

"You should come out on the boat. Racing over the water at high speed tends to take your mind off your problems. And it promises to be a lot more fun than hanging around old Brandon."

"We came to ask you some questions," Brandon said.

"Questions?" Cliff kept his gaze glued to Marie. "About what?"

"The recent deaths at Drake House. My father and Charlotte."

Cliff finally glanced at Brandon, as if gauging his nephew's reaction to his dead wife's name.

Brandon didn't move a muscle. Wavelets lapped against the pier's pilings.

Cliff looked back to Marie. "Tragedies, to be sure. What makes you think I can tell you anything?"

"You're part of the family. You live nearby."

"I do live nearby, but if you hadn't figured this out yet, the Drake family isn't exactly close."

Marie looked past Cliff to where Isabella was climbing out of the speedboat and onto the pier. Apparently she'd grown tired of being out of the spotlight and intended to take it back.

Marie gave Cliff a businesslike smile. "I know you have plans, so I'll make this short."

A lazy grin spread over Cliff's lips. He glanced in Brandon's direction and lowered one lid in a wink. "What can I say? I'm in demand."

"What are you men talking about?" Walking up behind Brandon, Isabella slipped her hands onto his shoulders and started kneading his muscles.

Brandon stiffened.

Cliff's easy smile faded. He shot Isabella a warning stare.

Isabella withdrew her hands and wormed her way into the circle, Brandon and Cliff on either side.

Marie shook her head. Let Isabella play her games. Marie had more important things to focus on. "Mr.

Drake? Did you see either Charlotte or my father around the time of their deaths?"

"I told you, it's Cliff. And yes, I saw your father a day or two before he died."

Of the two, Marie would have guessed it more likely for Cliff to have seen Charlotte. Or at least to have noticed her. But six months was a long time. Maybe he didn't remember, provided he didn't have anything to do with killing her. "Where was my father when you saw him?"

"Near the harbor. You know that bed-and-breakfast called The Seven Gables or some such?"

"Sophie Caldwell's place? Was he with her?"

"No. He was talking to that pain-in-the-ass developer. Perry. And let me tell you, your father didn't look too happy."

Marie could imagine. Shelley had said Ned Perry was trying to buy waterfront, including Drake House, and build condos. No idea would insult her father's sensibilities more. "What about Charlotte? Did you see her before her death?"

"No."

Marie and Brandon exchanged looks. He seemed to be as uneasy with Cliff's answer as she was. The abrupt answer felt a little too quick, a little too pat. "You're sure?"

"Absolutely."

Brandon eyed his uncle. "Charlotte died six months ago. That's a long time."

"You want an alibi?" Cliff chuckled, the sound more taunt than real laugh. "I was sailing. A regatta in the U.K. Stop by the yacht club. I'll take you on the yacht that won and show you the trophy."

Marie's stomach sank. Beyond Cliff, she didn't have much of a list of people who could benefit from Charlotte's death. She had no leads. All she had were the words of a ghost. Words Brandon didn't even believe.

Cliff narrowed his eyes on his nephew. "So why are you playing like this is some sort of murder investigation? I know about the vodka bottle. You might have been able to keep that part out of the papers, but I have my sources." He shot Isabella a little smile.

The maid tilted her chin up and gave Cliff a frown. She laid a hand on Brandon's arm. "I'm sorry, Brandon. I didn't mean to say anything. Really I didn't. I was just so upset that she would do that to you. She didn't deserve what she had. Drake House. You. She didn't deserve any of it." Flirty lilt gone, Isabella's voice rang with a hard edge.

Brandon's lips flattened. "Isabella, stop."

"It's true. I was hoping you'd see it after she died." The maid tilted her head in Marie's direction. "And if you think this one deserves you, you're going to be disappointed all over again."

BRANDON HAD NEVER BEEN as glad to leave a place as he was walking back to the car from Cliff's boathouse. Every moment of that encounter had been awkward and painful and teeth-grindingly frustrating.

"Did you hear the venom in her voice?" Marie asked.

"Isabella has a few issues." To put it mildly.

"Issues like she wants to be the lady of Drake House."

"Or The Manor at Drake Acres. I don't think it matters much to her." He let out a pent-up breath. "I think we're going to need to keep an eye on her."

"Do you think she might have killed Charlotte?"

"I don't see it. She couldn't have gotten Charlotte into the car and crashed it by herself." He still wasn't sure how anyone could have done that except for Charlotte herself. But since he wasn't about to get into a debate with Marie about the existence of ghosts, he'd let that part slide for now. "Isabella could have gotten someone to help her. She's good at convincing men to do things for her."

"Men? Like who? Cliff was racing one of his yachts."

"There are men besides Cliff." They rounded the far corner of the house and started toward the circle in front of the house's grand entrance where his car waited. Josef spotted them and climbed out of the car. Brandon kept his voice low. "Take Josef. He lost his fiancée about a year ago. He's got to be lonely. And he knows his way around cars."

"You think Josef—"

"Or Phil Cardon."

Marie frowned, as if searching her memory for the name. "The guy who works at Thornton Garden Center?"

Brandon nodded. "He has done some work at Drake House from time to time. And he worked on the gardens with Lexie. He was pretty interested in Isabella."

"I can imagine. But was he interested enough to help her commit murder?"

Brandon shrugged.

"How about the guy from Drake Enterprises? The one who came to Drake House?"

"Doug Heller? I could see it." Truthfully, he couldn't see it at all. Any of it. He still couldn't wrap his mind around the idea that Charlotte was murdered. That someone he knew was responsible. Maybe he was just in denial, but this whole conversation with Marie didn't seem real to him. More like a guessing game played purely for amusement. He was much more concerned with finding who had tried to kill Marie. "Do you think Isabella could have been the one who tried to throw you off the roof last night?"

Marie's steps slowed. "Maybe. She's taller than I am. And strong. I don't know."

"Maybe that's what we should focus on."

"I told you, I think it's all related."

He nodded. He was waiting for her to say that. "Think and know are two different things. And until we know it's related and know who wants you dead, we need to keep our options open. I don't want to overlook anyone."

They walked for a moment without speaking, the click of their shoes on the brick path the only sound. The sun beamed down from a sky that seemed shockingly blue after the dreariness of the day before. Too bad their situation wasn't as clear and pleasant as the weather.

"So what do we do?"

He wanted to suggest buying her a plane ticket, sending her back to Michigan where she'd be safe…and away from him. But he knew what her reaction would be. "Set some traps and see what happens."

As they approached the car, Josef opened the back door. Marie climbed inside. The chauffeur circled the car and opened the opposite door for Brandon. When it came to his job, Josef was precise and efficient. Could he be as precise and efficient when it came to killing someone? Especially if a young redhead, beautiful beyond his dreams, seduced him into it?

Brandon lowered himself into the car and waited for Josef to take his place behind the wheel. "Josef?"

"Yes, sir?" His accent was thick and warm and tinged with respect. Just the right tone.

"Take us back to Drake House. Then you can have the rest of the day off. And the night. We'll see you again tomorrow morning."

"Sir? May I ask why?"

"I've been asking a lot of you the past few days." He paused for dramatic effect…he hoped. "And we've learned something very disturbing about Isabella Faust. I'd like to handle it myself. If we need to go anywhere, we'll use Ms. Leonard's rental car."

Josef nodded and pulled away, leaving The Manor at Drake Acres behind. "Very good, sir."

SITTING IN A CRAMPED RENTAL CAR with a leg injury was not a good idea. Too bad Brandon hadn't realized that before he and Marie had jumped in her car in a damn fool attempt to follow Isabella's little yellow sports car when she'd returned from her day with Cliff. The trap he'd set for Josef turned out to be nothing. Nothing at all. The chauffeur had made no move to warn Isabella of their suspicions. He hadn't gone anywhere, and a call to the phone company had proved he hadn't made any phone calls.

Brandon shifted his leg into a more comfortable position. "I feel like an idiot spying on my employees. Especially since they don't seem to be doing a damn thing out of the ordinary."

Eyes on the road and the yellow car in front of them, Marie let out a sigh. The lights from the dash cast her face in a green glow, a color that would make anyone look like death warmed over. But not Marie. She looked as vibrant and determined as ever.

God help him.

"What is it?" he asked her.

"Nothing, really. I'm relieved Josef isn't tangled up with Isabella, but his life seems kind of sad."

"How so?"

"I don't know. Just what Shelley told me. Moving to a country where he doesn't know anyone. Losing his fiancée. He seems so alone."

Brandon nodded. Widowed. Alone. As Brandon himself had been before Marie had returned. As he would be again after she left.

He shook his head. If only he could forget all that, accept it. But it was impossible with her sitting only inches away. The scent of her, warm and spicy, wrapped around him, and he longed to feel the softness of her skin again.

Riding around with Marie in this cramped little car wasn't one of his best ideas.

He gripped his cane in both hands and remembered the bruising hidden under the high collar of her coat. He couldn't have Marie. He couldn't even let himself want her. But he could protect her. He could keep her safe.

"I finally got a hold of Lexie." Marie kept her focus on the road. "She said her records show Phil Cardon was working with her on a garden in Easton when Charlotte died. She said they were on the job site until sunset every night. There's no way he could have driven all the way to Drake House before the time of Charlotte's accident."

Another name off the list. "Doug is stopping by Drake House for a chat tomorrow. But I can't imagine he has anything to do with this."

Marie piloted the car down Main Street and into the heart of town. Shops and cafés lined the street, festooned with wreaths and lights and tinsel.

Christmas.

An ache settled into Brandon's gut. From the time he could remember, Christmas had been centered on the ball and charity auction. He remembered his mother presiding over the decoration. Then Edwin and, to a lesser extent, Charlotte. When he'd lost all of them, there had seemed no point to go on. He hadn't even felt bad about letting the tradition die. Or maybe he'd felt so bad about everything else that he hadn't noticed.

But now?

The time Marie had been here had been filled with turmoil and pain. Still, by comparison, he felt more alive than he had in years. And for the first time, the thought of Jenkins Cove going through a Christmas season without the charity ball felt…not right.

As the yellow car reached the outskirts of town, it slowed and turned into a lot. Brandon glanced at Marie. "Did you see that?"

"Yes." Marie drove to a spot near the street where Isabella turned, and pulled to the curb. Beyond a small parking lot sat a little restaurant and bar known to the locals as the spot for soft-shell crab in season and cheap booze all year-round. The Duck Blind.

"Does Rufus Shea still own this place?"

"I think so." Brandon frowned. Even though Rufus Shea had cleaned up his act and his tavern in recent years, the former town drunk wasn't the type of man Brandon could picture Marie having anything to do with. "How do you know Rufus Shea?"

"I knew his son."

Brandon nodded. He'd known Rufus's son, Simon, too, though not well. The kid had been younger. The quintessential troublemaker from the wrong side of the tracks. Brandon had been at Harvard when he'd heard about the kid's death. A lifetime ago. "I wonder what brings Isabella here?" He nodded out the window as the auburn-haired beauty pulled the door open and slipped inside.

"Should we find out?" Marie took the key from the ignition and got out of the car.

Brandon followed. They entered in time to catch Isabella stride past the counter and bar stools and turn into the restaurant. They followed. Sturdy round tables covered with red and green tablecloths dotted the modest-sized room. A good crowd of people filled the place, dining on plates of crab cakes and passing bowls of stewed tomatoes and lima beans served family style. The din of conversation bounced off paneled walls, and the sweet and tangy scent of seafood hung in the air.

Isabella made a beeline for a table in the far corner. She slipped into a chair beside a man.

A man Brandon recognized immediately.

He grabbed Marie's arm, stopping her before she was spotted. He leaned close and spoke into her ear. "Ned Perry. She's meeting with Ned Perry."

Marie looked toward the table, eyes wide. "The real estate developer? Do you think this might have something to do with Drake House?"

"I don't know. But I aim to find out."

MARIE SNUGGLED her coat tight around her shoulders against the cool morning. Kneeling down beside

Brandon's town car, she examined the tire. The white chalk line was still there, untouched.

She'd gotten the idea from her parking hassles in college. It was a trick the parking authority used. Mark the tire with chalk. If the chalk is still there, the car hasn't moved. In this case, that meant Josef hadn't moved. Not the entire night.

At least they could cross him off the list. Cliff as well. And probably Phil Cardon. But Isabella seemed to be neck deep in whatever was going on. And Marie was betting Ned Perry was helping her.

Marie wound through the east garden and back to the kitchen. Frost sparkled on the concrete bench, the fountain and the white shells that covered the path. Not quite like snow at Christmastime, but the extra sparkle lent Drake House a little magic of the season. Magic that was sorely lacking.

She found Brandon in the kitchen, sitting at the stone counter where she'd eaten cookies as a child. He sipped a cup of coffee and watched Shelley sauté vegetables for one of her extravagant breakfasts. Mouthwatering aromas and thick steam wafted from the pan. Brandon looked up at Marie and arched his brows in silent question.

She shook her head.

He leaned back in his chair, relieved.

One more name off the suspect list. Marie took a cup of coffee and tried to concentrate on drinking it without burning her lips and tongue.

A knock sounded on the kitchen door.

Marie jumped at the sound. She glanced through the mullioned glass. A pair of watery blue eyes stared straight at her.

Shelley wiped her hands and scampered to open the door.

The operations manager of Drake Enterprises stepped inside. "Brandon?"

Brandon nodded and stood, leaning heavily on his cane. "Thanks for coming, Doug. We'll talk in the office." Giving Marie a glance, he led Doug Heller from the kitchen. Brandon had told her he planned to pump the manager for information about Perry. And, of course, he wanted to ask a few questions of Heller himself.

As soon as they disappeared into the household office and closed the door behind them, Shelley made a tsking noise under her breath.

Marie focused on the housekeeper. "What is it, Shelley?"

"I can just imagine. Probably Ned Perry again."

Marie nodded vaguely, not wanting to let on that Shelley's guess was right on the nose. "Does this Mr. Perry stop by often?"

"No. He hasn't for a while. He doesn't have the nerve. But then he doesn't have to when he has someone already in the house lobbying for him."

"Someone in the house? Who?"

"Isabella."

Marie's pulse launched into double time. She didn't know why she hadn't thought of asking Shelley about this sooner. The woman seemed to know everyone's business. And she had no qualms about spreading the news around. "Why would Isabella lobby for Ned Perry?"

"They have a deal."

"A deal?" This was getting better all the time.

"She says she's buying one of the condos down by

the yacht club. But I think she wants a piece of Drake House. She's always wanted Drake House, you know. Although I don't know how she thinks Ned Perry is going to get his hands on it."

It hadn't occurred to Marie that Isabella wanted Drake House, not until her performance yesterday. What other secrets could Shelley tell her? "Why do you think Isabella wants Drake House?"

"Just ask her." Shelley pulled a knife from the block and started dicing shallots with more gusto than called for. The knife made a sharp snap each time it hit the cutting board. "When she first came to work here, she told me that one day she'd be lady of the house. 'It's only a matter of time,' she'd say. Hogwash. Mr. Brandon saw nothing in her. He only saw his Charlotte."

Shelley shook her head. Scooping up the shallots with the flat of her blade, she feathered them into the sauté pan and turned up the heat. An onionlike tang flavored the air. "After Charlotte died, Isabella got more aggressive. I told her it was no use. And it wasn't. Mr. Brandon is heartbroken. He lives only for his foundation and this house. He'll never marry again. Charlotte was the only woman he could ever love. She was perfect. You'd do well to remember that, too."

"Me?" If Marie hadn't been sitting, she would have stepped back under the assault. "What does this have to do with me?"

"I've seen you with him. Trying to make him smile. Trying to make him do things for you. You'd be better off leaving him alone." Shelley gathered a handful of dirty utensils and carried them to one of the huge sinks. She pushed up the sleeves of her blouse, revealing muscled arms. "I'm not trying to be mean. I'm telling you for your own good. He belongs to Charlotte. No other woman is wanted around here."

Marie stared at Shelley, not sure she heard the woman right. Hadn't she joked to herself about Shelley's resemblance to the fictional Mrs. Danvers? And now this on the heels of Isabella's comments yesterday? "Anything between Brandon and me is in the past, Shelley. It's over. You don't have to feel threatened by me."

"I'm just telling you the way things are. You seem like a nice girl, and I always respected your father. I wouldn't like to see you get hurt."

Marie nodded, not sure if Shelley's words held more motherly concern or threat.

Shelley thrust the utensils under running water. The scent of dishwashing soap mixed with the aroma from the stove. "While we're on the subject, I've talked to a handyman who occasionally does work around here. Phil Cardon. He has some hours free later today, so I hired him to help you pack up your father's things."

So Shelley was shoving her out of the house. Protecting Brandon's honor and Charlotte's memory, no doubt. Unless she had a more personal agenda. "I have time. I'm on personal leave from my job. There's no hurry."

"Well, you aren't the only one this affects, Marie. We have to think about Brandon. He likes his privacy. Having a guest in the house is tough on him."

Marie pushed herself back from the counter and picked up her coffee. She was getting a little tired of being in Shelley's crosshairs this morning. And while Marie knew her presence wasn't any easier on Brandon than it was on her, she wasn't going to let the housekeeper chase her out before she got her answers. "Maybe we should ask Brandon."

"There are other concerns, too." Shelley smiled, backpedaling.

Marie should just walk out of the room, leave Shelley stewing. Unfortunately she was never one to leave a leading comment hanging in the air without asking the question that went with it. "Such as?"

"It's very difficult to run the house when I'm not living here."

Now it was becoming clear. "You want to move into my father's quarters."

"Those rooms are for the person who is running Drake House. They aren't your father's personal property."

Marie couldn't argue with that, even though her father had lived in those rooms for forty years. "As soon as I finish tying up some loose ends, you can have your rooms."

Shelley nodded her graying head. "Good. I'm glad we understand each other."

Marie gave Shelley a broad smile. "Yes. We understand each other. But I don't need your handyman's help. No one is to touch my father's things but me."

Shelley didn't answer.

Marie clenched the hot mug. The moment she left the house, Shelley would probably have an army of handymen erasing her father's presence from Drake House. She'd have to ask Brandon to make sure that didn't happen.

"Perhaps you'd do a favor for me now."

The woman was asking for a favor? After everything she'd thrown at Marie in the past few minutes?

"I need you to move your car to the parking area

next to the carriage house. I have a decorator coming in to take measurements, and your vehicle will be in the way."

Marie had the sneaking suspicion Shelley thought everything about her was in the way. But as much as Shelley's grasping annoyed her, she had to admit life went on. An old and important mansion like Drake House needed a full-time caretaker, and Brandon had given the job to Shelley. With the job came the living quarters. She couldn't deny Shelley that.

But that didn't mean she'd let the woman push her out before she'd exhausted every lead. Finding her father's killer, and Charlotte's as well, came first. "Measure all you want, Shelley, but don't touch my father's things. Do you understand me?"

Shelley pursed her lips and raised her chin. "As long as you clear out the rooms in a timely manner. Now will you move your vehicle? My decorator will be here any minute." She glanced at a clock on the wall for emphasis.

Marie plunked her mug on the countertop, grabbed her keys and coat and gladly left the kitchen to Shelley Zachary.

Out in the cool morning, her car started on the third try. She'd have to take it in to the rental agency. Have them replace the battery or give her a new car.

She piloted the rental around the kitchen entrance's circle drive and joined with the drive leading to the carriage house, curving along the edge of the water.

Steely waves echoed the color of the sky and pounded rocks edging the shoreline. She approached the turn to the carriage house. Although the land around Drake House was fairly flat, this part of the drive dipped slightly, making her car accelerate. She pressed her foot to the brake pedal. It gripped, then softened.

Then plunged to the floorboards.

Marie tried the brakes again. Again they pushed to the floor. She didn't have time to think. Didn't even have time to panic. Blood rushing in her ears, she gripped the wheel and steered. The car canted to the side. Tires skidded on loose gravel.

The car jolted over rock and plunged into water.

Chapter Eleven

Marie hung forward in her seat belt. The air bag softened in front of her like a limp balloon, only dregs of air left. Her ears rang. Her already sore head and neck ached. Her feet felt so very cold.

Pushing down the air bag, she fought to clear her mind. Water sloshed over the car's hood. It covered the pedals and crept up the floor mat, swamping her feet to the ankles.

What a mess.

She looked out the driver's window. The car balanced on the gray rock that lined the shoreline, preventing erosion. Even though the nose tilted down into the water, the back end of the car was still high, if not totally dry.

She was lucky. If she had been going faster, she'd be out in the bay right now. As it was, she might have to do a little swimming, or at least wading, but she still had time to get out.

Trying to steady her trembling fingers, she found the buckle of her seat belt and released it. She groped the armrest, locating the controls for the power windows. She pressed the button to lower the driver's side.

Nothing happened.

She tried again. Damn. The water or the impact must have shorted out the car's battery or jostled the wires free. Not that it hadn't been half drained before she'd even gotten behind the wheel.

There was no reason to panic. Although the water seemed to creep higher by the second, she still had time to escape. But she needed to move.

She grasped the lock and pulled it up, releasing it manually. Fitting her fingers into the handle, she pulled it and shoved her shoulder into the door at the same time.

The door didn't budge.

A sob caught in her throat. She tried again. Again, it wouldn't open. Water bore down on the door, sealing it from the outside.

What was she going to do?

She closed her eyes and focused on her breathing. In and out. In and out. She couldn't let herself panic. There had to be a way out. She just had to stay calm enough to think, stay calm enough to find it.

If water pressure from the outside was forcing the door closed, then equaling the pressure would free the door. She just had to wait for the car to sink. The slight odor of fish clogged her throat. The relentless lap of waves drummed in beat with her pulse.

She'd never been afraid of water. Her father had insisted she take swimming lessons so she wouldn't suffer from the fear as he had. But the thought of letting the car sink, letting herself be trapped underwater…she didn't know if she could go through with it.

The car listed farther forward, the heavy engine dragging it down. The water rose to her knees. It crept over the seat.

A shudder came from the back of the vehicle. Marie twisted in her seat. Sore muscles in her neck protesting, she strained to see where the movement had come from.

Behind her, the shoreline seemed to move away.

The car jolted again. Oh God. She knew what was happening. The back wheels were thunking down the rocks along the shoreline. Without brakes to stop them, they would keep rolling, pushing the car farther into the bay.

Where the water was deep.

A sound came from her throat, an involuntary whimper.

She pulled the emergency brake. The lever moved easily. Too easily. It wasn't working, either.

She tried to breathe, struggling to remember the way Sophie had showed her. All she could think about was the car's nose diving deep. The car flipping over. Would she be able to get out if that happened? Would she even be conscious by the time it settled on the bottom?

She couldn't wait. She had to do something now.

She pulled her feet up out of the water. Twisting out from behind the steering wheel, she aimed the heels of her boots at the driver's window. Pulling her knees up to her chest, she gasped in a lungful of oxygen and kicked with all her strength.

Glass exploded into tiny pieces.

CURSING HIS LEG, Brandon raced for the edge of the water. He'd been walking Doug Heller to the door when he'd seen Marie's car go over the edge. For a second, he'd been stunned and confused. His body had burst into a run before his brain had caught up.

Marie was in the water. Maybe trapped in her car. Maybe hurt. He had to move. He had to reach her in time.

Pain clawed through his damaged tendons with each stride. He gripped his cane, stabbing it into the ground, pushing his legs faster.

He wouldn't lose Marie.

He reached the crest of the shoreline. Water stretched in front of him, waves lapping on rock. A light mass showed through the undulating waves. The car. It was submerged.

He stumbled on the rock, almost going down to his knees. She couldn't—

"Brandon."

He turned to the sound of her voice.

She huddled on the sharp rock, ten yards down the shoreline. Her clothing was soaked, her hair dark with water. She struggled to stand.

He scrambled over rock. His cane slipped from his hand and clattered into a crevice. He didn't care. He kept going. The only important thing was reaching Marie. The only important thing was that she was safe.

He wrapped her in his arms.

She clung to him, wet and cold and shaking. She looked up at him, her breath warm on his face.

He brought his mouth down on hers. Needy. Devouring the very life force of her. She tasted just the way he remembered. Warm and strong and oh so alive. He moved his lips over her face, her neck. Taking in all of her. Soaking in the feel of her body, the beat of her heart against his. He felt he'd waited forever for this. Wanted it. Dreamed about it. Pushed the dreams away. But he didn't deny himself now. He couldn't. It didn't matter that it was all wrong. That they'd get hurt in the end. That it could go nowhere. He'd almost lost her, but she was here. She'd almost died, but now she lived.

And God help him, whatever happened next, he didn't know how he'd ever let her go.

MARIE PULLED her big wool sweater tight around her shoulders and shifted closer to the fire. Her neck had changed from painful to stiff and painful. And although she was now dry, the chill hadn't left her bones. It felt as if it never would.

"Here." Brandon pushed a fresh cup of hot tea into her hands.

"Thanks." She wrapped her fingers around the cup's heat. He'd been hovering over her since he'd found her on the rocks, having escaped from the car and swum to shore. And even though she hated to admit it, she loved him taking care of her. It had been a long time since someone took care of her. Since she'd last lived at Drake House with a father who took care of everybody.

But Brandon wasn't anything like her father.

She could still feel the desperate press of his body against hers. She could still taste his kiss. It had been everything she wanted, the passion between them unleashed, the barriers broken. But even though he looked at her now with the same fire in his eyes, she knew their moment had changed nothing.

And that was what confused her the most.

Brandon lowered himself into a nearby chair.

How she wished he'd sit closer. How she wanted him to wrap his arm around her and kiss her again. She knew he'd do it if she asked. After that kiss she was even pretty sure he still loved her. Not that he'd admit it. Not that it mattered.

Brandon blamed himself for loving her. He blamed his feelings for causing his wife's death. And unless she proved to him Charlotte hadn't taken her own life, there was no way he'd forgive himself. Not enough to find happiness. At least not happiness with Marie.

And there was no way she wanted to suffer that kind of heartbreak again. She knew better this time.

Brandon checked his watch. "Hammer should be here any minute."

Marie almost groaned. "I'm not looking forward to explaining this to Hammer. He already thinks I'm making things up. My father's murder. The break-in. Even the roof. He's going to think I drove into the water myself. He's going to be more convinced than ever that I'm a crackpot."

Brandon didn't disagree. Instead he leaned forward and looked her in the eye. "Don't mention your father's murder. Or Charlotte's."

She wanted to protest that it was all related, but she'd told him that too many times before. "I won't. He'll have me committed for sure."

"Just focus on the attempts to hurt you. That's all we can do. It's all Hammer can help with, anyway."

And it was all Brandon believed.

A heavy feeling settled into the pit of Marie's stomach. This whole thing was a no-win situation. Finding evidence that didn't exist. Falling in love with Brandon all over again when she could only hope for more of the same pain.

Brandon shifted in his chair. "Where were you going this morning? The last I saw, you were having coffee."

He looked up at her again, this time his expression less insistent and more filled with worry.

"I wasn't going anywhere. Shelley asked me to move my car."

"Why?"

She explained about the decorator and Shelley's pressure to clean out her father's things. She wanted to tell him the rest, too. The way Shelley worshiped Charlotte. The way she'd warned Marie to stay away. But it all seemed too close after the kiss. Shelley was more perceptive than Marie had given her credit for.

Brandon groaned. "I should have been more on top of that. You'll have as much time as you need."

"Thanks."

He kept his eyes on her face. His brows dipped low. "What else?"

"I'm going back to the psychomanteum." She hadn't known that was her plan until she said it. But once the words were out, she knew it was what she needed to do.

"Are you sure?"

The thought made her nervous. But not more nervous than the idea of never finding out who killed her father and Charlotte. Not more nervous than waiting for the police to track down whoever was trying to kill her, especially when Chief Hammer seemed determined to chalk it up to her paranoid imagination. And it didn't make her more nervous than the growing feelings she had for Brandon and the certainty that she was heading for the same anguish she'd suffered ten years before. "I'm sure."

It seemed to take a lot of effort for Brandon to nod this

time. "Then I'll take you. I'm not letting you out of my sight until you're safely on a plane back to Michigan."

The cold settled deeper into her bones.

"Mr. Brandon?" Shelley called from the doorway. "Chief Hammer and Officer Draper are here."

Marie took a deep breath and braced herself for another round with the Jenkins Cove police.

MARIE STARED at the flickering candlelight reflected in the mirror. She tried to clear her mind, to relax, but a jitter circulated through her bloodstream like too much espresso, and she didn't seem to be able to focus on anything. After more than an hour, she'd given up trying to reach her father. Now she'd switched her focus to Charlotte. If this didn't work, she was out of options.

She breathed deeply, as Sophie had instructed. In and out. In and out. But all she smelled was the dusty odor of an old house. All she felt was a light head.

"Charlotte? Where are you?"

No scent. No voice.

"Charlotte? Please. I need your help."

Again nothing.

Marie stared at the mirror. Her own face stared back. She didn't get it. If Charlotte had been trying to tell her she'd been murdered, if she'd wanted Marie to find proof and seek justice, why wasn't she answering? Why wasn't she helping now?

"I can't find anything to prove your murder. I don't know where to look." She buried her head in her hands. If Charlotte couldn't communicate anymore, all this was no use. She might as well go back to Michigan. At least that way, she'd get far away from Brandon. She'd save herself the heartbreak of loving a man who wouldn't let himself love her back.

Tears stung the back of her eyes. She drew in a shuddering breath.

Jasmine.

Marie raised her head. Swiping at her eyes, she stared at the mirror. She felt something. A pressure. A presence. Candlelight flickered from behind her. Her vision became unfocused. "Charlotte? Tell me who killed you. Give me some kind of sign."

The scent of jasmine faded. Another odor took over the room. Something harsh. Sharp fumes stung her eyes.

Gasoline.

The whoosh of flame stole the air from her lungs. Heat seared her skin. Pain. Burning.

A scream ripped from Marie's throat. She shielded her face with her hands. She wasn't on fire. It wasn't real. She knew it…and yet the brightness flooded her vision, the roar of flame deafened her, the heat made her feel as if she were dying. "Charlotte, please. Who did this? Who did this to you?"

Footsteps thunked up the stairs.

She dragged her hands from her face and stared into the mirror.

The image was faint, like a cloud on her vision from the pressure of fingertips against closed lids. Petals. A stem. A single leaf.

A childlike etching of a simple flower took shape. A flower with cupped petals. A tulip.

The door flew open behind her. Brandon's reflection filled the mirror. Broad shoulders, dark brows, worried eyes. "Marie! For God's sake, what happened?"

Marie stared deeply into the silvered glass, but the

image had faded and was gone. All she could see was candlelight and shadows playing over Brandon's face.

Sophie joined him in the doorway. "Sweetheart? Are you okay?"

She felt weak. Sick. And although the burning sensation had stopped, she felt numb as if she were now covered with thick scars. "No, I'm not. I'm not okay at all."

Chapter Twelve

"I know you don't believe me."

Brandon's throat pinched. He followed her up the stairs that led to the upper floors of the east wing. Swallowing what she'd experienced in the psychomanteum was definitely a challenge. He'd never been one to believe in things he couldn't see with his own eyes, hear with his own ears, touch with his own hand. "I've never had experiences like that, Marie. I'm trying to understand."

She stopped on the landing and spun to face him. "Go to the psychomanteum. Obviously Charlotte is trying to contact you. She's just using me to do it."

"I don't need to sit in Sophie Caldwell's room, Marie. I know what Charlotte went through. I was there."

Even in the dim light he could see her gaze flit over the right side of his face.

He clutched the head of his cane. He hated the thought that Marie could see his scars and imperfections every time she looked at his face or witnessed his limp. He wished he could be the same man for her that he'd been that summer ten years ago. Despite the raw emotion still between them, he knew damn well it was too late for that.

Just as it was too late for Charlotte.

"What are you looking for up here?"

Marie resumed climbing the stairs. "The other night I smelled Charlotte's scent near the window in her study. I looked around, but couldn't find anything."

"I had Edwin give Charlotte's personal things to her family and the rest to charity. He wanted to auction off the furniture at the Christmas Ball."

"Shelley said you canceled the ball."

"Edwin and Charlotte put on the ball. It just didn't seem right to do it without them. And to tell you the truth, I didn't feel up to having people in the house."

"My father loved the ball. He loved Christmas."

"Which is why I can't see having it without him."

Reaching the top of the stairs, she paused once again to face him. "I think he would like it to go on. I think it would be a fitting tribute, to both my father and Charlotte. Besides, the Drake Foundation does wonderful things with the auction money, things that help a lot of people."

Leave it to Marie to see past the pain, to focus on the people in need and a tribute to the memories of those gone. "You are a strong woman, Marie." He wanted to touch her, to run his fingers through her hair, to kiss her the way he had by the water. He wished he could kiss her like that every day for the rest of his life. He gripped his cane in both fists.

"Thanks. I don't feel very strong."

"Well, you are. That's probably why Charlotte has contacted you instead of me. She knows you can handle it. She knows you're a fighter."

"You're a fighter, too." Her wide, caramel eyes looked straight into his, as though she believed what she was saying, as though she meant every word.

"I like the man I am in your eyes. I always have."

"You are that man, Brandon."

How he wished he could believe that. How he wished all the mistakes he'd made in his life would disappear and he could be as pure and strong and righteous as he'd felt when he'd fallen in love with Marie all those years ago.

But even then he'd already given Charlotte his mother's ring. Even then he hadn't lived up to Marie's image of him. "I'm not. I don't know if I ever was. But when you look at me, I can pretend. And that will have to be enough."

She reached out and took his hand.

He clasped her fingers. Her skin felt impossibly soft, her bones fragile. But it was all an illusion. Marie was strong and tough and unflinching in her caring for others and in her belief that good would win in the end. She was everything he was not. Everything he'd lost over the years. Everything he'd never had. It was impossible to go back, impossible to change things. But at least for the moment, he could hold her hand and pretend. "Lead on."

"Do you smell it?" Marie leaned close to the desk where she'd smelled the jasmine before she'd been dragged to the roof. The scent tickled her nose, light and sweet. Barely there, yet every bit grounded in reality.

Brandon tilted his head and gave the air a sniff. "Where?"

It grew stronger. She gestured for him to move closer. "Right here. All around."

He stepped beside her. Almost close enough for her to feel his body heat. Almost close enough that if she shifted to the side, their arms would touch.

Breathing slowly, he finally shook his head. "Where does it seem to be coming from?"

She leaned toward the window. Sure enough, it was stronger here. "Not the desk. Maybe the window."

He followed, breathing deep, a frown still lining his brow.

Marie stood still. Cold flowed over her, digging deep and sucking the warmth from her skin. She glanced back at Brandon. "Do you feel that?"

"The draft?"

"A few days ago I would have thought it was a draft, too." She raised her palm to the window. The air felt still. "This is not coming from outside. But the scent is strongest here." She gestured to the mullioned window.

"I…I can smell it." Brandon's voice rang low and steady, not questioning anymore, but sure.

Goosebumps peppered Marie's skin. "Do you feel her?"

"I…maybe. No. I don't know."

Marie peered through the rippled glass. The faint light of a slivered moon reflected off the waves of Chesapeake Bay. Below the window, the east garden nestled, ready for winter.

The garden where she'd first felt the still cold that was surrounding them now. "The garden."

"Edwin had that garden redesigned this fall."

Yes. She remembered that. But she hadn't put it all together. A trill reverberated along her nerves. "Maybe that's it. Let's go down to the garden." It didn't take them long to retrace their steps down the staircase. They wound through the dimly lit house to the kitchen and headed for the exit.

"Mr. Brandon?"

Marie jumped at the woman's voice.

Brandon spun around. "Shelley? Isn't it kind of late? What are you doing here?"

Shelley smiled sweetly at her boss. "Just taking care of some loose ends. Can I get you something?" She glanced at Marie, at their joined hands. The smile faded.

"No. We're fine. It's late." Brandon gave Marie's hand a little squeeze, then slipped his fingers free.

A weight shifted into Marie's chest.

"It's a big house. A lot to do," Shelley rattled on. "I can see why Edwin lived in the house. It's the only way to get everything done. And he didn't have anything to do with the cooking."

Marie knew Brandon wasn't going to offer the butler quarters, not until she was done with them. But she half expected him to let Shelley move into one of the guest rooms. And she had to admit, having someone else living in the house would make it easier for him to keep his distance, easier for them both.

"You're right, Shelley," Brandon said. "You are trying to do way too much. We'll have to start interviewing for cooks. Let me know when you have some good prospects lined up."

"Cooks?"

"Unless you'd rather take applicants for the butler's job."

"I'll get some cooks lined up right away, sir." She glanced at Marie, and gave her a somewhat apologetic smile.

"Good night." Brandon gave Shelley a nod. He held

the door open for Marie, and she slipped through into the night.

Oyster shells crunched under their feet. The night was cool, but even so, it felt balmy compared to the frigid air in Charlotte's study. Marie had heard cold spots were thought to be caused by spirits' attempt to manifest themselves. But she hadn't really connected those dots the first time she'd passed through the east garden. She wouldn't miss it again.

They wound their way to the garden. Holly and boxwood flanked the path. A plastic-covered fountain hulked near the house, its musical trickle silenced in preparation for the freezing temperatures of winter. The white concrete bench she'd spotted from the window glowed in the artful landscape lighting, nearly as bright as the shells at their feet.

"What are we looking for?"

"Search me." Brandon jabbed the fountain's covering with the tip of his cane. "This garden was redone after Charlotte's death. What was your father's favorite feature of this garden?"

Marie glanced at him. Did he now believe? She didn't know. Maybe he didn't, either. But at least he was trying. He was keeping his mind open. He was supporting her.

"My father. What did he like?" Marie blew a breath through tense lips. "I have no clue. My father was never into nature."

"Charlotte loved the rose garden on the west side of the house. And the gardens around the boathouse."

Marie shook her head. "I have a feeling it's this garden." The scent tickled Marie's senses, as if a confirmation of her belief. "Jasmine."

"Where?"

She turned around slowly. It seemed to be everywhere, faint in the outside air. Too faint. "I can't tell. I can hardly smell it."

"There must have been something about this garden that your father liked. He was the one who had it redesigned. I left it all up to him. I couldn't have cared less at the time."

What did her father like? "I don't know what it would be. I didn't know him to ever be passionate about gardens. Drake House, that's all he really cared about. He loved Drake House."

"That doesn't tell us anything."

"Wait. Maybe it does. I have an idea." She took the side path and wound her way through loosely mulched plants. She stopped at the concrete bench and sat down facing the house.

Landscape lighting shot upward, highlighting the house. The dark bushes stood out in sharp relief against the mansion's snow-white siding. Columns soared up to the third floor where the slate roof took over, all sharp angles and graceful slopes. In the summer, the fountain's magic would play against the backdrop of it all, its music adding to the mansion's grandeur.

Brandon sat down beside her.

Shivers prickled over her skin. "This is it. This is my father's favorite part of this garden."

He squinted at the bushes, the fountain, the smaller plants protected by mulch. "What is it?"

"My father loved Drake House more than anything, except maybe me. You have to admit, the house looks spectacular from this vantage point."

Brandon didn't look up. His eyes were still locked on the mulched plants at the bench's base. "What's this?" He reached into a patch of ivy and pulled something out. He held it in the air for her to see. A barrel key.

Marie's pulse fluttered. "Any ideas where it's from?"

Brandon shrugged and held it up higher to catch the landscape lighting. The key carried the patina of age and had a leaf-shaped end. "There are a few of the old doors in the house that use a key like this, but this looks like the wrong size."

"Where else could it have come from?"

"Lexie Thornton had a crew here working on the garden. Maybe it belongs to one of them."

Of course. Lexie had designed the garden. Her family's landscaping company had provided all the plants, the fountain and the bench. "Maybe Lexie could tell us more, not just about the key. Maybe she can help point us to whatever it is we're looking for."

"How late is too late to give her a call?" Brandon glanced down at his watch.

"I don't know. She works so hard, I'd hate to wake her. Maybe we should look around a little more first, try some of the doors in the house."

"Sure. I'll ask Shelley if she knows anything about the key, if she's still here."

"And Isabella?" Marie couldn't help thinking the key had to be related to something that had been going on. And Isabella seemed to be hiding the most secrets of anyone at Drake House.

Brandon nodded. "Right."

They pushed up from the bench at the same time.

Beneath them, the concrete shifted. Brandon grabbed Marie's arm, steadying them both.

"What was that?" Marie said.

Brandon gripped the top of the bench and pushed. It moved under his hand.

For a split second, Marie thought she saw a hollow space in the base of the bench. A space with something that looked like paper tucked inside. "Wait. Do that again."

Brandon lifted the edge of the bench.

Marie leaned close, her pulse racing. This had to be it. She peered into the dark space. "The legs of the bench are hollow. And there's something…" She dipped her hand inside. Her fingers touched the edge of a rolled piece of paper. She pulled it out.

Brandon lowered the bench's seat back into place. "What is it?"

Marie unrolled the paper. At first she wasn't sure. All she could see were penciled lines. "This is strange. It looks like a drawing of some sort."

Brandon studied it over her shoulder. He guided her hand, positioning the paper to take advantage of the landscape lighting. "It looks like a diagram. A sketch of the undercarriage of a car."

Sure enough. She could make out the wheels and the axles, the engine area and the gas tank. "What is this?" She indicated a pointy object near the gas tank.

"Some sort of spike?" He raised dark eyes to meet Marie's. "It's positioned to puncture the gas tank."

A pop split the air and echoed off Drake House.

Marie's heart jumped. "What was that?"

Brandon stiffened. He spun around, looking for the source of the sound.

Another pop. The bench made a snapping sound and something hit Marie in the leg.

"Get down!" Brandon threw his arms around her. His body slammed into her, and both of them tumbled to the ground.

Chapter Thirteen

Brandon could feel the air rush out of Marie's lungs as he came down on top of her. He raised himself up on his elbows, trying to lift his weight off her. "Marie, are you okay? Say something." He held his breath, willing her to speak, to be all right.

She coughed, gasped, nodded her head. Her breath sputtered and caught. Scooping air into her lungs, she looked at him with wide eyes. "I'm fine. I'm… What *was* that?"

"A gun."

"Someone is shooting at us?"

"Yes." And Brandon had to get Marie out of here. He had to get her someplace safe. "Can you move?"

"I don't know. I think something hit my leg."

A bullet? Brandon's gut tensed. Had Marie been shot? "Where?"

She moved her left leg under him. "I can't… You'll have to get up."

"Not until you're out of the line of fire." Marie might already be shot. He wasn't going to move aside and risk her being hit again. "Move to the other side of the bench. I'll shield you."

"But you—"

"No arguments." He glared directly into her eyes. She had to listen to him. She had to do what he said. "Go."

She gave a nod.

He lifted his weight off her, balancing on hands and toes, as if he were doing a push-up.

Marie rolled in one place until she lay on her stomach. She started crawling.

Pain screamed up Brandon's damaged leg. Gritting his teeth, he held on, trying to compensate with his good leg and arms.

She moved out from under him. As she cleared his body, he could smell blood. Something dark glistened on one leg of her jeans.

Damn. He hadn't been fast enough. It had taken too long for him to recognize the popping sound, to realize what it was. And his failure had left Marie hurt. Shot.

Reaching the corner of the bench, Marie rose to hands and knees. She moved faster, slipping between the holly bush and the bench.

Another pop echoed off the house. Something hit the concrete bench close to Marie's head. Too close.

"Get down!" Brandon yelled. He struggled to his knees. To his feet.

"Brandon!" Marie screamed. She popped up behind the bench, as if she was going to jump out and save him. "You'll be shot!"

"Stay there."

Another shot cracked in his ear. Again, something hit the bench. The bench. Not him. Even though he was standing in plain view. Even though he was a big, open target. Even though he'd done everything he could think of to draw the fire to him and away from Marie.

"Marie, stay down." He raced for the bench. He climbed into a spot next to her. He brought his hand down on her head, physically pushing her head lower, under the protection of the bench. He laid his chest on top of her and he wrapped his arms around her body.

She hunkered down, making room for him. She trembled all over.

Brandon held her tighter. Anger balled in his chest like a hard fist. Marie had almost been hit again. She'd almost died. No matter how careful he'd been, no matter how hard he'd tried to shield her, protect her, she'd come so close to losing her life he could hardly breathe. "Why didn't you get down? Why didn't you do what I said?"

She shuddered, as if letting out a silent sob. "I thought…I thought you were going to be killed."

He forced a breath into tight lungs. She didn't understand. In true Marie fashion, she'd thought only about saving him. Only about making sure he was safe. "Whoever is out there, he's not gunning for me."

She shook her head, as if she didn't want to believe the obvious.

It didn't matter. Not now. Now the only thing that meant a damn was getting Marie out of this mess. And the first thing he had to do was douse these lights.

He peered over the bench. His cane lay in the center of the path, its wood dark against the oyster shells. Too far to reach. Even if the shooter wasn't gunning for him, Brandon couldn't chance it. He didn't dare move that far from Marie.

He looked down at his feet. What he wouldn't give to be wearing hiking boots about now. Or a pair of the steel-toed work boots Doug Heller preferred. His Bruno

Maglis would have to do. Any luck and their sheer expense would make up for what they lacked in heft. Yeah, right.

Forcing his arms to release Marie, he slipped one shoe off.

"What are you doing?"

"Giving us some cover. Stay down." He slid between Marie and the prickly wall of holly. Using his hands and one foot, he pulled his body forward until he reached one of the landscape lights, a canister pointing up toward the siding of Drake House. Holding the shoe by its toe box, he brought the heel down hard against glass.

The lense protecting the light cracked but held.

He struck it again. And again.

Finally it shattered. One more blow and the light went dark.

He moved to the next light, the only one left that illuminated the bench area where they hid. He pulled back his shoe, ready to strike again.

A gunshot split the air.

Brandon ducked. His heart pounded; his breath rushed in his ears. He twisted back to check on Marie. She hadn't moved. "Marie?"

"I'm okay."

Had that bullet been meant for him? He didn't think so. The other shots had been fired close to Marie, too close. If the shooter had aimed at him this time, he should have been able to do a better job of hitting his target than that.

Unless he was just trying to scare Brandon. Trying to get him to abandon breaking the second light.

Hands clammy, he grasped the shoe and brought it down on the lens. Two more blows and the bulb was broken. The area was dark.

He scrambled back to Marie. The shells around the bench dug into his hands, his good knee. Now that the would-be killer had lost his spotlight, Marie was safer. But he still knew where she was hiding.

Brandon scanned the garden, searching for another spot to hide. But most of the garden was young, the plants still small. Only the holly and boxwood were left from the old east garden. Only they were large enough to conceal two adults. And only the bench could stop a bullet.

There was nowhere else to go.

Brandon looked down at the shoe still clutched in his hand. Maybe Marie and he didn't have to find a new hiding place. Maybe they only had to make the shooter think they had.

He dragged the shoe against the shells, making a shuffling sound. After several seconds of that, he flung it into a far section of the garden. Slipping off the second shoe, he flung that one as well.

Now to get back to Marie.

He moved slowly, careful to make no sound, careful to avoid rustling against the bushes. When he reached Marie, he slipped his arms around her as he had before. Lying flat behind the bench, he held her back tight to his chest. He brought his lips to her ear, her hair like silk against his cheek. "Shh."

She nodded. She didn't move. She barely seemed to breathe.

A minute passed. Two. It seemed like forever. Finally Brandon could hear the crunch of oyster shells underfoot.

He listened, struggling to hear the sound, to track it, over the beat of his own pulse, the hiss of his own breathing.

It came closer. Closer. It stopped.

Beneath him, Marie trembled. He could feel the rise and fall of her chest cease as she held her breath.

He wrapped her close, shielding her. If only he had a weapon. His cane. Even one of his shoes. Anything. He'd fight. But he'd used everything he could think of. Everything he had. And all that was left was to wait and see if it was enough.

A siren screamed from the direction of the highway.

The police. Thank God.

Footsteps crunched on shells. But this time going away, getting faint.

The siren drew closer. Red and blue light flashed from the other side of Drake House, radiating out from the corner of the east wing like an aurora during an eclipse.

Unless the gunman was an idiot, he had kept running and was long gone by now. Brandon closed his eyes and scooped in a deep breath of Marie's scent. He lay there for several seconds, soaking in the feel of her, the knowledge that she was safe.

Finally he forced his arms to release her. He forced his body to move away. Cold air filled the warmth where she'd been. His chest ached with it. It was all he could do to keep himself from gathering her against him again.

He looked at her, wanting to make sure she was okay. His gaze landed on her bloody jeans. "Let me see your leg."

She sat up. Grimacing, she pulled the leg of her jeans up to her knee. A red stain darkened her calf.

He moved to the side to get a better view of her wound. He could see a cut. He could see blood, but not as much blood as he'd expected.

"It's not too bad," Marie said. "I think it's just a cut. Maybe from a fragment of the bench."

She was probably right. In everyday life, the size of the cut and amount of blood would have horrified him. After all Marie had faced in the past few days, it seemed like nothing. She was alive, after all.

She was alive.

He could hear footsteps circling the house from either side, and low, official voices. The police. Josef must have called. Or Shelley.

"Whoever was shooting at us must think I found something. That I know something. That's why he's trying to kill me. To keep me quiet. Like he did my father."

Marie had voiced that theory before. And it made sense. But to Brandon, it didn't feel right. He'd been asking as many questions as Marie. He'd been with her, in her father's quarters, in Charlotte's study, in the garden fishing the sketch from the bench. So why didn't the shooter see him as a threat, too? Why wasn't the shooter just as eager to kill him?

The words Marie heard in the psychomanteum filtered through his mind. *All Brandon loves will die.* And who did he love? Who had he always loved?

Marie.

TO BRANDON'S RELIEF, it didn't take long for the police officers to secure the house and grounds and lead Brandon and Marie safely inside. A few minutes later, Chief Hammer joined them. Dressed in jeans with what little hair he had left plastered flat to one side of his head, he obviously hadn't been at the station this time. He'd no doubt been sleeping comfortably in his bed beside Mrs. Hammer. And although Brandon didn't have unshakable confidence in the Jenkins Cove Police Department or their leader, he was unspeakably glad they were here.

They'd saved Marie's life.

He answered the door himself, ushering the chief inside. "Thanks for coming personally, Chief. I know it's late."

"Not a problem. You know that, Brandon. It's a good thing your housekeeper called about the gunshots. I'm glad we were able to get here in time."

"Your men did a good job."

"Glad to hear it. They're good boys. I just had a word with Benson over by the carriage house before I came in."

Guilt jolted through Brandon with the force of an electric shock. He gripped his cane in both hands. He hadn't even thought to check on Josef. "My chauffeur. Is he all right?"

"Seems okay. Pretty scared. Poor guy was shaking."

Brandon would have to find a way to make it up to him. Extra vacation time. Trip to Florida. Something. Shelley, too. She'd kept her head and called the police. Interesting that the one employee he couldn't account for was the one he and Marie had the most reason to suspect. "You might want to send a car over to my maid's house. Isabella Faust."

"Why is that?"

"She's been acting a little strange lately. And I have reason to believe she might be out to get Marie."

"Marie? You're sure she was the target in this incident, too?"

"She was the target. Believe me, if whoever was

shooting that gun had wanted me dead, I wouldn't be talking to you now. He was gunning for Marie."

Brandon tried to read the chief's eyes. Hammer didn't like Marie, and he didn't believe much of what she said. He'd made that much clear. Maybe once she showed him the sketch they'd found, he'd reassess her theories.

Brandon sure had. At least he wanted to.

Hammer finally nodded. "All right. I'll have someone check up on Ms. Faust. Anyone else I should know about?"

Brandon thought for a moment. "Ned Perry, the developer."

Hammer nodded. "So he's been after you, too? I should have known. The man is a making a nuisance of himself. Badgering folks all around town to sell their waterfront."

"I think he and Isabella might be doing a little scheming to get their hands on Drake House."

"Scheming? How would shooting at Marie Leonard help them get Drake House?"

"Marie thinks they want to cover up something she has found."

"Marie thinks, eh?" The chief didn't look impressed. "And what do you think?"

Good damn question. Brandon shifted his feet on the thick oriental rug. He gripped the head of his cane. Marie's theory still didn't feel right to him. But what was the alternative? The words of a ghost? Words he hadn't even heard himself? "I'm with Marie."

The chief smiled in an unsuccessful attempt to cover up his skepticism. "All right, then. I'll hear Ms. Leonard out. Any more ideas about who might have declared target practice tonight?"

None that had panned out. "Come on in the kitchen. Marie's in there and she has something to show you. It might make everything more clear." At least Brandon could hope. He led Hammer through the halls, past the formal dining room and into the kitchen.

Marie and Shelley stood in the food preparation area, leaning on opposite countertops. Even though Brandon had helped Marie bandage her leg and had given her instructions to keep it elevated, she was back on her feet, probably still feeling too shaken to sit for long.

Hammer focused on Marie. The lines in his jowly face deepened with concern. "How is it you were involved in two life-threatening incidents in one day, Miss Leonard?"

Marie met his eyes. Her back stiffened just a little. "Not by choice, Chief."

"Brandon said you have something to show me?"

"I do." She pushed away from the counter and held out the rolled paper. "We found this hidden in the hollow base of a bench in the east garden. I think my father stashed it there."

The chief unfurled the roll. Plucking a pair of reading glasses out of his pocket, he slipped them on his pudgy nose and squinted down at the sketch. "A car?"

Shelley inched closer, craning her neck to see. She cradled a tea cup in her hands, a sweet scent wafting over the brim.

"The undercarriage of a car," Brandon said. "And look at the spike positioned by the gas tank."

Hammer frowned. "What is this supposed to be?"

"The evidence you wanted." Marie's voice was low but rang with conviction.

Brandon hoped Hammer would see it the same way.

The chief focused on Marie. "Evidence of what?"

Marie didn't miss a beat. "Charlotte Drake's murder."

A choked whimper came from Shelley's throat.

The chief held the paper at arm's length, as if suddenly afraid it would bite him. "Is this real?"

Marie's eyes flashed. Her hands tightened to fists by her sides. "You mean did I quickly draw it up?" she said sarcastically. "Of course it's real. It's just what I told you it is."

Brandon moved to Marie's side. He knew she was frustrated with her push and pull with the police. But if she wanted Hammer to look into the case, if she wanted him to switch the deaths from accidents to murders, if she wanted him to call in the state police to investigate, she had to be more diplomatic. He rested a hand on her arm.

She let out a pent-up breath. "I'm sorry, Chief. I've had a tough day."

"No offense taken, young lady. I'll take this back to the station and look into it along with the rest of the leads we find."

"No." Marie reached out to grasp the paper.

Hammer pulled it out of her range. "What do you mean, no?"

"I want to see your photos of the vehicle," Marie said. "The one Charlotte died in."

Brandon was aware of Shelley stepping closer behind him.

Hammer kept his eyes on Marie. He shook his head. "I'm sorry. I can't let you do that."

"Why not?"

"You aren't family. You don't own the car. You're not

part of the investigation. In short, I have no reason to show you anything."

Brandon took a deep breath. "Then maybe you can show me."

Marie whirled to glance up at him. Turning back to Hammer, she nodded. "You can't say Brandon doesn't have reason to look at the photos."

Hammer watched Brandon intently, as if trying to read his thoughts.

Strange. Brandon hadn't felt scrutinized like this by a police officer since he'd been caught drinking beer underage during his first year of college. A lifetime ago. He was more used to the chief of police handling his routine calls personally, not searching for the truth in his eyes.

Finally the chief nodded, as if he'd made up his mind about something. "There are no photos."

"No photos?" If it was possible for Marie's eyes to grow wider, they did. "What do you mean? Aren't they part of the accident report? Isn't taking pictures of a car involved in a fatal accident routine?"

"My officers must have overlooked it."

An uneasy feeling crept up the back of Brandon's neck. That could be true, except an officer hadn't overseen the accident report. As with most of the things involving the Drakes, Chief Hammer had hovered over the incident personally. And although Hammer had a reputation for being lazy, Brandon couldn't believe he was this lazy, not about something as serious as a death, accidental or not. "Why weren't pictures taken, Chief?"

Hammer looked down at the tile floor, the overhead lights reflecting off his scalp. "I thought…I thought it might get…inconvenient."

"Inconvenient?" Brandon parroted. "What in the hell does that mean?"

Hammer raised his eyes. "I don't think you want me to spell it out."

What was he getting at? Brandon had no clue. And he wasn't sure he wanted to know.

"You don't need pictures of her car," Shelley said.

All of them turned to look at the housekeeper.

She gripped her tea, her hands shaking so badly the steaming liquid sloshed over the edge of the cup and onto reddened fingers. She stared from Brandon to Marie, as if unaware she was burning herself. "The car itself. Her car. It's in a salvage yard outside town."

"It's still around?" The chief stared at Shelley as if she were speaking another language. "It was supposed to go to a crusher. It was supposed to be destroyed." He glanced at Brandon, his expression strangely apologetic.

"Shelley, are you sure it's still there?" Marie asked.

The woman nodded her gray head vigorously. "I see it every week."

"You must be mistaken." Again Hammer shot Brandon that strange look.

"I'm not mistaken. Believe me. I pay the rent, and Joey keeps it for me. Just like it was. I visit it every week. It helps me remember. Helps me keep her alive."

Brandon stared at his housekeeper. The woman visited the car in which Charlotte died? She paid someone to keep it for her? The idea was disturbing. Twisted.

Shelley's face crumpled. Tears rolled down her taut cheeks. "That paper, what does it say? What does it mean?"

Marie stepped toward Shelley. She laid a gentle hand on the woman's arm. "Charlotte didn't die in an accident, Shelley. I'm so sorry."

"What are you saying?"

"That paper and the car you've been caring for prove that Charlotte was murdered."

"Just a minute, Ms. Leonard," the chief boomed. "It doesn't prove any such thing."

"It will when we examine the car," Marie insisted. "We'll know then."

Shelley's tears gushed harder. The woman's wiry body convulsed in a sob. "Who could have done that?" She focused on Marie, and for a moment Brandon thought he saw a flash of hatred in her eyes.

"Calm down, Shelley," he commanded. "It wasn't Marie, for God's sake. But with your help, we can find out who did it. We're going to find out."

Shelley drew in a shuddering breath and nodded. Blindly she set her cup on the counter, then covered her face and softly cried.

Marie stepped beside her and placed a tender hand on the woman's shoulder. She said something soft in her ear, too quiet for Brandon to catch.

"I'm sorry," Shelley whispered. "So sorry." She reached for Marie, and Marie wrapped the woman in her arms.

Brandon looked back at Hammer. "I think you should call in the state police."

"You really want to do that?"

Brandon frowned. Strange. The chief's words sounded ominous, almost threatening, but his tone of voice was just plain worried. "Why wouldn't I?"

"You want it straight?" Hammer asked in a low voice.

Brandon answered with a nod.

"Because if your wife was murdered, the state's first suspect is going to be the husband, that's why."

Understanding rippled through Brandon. Suddenly it all made sense. The chief's hovering. His laziness in taking photos of Charlotte's car. Maybe even his reluctance to look at Edwin's death as anything but an accident. "You think *I* was responsible?"

Hammer waved off the words. "I don't think anything."

"You do. And you're protecting me."

Hammer didn't confirm or deny, he just held up the paper in his hand. "What do you want me to do with this? I'll handle it however you say."

Brandon shook his head. He'd never needed Chief Hammer's special protection. He'd never asked for it, never wanted it. And although he now realized it was merely part of his birthright, part of being a Drake in a town like Jenkins Cove, he felt a little sick at the double standard wealth gave him.

He looked Hammer straight in the eye. "Give the sketch to the state police. And while you're at it, call them right now and have someone meet us at the salvage yard owned by Shelley's friend. We have a car to examine."

Chapter Fourteen

The sun was starting to pink the eastern sky by the time Marie, Brandon and Chief Hammer met a Maryland state police detective named Randall McClellan at Joey Jansen's Auto Salvage east of Jenkins Cove on Route 43. Tucked into the base of a narrow neck of land clustered with vacation homes, the junkyard consisted of two corrugated buildings surrounded by rusted and twisted skeletons of cars and signs proclaiming Off-Season Boat Storage, Cheap Prices!

Joey, a man young enough to be Shelley's son and with a facial tick that looked to Marie as if he were constantly winking at her, led them to one of the steel sheds. He unlocked the door, apologized that there were no electric lights in the place, then announced he was going back to bed.

Marie let the men lead the way. A mixture of covered boats and a few pieces of farm machinery packed the large shed. The detective led them through the narrow paths between covered hulks with the flashlight he'd brought from his car. Finally his beam shone on a blackened and twisted steel skeleton against the back wall.

Charlotte's sports car.

Even though it had been six months since the fire, the stench of burned plastic and upholstery made Marie's eyes water as she stepped close. Oily and thick, the odor clogged her throat just as it had in the psycho-manteum. She could still hear the roar of the fire echoing through her memory.

Marie watched Brandon as he studied the car. Seeing the vehicle where Charlotte had died was hard enough for her. It had to be excruciating for him. Without thinking, she reached for his hand.

He squeezed her fingers and offered a tight-lipped grimace. "I'll look under the rear bumper, see if the spike is there."

His eyes looked tired, empty. Marie knew he was torturing himself by making himself face Charlotte's death all over again. But to what end? To punish himself for past mistakes? To reinforce the wall he'd built around his feelings for Marie? To give him the impetus to push her away again? She couldn't let him do it. Not now that they were so close to resolving this, so close to proving he had no reason for his crippling guilt.

She held his hand fast. "Let the detective look."

He held her gaze for a moment. And for that moment, time seemed to stop. Finally he nodded. "You're right. It's up to the police now, not us. Not anymore." He glanced at the detective and shifted to the side, giving him room to pass.

As if purposely unaware of their drama, Detective McClellan took one last look at the sketch they'd given him and moved to the car's rear. He crouched low and directed his beam under the back bumper, sweeping the undercarriage with light.

Marie forced herself to breathe. If the spike was no

longer attached to the car, she didn't know what she would do. She was out of leads and she was almost out of hope. Tonight, for the first time, the reality that someone wanted her dead had finally penetrated her thick skull. And worse, she understood that in protecting her, Brandon was in danger, too. She wanted to be done with this investigating stuff. She wanted the professionals to take over. She wanted the sketch to be out of her hands, and there be no more reason for fear.

But more than any yearning she had for safety, she wanted Brandon to know Charlotte hadn't killed herself. That for all his mistakes, all the mistakes everyone had made ten years ago, there was still a future for him and for her. Maybe even the promise of happiness.

Detective McClellan straightened, nearly as tall as Brandon himself. Marie searched his face for a clue of what he'd seen, but his flinty eyes were unreadable. He turned to Brandon. "We'll have to take the car."

"Fine with me."

"And I'd like to look around your property. And inside the house. I can have an evidence crew there this afternoon. Is that a problem, or should I call a judge?"

"You don't need a warrant. You'll have free run of the place."

A trill shimmered up Marie's spine. She wanted this so badly, she was afraid to speak, afraid to hope. But she had to know. She forced the words from her mouth. "Does this mean you'll look into Charlotte's and my father's deaths?"

Detective McClellan's mouth flattened to a line. "I have evidence sufficient to believe Charlotte Drake was murdered."

Relief warmed her like a double shot of brandy, making her feel light-headed and unsteady on her feet. "And my father?"

The detective peered down at her, his expression unchanging. "I'm sorry. Unless more evidence comes to light in your father's case, I have no reason to believe a crime was committed."

"I'LL HIRE A PRIVATE INVESTIGATOR. A professional. Someone good. He'll find the evidence the police need." Brandon watched Marie's face as Josef drove them back to Drake House. The morning sun had crept into the eastern sky, but even its warm rays couldn't dispel the darkness of the state police detective's pronouncement about Edwin's case.

Marie shook her head. "I'll keep looking. I still have some of his things to go through. I'm sure I'll find something… Something has to help."

She looked tired. Hurting. And Brandon didn't know what to do about it. He'd never felt so powerless in his life. "Now that the police believe Charlotte was murdered, it's only a matter of time. You know that, right? Edwin had to be the one who hid that sketch. He had to be killed because he knew who murdered Charlotte. When Detective McClellan finds who that is, he'll solve Edwin's murder as well."

"I know." She smiled up at him. "The important thing is that you know Charlotte didn't commit suicide. You know it wasn't your fault."

He let her words sink into him, let them circulate through his bloodstream, warming him to the core. But as good as it felt, he knew it wasn't that simple. Even though he knew Charlotte hadn't killed herself, he wasn't absolved of everything. "I made a lot of mistakes. I hurt Charlotte. I hurt you."

"You hurt yourself."

He nodded. But that wasn't important. Not as important as the burden of knowing he hurt people he cared for, people who cared for him. He looked down at his hands, suddenly aware he was twisting the wedding band on his finger.

He hadn't felt right about removing it when Charlotte died. He'd worn it like a penance. A constant reminder of what he'd done to her, the tragedy he'd caused. But now that he knew he hadn't caused that tragedy, it felt blasphemous to treat a wedding band as punishment. Somehow it felt disrespectful to Charlotte. To the wonderful woman she was.

He slipped it off.

Marie said nothing, but he could feel her watching. He could feel her body close and smell her delicious, spicy scent.

If only he'd trusted his feelings for her ten years ago. If only he'd stood up to what was expected of him and listened to his heart. He still would have hurt Charlotte, still would have been unfair to her. But her hurt would have faded, and she would have had a good life. Marie and he would have had a good life.

Despite the unease still niggling at the back of his mind, he'd like to believe they could have that good life now.

The car slowed and turned. Passing the redbrick and iron gate of the Manor at Drake Acres, it went through the simple white pillars announcing Drake House. Brandon pulled in a breath and peered out the window.

Black soot still stained the gray stone wall. A bouquet of flowers lay at the foot of the small cross Edwin had placed on the site. Flowers arranged by Shelley, no doubt, and placed with the utmost care. "Stop for a moment, Josef. Will you?"

The car slowed to a stop.

Brandon sat still, watching out the window. "I've never looked at that spot. Not since that night. Every time Josef drove me past, I averted my eyes. I just couldn't..."

"It's different now." Marie's voice sounded hushed, respectful and so wise.

"Yes. It looks different in the sun." He thought about placing the ring on the cross. Thought about bringing it to her grave outside Jenkins Cove Chapel. But in the end, he knew neither option felt right. He slipped it into his pocket. Charlotte was a part of him. A part of his past. And even though he would never again wear it, he would keep the symbol of their marriage with him. To remember the good things...and the mistakes.

"Go ahead, Josef."

The car resumed moving down the drive. He didn't remember getting out. Didn't remember walking to the house and unlocking the door. Didn't remember turning off the alarm and ensuring that the house was empty. All he remembered was taking Marie's hand in his and leading her upstairs.

He felt as though he'd waited ten years for this. He supposed he had. He peeled off her coat, her blouse. He pulled off her jeans tenderly over her bandaged leg and stripped her panties and bra.

The soft light of morning glowed through the bedroom window and kissed her skin.

When he'd last made love to Marie, she'd been a girl.

Now the naked body before him was that of a woman. And he couldn't quite catch his breath. "You're beautiful."

She looked down at the floor.

He slipped his hand to her face and tilted her chin up. "You're the most beautiful woman I've ever known."

He brought his mouth down on hers, tasting her, savoring her. She kissed as she had in his dreams, light and caring one moment, passionate and needy the next. Smelling her scent aroused him. Touching her filled him up.

She raised her hands to his shoulders, combed her fingers through his hair. She moved one hand to his face as they kissed, and traced her fingertips over his cheek.

The skin had once been so tender, so sensitive that a whisper of air inspired agony. Back then, after the car fire, he'd wished he couldn't feel anything. He'd prayed for it. Now her touch felt faint, his nerve endings protected by scar tissue. And for the first time he wanted to scrape it off, to dig deep, to feel.

For the first time he wanted more.

Without releasing her lips, he shucked his clothes. She helped him, unbuttoning his shirt, pushing his pants down his legs. He wanted to be as naked as she was. He wanted to feel every inch of her skin with every inch of his.

When the last piece of clothing fell, he picked her up in his arms and carried her the few steps to the bed. It was an old-fashioned move. Something he'd seen in the movies. Something he'd never thought a modern man would do. But it felt fitting. It felt right.

He lowered her to the bed, gently, so gently. He feathered kisses down her neck and over her collarbone. He worshiped her breasts with his mouth, his tongue, his teeth. He'd never wanted another woman this way, only Marie. He'd never felt so powerful and strong and important as when he looked into her eyes.

He kissed her whole body. Her belly. Her thighs. Between her legs. And when shudder after shudder took her, it was the best feeling in the world.

When he kissed his way back to her mouth, she rolled him to his back and smiled. Moving down to his legs, she traced her tongue up the scars on his legs before devouring him with her warm, wet mouth.

She moved her lips up and down his length, stoking his want, drawing out his need. He felt as though he'd explode—with need, with love, with more happiness than he'd ever dared to dream. And when she came back to his lips, he took her mouth, tasting himself, tasting her, wanting more.

She sat up, arching her back. Sun caressed the curve of her breasts, lit her taut, reddened nipples. She moved over him and positioned him between her legs.

Sinking down, she accepted him inside.

He groaned as her slick heat enveloped him. Swallowed him. Claimed him. He covered her breasts with his hands, feeling her softness, reveling in her strength. He didn't know how long they moved like that, her on top, him on top, every way they could invent. Not long enough. Too long. It didn't really matter. Finally pleasure shuddered through her and spread to him as well. Release. Redemption. And when their bodies calmed and the sweat slicking their skin cooled, he cuddled her close. "I love you, Marie. I always have. More than I thought I could love anyone."

She smiled, a beautiful, open smile. "I love you, too, Brandon. And I'll never stop."

Her voice curled inside him. Her scent marked him. Her body melded to his. She was so precious to him, so perfect. He always wanted to hold her. Never wanted to lose her.

To lose her.

He pushed the thought away and snuggled a kiss into the crook of her neck.

Her giggle bubbled through him. Light. Carefree. Just what he wanted. To be carefree. To be untroubled. For once in his life to be happy.

But he wouldn't have those things. Not if something tragic happened. Not if he lost her.

His chest felt tight. His leg started to ache. He was being morose, but he couldn't help it. He had everything he wanted—right now, right here—yet he was more conscious than ever of how quickly it all could be taken away. How quickly Marie could be taken away.

All Brandon loves will die.

The words beat in the back of his mind like a war drum. Matching the beat of his heart. Overwhelming it. He didn't believe in ghosts. Not really. He'd never seen one, never heard one. Why would he believe a ghost's words?

He rolled his shoulders to loosen them. He tried to breathe deep, to draw in her scent, to pull oxygen into his starving lungs, but the pressure was too strong to shrug off. The fear was too strong to push away.

Maybe it wasn't about believing or ghosts or any of that. Maybe it was just about Marie. And if there was even the slightest chance that loving him was putting her in danger, it was a risk he couldn't take.

Chapter Fifteen

Marie didn't want to get out of bed. She didn't want to move away from Brandon. She didn't want to shower and wash off Brandon's scent from her skin. She felt if she disturbed this perfect moment, this perfect scene, the magic they had finally found might slip away.

Chimes rang through the house. The doorbell downstairs. She could hear the click of Isabella's footsteps crossing the marble foyer.

She flinched. "I don't want to move."

Brandon ruffled her hair with his fingers. "Can you see the surprise on Detective McClellan's and his evidence team's faces when they come up to search the master bedroom and find us naked in bed?" Brandon's words were light and joking, but something in his voice made Marie uneasy.

She propped up on an elbow and studied his face. "What's wrong?"

He shook his head, but he didn't meet her eyes.

"Please, tell me." Her voice sounded strained, frightened to her own ears. She *was* frightened. The way he'd avoided looking at her scared her to death.

She was probably overreacting. The last time she'd

made love with Brandon and let herself feel this happy, her whole world had come tumbling down around her. But things were different this time. Weren't they? There was no pending marriage. Their age difference didn't matter anymore. And after this morning's revelation, nothing was in their way. Everything had changed.

Brandon cupped the back of her head in his hand and pulled her snug against him.

Marie leaned her head against the solid strength of his shoulder. She knew there would be tough times ahead. She knew everything wouldn't be magically okay. That was fine. Brandon would never totally put the pain of the past behind him. Neither would she. But now that they had each other, maybe they could move forward. Bit by bit. Day by day. They could be happy together. At least after this morning, she dared to hope. "Whatever it is, you don't have to worry. We'll handle it. Together."

He didn't answer.

She could feel her heart rate rise, beating against his chest. Her throat grew dry. "Brandon?"

"You need to go back to Michigan."

His words jangled through her with the force of an electric shock. She sat up. As an afterthought, she pulled the sheet up, covering her breasts. "What do you mean, go back to Michigan?"

"You'll be safe there."

"I'll be safe here. The police—"

"Don't need your help."

"I wish that was true. But they wouldn't even have looked into this if we hadn't made them."

"But we did. And they are." He reached up and ran his fingers over her shoulder, down her arm. "It's up to the police now. Remember? You helped me see that. You helped me step away and go on with my life. Now let me help you."

"But I don't have to go back to Michigan for that. I'll look for teaching jobs in Baltimore or D.C. My life is here now."

He pushed himself up from the pillow. The soft glow of the afternoon sun lit his bare chest.

"Isn't my life here?" Panic clawed inside her. She struggled to remain still. To not grab him. Shake him. "Brandon?"

He thrust himself from the bed. He stepped to the chair and stood there, naked.

Marie scanned his face. His body. Her focus landed on the long scar marking his leg. Brandon had other scars, not so visible. Scars not totally healed.

"How can you send me away?" Her voice cracked. She sounded hysterical. She felt hysterical. This couldn't be happening. Not now that he knew Charlotte hadn't committed suicide. Not after they'd made love. Not after he'd told her he loved her. "We're supposed to be together. We're supposed to be happy. How can you ask me to leave?"

He grabbed a thick terry cloth robe from the back of the chair. He pulled it on and tied it at the waist, covering himself. "It's temporary. It's for your own protection. Once Detective McClellan finds out who killed Charlotte and your father, you can come back."

She shook her head. She knew what he was saying was smart. It was safe. It made sense. But logical or not, she had the feeling that once she left, what she and Brandon had found would be gone. That once she walked out of Drake House, she couldn't come back again. "I love you, Brandon. I don't want to lose you again."

"You won't lose me."

"If I leave, I will. I'll lose you. I know it. I don't want to leave."

"No, Marie. If you *don't* leave, I'm afraid *I'll* lose *you*."

A wave of cold swept through her and penetrated her bones. She clutched the sheet tighter against her breasts. "What? Why? The police have the sketch. It's out of my hands now."

He shook his head. He raked a hand through his hair. He seemed conflicted. Desperate. As tortured as when he'd believed he was the cause of Charlotte's death.

Now he was really frightening her. "What is it, Brandon? Tell me."

He met her eyes. "'All Brandon loves will die.'"

He didn't have to explain where the quote came from. She'd heard it with her own ears, and she'd never forget. "Did Charlotte speak to you?"

"No."

"Then what has changed since this morning?"

He stared at her as if he wasn't sure how to answer.

"You told me you loved me this morning," she said. "You made love to me. I thought you wanted us to be together."

"I did. I do."

"I told you what Charlotte's spirit said *days* ago."

He raked his hair again. "I know. I just didn't really understand what it meant until now."

Her throat felt tight. As if she could scream and scream and never get the pressure to loosen. "What does it mean, Brandon? What does it mean to *you*?"

"That I could lose you." He tested the belt of his robe, as if it wasn't tight enough, as if he'd felt it coming loose. "What if it isn't just about who killed Charlotte and your father? What if it isn't about you snooping around?"

"What are you trying to say?"

He splayed his hands out in front of him, begging for her to understand. "I've been investigating this, too. I've been asking questions. I even helped you find that damn sketch. But someone tried to throw *you* off the roof. They cut the brakes in *your* car. They shot at *you* alone, even though I was a much easier target."

"All that stuff is about covering up the murders."

"What if it isn't?"

"Are you saying you're afraid I'm a marked woman?"

"No. I'm saying what if by loving you, I've *made* you a marked woman?"

She shook her head. She was hoping things had changed. She was hoping the proof that Charlotte was murdered had taken away Brandon's guilt. Taken away his fear. But she'd failed to realize the fear wasn't really about Charlotte. Maybe it had never been. Maybe it was older than his marriage to Charlotte and his summer with Marie. Maybe it was something rooted deep in Brandon himself.

Tears filled her eyes, making the room blur. She turned away. "You're blaming yourself again. Just like you did with Charlotte. Just like you always do. What are you so afraid of?"

He was in front of her in two steps. He gripped her shoulders, turning her back toward him, forcing her to look into his eyes. "'All Brandon loves will die.' You said you heard Charlotte's spirit speak those words." His voice was hard, almost accusing.

"I did."

"Do you believe in ghosts, Marie? Because it seems like if you believe in ghosts, you should listen to the things they tell you. You should believe the words they say."

Her throat felt thick. Her heart ached with each beat. For him. For her. "Loss is part of life, Brandon."

He released her arms. Shaking his head, he limped to the fireplace and grabbed his cane.

Tears rolled down her cheeks, but she didn't push them away. She understood what he felt. Understood what he feared. "Last week when I talked to my father, our discussion was so ordinary. The snow in Michigan. His plans to visit me at Christmas. The box of ornaments he sent me from when I was a kid. I never guessed I wouldn't hear his voice again. And when he died, all I could think about was all the things I wanted to say that I can never say now. But you know what?"

"What?"

"It isn't about the things I didn't say. It's about the time we spent together. Like every ordinary minute of that conversation. That's the stuff that is life. That's the stuff that makes up love. And if you send me away, that's the stuff you and I will never have."

"I love you, Marie. How can I not protect you?"

"You can't protect me from everything."

He shook his head slowly, as if he could hardly summon the energy. "I can't accept that."

Tears clogged her throat, choked her words. "Everyone will die. It's just the way things are. We don't get to decide. But, Brandon, we do get to decide how we live. Who we share our days and nights with. Who we love."

He paused in front of the mantel, clutching his cane in both hands, leaning on it as if he couldn't stand on his own. "I'll book you a flight for tomorrow morning. That should give you enough time to finish packing your father's things."

MARIE TAPED THE LAST BOX of her father's papers and wrote her address on the label. Shelley would mail the papers, a few family heirlooms and a handful of photo albums to her address in Michigan. His clothing, shoes and most of his furniture would go to charity. And the rooms themselves would finally belong to Shelley.

Marie didn't cry as she looked around the space. She didn't have tears left. Not anymore. Ten years ago, when she'd left this place, she'd thought her heart was permanently broken. Now Brandon had mended it this morning only to shatter it again.

This time she knew it was unfixable.

Her father had been right. Brandon would never open himself to love. If it wasn't his engagement to Charlotte keeping them apart, he'd find something else. And he had. The real issue. Fear.

Marie walked into the bedroom. It had taken her all day, but the room was bare. Only her mostly packed suitcase remained in the corner. The bedsheets and spread were still tucked in neatly on the bed. Her flight to Michigan left in the morning, which meant she'd be sleeping at Drake House one last time.

Sleep. She almost laughed. There wasn't a chance she'd be able to sleep. She might not have any cry left in her, but her heart squeezed with each beat. Her ears kept hearing Brandon's words over and over. Her mind searched for things she could have said or done to make this turn out differently.

Too bad those perfect words and deeds didn't exist.

Shaking her head, she sat on the edge of the bed. Even if she couldn't doze off, she might as well go through the motions. She had nothing else to do. Nothing else to pack. And she could stomach no more goodbyes.

She slipped off one boot, then the other and dropped them on the floor. One hit something, producing a metallic clink. What was that? Had she missed something? She shoved off the bed and peered under the white spread. A watch lay on the rug. One of her father's old pocket watches.

She plunked down on the floor and cradled the watch in her hands. When Jonathan Drake was alive, he'd given his butler a new pocket watch every Christmas, and her father treasured them, wearing a different one each day. The thought that she'd almost left one behind made her stomach twist.

What else might she have missed?

Sniffing back her tears, she flipped the edge of the bedspread back. Crouching on hands and knees, she scanned under the bed. Even though the rug seemed clean, her nose tickled with dust. The edge of a small notebook caught her eye. She grasped it and brought it into the light.

At first it seemed like nothing, just a pad of paper he might have jotted messages or to-do lists on. Then she saw the indentations left from pressing the pencil or pen on the sheet above.

Marie's heart jolted. She scrambled to her feet and

raced into the sitting room. She ripped open the box holding items from his desk and fished out a pencil. Rubbing the pencil back and forth lightly across the indentations in the notebook paper, she started to see the indentations take shape. A short, curved stem emerged on the page…a simple leaf…and finally the U-shaped petals of a tulip.

Identical to the image she'd seen in the psychomanteum mirror.

She squeezed her arms close against her sides to steady herself, to try to keep her hands from shaking. Her father had seen the image, too. He'd copied it. And there was more.

She rubbed the pencil over the other indentations on the notebook page. Numbers formed in her father's abrupt script. No, not numbers. Letters. A name.

JENKINS COVE CHAPEL CEMETERY.

The graveyard where her father was buried.

Chapter Sixteen

Brandon paced the third floor. His leg ached to high heaven, but he couldn't care less. He was doing the right thing. He was. Wasn't he?

He wished tomorrow morning was already here, that Marie was on the plane, that she was safe. Every second that ticked by made him more nervous. Every creak of the old house made him long to run downstairs to gather her into his arms. To protect her? Or to tell her he'd changed his mind? To beg her to stay with him forever?

He didn't know.

The distant sound of an engine hummed from the front of the house. What the hell?

He raced to the door of his sitting room and across the hall to his study. He pulled aside drapes covering the windows facing the forest and driveway at the front of the house. This was where he'd seen the fire that had taken Charlotte's life. A small orange glow through the trees at the stone wall. But he didn't see a fire now. He didn't see a crash.

He saw headlights shining down the drive, moving

away. And immediately he knew the car, even though it had only arrived from the rental agency the day before.

Where did Marie think she was going?

MARIE WRAPPED HER JACKET around her shoulders and quickened her steps up the redbrick path that wound between boxwood hedges. The gray stone church and walled graveyard were smack in the middle of town, right on Main Street. But that didn't seem to matter to her jumpy nerves.

A cemetery was still a cemetery.

She'd tried Sophie's breathing exercises. They didn't work. The only thing she could think of as she was scooping in those big, slow breaths was that she could hear sounds around her. Footsteps following up the path behind her. The creak of someone watching from the willow oaks overhead. Moans from among the gray, lichen-covered stones.

She had to reel in her imagination.

She pulled the notebook from her bag and tilted the page toward the light from the nearby street. Why had her father included both the sketch and the cemetery name on that page? She knew they were related. The two things were grouped too deliberately on the page not to be. Had he seen both the tulip and the name of the graveyard in the psychomanteum mirror? She'd seen the tulip right before Brandon had rushed into the room, responding to her scream. If she hadn't been interrupted, would Charlotte have shown her the rest?

Charlotte.

Charlotte was buried in this cemetery. Generations of Drakes were, as were many of their loyal servants who attended the chapel alongside the family. Would finding Charlotte's grave make the tulip's meaning clear? But how could she locate the grave in the darkness?

Maybe she should have roused Brandon and asked him to come with her. He would be able to lead her directly to Charlotte's headstone. And as painful as it would be to spend her last hours in Jenkins Cove with him after he'd pushed her away, at least she wouldn't be walking through graves alone.

No. He would never have let her come. Not as determined to protect her as he was. Once he made his decision, she knew he wouldn't let her go anywhere but to the airport. He would insist she turn the notebook over to the police. And they would file it away, never knowing what importance the drawing held.

Not that she knew, either. At least not yet.

She glanced around the perimeter of the yard. Just over the redbrick wall, she could hear a car's engine as it buzzed down the street. She could see the night-lights of the stores along Main Street. Some insomniac soul was burning the night oil in a nearby house.

She'd never been afraid to walk around Jenkins Cove by herself. No one was. Half the residents still didn't lock their doors, at least not during the off-season. She didn't need Brandon's protection. And she didn't need his help finding Charlotte's grave, either.

She could do it herself.

She reached an opening in the boxwood. She stepped off the path onto the sparse, winter grass. The dappled glow of nearby streetlights kissed the cemetery, filtered through thick, evergreen leaves of magnolia and wispy branches of willow oak. Tombstones of different shapes and sizes jutted from the ground like jagged teeth. They crowded every space between tree trunks and shrubs, some old as the town itself, some new…like her father's.

Marie hadn't noticed Charlotte's grave during her father's funeral, but then she'd been focusing on holding herself together and on the upcoming discussion she'd planned with Police Chief Hammer. It could be in the same area, and she'd simply missed it. At least she knew some Drakes were buried in that area. It was a place to start.

She wound through the stones, rubbing her arms to ward off the chill. If spirits roamed Drake House, surely they must roam this place. She thought she could feel them. The cold pockets of still air. The hair rising on the back of her neck. The soft beat in her ears that she swore had to be footsteps.

Or maybe the beat of a heart.

She shivered again, tamping down her imagination. She had to focus on the tulip. She had to find what it meant, what connection it had to the cemetery. She rounded a tree and spotted a white spire thrusting into the night.

The marker of Brandon's father, Jonathan Drake.

She remembered the tall column of stone, reminiscent of the Washington Memorial across the Chesapeake in the nation's capital. She couldn't help thinking of Brandon's uncle. When Clifford Drake died, no doubt his memorial would be twice as tall.

A twig cracked behind her.

She whirled around, but all she could see were stones, trees, shadows. She pushed out a tense breath and moved on. One by one, the Drake name started popping up on the headstones around her. Her father's grave was closer to the wall, deeper in the cemetery. But judging by the increased frequency of the Drake family graves, Charlotte's had to be close by.

She scanned each name. Mirabelle Drake, who died in 1933. Samuel Drake, who died as an infant twenty years earlier. William Drake, 1883, possibly one of the first Drakes buried in the yard.

Charlotte Drake.

Charlotte's stone was smooth. No mark of a tulip. No sign of the violence that had taken her life. Just beautiful, flawless, white.

Marie swallowed into an aching throat. She'd never liked Charlotte, but that wasn't due to anything Charlotte had done. It was because of what she had. It was because she was living the life Marie had dreamed of. It was because of jealousy and envy and bitter resentment.

Marie felt ashamed of those feelings now. She felt ashamed she'd been so hard on Brandon's wife. "I'm sorry, Charlotte. I'm sorry things worked out so badly for you. I'm sorry things worked out so badly for me. And most of all, I'm sorry Brandon will never know happiness."

The chill surrounding her faded and the air warmed. Marie blinked back the tears pooling in her eyes and scanned the stones around her. Maybe there was no tulip. Maybe Charlotte was the reason she had to come here tonight. To speak to her one last time. To put everything between them to rest.

Feeling less tense, Marie walked to her father's grave, the earth on top still rough and mounded. She'd felt Charlotte's presence in the graveyard, but she could tell right away her father wasn't there. His stone felt like just a stone. The mound of dirt covering his casket was just dirt. She pressed her lips together and studied the flowers clustered around his grave. "Goodbye, Daddy. Wherever you are. I'll miss you every day."

She turned away from the stone and wiped her eyes. She shed still more tears. A miracle. When her vision cleared, she focused on the brick wall. Concrete squares lined the length of the wall, vaults for cremated human remains. Each one held another name, another loved one who would never come back. The dates they died. The special bonds they had with family and friends and community.

And one held the simple etching of a tulip.

Marie sucked in a breath. She stumbled to the marker and fell to her knees.

She didn't have to compare the image to the one her father had drawn in the notebook. It had been burned into her brain in the psychomanteum. She read the name.

Lala Falat.

A foreign name. Maybe Eastern European.

The story Chelsea and Michael told her after her experience on the roof filtered through her mind. They'd said the doctor, Janecek, had smuggled people into the United States from Eastern Europe. He'd made them pay for their passage by donating their organs. Many had died. The state police were still counting the bodies.

Could Lala Falat be tied to the mass grave? And if so, what could she possibly have to do with Charlotte Drake? And why did her father think her grave was important?

Marie dug into her bag. Her hand closed over her digital camera. She pulled it out and focused the camera on the wall marker.

And the world went black.

"MARIE?" Brandon quickened his pace. He swore he'd heard the low whisper of her voice on this side of the graveyard. "Marie? Are you in here?"

Damn this leg. By the time he'd awakened Josef to drive him, Marie had a substantial head start. He wouldn't even have known where she'd gone if she hadn't parked her car right on Main Street in front of the Jenkins Cove Chapel.

He wound through the headstones, making his way to her father's marker. What on earth would make her so intent on visiting his grave that she had to drive here in the middle of the night? And what had possessed her to come here alone?

He knew the answer. Or at least he could guess. She'd assumed he would nix the idea in an effort to protect her.

And the worst thing was that she was probably right.

He reached Edwin's grave site.

No Marie.

He made his way to the brick wall. Maybe if he walked the perimeter, he could locate her.

His foot hit something in the grass.

He bent down and picked up a camera. And not five feet away lay Marie's purse.

His lungs constricted. His pulse thundered in his ears. She never would have dropped these things. Not unless she was forced to. Not unless she was attacked.

He spun and headed back to the dark, squared outlines of the boxwood hedges. He had to reach the car. He had to find Marie. "Josef!"

The chauffeur didn't answer. Or at least, Brandon didn't hear him. He couldn't hear anything above the roar of his breath and the beat of his heart. "Josef!"

He reached the boxwood. He could move faster on the path's hard, brick surface, but still not fast enough. He approached Main Street and strode through the church's gate.

Marie's second rental was still parked at the curb. The black shadow of his town car hulked behind it. A man stood behind the town car, raised the car's trunk.

"Josef?"

The man bent down and picked up a large object. Something wrapped in a blanket or a bag. The way he strained, Brandon could see it was heavy. The package seemed to move. The man dumped it in the trunk.

No. Not a package… A body.

Marie.

Josef slammed the trunk and looked up at Brandon.

Brandon raced for the car. Pain shot up his leg. He gritted this teeth and pushed faster.

The chauffeur jumped in the driver's seat. The engine hummed to life.

Brandon reached the curb. He slammed into the passenger door and grabbed at the door handle. But the car jolted into gear. It shot away from the curb, tires screeching.

The door swung open under Brandon's hand. He ran, trying to keep up, trying to jump inside. His legs faltered.

The door handle ripped from his grasp. He staggered and fell to his knees in the street.

The taillights faded into the distance.

Chapter Seventeen

She had to find a way out.

Marie pulled in the moist air of her own breath into her lungs. The bag he'd slipped over her head and shoulders clung tightly to her skin. Duct tape cut into her wrists and ankles. She fought the need to scream. It wouldn't do any good. Once he'd taped her hands and feet, he'd stuffed a gag into her mouth and secured it with more tape before replacing the bag. The gag wouldn't allow her to make much noise. Not enough for anyone to hear.

All she could do was thump her feet against the wall of the trunk, and even then she didn't have enough space to get power into her kick.

Josef.

She'd heard his voice when she'd kicked him. His accent. The strange language he spoke with a fluent tongue. She still couldn't believe he was doing this. She couldn't understand it. He'd seemed so meek, so courteous. Why would he want to hurt her? What had she ever done to him?

She could feel the car slow beneath her. She could feel it turn. More driving, over loose gravel this time. Around twists and bends. Finally the motion stopped.

A door slammed. Footsteps moved to the back of the car. The trunk lock clicked its release. Cool air rushed over Marie's sweat-slick skin. The crash of waves against rock whipped on the wind.

His rough hand gripped her arm. He pulled her to a sitting position, strong fingers bruising her flesh.

She didn't know what he planned to do, but she wasn't going to let him do it easily. She twisted her body, wrenching from his grasp. Flopping back down in the trunk, she lashed out with her feet.

She hit something solid.

A grunt broke from his lips, followed by swearing in that other language. He gripped her arm again. His fist crashed down on her neck and shoulder.

Breath shuddered from her lungs. For a moment, she couldn't think, couldn't move. Pain shuddered through her.

He lifted her from the trunk and slung her over his shoulder.

A whimper stuck in Marie's throat. She swallowed it back. She couldn't give in. She wouldn't.

She willed her mind to clear, willed the pain to fade. She wasn't strong enough to fight him. And trying wasn't going to get her anything but hurt…or killed. She had to be smarter. Had to strike when she could make it matter. *If* she could make it matter.

He walked on, her body swaying on his shoulder with each stride. The scent of water rode the wind along with the sound of the lapping waves. Then Josef stopped. She heard a lock rattle. Her body brushed against what felt like the jamb of a door. His heavy footfalls moved over what sounded like a marble floor.

Drake House.

She'd heard Brandon calling her name in the grave-yard, even though she couldn't answer loud enough for him to hear. He must still be at the chapel. Without Josef, without the car, he'd have no way to get back to Drake House. No way to help her until it was too late.

She had to find a way out of this on her own.

Stairs creaked. She could feel the sensation of moving upward. He was taking her upstairs. To do what? She tried to think, tried to stay calm. There had to be a way to escape. There had to.

"You kick again, I beat your head." His voice was low, dead, as if bled of any emotion, any humanity.

He lowered her down, letting her fall the last two feet to the parquet floor.

Oxygen rushed from her lungs. She tried to breathe, but took in dust. She coughed and sputtered.

He pulled her up to a sitting position and yanked the bag off her head. Without saying a word, he strode out of the room.

She blinked against the light. She didn't recognize the room at first, but the molding along the ceiling and the carved woodwork proved they were in Drake House. The room smelled dusty, as if it hadn't been used in a long time. She focused on the trees outside the uncov-ered window. The room was facing the south side of the house, away from the water. She blinked her eyes. Her vision cleared. Details came into focus. Animals circled the room, carved into the moldings. They rimmed the fireplace mantel. They had to be in the nursery.

Josef thunked back into the room. Rugs and paper and broken sticks of furniture overflowed his arms. He dropped them near the front bank of windows. He walked back out, returning with another armload, as if he was raiding whatever he could find and piling it in here.

As if he was building a bonfire.

Marie's throat constricted. She struggled to breathe around the gag. She had to think. Clearly she couldn't fight Josef. Not only was she tied, but he was twice as strong. She'd found that out the hard way. But maybe she could talk to him. Reason with him. Convince him that she was a person, too, that he couldn't just burn her like trash.

She offered a pleading look and made a noise deep in her throat, words impossible to squeeze past the rag jamming her mouth.

"You have something to say?"

She fought the urge to flinch from the harshness of his voice. Instead, she forced her head to nod.

He stepped beside her. Grabbing the duct tape, he ripped it from her lips.

Her skin burned. The room blurred with tears. She coughed, spitting the rag onto the floor. "Why are you doing this?"

He looked at her as if he didn't understand the question.

"I've never done anything to you," she said. "I never would."

"I am not doing this to you."

Marie stared at him. His words made no sense. "Of course you're doing it to me. You're hurting me right now."

He shook his head as if she were the one speaking gibberish. "I am doing it to him. Like he did to me. I am paying him back." As if that was all he needed to say, he turned and plodded from the room.

There was only one "him" Marie could think of, but

it didn't make sense. Why would Josef want to hurt Brandon? Nothing the chauffeur was saying or doing made sense. She twisted, looking around the room. She had to find a way out.

Her gaze landed on the old radiator along the wall. It was made of metal. Some pieces of it might even be sharp. It was her only chance.

She pushed herself across the floor, a combination of scooting on the wood and moving her legs like an inchworm. Reaching the radiator, she positioned her back against its warmth and felt the bottom edges with her hands.

Her fingers touched hard edges. Not exactly sharp, but if she had some time, if she could stall, she might be able to rub the tape enough to weaken it. She might be able to set herself free.

She just needed time.

Footsteps stomped in the hall, approaching. Josef bulled through the door, his arms filled with another load. More fuel for his bonfire.

He threw the armful on the pile and turned to stare at her. "You moved."

"I needed to lean against the wall. My back is sore." Marie didn't have to act. The muscles in her back were sore. And with her ankles taped, she had a hard time sitting in the middle of the floor with nothing to lean on.

Josef grunted. He started back to the door.

"Wait!"

He stopped and glared at her.

"You said you were doing this to someone else, not me. That you were paying him back. Who? Who are you paying back? Brandon?"

"Yes, Brandon."

"Why? What did Brandon ever do to you?"

A shadow of something passed over his brutal face. Anger. Sorrow. "He took away my Lala."

Lala? "The woman whose ashes are in the wall vault? She has the tulip on her marker?"

"Lala means tulip. She was my tulip. She and I were to be married. Now she is dead. Murdered."

The fiancée who died. Shelley and Brandon had both mentioned the woman, and how devastated Josef was when she died. "But I thought she was sick. Didn't she die in the hospital?"

"An infection. That's what they said. An infection from the surgery."

She couldn't follow. She knew Brandon provided health insurance to all his employees, just as his father had. She'd grown up on that insurance. So how could Josef blame Brandon for his fiancée's death? "I don't understand. It's not Brandon's fault she died."

He stared at her, his eyes hard, his boxer's nose red with the burst capillaries of a heavy drinker. A man who'd tried to forget. A man in pain. "It is his fault."

She kept rubbing the tape. The man looked as though he was rapidly reaching the end of his patience. She didn't have time to waste. "How?"

"He made her have the surgery." He walked from the room.

Now she was really lost. He wasn't making sense. Why would Brandon make anyone have surgery? Maybe Josef was suffering some kind of psychotic breakdown. Maybe Lala simply had a life-threatening illness and Brandon was there helping Josef through it. Maybe that's why Josef blamed his feelings of helplessness and frustration on Brandon.

She rubbed the tape, pressing it against the iron radiator as hard as she could. Moving it as fast as she could. It wasn't working. The tape was weakening a little, maybe, stretching a little. But it wasn't happening fast enough. She was running out of time.

She groped under the radiator again. There had to be a valve somewhere. Maybe that would give her the sharp edge she needed. She touched something circular, ridged like the serrated edge of a knife, but not as sharp. It would have to do.

The heavy footfalls returned. Josef carried an armful of gossamer draperies, something large and red underneath. He threw the drapes on the pile. Then she saw what else he carried. A fuel can. He twisted off the cover.

The sharp scent of gasoline assaulted Marie's senses. She had to delay him. She needed more time. "There's something I don't understand. Why would Brandon force Lala to have surgery?"

"She needed to pay." His voice growled low with anger. It shook with frustration. "She had no money. I had no money. She needed to pay, and I could not help her."

"She needed to pay what?"

"For coming to this country. She needed to pay. Dr. Janecek would not let her come without the surgery. Without giving something to pay for her passage. He would not let her come to me." A sob broke from his lips, deep and low and full of agony.

The pieces fell into place in Marie's mind. "The human trafficking? The mass grave? Lala was one of the people Janecek smuggled? He forced her to give him an organ to pay for smuggling her into the country?"

Josef made a keening sound low in his throat.

Marie's head hurt. She rubbed the tape harder. Faster. Even though she'd tied the pieces together, what Josef was saying still didn't make sense. "It was Janecek who did those things. It was him who forced Lala to have the surgery. It was him who caused the infection. Why do you keep saying it was Brandon?"

He splashed gasoline on the draperies and rugs. "The Drakes. Brandon and his uncle. I break his uncle's things. I try to make him pay. But he does not care about anything like I care for Lala. Brandon does."

She remembered overhearing Brandon talking to Chief Hammer about some vandalism at his uncle Cliff's. That was Josef? None of this made sense. Why would he target the Drakes? "I don't know about Cliff, but Brandon would never do anything to hurt you."

He shook his head. "He would. He did. I saw the ship. I was brought in, too. Before Lala."

"What ship?"

"A big ship. It said Drake right on the bow."

"The ship used for smuggling?"

"Yes."

"Are you sure?"

"I lost my Lala. I must live alone. I will have no children." He looked at the carved moldings at the top of the nursery walls. Tears wet his rough cheeks. "My life is dead, yet I must live on. Well, if I must, then Brandon Drake must, too. He will know how it feels."

The words she heard in the psychomanteum echoed in Marie's mind. *All Brandon loves will die.* Was Brandon right? Were the people who cared about him marked for death? All to serve Josef's need for revenge?

"Charlotte?" She felt the tape give. Not entirely, but

a little. Her hands trembled and burned. The odor of gasoline stung her eyes. She held Josef's gaze and pushed on. She had to know. "Did you weld the spike near the gas tank? Did you crash Charlotte's car into the wall?"

"Lala came here to marry me. He took my wife. He did not deserve one of his own."

"And my father?"

He stuffed his hands into his pockets and stared down at the floor. "I could not let him tell. I am sorry."

"And now me?"

"You most of all. He loves you like I loved Lala. I cannot let him have you."

"You'll never get away with this. The police will know you did this."

He brought his hands out of his pockets, something in his fist. He looked up at her, his eyes dead. "I am not trying to get away. I am going with you. I am going to be with Lala, where I belong." He struck the match and threw it in the pile.

Chapter Eighteen

Brandon noticed the orange glow in the sky before he could see the house. It pulsated beyond the twisted, bare branches of oak, sycamore and wisps of willow, radiating like the eerie light of a coming storm. He pushed the accelerator harder. The engine of Marie's little rental whined. Its tires jolted over dips in the long drive.

A curve in the drive rushed toward him. Gritting his teeth, he forced his leg to respond. He lifted his foot from the accelerator. Hot pain shot through his thigh and hip, pulsed up his spine. He jammed his left foot to the brake. The little car fishtailed around the turn. He steered into the slide. The car righted itself. Remembering to breathe, he hit the accelerator again.

He'd lost so much time rushing back into the graveyard and finding Marie's purse. Time he couldn't afford to give Josef. But at least he'd found her cell phone and the keys to her car. At least he could call for help. At least he had wheels to get back.

At first he hadn't been sure where the chauffeur would take Marie. Then it came to him. Drake House. He could have killed her in the graveyard. It would have been easier. Cleaner. But his focus wasn't simply on killing her. He wanted to kill her at Drake House. The place where he'd tried to kill her the other times. And where he'd chosen to kill Charlotte.

All Brandon loves will die.

The words were true, just as he'd feared. It was all about him. Not Charlotte. Not Edwin. Not Marie. Whatever Josef had against him was personal. He'd want to do it at Drake House. He'd want to bring it home to Brandon.

The only thing Brandon couldn't figure out was why.

He fishtailed around another bend in the tree-lined drive. The trunk of a sycamore rushed at him. The car door missed the tree by inches.

He stomped on the gas.

He'd been so damn stupid. So stupid. He'd pushed Marie away. He'd tried to make her leave. He'd told himself he was protecting her, shielding her from a killer. But all he'd done was leave her alone and vulnerable. And tonight he'd brought Josef straight to her.

He hadn't protected her at all.

The car broke from the trees. Nothing obscured the fire now. It licked from the front windows of the east wing. Black smoke gushed into the air and engulfed the balcony. It carried on the air and made him choke.

He couldn't be too late. He couldn't.

He stomped the brake and the car skidded to a stop. He shoved his way out the door. He pushed as fast as he could go, jabbing his cane into the ground, pulling his legs along.

He shoved the front door open. Smoke hung in the air, making the grand staircase appear dim and gray. The fire was in the east wing. He'd noticed from outside. The nursery.

He raced over the marble foyer. Clutching the banister, he half pulled himself, half ran to the top of the staircase.

The air grew hot. His eyes stung and watered. Smoke thickened, choking out oxygen, making it hard to see.

He groped through the dark hallways. Low. He had to get low to the floor. The smoke would be thinner there. He could breathe.

He crouched down. It was easier to breathe, but he still couldn't see. Tears streamed down his cheeks. His eyes felt as if they were burning out of his head. He groped the wall as a guide and crawled.

He hoped to God Marie wasn't in the nursery. The way the flames were leaping from the front windows, if she was in that room, she was likely dead.

He couldn't believe that. He wouldn't.

A loud thunk shook the house. A cough rose above the crackle and hiss of fire.

A woman's cough.

Not from the nursery. It came from down the hall. He could swear it.

He crawled faster. His leg screamed with pain, but he didn't care. If he didn't find Marie, if he didn't reach her in time, he didn't care about anything. Not his leg, not getting out of Drake House, not living until tomorrow.

UNABLE TO REMOVE THE TAPE that bound them, Marie dragged her useless legs down the hall. She didn't know where Josef was. Didn't even know if he was alive or swallowed by fire. She'd made her move when he'd thrown the match. Adrenaline, survival instinct, what it was she didn't know. But when the fire flared, sucking the oxygen from the room and imploding glass from the windows, she'd finally ripped the tape free. She'd pulled herself out of the room and down the hall. She'd gotten away.

And she'd taken a wrong turn.

Unthinkingly she'd turned down the hall, racing away from the fire instead of turning back for the staircase. And now she had to find her way back to one of the staircases before she was trapped.

Smoke billowed around her, enfolding her in its gray darkness. She was all turned around. She couldn't see, could hardly breathe.

"Marie!"

She gasped and coughed. How had he gotten here? How had he reached her? Tears ran from her eyes, but not from the smoke. "Brandon! I'm here!"

"Move toward my voice. Stay low."

As if she had a choice. She scooched on her stomach, dragging her legs behind. Along the hall, back toward the heat, the fire. *Toward Brandon.*

A shape came out of the smoke. Brandon? Was he here?

Something smacked the side of her head. Hard.

She slumped forward, her eyes blurring, her ears ringing.

"Marie? Are you okay? What happened?"

No. Josef was here. Josef had found her. And now he would find Brandon. He'd hurt him. He'd kill him. "Brandon! It's Josef! It's—"

Another blow hit her and she couldn't say anything more.

Chapter Nineteen

Brandon could see shapes through the smoke. One crouching, like him. One lying flat on the floor.

Marie.

Growling deep in his throat, he launched himself at the larger hulk. He lashed out with his cane.

The blow connected. Its force shuddered up the teak and into the handle. A masculine grunt rose above the din of the fire.

Brandon swung again, fighting his way forward to Marie.

Josef moved back.

Brandon swung again. This time he missed, his cane whooshing through nothing but smoky air.

Josef slipped around the side of the hall. He circled around behind Brandon.

No.

He couldn't let Josef cut them off from the stairs. The man had a death wish. He must. He never would have stayed in the fire if he hadn't intended to die along with Marie. He would do everything in his power to keep them from escaping. And now that he was between Marie and closest the staircase, he might succeed.

Unless Brandon stopped him.

Brandon struggled to his feet. Swinging the cane in front of him, he crouched low, following Josef down the hall, pushing him back. They reached the nursery door. The heat was intolerable, fiery as a blast oven. The smoke gushed out into the hall, too thick to see through despite the blinding light of the flames behind Josef and the blown-out windows all along the front of the wing.

Brandon's muscles ached, but he kept swinging. "Marie! Get out! If you can hear me, get out now!"

Josef backed up under Brandon's assault, retreating into the nursery.

No, not retreating. He darted to the side and grabbed something from the room. Something long. He swung it at Brandon.

Pain slammed into Brandon's thigh. He blinked back the agony.

The gray shape he knew was Josef drew back its weapon, angling to land another blow. Even though the thick cloud, Brandon could see it was a stick of some sort. A broken piece of furniture.

Josef swung again.

Brandon blocked the blow with his cane. He jumped back, out of the doorway. His leg crumpled under him and he fell to the floor.

A larger crash rumbled through Brandon's head, through the whole of Drake House. The orange flames leaped. The nursery's ceiling closed down on them, falling, crashing. A flaming piece of molding landed on Josef, pinning him to the floor.

His scream ripped through the roar of fire, deep, guttural, full of agony. Flame jumped around him. Heat sucked air from the room.

Brandon scurried back. He couldn't help Josef. But he could still save Marie.

Or die trying.

The fire was hot. So hot. Smoke clogged his throat. Sweat dripped in his eyes.

He closed his eyes and felt his way along the hall back to the spot where he'd left Marie. The trek seemed to take forever. His hands touched nothing but smooth floor and wall moldings. The heat seemed to close in behind him.

His fingers brushed something soft. Silky strands of hair. He ran his hands over her, gripping the wool of her coat.

She stirred.

She was alive. Still alive. "Marie? Can you move? I need to get you out of here."

She made a sound, but he couldn't decipher words. She struggled to her elbows. "Feet."

He ran his hands down her legs. Duct tape affixed her ankles. He couldn't get it off, not without scissors or a knife to cut it. He'd have to carry her. "I got you. I'm going to lift you to my shoulder. I need you to hang on. Can you do that?"

He felt her nod.

He hefted her to one shoulder. She helped him shift her body into a fireman's carry position, slung over his shoulders and behind his neck. She locked her hands around his left arm. He threaded his right between her bound legs. They had to move.

Slowly, too slowly, he crawled down the hall. The nursery was engulfed in flame now, the air in the hallway too thick to breathe, the heat too intense to slow down.

Josef's screams had stopped.

Brandon pushed the chauffeur from his mind. He had to focus. He had to get Marie and himself out, or they would suffer the same fate as Josef.

He made his way down the staircase, half stumbling, half falling. He forced his feet to carry them across the marble foyer. He pushed his way outside.

Sirens screamed from the highway.

Brandon staggered to the lawn and fell to his knees. He released Marie's legs and lowered her to the cool grass.

She looked up at him, her face streaked with soot and tears. Her eyes red and swollen. Bruises bloomed on her delicate cheek. "Josef?"

"Dead."

She swallowed, flinching as if the action was painful. Her throat must be as swollen from the smoke as his. No, more swollen since she had breathed it longer.

"Police are on their way. Probably fire, too. Para-medics."

"I'm okay."

"No, you're not. Me, either. But we will be."

"You were right. Josef was trying to destroy every-thing you love. Charlotte, my father, me, Drake House." Her voice sounded choked. She swallowed hard and went on. "His fiancée was one of the people Dr. Janecek smuggled into the country. She died from an infection after the surgery."

It was a sad story. A tragic story. But it didn't explain a thing. "What does all that have to do with me?"

"He said she was smuggled into the country aboard a Drake ship."

"Drake Enterprises? A cargo ship or the yacht?"

She moved one shoulder as if trying to shrug. Flinching from pain, she aborted the move. "He said the name *Drake* was on the bow."

"Damn. I'll have to talk to Cliff about that. And Detective McClellan."

"Josef tried to hurt Cliff, too. The vandalism."

He nodded. The surest way to hurt Cliff was to destroy his toys. And the surest way to hurt Brandon was…

He felt sick. His throat ached, not just from the smoke. "I brought him right to you. He wouldn't have even known you were at the chapel graveyard except I asked him to drive me there."

Marie reached a hand to him. She traced her fingers over his face, his cheek, his scar. "It's not your fault. You couldn't have known."

"Maybe not about Josef, but I should have known enough to keep you by my side. To never let you go." He hadn't let himself think of it. Not since he'd seen her purse on the cemetery lawn. But he knew that was his mistake. That had been his mistake all along. "I've wanted you so long, Marie, that once I had you in my arms again, all I could think about was losing you. I couldn't let myself believe we could be together. It just felt too…"

"Fragile."

He nodded. And *he'd* felt fragile. Raw. Exposed. Vulnerable. "I didn't see until I lost you. I didn't understand until…"

"It's okay."

He shook his head. He had to explain this. He had to

make her see. "When I lost you, all I could think about was how I threw my chance away. Again. Our chance to be together."

Police cars flew into the clearing and screeched to stops in the yard. Another siren screamed up the drive. Lights flashed red against the bare trees. A fire truck barreled toward the house. Another screamed out at the highway.

He looked back to Marie. He had to finish. He had to make her see that he understood. He needed to know if she could forgive him. If she could trust him again. If she could love him. "I get it now. I understand. I can't protect myself from losing you. If you're here or in Michigan or halfway around the world, it's going to feel the same. It's going to destroy me."

Tears streamed down her face and sparkled in the fire's radiant glow. "You're not going to lose me, Brandon. I'm here. I love you. And I'm not going anywhere."

They were the most beautiful words he'd ever heard, and he soaked them up and held them in his heart. "I want to spend the rest of my ordinary moments loving you, Marie."

"Oh, Brandon. I—"

He hovered a finger over her lips. "Let me talk. I need to say this." It might not be poetic. He was sure it wouldn't be. But he had to say it. And he needed her to hear.

She nodded.

"I want all that stuff you were talking about. All that ordinary stuff, every day for the rest of our lives." He swallowed into a burning throat. "However long that will be."

A smile curved her lips. "It will be long, Brandon.

We'll have children and they'll have their own children. We'll grow old together."

More beautiful words. And looking into her eyes, he believed them. He knew from now on, he always would.

MARIE WATCHED LEXIE'S WORKERS bustle into the ballroom, hauling armfuls of the most luxurious poinsettias she'd ever seen, the first step in getting the room ready for the Drake Foundation's Christmas Ball. She was so glad they were going through with the ball. It seemed right. A fitting tribute to her father and to Charlotte. And a sign of the life and vibrancy she and Brandon intended to bring back to Drake House.

The cleaning crews had been amazing. She could barely smell the smoke from the east wing fire. And Lexie's plan of filling the room with pots of flowers to add more freshness to the air should take care of the problem nicely.

Even Isabella and Shelley had pitched in long hours without complaint. And although Marie was still a little guarded around the two of them, she felt they'd reached some kind of truce. Shelley had even warmed to her after their talk in the kitchen that night. Isabella had focused her romantic ambitions fully on Brandon's uncle Cliff. And even though Ned Perry was still out there buying up land for condos, the fact that he wasn't killing people to get it made Marie feel a lot more charitable toward him as well.

It was the season for giving, after all.

And now it was the season for deciding what she thought of Lexie's new ideas for decorating the ballroom before her friend came down from the balcony and demanded her verdict. But try as she might, she was having a heck of a time looking around the ballroom and making the sketches Lexie had shown her come to life in her mind's eye.

Marie tilted her head to the side, despite the residual soreness in her neck, and studied the mantle of the ballroom's grand fireplace. She just didn't have the talent for design that her friend had. Or the good taste of her father, for that matter. Although Lexie had explained her plans for garlands around the glass doors, a evergreen swag and candles on the fireplace mantel and a lighting effect that would look like snow falling from the sky, Marie couldn't see it. And she didn't want to let her friend down.

Brandon walked up beside her and slipped an arm around her shoulder. "What is it?"

"Lexie wants to know what I think of her plans."

"So what do you think?"

"I don't know. She knows this stuff better than I do. I wish she wouldn't ask me. I trust whatever she decides will look great."

"Then tell her that."

"I tried. She said she always ran things by my father. She wants my opinion."

"Tell her it will look beautiful."

"Unless I can really imagine it, she'll know I'm just saying the words."

"I think it's beautiful. In fact, I think it's absolutely perfect." But he wasn't looking at the mantel or the mirror above. He was staring straight at her.

She backhanded him in the ribs.

"Ow."

"Yeah, that hurt. Sure."

"Okay. It didn't hurt. But I like tickling better. Or kissing."

She let out a sigh. She couldn't help but smile. After all they'd been through, they'd finally found a way to be together. To share their love. To live their lives. Every ordinary minute they had left. "I'm happy."

"Are you?" Brandon gave her a grin. "I'm glad. I'm happy, too."

"I only wish…"

"What?"

"That my father was here. That he could see Lexie's plans. That he could let us know what he thinks."

Brandon's grin softened. He rubbed her arm gently with his fingertips. "You want his approval."

"Yes."

"You're not just talking about the Christmas decorations, are you?"

A tingling sensation stole over her. "No. I guess I'm not."

He leaned down and kissed her, light and gentle, a confirmation of their love and a promise of more love to come. "I have something for you." He took her left hand in his and slipped something onto her finger.

Marie held her breath. She lifted her hand and studied the ring.

It was a marquis solitaire diamond on a platinum band, sleek, classic, beautiful. And bigger than any diamond she'd ever seen. Not his mother's ring, but a new one. A fresh one. A ring just for her. "I love it."

He leaned on his cane. He grimaced as he lowered himself to a knee. "To make it official, you know."

Her throat felt thick. "I would love to marry you."

He shook his head. "You have to wait until I ask."

"Then ask, already." She couldn't help being impatient. She'd waited ten years for this. But the ten years had been worth it to see his smile now. To feel his unreserved happiness. To bask in happiness of her own.

"I love you, Marie Leonard. And I would be honored and humbled if you would agree to be my wife."

Marie smiled and nodded, unsure her voice would work.

He crooked his eyebrows. "Is that a yes? Because my leg is killing me."

She gripped his arm and pulled him to his feet. "It's a yes. Always and forever a yes."

He gave her a peck on the lips and glanced around the ballroom, watching the workers carry in another round of colorful plants. "I think Edwin would be happy. I think he would heartily approve." He kissed her, longer this time, deeper, and when he finished, he held her close against his side.

Marie's eyes misted. They had wonderful days ahead, wonderful years. And with luck, children to fill the new nursery that would rise from the old nursery's ashes. Rebuilt with detail and care to match the rest of Drake House.

She blinked back the tears and looked into the mirror above the mantel. Suddenly Lexie's decorating plans came alive in her imagination. Greenery draped on the mantel. Candles of different heights rose gracefully, their flames reflected in the glass. Light drifted through the ballroom like floating flakes of snow. Perfect.

And deep in the mirror's antique silvered glass, as real as her happiness, she could see her father's smile.

* * * * *

CHRISTMAS DELIVERY

BY
PATRICIA ROSEMOOR

Patricia Rosemoor has always had a fascination with dangerous love. She loves bringing a mix of thrills and chills and romance to Intrigue readers. She's won a Golden Heart from Romance Writers of America and Reviewers' Choice and Career Achievement Awards from *RT Book Reviews*. She teaches Writing Popular Fiction and Suspense-Thriller Writing in the Fiction Writing department of Columbia College Chicago. Check out her website, www.patriciarosemoor.com. You can contact Patricia via e-mail at Patricia@ PatriciaRosemoor.com.

Since the theme of *Christmas Delivery* has to do with getting justice for the evil that is done to others, I would like to dedicate the book to the relentless Task Force that, after three years, identified and arrested my father's murderer using DNA evidence.

Prologue

Christmas Eve, thirteen years ago

Wind howled along the Chesapeake and drove a stinging wall of snow at Simon Shea, virtually blinding him. Somehow he made it off the road and into the woods, where the unusually fierce winter storm abated some. Dropping his duffel bag, he stopped for a moment and leaned against the trunk of a pine to catch his breath. He could hardly move, could hardly think, what with weather conditions that threatened to ruin his carefully made plans.

Even in the woods, the wind haunted him, moaning and rattling ice-covered tree branches overhead. Geared up to get free of Jenkins Cove—to get away from his drunk of a father, from his cold, bitter life—he had to do it tonight.

Thank God, Lexie was coming with him.

That's all Simon had been thinking about since convincing her to run the night before, as they lay together, snug in their wooded shelter, his angular body protectively wrapped around her soft one. Being with her…starting a new life together…waking up happy with her in his arms every morning for the rest of their lives—they were the best Christmas presents in the world!

She'd hesitated at first and he'd understood her arguments. They were awfully young to go off on their own. She hadn't finished high school yet. And what about college? But Simon had sworn that he would protect her and provide for her and find a way for her to do everything she ever wanted. She'd smiled at him then—that crooked, heart-wrenching, only-for-him smile that had made him fall for her in the first place—and he'd known everything was going to be all right.

He'd better get going. Didn't want to be late. Didn't want to scare Lexie into thinking he'd gotten cold feet. They were to meet behind the church at half-past midnight to start their new life together on Christmas morning.

Picking up the duffel bag, he decided to stay off the main road and take the shortcut through the woods into town. Luckily, he knew those woods like the back of his hand. Every path, every detour around danger. There were a couple of swampy areas the locals stayed away from. They could trap a man, suck him down and bury him alive. Not much different than living with Rufus Shea, Simon thought, fighting guilt that he was leaving his old man alone. He just couldn't take it anymore—couldn't take being caregiver to a drunk who'd given up—not when he could start a decent life with Lexie.

Simon was so engrossed in thoughts of their future, that at first he didn't hear the approaching sounds until they exploded through the trees.

A series of shouts raised the short hairs on the back of his neck and made his pulse jag. He stopped dead in his tracks. What the hell was going on?

He looked around in confusion, caught blurred movement through the trees and zeroed in on a kid flying through the woods as if his life depended on it.

Another teenager, younger than him, Simon thought, heart

thumping against his ribs now. Snow dusted the mop of curly pale hair. The kid wasn't dressed for the cold; he had on only a thin leather jacket and ripped jeans. He was no one Simon recognized.

Still, something made him call out to the terrified kid. "Hey! You need help?"

But the kid threw a fast, panicked look behind him and kept running until a whine shattered the quiet. Then he led with his chest, head and arms flung back as his body snapped into an impossible arch before he fell first to his knees, then face forward onto the snow-covered ground.

Not knowing whether he should see if he could help the kid or run for town, Simon hesitated a moment.

His mistake.

Chapter One

Turning the Drake House ballroom into a winter wonderland for the annual Christmas charity ball should make her happier, Lexie Thornton thought. The main room in the west wing was two stories high, with a balcony off the second-floor parlors, and nearly one hundred feet long, fifty wide. Doors with glass insets lined one wall, leading to an outside balcony with a view of the gardens and the Chesapeake Bay beyond. Decorating the mansion for the ball was quite a feat and would take several days to complete.

Lexie pushed up the sleeves of her sweater, looked around the ballroom, then glanced down to her laptop to review the design she'd planned out.

"Hey, Lexie, where do we put these?"

She looked up to see two of her garden shop workers hauling in large poinsettia plants, each planter encased in red or green foil and wrapped with a huge gold bow. "Just set them in an area free of drafts for now."

Today would be devoted to the basics—dividing the ballroom with its gleaming wood floors and trim into several distinct areas for dancing and socializing over drinks and displaying the silent auction items. Virtually the whole town of

Jenkins Cove would show up for the ball, and Lexie would make the most of every inch of available space.

That she would be responsible for giving so many people pleasure didn't bring a smile to her face. Ironic that Christmas was so important to Thornton Garden Center, the family business that she now ran. Her parents both still worked there, but in more relaxed capacities. They were both retirement age, but refused to retire, saying it would make them feel old. Decorating public areas as well as private estates and businesses for Christmas brought in a solid portion of the year's income, so Lexie couldn't hide from the holiday.

Call her the Christmas Grinch, especially since the ball and the silent auction would raise money for the Drake Foundation, which supported several local charities. This included one that helped impoverished single mothers and their children—a cause dear to Lexie's heart, since she was a single mother herself.

Frowning at the further reminder of why Christmas always made her so sad, she looked for her best friend.

Marie Leonard stood in front of the fireplace, the focal point of the room, and stared into the large, antique mirror hanging over the mantel. When she turned away from the mirror, her expression went beyond happy—she was glowing, actually, so that the color in her cheeks intensified the chestnut color of her hair. For the first time since she'd returned to Jenkins Cove after her father's death, Marie seemed at peace.

Lexie was happy for her dear friend, who was about to start a new life. Marie was madly in love with Brandon Drake, owner of this estate, and their engagement was to be officially announced at the ball. Which Lexie would be forced to attend, making her relive her loss all over again.

Christmas Eve…

Thirteen years and she wasn't over the heartbreak.

Thirteen years ago, instead of meeting her behind the church as planned, Simon had gotten himself killed in an accident taking the shortcut through the woods. Even after all this time, thinking about it brought a lump to her throat and a tightness in her chest.

"Hey, those are gorgeous plants," Marie said, crossing to her.

"Thanks. Gorgeous plants for a gorgeous room."

Though Lexie tried to inject enthusiasm into her voice, she knew she failed when Marie gave her that look that told her if she wanted to talk, Marie was there for her. Not that Lexie was planning to take her friend up on that. She didn't want to talk about Simon anymore, didn't want to think about him, didn't want to remember...only, considering the circumstances, how could she ever forget?

Before Marie could try to force the conversation, noise from the foyer had the other woman turning toward the entry. "Ah, the caterer has arrived. I need to talk to her, see what final selections she made for the buffet." She moved in that direction, glancing back at Lexie to say, "But don't imagine *you're* home free."

Lexie groaned at her friend's implied threat. Then she got back to work, referring to the checklist and the decorating design on her laptop to see where she was.

Dozens of poinsettias had been brought in. Hopefully, she'd planned enough plants and greenery for the ballroom to help improve the air quality. The fire that had damaged the east wing of Drake House had left a thick stench that was difficult to mask, despite the clean-up efforts of a professional crew. Later, she would add dozens of pots of mums and gerbera daisies to the decor—both would help purify the air.

The first order of business was to distribute the poinsettias the way she'd mapped them out in the room. So she spent the next hour with her landscape workers, making sure every plant was in its proper place. Then she had her workers fetch the mantel swag and the garlands that would be hung around every door—a time-consuming job, but one that would help transform the old mansion for the season.

A familiar laugh echoed from the entranceway. Lexie went to investigate the foyer, where the master staircase split upward to each wing. Well, one wing now. The private wing was unlivable because part of the roof had collapsed during a fire, so it was cordoned off and would be for some time to come. Marie and Brandon were occupying rooms in the public wing and the servants were all housed off grounds.

In the foyer, Lexie found Marie with Chelsea Caldwell, looking soft and lovely in a white cashmere sweater and matching beret, and her fiancé, Michael Bryant.

"For the silent auction," the blonde said, handing Marie a painting.

"Oh, nice." Marie waved Lexie over.

A quick look and Lexie's brows shot up. Chelsea had painted a view of Jenkins Creek. While water was a good part of the canvas, the focus was the dueling estates perched on points that faced each other—Drake House on one side and the Manor at Drake Acres on the other. Brandon had inherited the older estate from his father, Jonathan. Always competitive, his uncle Cliff, the younger of the brothers, had built what he'd considered a bigger and better estate.

"Hmm, I have a feeling I know who will be bidding against each other on this item." Knowing Cliff, Lexie thought he would pay any amount to keep the piece from his nephew.

"That was the idea," Chelsea admitted. "More money for charity."

"You would have had bidders competing against each other no matter which painting you donated," Michael murmured, pulling her closer.

Chelsea blushed and grinned and Lexie noted the diamond ring on the other woman's left hand. So the engagement was official. Lexie quickly looked away.

"Rumor has it you have a new book contract," Marie said to Michael.

But it was Chelsea who enthusiastically said, "Michael is going to write a fictional account of the human trafficking that went on here for decades."

"All names changed to protect the innocent," Michael promised.

"Congratulations," Lexie said, zeroing her attention onto one of her workers waving to her. "I need to get back to work. I'll see you both at the ball."

Seeing how right Chelsea and Michael were for each other, as were Brandon and Marie, Lexie felt a sharp pang of longing. Would *she* ever find someone to love, to share things with again?

Would she ever have a second chance at a real life?

It was that idea of wanting a second chance that finally convinced Lexie to accept Marie's dare to try the psychomanteum at the House of Seven Gables, the bed-and-breakfast run by Chelsea's aunt, Sophie Caldwell. Marie had tried to push Lexie into doing it before, but pragmatic Lexie had resisted.

Since she'd ridden out to Drake House in one of the garden center's trucks with her workers, Marie drove her into town. They left the car in the parking lot near the church and walked the short distance to the B&B, which was situated on the harbor.

"I just wish you the same happiness I rediscovered with Brandon." The sun had set and Marie pulled her wool coat closer. "I never thought it would happen, but it did. Who's to say it can't happen for you? You just have to learn to let go."

"Katie is my life."

"I didn't mean let go of *her,* just…"

"I know. But every time I look into her eyes, I see Simon. Maybe I'm not meant to be with anyone else."

Maybe that's why her life consisted of running the family business and raising her twelve-year-old daughter. Period. No time off for good behavior.

"Or maybe you've just decided to protect yourself against potential loss," Marie said. "You don't know what will happen in that room. Maybe you'll learn the truth about what happened to Simon. Isn't that worth the risk? The truth can give you peace. And then you can move on. You can't protect yourself from love forever, Lexie. Love is a *good* thing. Simon wouldn't want you to be alone. He would want you to find someone to fulfill you as a woman, as well as a mother."

Lexie sighed. "Now you're romanticizing."

"You could *use* a little romanticizing. If only you could commune with Simon, perhaps you could let him go, move on to someone new. It's more than time, Lexie."

"When you're right, you're right."

No use arguing with Marie when she got an idea into her head.

Lexie figured that giving in to her friend's insistence that she visit the psychomanteum was romantic enough for anyone. Basically, she'd agreed in order to get Marie to stop fretting over her. And, she had to admit, there was something else.

Even though she wasn't a believer, a little part of her wished she could see Simon one last time….

They circled the House of the Seven Gables with its long, two-story porch. The bed-and-breakfast faced the harbor and was situated directly across from a seafood restaurant, a prime stopping place for tourists who came to sail or take boat rides to see the waterfront estates.

As they turned the corner, the wind whipped up with an odd wail and Lexie pulled the front of her brown suede Sherpa jacket closed against the chill. The wind out of nowhere and the late afternoon mist coming off the water seemed to be omens of some kind.

Either that or her imagination was working overtime.

The long building of white clapboard had dormer windows under the gabled roof. Lexie quickly took the steps up to the front door, Marie following. The Christmas wreath hanging there was decorated with miniature duck decoys, small sailboats and Maryland crabs. Lexie couldn't take credit for the unusual holiday decor. Sophie Caldwell had her own unique ideas.

Like the psychomanteum.

"Ah, there you are," Sophie said when they entered the hall.

Just coming out of the office, the owner of the B&B retied the lace-trimmed apron covering her dark skirt. Attached to her green blouse was a pin as striking as the porch decorations— Rudolph the reindeer, his red nose blinking on and off. As usual, her graying blond hair was pulled into a neat bun at the nape of her neck, and a gentle smile played over her lips.

"Sorry we're late," Marie said. "But Chelsea stopped by with her painting for the auction, and I guess we lost track of time."

At the mention of her niece, Sophie beamed. "Is that all?" She looked to Lexie. "I was afraid that you'd changed your mind."

"Hard to do when someone's twisting your arm behind your back," Lexie muttered.

Sophie checked Lexie's arm as if expecting to see it in Marie's grasp. Then she shook her head and said, "Can I get you girls something? Tea and some fresh cookies?"

"Oh, no, not for me." A spiraling sensation Lexie defined as pure fear shot through her, making her stomach cramp at the thought of food. "Just the…um…"

"Upstairs," Sophie said kindly, then turned to Marie. "While you wait, you and I can have a nice catch-up in the kitchen, dear."

"Sure," Marie said, though she was staring at Lexie as if for a cue.

"Go." Lexie shushed her off and headed for the stairs. "I need to do this alone anyway."

Before she could talk herself out of it, Lexie proceeded up to the third floor and headed down the hallway, stopping only in front of the door to the psychomanteum. This was just plain silly. A pragmatic person, Lexie didn't succumb to flights of fancy. Why, then, did she feel as if her limbs were made of lead?

Taking a deep breath, she opened the door and stepped into the room whose ceiling was painted black and whose walls were hung with black curtains. Her heart was beating double time and her stomach was knotting as she looked around. A chair in the middle of the room faced an ornately framed mirror that leaned against a wall. Chests and small tables around the room held candles of various sizes. Lexie dimmed the ceiling fixture and the room immediately became spookier.

Her legs felt like rubber as she moved to the chair and sat facing the mirror.

Now what?

She supposed she should light the candles, but it was as if something had a grip on her and she couldn't move. The back of her neck prickled and her breath came harsh and she had to force it through stiff lips.

Stop it… This is silly!

It was. Really. And yet she couldn't make herself leave. She sat there, frozen, staring into the mirror. She let her own image go out of focus and instead thought of Simon as she had last seen him—tall and rangy, shaggy light brown hair framing a rugged face and heavy-lidded deep green eyes.

"Simon, why did you have to die?" she whispered, her stomach churning. "Why did you have to leave me?"

Questions she'd asked the ether over and over again through the years, especially when she'd learned that she was pregnant and again after having a baby she'd vowed to raise on her own.

She got no answers. Not then. Not now.

She concentrated harder.

Remembered the first time Simon had pulled her braids and teased her when she was six.

Remembered the first time he'd pushed a bully away from her when she was eleven.

Remembered the first time he'd kissed her when she was fifteen.

So many memories, each one treasured, never to be forgotten, all to be taken out and examined at will, usually when the loneliness got to her. Times when she found it hard to believe he was dead at all. Surely part of her would have died with him!

She'd never felt lonelier than now, when her vow was to leave all those memories behind and go on. To make new ones. Maybe to meet someone she could love who wasn't Simon Shea.

Could she do it?

"Simon, if you can…if it's possible…come back to me now, even if only for a moment. Assure me that I can trust the future. Let me say goodbye properly."

Not just by spilling tears over his grave.

For years, she'd dreamed of Simon. Dreamed of the first and only time they'd slept together. Dreamed that they'd run away together as they'd planned. Dreamed that he wasn't dead at all, but was by her side, raising their daughter.

Dreamed that she was happy when she was anything but.

Could she abandon her dream world to the real one and trust that if she found someone new to love he wouldn't leave her alone and brokenhearted as Simon had? Could Simon reassure her that wouldn't happen?

No matter how hard she tried to see her ghostly love in the mirror, no matter how much she needed to do so, Lexie simply couldn't.

Her anxiety receded.

Her stomach leveled.

Her heart slowed to a normal beat.

"Goodbye, then," she whispered and left the room.

She raced downstairs to the kitchen where Marie and Sophie were laughing and scooping cookies off metal baking sheets. They looked up and when Marie's gaze met Lexie's, her expression fell. "No luck?" she asked.

Lexie shook her head. "Thanks anyway, Sophie." To Marie she said, "I need to get home, so I'll see you tomorrow."

"Wait, I'll drive you."

"No need. I could use a run."

Lexie was already backpedaling out of the kitchen. She practically ran from the B&B out into a pea-soup fog. Slowing, she felt for the stairs, then once on solid ground picked up her pace once more.

She hadn't been kidding about needing a run—she felt as if she were being chased by memories—but took it slower than she might have because of the fog. The boots she wore were practical for her work, but not for running. Jogging parallel to town, she waited until she could steer clear of the shops and anyone she knew and then crossed over to the other side.

Avoiding Thornton Garden Center and any employees still around who might detain her, she zigzagged the few blocks to a gravel road that fronted a couple of properties, including her own. The house was closer to the water than the road.

Taking the shortcut through the woods, Lexie once more got that weird feeling she'd had when forcing herself into the psychomanteum. Her pulse was racing and her stomach cramping.

Man, she'd really spooked herself! There was no reason to fear crossing through the familiar woods.

So why did she?

The pines seemed to close in on her and the wind whistled a message she couldn't understand.

A warning?

Weird things had been going on in Jenkins Cove, but not around here. And they were over. The criminals were dead or behind bars.

So why did she get the distinct feeling that danger lurked right around the corner?

"Thank you, Marie," she muttered. Her friend had opened her to unrealistic expectations. It was her own fault that she was turning them into something else.

Slowing to a stop, she stooped over to catch her breath. And regain her sanity. She took a moment to look around, peer deep into the surrounding fog.

There was nothing threatening her other than her own imagination.

No danger.

No nothing.

Or was there?

A rustle was followed by ghostly movement deep in the woods.

A deer, Lexie told herself. Just a deer.

Even so, she backed off, toward the house, her gaze pinned to the very spot through the trees where she'd seen something…

Only when she was just about there did the fog shift for a moment.

And for a moment—just that moment she had wished for—Simon Shea stared back at her.

Chapter Two

Simon pulled back, making himself invisible a moment too late. An expert tactical fighter, he should have known better than to expose himself like that.

He'd simply wanted to get closer.

With senses honed sharper than the average person's, he watched her ghostlike figure through the fog as she gazed around, seeming alarmed. And confused. She continued on her way, faster now, every so often glancing over her shoulder as if her nerves had gotten the better of her. As if she were expecting to see him there, behind her.

But was it *him* that she'd seen?

Had she actually recognized him?

Doubtful, he thought. He wasn't the boy who'd left Jenkins Cove all those years ago. He'd matured. Had bulked up. Had grown harder. Though the last wasn't necessarily something she would notice, at least not at a distance. But both time and a life working as a mercenary had changed him.

He might have grown harder—a requisite for his survival— but the moment he'd spotted Lexie coming from the dock area, Simon had known he still had a soft spot for the girl he'd been forced to abandon. He'd recognized her tall, graceful form immediately, and a closer look made him feel as if time had stood still. Her dark hair was as long and as thick as ever, her skin as pale and smooth, her gray eyes as large and inviting. And though she wore a sheepskin jacket, he had a sense of familiar curves more lush than ever.

Wanting to know more about the woman Lexie Thornton had become, Simon hadn't been able to stop himself from following her.

He hadn't meant to scare her, but of course he had. Too familiar with the vibes put out by fear—mostly people who'd feared *him*—he could sense what Lexie was feeling and therefore was extra careful not to repeat his mistake.

He didn't want her to know he was here in town, at least not yet.

He didn't want anyone in Jenkins Cove to know.

Until he learned the truth about what had happened to him thirteen years ago, he wanted to remain a ghost.

Only after seeing the news flash about a mass grave found a couple of miles outside of the town proper—and that those buried there had had their organs harvested—did he realize that he had to return to Maryland and learn how he'd ended up in some third world country bearing arms. He'd been a victim of human trafficking as much as any of the victims in that grave. The only difference was that he was still alive.

At least his body was.

Before the media had its field day with the story, he'd been wandering the States, aimless, having freed himself at last from the company that had controlled his life for so long. Employment as a soldier in a private army had its financial rewards, however, and when he'd left, he'd had more money than he'd needed.

What he hadn't had was a life.

Not that he'd come here to reclaim his. Simon knew it was

too late for that. In more than a decade working for Shadow Ops, a private military company hired by the CIA to run "peace-keeping" operations in third world countries, he'd done things he'd never imagined doing. Like the time a month into his enforced service when, after delivering medical supplies to a village in Somalia, he'd been surrounded by an angry mob. He'd thought he could bluff his way past them and back to his unit, until he'd been caught from behind and a man with a knife came at him. If he hadn't reacted fast, Simon would have been stabbed to death.

In the end, the assailant lay dead, the one who'd held him wounded. Afterward he didn't even remember what had happened. It was only much later that he'd reacted to his first kill.

He'd been brought to his knees, his stomach emptying.

The dead man's ghost had haunted him day and night for months afterward.

Eventually, Simon had hardened himself against the reality of war, the only way he could deal with it, since violence had quickly become a way of life.

Just because he finally freed himself of that life didn't cleanse him of what he'd been forced to do. He couldn't escape his past, and he wouldn't wish himself on any other human being, certainly not on a woman he'd once loved.

His jaw tightened at his reaction to seeing Lexie again.

She reached a house set in a semicircular stand of pines. It was a neat two-story with an upper deck overlooking the woods. Did she get to the deck from her bedroom? Suddenly imagining himself on the bed there with her, Simon cursed. What was he thinking? She was probably married with a couple of kids. No room for someone like him in her life.

Unlocking the front door, Lexie stepped halfway inside before turning again to look his way. Even protected by the deepening woods and fog, Simon slid behind a tree and leaned his back against it. He closed his eyes for a moment and cursed himself for following her.

Now Lexie would be afraid because of him.

He'd never meant for that to happen.

He simply hadn't been able to help himself. He'd had to follow her, would have to learn everything he could about her and her life.

His mistake.

Again.

Because now Simon knew something irrefutable, something that would only bring him more misery, more heartache, something he didn't want to admit, didn't want to think about.

Thirteen years might as well have been thirteen days.

He was still in love with Lexie Thornton.

WEIRDED OUT thinking she'd seen Simon, Lexie hovered around the door and every few seconds looked out the window. But if anyone had truly been out there, he was gone now.

What had she really seen?

Nothing had happened in the psychomanteum, but what if the effects had followed her and once she'd relaxed...

Had she really seen Simon's ghost?

Was it possible?

Or was her mind playing tricks on her because she'd been thinking about him so intently?

She closed her eyes and replayed the moment in her mind. The Simon she had seen had been tall, but not rangy. He'd had light brown hair, but it was short and spiked, not shaggy and unkempt. His features had been familiar and yet not. They'd been older, mature, more rugged. They'd seemed closed and hard, especially his mouth, which had been set in a straight line.

The one thing that had been the same—exactly the same—had been his eyes. She'd been too far away to see the color, but they'd been heavy-lidded, incredibly sexy.

Simon's eyes had been the first thing that had attracted her to him. They'd held a promise that he had indeed kept. They were eyes that haunted her dreams. And her waking hours.

So what had she seen? A ghost?

If so, this ghost was of a man her age, not a teenager.

More than likely, her imagination had been playing tricks on her, creating what she'd wanted to see most.

Or…what if it had been a real man following her and her imagination had turned him into a mature Simon?

That set her heart to racing and she looked more intently toward the tree line, fearing she might see some stalker watching the house, waiting for her to leave again.

"Hey, Mom, what's up? Is something out there?"

Starting, heart pounding, Lexie turned to find Katie coming down the stairs. Her daughter shared her own features—all except her eyes. "I don't know. Fog's too thick." She looked into Katie's green eyes—Simon's eyes—and lied. "I heard something before coming in. A deer or raccoon probably." No way was she going to share her thoughts with her daughter and scare the kid out of her wits.

"Oh." Athletic and wiry, curves only now starting to soften her hips and chest, Katie shrugged and bounced down the last few stairs. "What did you bring home for dinner?"

"Dinner? Oh, no, I forgot I said I'd pick something up." That she'd been too distracted with thoughts of Simon to remember made her feel awful. "I don't think there's anything in the freezer, either."

Katie groaned. "Canned soup and sandwiches again?"

"Sorry, sorry, sorry!"

"Other mothers cook."

"Other mothers don't run family businesses."

Katie heaved a sigh. "Fine. Your not cooking hasn't killed me yet."

Lexie put her arms around her daughter and kissed the top of her head. She had to rise up on her toes to do so these days. Though only twelve, Katie was nearly as tall as she was. Still freaked after thinking she had seen Simon, Lexie held on tight to his daughter. Too tight.

Squirming out of her arms with a "Mo-o-om!" Katie headed for the refrigerator.

Not only was her little girl not so little anymore, she was getting uncomfortable with big shows of affection. Lexie sighed, knowing their relationship was bound to change as Katie matured. Lexie understood that, understood that she would have to loosen the reins.

She didn't have to like it.

She hung her jacket on the hall tree, kicked off her wet boots, slipped her feet into a pair of clogs she kept by the front door, then joined her daughter in the kitchen.

They worked together preparing the meal, smoothly as always. Lexie started the sandwiches, while Katie opened the can of soup and poured it into a pot on the stove.

The kitchen was old-fashioned—hickory cabinets, butcher block counters, big single porcelain sink, plank wood floors, old appliances—but Lexie liked it exactly as the last owners had left it, so she'd never even thought about updating. The only thing she'd done was paint the walls a deep gold and had the original window replaced with a garden window so she could grow fresh herbs all year round.

Even if she didn't have time to cook meals from scratch very often, the herbs looked pretty and smelled wonderful.

"Nana said she'd teach me to cook," Katie said, as if reading her mind.

"That's nice of her, but I don't want you to think it's your responsibility to make dinner."

"I'd just like to know how, in case I wanted to."

"Okay."

Katie was aware that her grandmother was the better cook by far. Lexie knew they would enjoy spending the extra time together.

"We're going to start with Christmas cookies tomorrow night."

"On Thursday? What about school on Friday? I remember how Mom gets carried away with her baking and doesn't know when to stop. You need your sleep."

"Nothing goes on in school the last day before the holiday but parties. Actually, Nana wants me to stay for a couple of nights so we can have a marathon cookie-making session. Don't worry. She'll make sure I get enough sleep. Aunt Carole's going to help, too, when she's not at the garden center."

Hardly a domestic goddess herself, Lexie wasn't surprised that no one had invited *her.* No doubt because her mother knew that if she went it would simply be to eat the cookies everyone else made, as she had done when she was a teenager.

Knowing she was going to be too busy finishing up the decorating for the charity ball to have time to spend with her daughter this weekend, Lexie said, "As long as you promise to bring tons of cookies home for me."

Katie grinned. "Deal."

Lexie smacked her lips in anticipation and set the sandwiches on the table.

Dinner, such as it was, allowed Lexie to spend precious time with Katie. Between her own work and Katie's school and activities with her friends, breakfast and dinner were the only times she could count on their being together during the school year. A top student, Katie would spend the rest of the evening holed up in her room doing homework. And, no doubt, e-mailing or text-messaging her friends.

But for half an hour, Lexie got the update on Katie's school-work, her activities, the other kids. She appreciated every precious moment.

"So when are we gonna go pick out a Christmas tree?" Katie asked.

"After I recover from the ball at Drake House."

Katie gave her a big sigh. "Cutting it close again. That means Christmas Eve."

"I know, sweetheart. I'm sorry. But you know how important this season is to the business."

"Someday I wish we could put up our decorations before you get so busy."

Lexie laughed. "You mean right after Halloween?"

"Why not?"

"We'd have to get a fake tree, then. A real one wouldn't last until New Year's."

"Might be worth it."

"If you want to do that next year, it's a done deal."

"Cool." Katie grinned at her and Lexie grinned back.

In reality, she knew Katie would change her mind when the time came. Picking out a real tree together and cutting it down themselves was a time-honored tradition they both loved. And Katie would purposely sleep on the couch some nights because she loved being surrounded by the pine scent. Even so, they could at least put up lights in the windows and do some other early decorating as a compromise.

Though Katie was finished eating, she sat there a while, as if she had something else on her mind.

Finally, she said, "So there's a Christmas party Saturday night, but Nana says I need your permission to go."

"Christmas party where? At school?"

"No. It's a private party. In a house."

"Whose house?"

"Josh Pearson's."

"Josh Pearson." Lexie tried to place him. "Have I met him? Has he been here?" She'd always encouraged Katie to invite her friends over, so that she would get to know who her daughter hung out with.

"Um, no."

"But he's in your class."

Katie bit her lip, then said, "No, he's in high school."

"How old is he?"

"Sixteen." Now Katie sounded truculent.

"Katie, you're twelve."

"I just want to go to a party—"

"For teenagers."

"So I'm a preteen."

A designation she'd given herself since she'd turned twelve.

"Even if you were thirteen I wouldn't let you go to a private party with high school kids," Lexie said. "You're only in seventh grade, for heaven's sake. Stop trying to grow up so fast!"

Katie jumped to her feet. "You just want to ruin my life!"

"Just for a little while longer," Lexie said, refusing to engage in a debate. "Please clear the table before you escape to your room."

Katie was clearly fighting tears as she did as ordered, then refused to say another word before rushing back upstairs.

Lexie sighed and shook her head. Her mother had always said it would serve Lexie right to have a daughter just like her—and she had. Just as long as Katie didn't get pregnant at seventeen the way she had. The time for the safe-and-respon-sible-sex talk was coming up, but Lexie hoped to delay it just a little longer.

Thinking about it made her think of Simon again. She tried to watch television to distract herself, but she couldn't concen-trate, no matter which program she tried. Her gaze was con-tinually pulled to the front door.

Eventually she gave up the sham and got off the couch, grabbed her jacket from the hall tree and went outside.

Not that she planned to go anywhere.

On the porch, she stared out toward the path she'd taken through the woods.

What had she seen earlier?

Some version of Simon, but whether ghost or her imagi-nation or some guy she put the wrong face to, she didn't know.

Even now, Lexie sensed something out there—ghost or man?—but no matter how hard she stared through the tree line, she saw nothing.

The damp cold got to her eventually, driving her back inside.

Unable to stop thinking of Simon, Lexie got ready for bed. She could hardly keep her eyes open, and when she climbed under the covers, her eyes drifted closed.

Even so, Simon's image stayed with her, fading only as she fell asleep....

He stood in the fog, staring at her as if silently calling her to him. Pulse fluttering, she moved closer, and when the fog swallowed him, she ran into the thick, wet air to catch up to him. She couldn't let him get away from her again!

Suddenly she was jerked off her feet. He caught her around the waist and spun her in his arms so that they were face-to-face. Breathless, she reached up and touched the features that were familiar and yet not.

"Simon?"

"I came back for you. I love you...always have..."

He kissed her then, and her heart swelled with happiness.

When he ran his hands down her sides and cupped her bottom and pulled her to him, she gasped with desire.

She held on tight...clung to him. She would never let him go again...

Chapter Three

Lexie drove her SUV to Drake House the next morning and told her workers to meet her there. Tired from a night of tossing and turning, and, yes, dreaming of Simon, she'd armed herself with an entire thermos of coffee.

She chugged down the last of a cup as she rode alongside the bay, noting a couple of boats slapping across the water even though it was past mid-December. She wondered why anyone would want to be out there in weather like this. In a few weeks, weather would force the owners to dock their boats for the rest of the winter.

When she pulled into the circular drive, it was right behind a red Jaguar. Cliff Drake had gotten there before her, and at an hour early for him. She wondered why he was there. When she went inside, Cliff was nowhere in sight.

Marie was standing in the foyer as if waiting for her.

"Hey," Marie said, sounding tentative, "everything okay this morning?"

Lexie wanted to come back with something about Simon's ghost avoiding her, but considering what she'd seen—or thought she'd seen—on the way home, she couldn't make jokes about it.

"I'm good. Tired, but good."

"You're not still angry with me, are you?"

"I wasn't angry with you, Marie. I just spooked myself is all, and I needed to walk it off."

"Oh."

Marie smiled and seemed to relax and Lexie gave her a great big hug. She knew her friend only wanted what was best for her.

Though Lexie was tempted to talk to Marie about what she thought she'd seen the night before, she simply couldn't. Marie would make a big deal over it, say it was a sign, and would pressure her about her personal life more than ever. Better to let Marie feel a little guilty and drop the issue.

"Cliff came by to make a donation to the silent auction," Marie said.

"So that's why he's here. I saw his Jag out front."

"You'll never believe what he's contributing. Think big," Marie said. "Too big to bring into the ballroom. We'll have to use a photo."

"One of his sports cars?"

"Try one of his speedboats."

"You're kidding." Not that Cliff actually needed more than the three he had. "Huh, wish *I* could afford to bid on it." Lexie was sure that, when new, the speedboat had cost him at least six figures. "Where is Cliff, anyway?"

"He and Doug Heller are with Brandon in his office discussing company business."

Looking out from the ballroom across the foyer where Brandon's office sat facing the drive, Lexie grimaced. "What, no shouting? No loud noises? No gunshots?"

Marie laughed. "Not so far."

Though Lexie was joking, she knew full well that Brandon and his Uncle Cliff didn't get along. Brandon had no respect for his fun-loving, hard-living playboy uncle.

The younger Drake brother by more than a decade, Cliff had always been in competition with Brandon's father, Jonathan. In addition to Drake House, Brandon had inherited his father's half of Drake Enterprises, which he'd had no desire to run. Now the steady, levelheaded one in the family, he contented himself with continuing to run the foundation and keeping an eye on his uncle.

Even though Cliff had taken over the CEO position of Drake Enterprises unopposed, he'd kept up the feud, doing his best to outdo, outshine and outfox Brandon. That led to some pretty intense meetings between the two Drake men.

The company was doing well enough, so Cliff must be doing something right, even if he was relying on his business manager, Doug Heller. At least Marie had *told* her Cliff relied heavily on Heller to make many of the decisions concerning the Eastern Shore properties.

Hearing a truck pull up outside, Lexie poked her head out the front door. "Ah, here's part of my crew now. Time to get started."

"Me, too," Marie said. "There are a thousand little details to take care of. Talk to you later."

After putting her crew to work decorating the huge staircase, Lexie reached for her cell phone and realized she'd left it in the SUV. Throwing on her jacket, she ran out and fetched it. The air was cold and crisp, the sky gray. Snow was imminent; it would replenish the half-melted piles on the ground, and just in time to accentuate the majesty of Drake House for the coming guests. Hopefully, it wouldn't actually snow on the night of the ball.

Opening the entry door, Lexie stepped inside and saw Cliff with the maid, Isabella Faust, a pretty young thing with huge blue eyes and waves of auburn hair. In her early twenties, Isabella was half Cliff's age, not that he wasn't attractive, his slim, six-foot frame usually hung in Armani or some other designer suit.

Marie had told Lexie that Isabella was Cliff's newest romantic interest, making Lexie wonder why he didn't have more discerning taste in women. Marie had also admitted that Isabella was a gold digger, and that the maid had seemed possessive of Brandon—not that Brandon had fallen for her charms.

"So you'll meet me at the Duck Blind as soon as you get off work?" Cliff asked the young maid.

"I might. Convince me."

Cliff leaned over and whispered something in her ear that made Isabella giggle.

Lexie rolled her eyes. Cliff couldn't resist flirting with an attractive woman. Not that he had ever flirted with her, maybe because she'd had Katie so young. He'd always treated both of them with respect.

"All right, then, it's a date," the maid said, her voice throaty as she sauntered off, rotating her hips for Cliff's maximum enjoyment. Indeed, he stared after her until she was out of sight.

Then Lexie said, "Hey, Cliff."

Cliff turned to face her, his handsome features lighting up and the corners of his green eyes crinkling with pleasure. "Oh, there are you are. I just had a look around. It's going to be the most beautiful setting for the charity ball ever. Such talent."

"You have to say that since I take care of the landscaping for Drake Enterprises, as well as for your home."

"You're more than a caretaker, Lexie. You're an artist. Never undersell yourself."

Lexie grinned. As far as she was concerned, Cliff wasn't a bad sort, despite his reputation.

"I heard about your very generous donation for the silent auction," she said. "Tired of plying the bay waters around here?"

"Hardly. It's one of my favorite pastimes."

"I thought maybe you were getting a new hobby."

"More like a new speedboat. You know me. XSMG builds the Bugatti Veyron of the sea. It travels over 100 miles per hour. I couldn't resist more speed!" His grin infectious, Cliff then sobered to ask, "So how's your Katie doing?"

"Growing up way too fast. My baby told me she's going to learn to cook."

"Good for her. She seems like a really good kid. One to make you proud."

"So proud it scares me sometimes." Lexie still remembered what growing up had been like. "I sometimes wonder if she has some secret life I don't know about."

Cliff's smile faded. "Secret life?"

"Just a mother's paranoia. You know, when something seems too good to be true, it often is."

Before Cliff could say anything more, the front door opened and Doug Heller came in. He ran a meaty hand over his close-cropped, sandy-brown hair. "Hey, boss, we gotta get going."

"In a minute, Heller."

Heller's jowly face tightened. "We got that meeting, remember."

Cliff's jaw clenched and unclenched. "All right." Then to Lexie, he said, "I'm just a slave to the job. You say hi to Katie for me, would you? And don't worry about her or any secret life she might be leading. If you think she's a good kid, then she is. Kids pick up on that, meet your expectations."

"Thanks, Cliff."

Lexie stared after him as he left, taken aback by his last statement.

Had he been talking about himself?

Had his father expected him to be the unreliable one and so he'd proven his father correct by becoming the town playboy? Whatever his reason for the advice, Lexie thought it was kind of him to be concerned about any worry she might have over her daughter.

Cliff Drake might be the wild playboy of the Drake family, but he had a good heart. Several years back, Thornton Garden Center had been in trouble. It had looked like they might have to close up shop—or at the very least scale back to a flower and plant shop, which wouldn't have made enough profit to support her and Katie, her parents and her sister, Carole.

Then Cliff personally had sought her out to redesign the landscaping at Drake Enterprises, when in truth, it hadn't needed to be redone. The following season, he'd hired her to redo the Manor at Drake Acres gardens.

Lexie had always wondered if Cliff had hired her because he felt sorry for her. His kindness had given the business a well-needed boost. In the meantime, word spread about her landscaping capabilities, and the next thing Lexie knew, she had enough work to keep the family business afloat.

She would always be grateful to Cliff for that.

Lexie got back to work. Rather than taking lunch, she ate the sandwich she'd brought while giving instructions to workers putting up small tables near the dance floor, set in front of a low stage that would hold the band. Two high school kids who'd begged her for a way to make some Christmas money came in after school and set up a trio of different-size balsam trees at the far end of the ballroom, decorating them with hundreds of tiny white lights.

By the end of the day, she was feeling good about their progress.

Before leaving, she went in search of Marie, who was in the huge kitchen equipped with stainless steel work areas to handle banquets and a more intimate marble counter area for the smaller family and employee meals. That's where she found Marie with Isabella and the housekeeper Shelley Zachary.

In her midfifties, Shelley had an iron strength—both physically and psychologically—despite her slender appearance. Her hair was pulled back from a narrow face and her thin brows were penciled over eyes that always seemed to be inquisitive. Or so Lexie thought, after Marie told her to watch what she said around Shelley, since the housekeeper was a known gossip. Rather than hiring another butler after the murder of Edwin Leonard, Marie's father, Brandon wanted Shelley to run the house, so the woman had moved into Edwin's quarters off the kitchen, making Lexie wonder if Marie's business was going to be all over town if she wasn't careful.

At the moment, Marie, Shelley and Isabella were at the marble counter area polishing the silver flatware that would be used at the ball.

"Wow, I can see I've got the easy job," Lexie said.

Marie grinned. "That's because you're not domesticated. I'd rather do this any day than haul plants and trees around." She held up a serving piece and inspected it. "There's something satisfying about bringing out the beauty in…well, anything silver."

"A woman in love will fool herself into thinking real work is fun," Lexie teased in return. "I just wanted to let you know I'm done for the day and everything is in good shape."

"Wait! Before you go…" Marie reached into her pocket to retrieve something. "I meant to ask you about this key yesterday, but it slipped my mind. It was found on the grounds where you and your crew did some winter prep work last week. I thought it might be yours."

All eyes were on the brass key as Lexie took it from Marie. Unique in design, it was solid and heavy—an old-fashioned, barrel-type key with a fancy leaf at the top.

"I've never seen this before," Lexie said, "but maybe it belongs to one of my crew."

"Keep it and show it to them, then. It doesn't fit any of the doors in this house."

"Will do."

Giving the key a last look, Lexie realized that Isabella and Shelley weren't the only ones interested. Ned Perry, nattily dressed as usual, his brown hair neatly combed to one side, was there, as well. The annoying land developer who was trying to get his hands on any available waterfront property was standing in the doorway, his gaze glued to the key. She quickly pocketed it in her sheepskin jacket.

Ned practically jumped and cleared his throat. He looked past her to the other women. "Is Brandon home?"

"No, he's not, Ned," Marie said. "And he's not interested in selling any shoreline land, either."

"I'm sure if he hears me out, he'll see things differently. New building would revitalize the area."

Lexie waved to Marie and quietly left the room.

As she headed down the hallway, she thought about how the cutthroat developer wanted the Drake Enterprises-held shoreline so that he could build luxury condominiums and make himself a fortune.

She was glad that Brandon didn't want to sell. So much new building would change Jenkins Cove, and not necessarily for the better. In summer the roads were already congested with tourist vehicles. A new development of the size that Ned envisioned would mean congested roads all year round. Not to mention the myriad other problems that would result from nearly doubling the population of a small community all at once.

Once outside, she took a deep breath of fresh air and tilted

...er face up to the sky. Snow was coming down in big, fat, lazy flakes. Smiling, she climbed into her SUV and took off.

Her smile didn't last long because she'd barely gone a mile before a higher area with scrubby brushes and pines came into view to her left. The sun had already set, casting long shadows over the area. She could see one of the pieces of heavy machinery parked there and a Jenkins Cove police vehicle parked off road, the cop inside apparently keeping an eye on the site. The state was still digging up the mass grave found earlier in the month as part of its investigation into human trafficking. They were still finding bodies.

So many deaths in such a small town...Lexie's mind went back to Simon dying so young. Marie really was right. Simon was gone and she had to stop thinking about him. Definitely had to stop dreaming about him, she thought, flushing.

Lexie was glad to reach Thornton Garden Center, a long, low brick building with big windows filled with glass sun catchers and red poinsettias and amaryllis.

Upon entering, Lexie looked for her mother. She gazed around the store, but didn't see her among the customers, who were mostly checking out the Christmas ornaments in baskets set among the plants in the windows. Her sister, Carole, an older, shorter version of Lexie, except for her henna-enhanced, reddish-brown hair, was at the register behind the counter.

"Hey, is Mom out back with Dad?"

Her father was in charge of the landscaping supplies sold in the attached sheltered area, and during the holiday season, the Christmas trees in the outside area beyond.

"Nope. She made him take her home early. She's in her cookie-making mode and couldn't think about anything else. Phil took over for Dad."

"I didn't get my invitation to join you."

Carole just laughed. "Is that why you're gunning for Mom?"

"If I didn't give her a hard time about it, she would think something was wrong."

Though she was exhausted, Lexie went to the far side of the counter and checked her desk/design center and found a message from one of her business customers requesting more poinsettia plants and a couple of wreaths for the company Christmas party next week. No sense in waiting until the morning. She called Phil on the intercom and told him what she needed just as the police chief entered and walked to the other end of the store, straight to the refrigeration unit holding floral arrangements.

A squat bulldog of a man, Chief Hammer was no one's favorite. He had a reputation for letting things slip by him. Lexie had always thought he was just plain lazy. Thankfully, the state had taken over the mass grave tragedy. If it was up to Hammer, he would probably have left the bodies where they were and buried the investigation. Pulling a bouquet from the refrigerator, he made his way to the counter just as Phil Cardon came from the back, carrying a couple of wreaths.

Probably in his early thirties, Phil was a seasonal worker for the garden center. He made his living doing odd jobs in town and looked the part, wearing scruffy jeans, work boots and a raggedy jacket.

"These are what we have left right now. Do you think they're big enough for a business?"

"They're on the small side." Lexie frowned. She didn't want to disappoint a good customer. "When you make the delivery, check with the administrative assistant, Rosemary. Tell her if she can wait until Monday, we can make up a few bigger ones for her."

"Okay." He turned to go.

Remembering that Phil had been part of her grounds crew

at Drake House, Lexie said, "Wait a minute." She pulled the key from her jacket pocket. "Someone lost this on Drake property. Any chance it's yours?"

Phil pushed straggly brown hair from his eyes and shook his head. "Not mine."

"If anyone mentions a lost key, let me know."

Phil nodded and headed toward the back.

"Lost key, huh?" Chief Hammer said from the counter, where Carole was wrapping his flowers. "Can I see it?"

Not knowing why, Lexie was reluctant to hand the key over to him. She let it nestle in her palm and kept it out of his reach.

"Unusual key." He held out his hand, indicating she should turn it over to him. "Maybe I should take it for safekeeping until the rightful owner claims it."

"It'll be safe enough with me." Lexie closed her hand. "I'll see my other workers tomorrow. I'm sure one of them dropped it."

"Here you go, Chief," Carole said.

Hammer stared at Lexie for a moment before turning to take his purchase.

What was that all about? she wondered as the police chief left. No doubt one of Hammer's little power plays. He liked being seen as the big man in town even if he didn't want to do the work that came with the designation.

Realizing that she still had the key in her hand, she slipped it into a back pocket where it would stay put.

"You look beat," Carole said. "Maybe you ought to go home and take a bubble bath or something."

"Or something," Lexie agreed, suppressing a yawn. Right now, her bed called to her. "Are you sure you don't need me?"

Carole rolled her eyes. "I lock up in less than half an hour. Just go."

"Okay, then." Lexie slipped into her jacket and headed for

the door. "Have a good time tonight. Tell Mom I expect to have enough cookies to gorge on."

Thoroughly exhausted, Lexie was glad the drive home was short. Snow was still falling, but there was little new accumulation. Five minutes later, she pulled up in the gravel parking area next to the house. Yawning while clambering out of the SUV, she dragged herself toward the front door and pulled her keys out of her shoulder bag.

Almost to the door, she heard a shuffle behind her. Heart thumping, she turned to see a figure dressed in dark clothing, face covered by a ski mask, advance on her.

The man she'd seen the night before?

Was he stalking her?

Though her chest squeezed tight, she tried not to panic.

Knowing she couldn't make it inside, Lexie threw her shoulder bag as hard as she could and hit him square in the face, then ran, her pulse jagging. She heard him curse and come after her. Not interested in money, then.

Her heart hammering, she ran flat out around the house, hoping to reach the wood stack in back, where she could arm herself with a split log. Maybe she could knock the man out, *then* get inside.

In the side yard, she slipped on the snowy grass and nearly fell, the interruption long enough for her attacker to catch up to her. Her scream for help was cut off when he tackled her.

She went down hard, her breath knocked out of her, yet struck back with the hand holding her keys. Before she could connect with his head, he grabbed her wrist and pounded it against the ground. The keys went flying into the snow. Undaunted, Lexie continued to fight and squirm away as the man started feeling her up.

Weirdly, the attack didn't seem sexual in nature. It was as if her assailant were searching for something…patting her jacket pockets and trying to get his hands inside them.

Though she bucked and struck out, she was unable to get him off her. "What do you want?"

When he didn't answer, she clawed at the mask.

He knocked her hand away and hit her in the head so hard her vision went out of focus and her limbs went limp so that she had to struggle to remain conscious.

He was slipping his hands under the jacket now, feeling the sides of her jeans. Had she been wrong about this not being sexual? Her stomach lurched and she was about to renew her battle, when suddenly her attacker rose off her as if by magic.

Lexie took a deep breath and scooted back to see her masked assailant struggling with another man. A tall and broad man with spiked, light brown hair and heavy-lidded eyes.

Unless she really was seeing a ghost, it was…

"Simon?"

Chapter Four

Lexie's cry caught Simon off guard and the bastard who'd attacked her got a moment's advantage, nearly delivering a kidney punch. Honed reflexes allowed Simon to drop and divert the blow. He landed on one knee, and when the attacker kicked out, he grabbed the bastard's foot and twisted. The man flipped around and landed on the ground.

Lexie was groaning, and Simon gave her a quick glance to see her struggling to her feet.

Enough time for the attacker to get to his feet and run off.

Though Simon would have liked to go after the bastard, he was more concerned about Lexie.

Fearing that she was hurt, he swept her up into his arms. "Let's get you into the house."

"Keys," she whispered with a groan, indicating the area to the right of where she had fallen.

Simon moved in that direction, carefully sweeping the snowy ground with his gaze. There was just enough light to see the skid marks made by the keys. He reached out blindly and felt around for a few seconds before feeling metal against his fingertips.

"Got 'em."

Lexie seemed to be coming back to herself. She started pushing against him. "Let me down. I can walk."

"I'm sure you can."

Not that Simon was about to let her down. He carried her around the house to the front door, picking up her shoulder bag along the way.

As he sorted through the keys, he felt Lexie's gaze on him, but he didn't look at her. He hadn't meant for this to happen. He'd been unable to keep himself from spying on her.

"I missed you all these years, Simon. You don't know how much. That's why I let Marie talk me into going to the psychomanteum yesterday." Seeming confused, only half-aware, Lexie continued babbling. "I wanted to see you one last time before I said goodbye forever. Now that I have, I don't want to let you go."

Simon realized that the smack from her attacker must have scrambled her brains. He got her inside, kicked the door closed behind them, then carried her to the oversize couch, upholstered in a brown and burgundy design, and gently set her down against the myriad pillows.

"Let me look into your eyes."

"I always loved it when you looked deep into my eyes and I looked into yours…"

She was trying to do that now.

"I want to make sure you don't have a concussion." Kneeling in front of her, he pulled a pencil-thin maglite from the pocket of his leather bomber jacket and, lifting her chin a bit, shone the light in her eyes. "Your pupils are even and dilating properly. No concussion."

So why was she so confused?

Psychomanteum? What the hell was that?

Suddenly Lexie blinked and her expression shifted. As if

testing, she poked him in the chest. "Wait a minute, you're no ghost! You're alive!"

Simon got to his feet and backed away. "That I am."

The confusion cleared, leaving shock in its place. "But they told me you were dead!"

"I assure you, I am very much alive, Lexie."

"Oh my God!" Lexie lunged off the couch and threw herself against him. "You're alive! You're really alive!" she said through her tears.

And then she kissed him, plunging him back thirteen years, to the night they'd made love, had made plans to start a life together, away from Jenkins Cove. Instead, he'd started a new life without her. A life he would never be able to forget…or share with her.

He didn't want her to know what he had become.

So it was he who broke the kiss and pushed away the one person in the world who meant anything to him. The only woman he'd ever loved.

"Simon?" Lexie blinked and wiped away her tears, focused on his face as if really seeing him for the first time. "Simon…if you weren't dead…why didn't you come for me? Why did you leave me? I've spent thirteen years mourning you. What happened? You simply chose to play dead and on the very night I was going to run away with you?"

"I had no choice in what happened to me."

Lexie shook her head. "We all have choices."

Her accusing expression and tone put Simon's back up. "Not always. Sometimes things are out of our control."

"For thirteen years? You walk out of my life and don't contact me? Don't let me know what happened or even that you're still alive?"

"I couldn't."

He couldn't at first. But by the time his situation had changed, so had he. He'd become a man Lexie didn't know. Wouldn't want to know. One he hadn't wanted her to know. He'd wanted her to be happy, to have a good life, and it looked like she did…though she wasn't wearing a ring and he didn't see signs of another man.

The room was all Lexie—casual yet with a hint of sophistication. The couch, a matching chair in front of the fireplace, a leather chair with a scrolled back by the windows, maybe for reading. The lamps had shades of stained glass or mica; the accessories on mission-style tables were feminine in design. Nothing to indicate that a man lived here.

That kiss Lexie had given him had certainly been hungry enough…

Suddenly she said, "Get out!" Her face was flushed, her expression angry.

"What? You were just attacked."

"Thank you for saving me," she said evenly. "I'm fine now, so you can go back to wherever you've been hiding for the last thirteen years. You know where to find the door."

"I'm not going anywhere. Someone has to protect you."

"I've had to do that for myself since you left, and you're not someone I can count on!"

The truth of that struck Simon like a physical blow. Too much time had gone by. He couldn't possibly connect with Lexie the way he had in that other life.

"Let me take you to see a doctor—"

"I'm fine. I don't need a doctor. I don't need *you*. Just go, please."

Simon clenched his jaw so he wouldn't argue with her. She probably *was* fine. He had a lot of experience dealing with injured men on the battlefield, and though she had exhibited some strange behavior, he chalked that up to the shock of seeing a dead man. She'd gotten over that quickly enough. She appeared ready to do battle again.

"At least tell me that you'll file a police report." Simon had every reason for staying dead for the moment, at least until he figured out who had sent him to that hell and why he hadn't simply been killed, as had the kid he'd seen murdered. He had to stay dead until he exacted the revenge he sought, his reason for being. "Just don't mention me."

"As far as I'm concerned," Lexie said caustically, "you're still dead and buried."

THE REAL SHOCK of Simon's being alive didn't hit Lexie until he finally left. Alive. After all these years. It hardly seemed real to her.

And then another thought hit her. Katie. What was she going to do about that? Her chest squeezed tight. If she told Simon he had a daughter, would he want to meet Katie only to abandon her, too? He hadn't said anything about staying and she couldn't bear to see her daughter's heart broken as hers had been. She knew just how awful that felt.

Protecting her daughter from emotional pain was her main responsibility here. Thankfully, Katie was staying with her grandparents for a few days. The pressure on her chest let up a little. She wouldn't have to make the decision as to whether to tell Simon just yet. Perhaps she would never see him again. How would she know?

Lexie called the police and got the runaround about no one being there; the chief would call her back. Fat chance. She waited half an hour, then decided to go in and make the report in person.

Trying to keep her teeming emotions under control, Lexie got her keys and started for the front door.

Afraid that her attacker might still be out there, however, she decided to check and went from window to window to stare out into the dark. Her pulse spiked, but she saw nothing, no one.

Not even Simon.

Heart hammering, Lexie grabbed her bag, slipped out of the house, raced to her SUV, got inside and immediately locked herself in. She drove straight to the police station, an old house a block off Main Street, bought by the city to house offices for its small force.

"Hey, Lexie," Martha, the dispatcher/receptionist at the front desk, said when she entered. "Chief Hammer just got in."

"Good." Without waiting to be announced, Lexie headed for his office. The door was open, so she walked right in. "I want to report an attempted robbery."

Frowning, Hammer looked up from his newspaper. "Something happen after I left the garden center?"

"Not there, at my home. I was attacked."

"What was stolen?"

"Nothing. I, uh, fought him off."

"If nothing was stolen…"

Lexie seethed. He didn't want to write up the report. As usual, Chief Hammer was trying to get out of doing any work.

"What if I was hurt?"

"Are you?"

"Not really." Though the side of her face was still a bit sore where the attacker had hit her.

"You know, Lexie, it was probably some out-of-towner just looking for money during the Christmas season. You should have given up your pocketbook and he would have fled."

Yeah, that would have made things easier for everyone. Lexie clenched and unclenched her jaw. "He didn't want my bag. He had me on the ground and his hands were all over me and—"

Hammer raised his hand for her to stop. "Draper!" he yelled. "I need you to take a report."

The police chief really *was* adept at avoiding work.

A young officer named Sam Draper appeared at the door and waved her out of the room and over to a desk where he took her report. He hemmed and hawed to himself a bit before saying, "If this guy was interested in robbing you, I don't get why he didn't just take your shoulder bag."

"You and me both." She didn't want to say she'd been rescued. She didn't want anyone to know that Simon was alive any more than he did.

"You say he had you on the ground and was feeling your, um, pockets?"

"Right."

"Any idea of what your attacker could have been looking for?"

She shook her head. "No." Not until that moment. Suddenly she thought of the key Marie had given her. The key she'd slipped into her back pocket. She stopped herself from feeling for it to make sure it was still there. She wiggled her butt against the back of the chair and felt something hard that must be the key. Thinking caution would serve her well at this point, she said, "No idea at all."

Draper said, "I really don't know that we'll be able to get this guy, being that he was wearing a mask and all. Are you sure you can't identify something about him? Height? Body type? Something about his hands?"

"Nothing. I'm sorry. I was so freaked…it…it seemed like a nightmare."

"Tell you what I'll do. I'll follow you home and drive around your place, give the area a good look-see to make sure the guy's gone."

Lexie nodded. "Thanks, I'd appreciate it."

"Let's go, then."

Only when she rose and turned to go did Lexie realize that Chief Hammer was leaning against his office doorjamb. He'd been watching her the whole time, but she had no clue what he was thinking. His face was expressionless.

Draper followed her home in the police vehicle, an SUV, then pulled up next to her and rolled down his window. "Stay put while I circle the area, make sure it's safe."

"Will do."

She followed Draper's progress with her gaze until his vehicle disappeared behind a stand of trees. Her thoughts wandered, going from the key and what her attacker might want from it to Simon.

Where had he been all these years? Why had he left in the first place? He'd said he had no choice. How was that possible? Lexie began regretting sending him away without getting answers to her many questions.

Startled from her thoughts as the police vehicle pulled up next to her again, she lowered her window. Moonlight silvered Draper's half-regretful expression.

"No one around," he said. "Wish I coulda got the guy for you, but at least you're safe. House looks locked up tight, too. I can check inside if you want."

"Thanks."

Lexie rolled up her window and grabbed her shoulder bag, then slid out of her SUV. Moving to the entrance, grateful that Draper was watching her back, she unlocked the door, then, pulse quickening, she let him in first and quickly followed. Minutes passed, seeming like forever. He came out of the kitchen, gave her a thumbs-up and headed upstairs. Lexie breathed normally only when he came back down.

"All clear."

"I really appreciate your looking out for me."

He gave her a crooked smile and tipped his hat. "My job."

"Thanks, anyway."

Closing the door after him, Lexie would like to think this was the end of it, that her attacker wouldn't be back, but she wasn't so certain that was true. She went around the house, closing the blinds.

At least Katie was with her parents and sister for a few nights and didn't have to be afraid. Her parents… She would have to call them. Sam Draper's wife was one of the town gossips. Shelley Zachary, Brandon's housekeeper, being the other. Lexie was sure that everyone would know what had happened by morning.

She couldn't let her parents hear it from someone else, so she would have to call them and tell them what happened, leaving Simon out of the story. Though she hated lying, Lexie couldn't tell anyone Simon was back. Not yet, anyway.

Before making the call, she needed to put the key someplace safe until she could figure out why it was so important. But where? She looked around the room, her eyes lighting on the staircase. There was a hollow in the newel. She and Katie had used it to hide messages to each other ever since Katie learned to write. No one else knew about their special hiding place. Since Katie wasn't going to be home for a couple of days, the key would be safe there.

Taking the key from her back pocket, she unscrewed the newel.

"Why are you so special someone would attack me to get hold of you?" she murmured, turning the key in her fingers.

No answer came to her. How would she ever figure it out?

Setting it in the hiding place, Lexie went to the phone to make that call to her parents.

Chapter Five

Not wanting his presence known until he figured out the mystery of his past and a way to avenge the horror that had been done to him, Simon had camped out where he and Lexie used to go to be alone—a fishing shack in a stand of trees about a hundred yards from the water. To get there, he had to pass the swampy area that everyone in town always avoided—which had just been revealed as a mass grave.

On the way to the shack now, Simon slowed his truck when he neared the Duck Blind, which his father owned, at the west end of town, where the commercial buildings trailed off. Rufus was just coming out of the bar-restaurant. His salt-and-pepper hair had thinned a bit as had his still-muscular body. Even from a distance, Simon could see the short, scraggly beard he'd always had. To Simon's surprise, his father didn't seem to be drunk. His hand was steady as he locked the door and he walked a straight line heading for the only car left in the small lot to one side of the building.

As far as Simon could tell, his old man was stone-cold sober.

Warmth flooded through him, and he realized that his father's apparent sobriety made him happy. There had been times when he'd felt his father really had loved him, though mostly that had been before his mother died and Rufus hadn't been drinking so heavily. Afterward, his father had immersed himself in booze.

Thinking about the old man had always plunged Simon in a dark mood. Now perhaps he would have reason to put those bad memories behind him. He only wished his father could have sobered up when he was still around. If he had, things would have gone very differently in Simon's life.

A thought that made him stay in the truck.

He wanted to catch up with his father, but he wasn't ready to do so just yet. Their rocky relationship was still too clear in his mind, especially the argument that had made Simon decide to run away. He'd tried to talk his father into cutting back on the drinking. He'd even poured half a bottle of whiskey down the drain. The old man had responded with his fists and by saying that Simon was no son of his.

That had broken Simon's heart.

The wound had never healed, and yet Simon watched from where he'd stopped near the tree line until his father drove off.

Then he went on his way, driving as far as he dared. He'd found a place to hide his truck in a stand of pine trees before reaching the swampy area where, as the media had reported, dozens of bodies had been found, some from deaths a century ago; many others more recent.

Who had done this to them? The same man responsible for his fate? He'd spent years dreaming about using the skills he was learning on the man. In his mind, he'd punished the bastard for what he'd done in every way possible.

But if the same man was responsible for this atrocity…

Tentacles of fog wove throughout the area, but Simon could still see the crime scene tape and several pieces of heavy equipment that had been left alongside the excavation. Usually there was a cop car somewhere around—the reason he didn't want to take his truck all the way to the fishing camp, lest he be spotted. But tonight the police seemed to be elsewhere.

Simon wondered how many more bodies would be found.

The mass grave reminded him of several incidents in the war-torn areas he'd fought in. There had been no time for funerals and neat graves with headstones commemorating the lives of the dead. They'd been piled one on top of the other, taking away the last of their dignity.

But these dead hadn't been part of a war. From what he understood, these poor souls had been tricked into coming to this country, thinking they would get a better life, but had ended up as spare parts for people who could afford to skip the donor lists.

So much evil in this world. Everywhere. But this was unfathomable.

Simon couldn't make his legs carry him past the mass grave, not without stopping and paying the victims his respect. He bowed his head and said a silent prayer for their souls.

And then he said one for his own.

He, too, had done unforgivable things—not out of choice, but out of necessity—and he was ready to do more. Those responsible for the nightmare he'd survived needed to be dealt with, and Simon didn't believe that justice would be done unless he made sure of it himself. And he was determined that justice would be done.

A chill suddenly swept over him, as if he were standing in a pocket of cold air.

When Simon raised his head and opened his eyes, he saw a figure materializing in the fog. In the stand of pine to the east of the mass grave, a man was staring at him. No, not a man. A teenager with a mop of pale hair over hollow eyes and wearing a light leather jacket and ripped jeans.

Simon's pulse jagged and, for a moment, he forgot to breathe.

The figure was so familiar. Simon would swear this was that kid he'd seen shot thirteen years ago!

It couldn't be.

"Hey!" Simon shouted, forgetting he was trying to stay undercover. "Who are you?"

The ghostly figure gestured to Simon as if asking him to follow before moving off in a swirl of fog. Unable to help himself, Simon complied and followed the kid on a path nearly straight back to his truck and realized this wasn't far from where he'd been taken while on his way to get Lexie that night so long ago. Pockets of icy air rippled along his skin. No matter how hard he tried, how fast he ran, Simon couldn't catch up to the wraith.

Simon absolutely believed that the souls of the departed haunted people. He'd lived with one—the man he'd killed in self-defense—for months in Somalia. Only when he had reconciled his own actions had the dead man's spirit crossed over. Over the years he'd been shadowed by other ghosts, but he'd learned to steel himself against them and they'd eventually left him alone.

Left him empty and hard…damaged goods…without a soul of his own.

So why was he being haunted now? He hadn't been responsible for the kid's death.

What did this lost soul want from him?

Once in his truck, he lost the apparition, had to go slow on the road, searching the land from the road to the water as he drove. He spotted the ghostly figure off and on in between the trees all the way to the edge of town, where he ditched the truck behind a warehouse and followed on foot.

The sidewalks were nearly clear of pedestrians, the streets of vehicles. No one seemed to notice the mist-shrouded kid.

Down the block, a stray dog was going about his business, but stopped when the kid drew near. It didn't make a sound, but it froze and its ruff went up and then it warily backed off.

Simon's ruff went up, too.

What the hell?

The kid walked along a red brick fence that surrounded the gray stone church at the center of town, Jenkins Cove Chapel. Suddenly, he disappeared through an opening.

Heart pounding, Simon ran faster so as not to lose him.

The fog was lighter here, the chill greater, and once past the fence's wooden gate, which had been left open, Simon realized where he was.

The cemetery.

Why had the kid brought him here?

Following the curving redbrick path lined by boxwood on both sides, Simon kept track of the kid's mop of pale hair, which appeared on the other side of the hedge, then lost him altogether. When he came to the open area dotted with gravestones and markers, Simon only half hoped he would actually find him again. He gazed around, past a couple of large willow oaks and a magnolia tree in the center of the graveyard, then spotted the kid at a far gravesite, touching the stone that identified its occupant.

Again, the kid looked up at him with hollow eyes and gestured that he should come.

Reluctantly, Simon did. Not wanting to cross anyone's grave—he'd had enough of that in his former life—he stayed on the brick path, keeping his gaze locked on the figure still summoning him.

One minute the fog seemed to circle the kid, the next he seemed to fade away into the mists.

"Wait! Don't go!"

But the demand came too late. The kid was already gone. And Simon was moving to the headstone he'd touched, had obviously wanted Simon to see.

A deep, arctic cold suddenly surrounded Simon and then the breath was knocked out of him as he stopped in the spot where the kid had disappeared. Looking down, Simon understood why Lexie believed he was dead and buried. The headstone bore his name and the dates of his birth and of his supposed death on Christmas Eve thirteen years before.

Not a man who easily believed in what he couldn't see, Simon had no doubts about who had led him here. Of who was buried in his grave. He was certain the kid he'd seen shot had taken his place.

Thirteen years ago and his ghost still wandered, unable to rest, Simon thought.

How many ghosts inhabited this area?

How many souls were denied eternal rest?

He reached out to touch the headstone as if he could communicate more easily with the dead. The stone was icy, but if he'd really thought he could bring back the kid's ghost or otherwise resurrect him, he would have been sorely disappointed. Nothing happened. No surprise.

Of one thing he was certain. The kid had been buried in his stead. How had they pulled that one off? He and the kid looked nothing alike. A closed coffin, then? How had he supposedly died so that no one would have raised the alarm? Who had been in on his supposed death?

More questions that needed answering.

Another reason for him to stay undercover awhile—to find the answers.

Did *ghosts* seek retribution? he wondered.

Considering the evil that had stalked the town unchecked, probably not.

But now the town had to deal with *him*.

Heart heavy, Simon headed for his truck and a short while later drove past the mass grave. Still no cop, so he drove all the way to the fishing shack and did the best he could to hide the vehicle on the camp's far side.

Had he really returned to Jenkins Cove to seek revenge for what had happened to him? Simon did want to identify the one responsible and learn the reason behind it, did want that person brought to justice, but somehow he wasn't as energized by the thought as he had been when the news about the mass grave had hit the media.

Then he'd convinced himself that's why he needed to come back—to expose everything associated with his own abduction—but the doctor responsible for harvesting organs was dead and his business ended, so what could he really accomplish? No doubt many secrets had died with the doctor, including ones that had to do with him.

Drake Enterprises had been implicated in the modern-day slave trade, but the authorities had barely begun their investigation. According to a newspaper article, the Drake connection didn't seem to hold water. There simply was no evidence, just the word of a man who was not only dead, but who had been crazed with grief at the loss of his wife, another victim.

Simon still wanted answers, certainly, and he wasn't above exacting retribution, as well.

But more than either, he wanted Lexie Thornton.

After seeing her, Simon faced the truth: He'd been lying to himself all along.

Even though he knew she wouldn't want him once she learned the truth about how he'd spent the last thirteen years, Simon admitted he'd come back to Jenkins Cove so that he could reclaim the woman he loved.

As he approached the shack, a crack like a twig breaking underfoot froze Simon to the spot. Someone was there, on the other side of the camp. The cop who should have been at the mass grave?

Silently backing up, Simon was about to step behind a tree when he spotted the silhouette of the intruder.

A silhouette he would know anywhere.

What the hell was Lexie doing out here?

AGITATED BY THE ATTEMPTED robbery and even more so by knowing that Simon wasn't really dead, Lexie hadn't been able to settle down for the night. She might not be able to do anything about the assault, but she sure as hell could do something about Simon. She could get the truth out of him. Then just maybe she would tell him about his daughter. Above all, she had to think of Katie. She no longer even knew this man who was her daughter's father, but she had to give him a chance to explain himself.

With that in mind, she'd left the house yet again and had driven to the spot where Katie had been conceived. Somehow she'd known Simon would be here. The moment she saw him, her pulse picked up and her breath shortened.

"What are you doing, Lexie, wandering around in the dark and after being attacked?"

Not exactly the welcome she'd hoped for, but then why should she have expected him to be any friendlier than she had been when she'd thrown him out. Her eyes were adjusting to the dark and there was just enough moonlight to see his mouth set in a straight line.

"We have some things to settle," she said.

"Such as?"

"The last thirteen years."

"I'd rather forget them."

"I can't forget, Simon. What happened? Why did you leave without me?" She'd been going over and over the possibilities and only one thing had occurred to her. "The kid who was buried in your grave… Was there some kind of…accident?"

"Don't you mean, was I responsible for his death?"

Lexie shuddered. She really didn't want to know the answer if it was yes, but she couldn't keep herself from asking, "Were you?"

"No."

His answer was flat, emotionless, like his expression. Lexie believed him. She sensed that he was closing himself off from her. Once that happened, he would never tell her anything, so she moved closer and tried to connect with him by placing a hand on his chest. His heart immediately sped up and she felt him soften toward her, despite the determination she remembered so well.

"Please, Simon, I need to know the truth." Touching him made her a little breathless. She stepped in even closer, looked up into his face, now only inches from hers. "When they told me you were dead, I wanted to die, too."

Simon grabbed her by both arms. "Lexie, don't ever say that. You don't know anything about death."

She could feel every one of his fingers leaving a print on her flesh. Energized from the contact, from the wanting he stirred in her, she asked, "And you do?"

"Too much."

"Now you have to tell me or my imagination will just make things up."

"Reality can be worse than anything you could imagine, believe me."

"My God, Simon," she whispered, moving into him and

laying her head on his chest as she used to. Tears filled her eyes as she asked, "What terrible things happened to you that you can't even talk about them?"

But suddenly knowing didn't seem as important as her being close to him. He wrapped his arms around her, pressed her to him so that she could hardly breathe. Her heart fluttered and a gasp escaped her.

How could she be so susceptible to him after so long? She felt exactly as she had thirteen years ago. Exactly as she had dreamed of ever since. She'd ached for this feeling that she'd had with Simon alone. She couldn't let it go. No other man had so stirred her emotions. Or her passion.

So when he kissed her, she couldn't resist.

And when he picked her up and carried her into the old shack that was barely more than half-rotting boards with a single window, she didn't protest.

And when he placed her on the sleeping bag near the cast-iron stove and covered her with his body, she didn't stop him.

Simon was a bigger man, weighed more than he had the last time—the only time they'd made love, but Lexie reveled in the difference, felt as if she couldn't get enough of him pressing against her, kissing her.

His kiss went so deep, she swore it touched her soul. She could drown in it. In him.

Closing her eyes, she let herself float, let herself dream. When he touched her through her clothing, she couldn't stand it, wanted to feel his flesh against hers, and so she pushed him back and sat up so she could pull off her coat and sweater. He did the same, and by the time the sweater was off her head, she saw him stripping down, the moonlight from the single window making his flesh look like silver-blue marble.

Even in the moonlight she could see that the marble was

not without flaws. For a moment, she froze, staring at the network of scars that started on the right side of his chest, slithered partway down his abdomen, and picked up halfway down his thigh.

She gaped at the souvenirs of whatever nightmare he had endured, then vowed to help make him forget it when he was with her.

Her fingers fumbled with the hooks of her bra and the next thing she knew he was kneeling and pulling off her boots, then her jeans. She was nude but for the damn bra, and he leaned forward and swept that off as easily as he had everything else.

"I've waited for you for so long," she whispered, running her hands on either side of his head. The crisp cut of his short hair prickled her palms and the sensation spread down her arms to her breasts.

He groaned and ground his mouth against hers as he swept his hand down her middle to her center, already wet with wanting him. He stroked her lightly, each time his fingers entering her more deeply, each time her legs spreading wider until she was fully open and arching up into him.

He found her as easily as if she was home to him. Their union felt like home to her, as well. She closed her eyes and arched harder so that he could go deeper. Her fingers clawed his back as though she could bring him closer, somehow make him part of her, somehow make it impossible for him ever to leave her again. Too quickly he propelled her to another place where the dark sky inside her mind lit with pinwheels of light.

Only when her cry softened to a sob of contentment did he let himself finish, riding her hard and deep, coming only after she dug her fingers into his buttocks and cried, "Now, Simon, now!"

Then he collapsed on her and she took his weight with gratitude. She felt as if all was right in her world, and hoped that this time, it would last forever.

Lexie had always known she would love Simon forever, and now she was convinced of it.

AS DAWN STREAKED through the cabin window after a night of continued abandon and little sleep, Lexie allowed her doubts to creep in.

Still snug in the sleeping bag with Simon wrapped around her, as if he never meant to let her go, she looked around the shack and noted what appeared to be the same rickety wooden table and two chairs, the cot with the same thin mattress they'd used last time. Nothing had changed.

No, everything had changed.

Simon's eyes were open, glued to her face. She pushed him until he let go of her, then found her clothes. Luckily sometime during the night, Simon had stacked the stove with wood and there remained embers to keep her warm as she dressed. Simon watched her every move without rising, without saying a word. His expression had closed again, as if he thought she were going to give him her back and walk out on him.

Not likely. Not until she had what she'd come for. The truth.

Suddenly Simon rose and got something out of his supply bag. Coffee. Nude, he set about making a pot on the wood-burning stove. Lexie's breath caught in her throat as sunlight revealed the full beauty of his body. His muscles looked as if they'd been sculpted, his abdomen was flat, his waist trim, his shoulders massive. And his butt—her favorite part of him—was rock hard. Blushing when he turned her way and she noted that wasn't the only part of him that was hard, she amended his butt to her second favorite body part.

"Are you going to have some coffee before you go?" he

asked as if she were someone who'd simply stopped by rather than the woman he'd made love to half the night.

"I was hoping for more."

"Let's see, I have beef jerky. And—"

"Not food. The truth, Simon," she said, pulling on her socks. "I was hoping for that."

His expression tightened. "You don't really want to hear it."

Or he really didn't want to tell her. "Let me decide for myself. How, for example, did you get those scars?"

Rather than answering immediately, he reached down, picked up his jeans and stepped into them. Finally, he said, "Human trafficking."

The breath caught in her throat. "Someone removed your organs?"

"Worse. They removed my soul." He didn't sit; rather, he paced, barefooted, the short length of the cabin. "I saw one of the victims killed that Christmas Eve. He was just a kid, younger than I was. He's the one buried in my grave. He was trying to escape and they shot him dead. I should have run. Maybe they would have shot me, too. That would have been better than what they did to me."

"What who did to you?"

"I don't know. I was knocked out, drugged, and when I came to, I was on a transport ship bound for Africa with a bunch of mercenaries working for a private army employed by the U.S. government." He grabbed his sweater and pulled it on. "They had a contract saying I'd agreed to go with them, to work for them for the next five years. Only it wasn't me who signed the papers."

"Work? You mean…fight?"

"If I hadn't, I really would have died. Maybe I should have."

"Don't say that!"

Her heart thumped against her ribs and Lexie knew that she really didn't want to hear…and that she had to.

"I had to do things that changed me, Lexie. Things you would never understand. I had no choice. I did as I was told and learned to use weapons and my own cunning to stay alive. It was a nightmare of a life—kill or be killed. I couldn't escape. I had no way to get out, no money. My salary was put into a bank account I couldn't access until my tour of duty was over."

"Five years, not thirteen."

How could he have stayed longer? How could he have chosen that life over one that he could have had with her?

"After my contract was fulfilled, I knew I could never come back here and face you. How could I after the life I'd been forced into? So I reupped. Believe it or not, Shadow Ops was a legitimate private military corporation, hired by the Department of Defense to do work for the CIA. They sent us to Somalia, Afghanistan and Iraq."

"We could have been together for years, but you chose to stay in something you hated?"

"I'm a different person than the one you knew."

"But you still have a soul or you wouldn't have worried about who you might hurt coming back here." Tension and doubt filled Lexie with confusion. She felt the same radiate from him. "We could have been together years ago, Simon. But you abandoned us."

"Us?"

Realizing her slip, Lexie said, "Me…your dad…"

"Why would you include him when you know how I felt about him?"

"But after you died…after we *thought* you died, he cleaned up his act."

Simon's gaze seared her. He didn't believe her.

Lexie knew she could go on lying, but he would no doubt eventually learn the truth. Torn between wanting to protect Katie and wanting to tell Simon they'd had a daughter together, she chose the latter and prayed it really was the right thing.

"About six weeks after we buried you, I learned I was pregnant. We have a twelve-year-old daughter, Simon. Her name is Katie."

His shocked expression would be comical if it weren't so tragic. Lexie's chest tightened as she waited for his response. One that didn't come. Why didn't he say something? Didn't he care that they had a daughter?

Suddenly furious, meaning to get out now, she pulled on her shoes and grabbed her coat. Simon took hold of her arm and stopped her from heading toward the door.

"Tell me."

"She's a good kid. Smart. Smart mouth, too, sometimes. Old for her age. She's had to be with only one parent who has to make a living to support her and take care of her. She looks pretty much like I did at that age, except for her eyes. Those are yours."

She gave him time to process the information. Minutes ticked by and he didn't respond. Didn't say how happy he was to learn he had a kid.

Maybe he wasn't.

Lexie pulled free, cursing herself for falling into Simon's arms so easily when obviously the last thirteen years had left him devoid of normal human feelings.

Chapter Six

Simon moved fast, blocking Lexie's access to the door. "I thought you wanted to talk."

Now all she wanted to do was get away from him before she dissolved into tears. "I'm talked out."

"Maybe I'm not."

"Maybe you're too late, Simon."

She should have known better than to think he cared about a kid he'd never seen, never even knew he'd fathered. She should have known better than to think he cared about her. After all, he'd made no declarations of love during the night.

It had been a mistake to tell him about Katie.

"We'll talk later, then, I promise," he said. "At least let me take you home."

"I have my own vehicle."

"I'll follow you, check the house before you go in."

"Why?"

"To make sure you're safe."

"And how long can I count on your doing that?" she asked, unable to keep the sarcasm from her voice. "For a few weeks? Days? Just this morning and then you disappear again for another thirteen years? Let me out. Now."

His expression tightening, Simon moved away from the door and Lexie left without looking back.

What a fool she'd been to sleep with him! Driven by hormones and nostalgia, she'd just made the biggest mistake of her life. How had she imagined that Simon Shea was the same person he had been thirteen years ago?

Lexie fumed about her stupidity all the way home. Only when she parked the SUV did her tension switch gears. The fog had lifted and the sun shone brightly. Nothing to alert her. Nothing to fear.

Even so, she held her breath and moved fast and was inside her house in a minute flat.

Only when she let go of her breath and turned from the front door did her heart begin to pound. Even with nothing but faint dawn light edging through the windows, she could see that the place was a mess. Cushions had been pulled from the couch, drawers from her desk. Papers were scattered everywhere. She was about to call the police, when a scraping sound coming from somewhere nearby stopped her.

Whoever it was hadn't left!

She turned to get out of the house, but the lock confounded her shaking hand, and by the time she got the door open a crack, she was grabbed from behind. She kicked back and used her elbows to help twist her way out of his grip and ran toward the rear door. No sooner did she reach the kitchen than her attacker caught up to her and tripped her. She went down hard and he was on her, searching her again.

Lexie fought, beating at him with both fists, trying to knee him, but missing. And this time there was no Simon to pull the bastard off her.

Then he got hold of both her hands.

"What do you want?"

"The key," he demanded. "Hand it over and you'll never be bothered again."

His voice was low and husky coming from behind the knit mask that hid his face.

So she'd been right about the key. What could be so important about it that someone would attack her twice to get it?

"What key?"

"Don't play dumb. You know I mean the one found on the grounds of Drake House."

"Oh, that one." She thought quickly. "I threw that key away."

Gripping both of her wrists together with one hand, he reached in his jacket pocket for something. Her eyes were adjusting to the dim early-morning light and she saw him pull out a roll of duct tape. The next thing she knew, he was taping her wrists together.

"Where is the damn key?" he demanded.

"I told you it's gone."

"Don't lie to me."

"What does it open?" Lexie asked, hoping he would say something that would give her a clue. "A safe-deposit box filled with money or bonds or jewels? Is that why you're so set on getting it?"

"Stop playing games. If you don't want to get hurt, tell me what I want to know."

Remembering that her attacker had hit her before, Lexie went stiff. Still, if the key was important enough to commit a crime to get, she couldn't just turn it over to this bastard.

"I asked around. No one claimed it, so I threw it away," she lied, hoping she sounded convincing.

"Where?"

"In town. The trash can between the police station and the library."

Now he was securing her ankles together with the tape. "I don't believe you."

"Why would I want to keep a key I couldn't use?" Lexie tried not to panic, but keeping an even head wasn't doing her any good. "I swear I don't have it anymore. Why is an old key so important?"

He placed a piece of the duct tape over her mouth. "Maybe I'll have to wait until your girl comes home and ask *her* about it."

Katie? He was threatening Katie now? Behind the duct tape, Lexie screamed.

Too bad no one could hear her.

SIMON WAS DEVASTATED. He'd missed the last dozen years with a kid who was his and Lexie's—years that he wouldn't ever want his child to know about. Perhaps, he thought, it would be better if Katie never knew about him, either.

Saddened by the thought, he sat in his truck down the road from Lexie's house, waiting for lights to go on somewhere. Despite her harsh words, he'd finished dressing quickly and had driven like a maniac until he'd gotten her SUV in sight. Well trained in the art of subterfuge, he'd followed at a discreet distance, and when she'd hit the gravel road, he turned off his truck's lights so that she wouldn't know anyone was behind her.

Still no light in the house.

Getting a bad feeling, Simon left his truck and walked in closer to the house, his gaze shooting from corner to corner. He couldn't see anything wrong, but his gut told him otherwise. When he got close to the front door, he saw that it was open, if just a crack.

His gut tightened.

Lexie would never leave her front door open, not after the attack the night before. He should have forced her to let him go with her, rather than staying in the background as he had.

Listening intently, Simon thought he heard a sound like a

muffled voice from another part of the house. Removing a knife from his jacket—carrying a weapon on him for thirteen years was a hard habit to break—he slowly edged the door open until he could see inside. The living room was a mess, but it was empty so he edged himself in and followed the low murmur of a male voice.

"Your girl will tell me what I want to know."

The answer was a muffled protest.

He was talking about Katie, Simon realized, silently moving forward until he saw a dark-clad figure standing over Lexie on the kitchen floor.

The bastard must have sensed him, because he threw a glance over his shoulder, then ran for the back door.

Simon stopped only long enough to cut the tape holding Lexie's hands and feet together, and pulled another strip from her mouth. Then he ran, too.

The assailant had already disappeared. Simon looked down at what was left of the snow on the ground. Tracks led back and forth to one side of the house. By the time he rounded the corner, however, he heard an engine start up. The bastard had parked his vehicle somewhere beyond the stand of trees, just far enough so that Simon couldn't see it until the lights went on. Too late.

He ran anyway, hoping at least to identify the vehicle, but all he got was a glimpse of something dark in the distance. He couldn't even distinguish whether it was a car or a truck or an SUV. Finding where it had been parked, he checked the tire tracks— and he suspected they were made by all-terrain tires with a lot of traction. He took a mental snapshot of the pattern, then shot back to the house.

Lexie wasn't in the kitchen. Hopefully, she was calling the police.

"Lexie?"

"In here."

He followed her voice. Rather than on the phone, he found her at the stairs that led to the second floor. She stood at the newel post, the carved finial in her hand.

"What are you doing?" he asked.

She reached into the shallow depression at the top of the newel post and pulled out something small. "A key. I just wanted to make sure this was still here. This is what he wanted. He said so."

"Then why didn't you give it over? It's not worth your life!"

"I don't know. Instinct. I get the feeling this key unlocks a mystery, as well as a lock."

"Did you call the police?"

She shook her head. "What if the chief's involved? Not that he attacked me himself. But what if he's the one who told the attacker I have the key? When I showed it to Phil—one of my workers at the garden center—Hammer was there. He seemed awfully interested in the key, wanted me to hand it over. I didn't."

"Even when I was a kid, I heard rumors that Hammer could be bought." He moved closer then, and his eyes lit on the vintage key in her hand. It was a barrel key with a decorative leaf at the end. He'd seen one like that before…. Then suddenly, the memory crystalized. "One of the men responsible for my disappearance had a key like that. I was drugged, but I remember seeing it before he slipped it into his pants pocket."

"Did you see his face?"

Simon shook his head. "I only came to for a few seconds and then was out until I awoke on the transport."

"You know what that means—the key must belong to someone involved in the human trafficking business here. Dr. Janecek was undoubtedly already dead when that key ended up on the Drake property. And his assistant, Franz Kreeger, had already committed suicide in his jail cell."

"I read that the authorities think there's something fishy about Kreeger's death, but they haven't been able to prove it," he said.

"Plus they're certain others must have been involved in transporting the people from Eastern Europe to this area to do the harvesting," Lexie said. "This key proves it. Even if the ring isn't operating now, someone involved is still out there, and for some reason this key is too important to him to let go."

Made sense, Simon thought. "If the state investigation turned up anything, it hasn't hit the media."

Lexie shivered visibly. "No, it hasn't. But this might be the clue they're looking for."

"Or at least the one *I'm* looking for," Simon said. "Maybe you'd better give it to me."

Lexie locked gazes with him. "You're not the only one affected by this."

"But I may be the only one who can solve it."

"Pitting yourself against professional investigators? Isn't that taking a bit too much credit?"

"I didn't just learn to kill while I was gone."

Lexie flinched at that. "I'm the one who has access to various places at this time of year—"

"You're not going to try to investigate yourself," he said.

"Why not? I have as much at stake as you do. You might have been shipped off by the owner of this key, but I was attacked for it, my house searched."

With that, Lexie returned the key to its hiding place in the top of the newel post and reattached the finial. Remembering how stubborn she could be, Simon didn't think he could change her mind.

But he could keep her—and their daughter—safe.

"Then we'll work together." He could move in, shadow her if necessary. "I'll bring my things here and—"

"I don't think so."

"You need protection. And don't tell me again how you can protect yourself, not after what just happened."

Lexie needed more than *his* protection unless he could be with her 24/7 until this case was solved, and he had the feeling that wasn't going to happen. It was time to call in reinforcements—professional bodyguards, ones who would have to keep their distance, since he was certain Lexie would never agree to that, either.

Bray Sloane, an old buddy of Simon's from his tour in Afghanistan, ran Five Star Security in Baltimore and had contracts all over the Eastern Shore. Simon had already contacted him; he had Bray's word that he would send help on the spot if Simon needed it.

Well, Simon needed it now to keep Lexie and their daughter safe.

In addition, Bray's wife, Claire, was making it her mission to see if she could find any of the survivors. With her computer skills, she was bound to find any leads available online and would follow them up.

In addition to which, Simon had her place ads for survivors in all the newspapers within a hundred-mile radius of Jenkins Cove. Simon was offering a very generous reward for anyone who would step forward and give him information. Then again, victims who'd been tricked once might not trust anyone to do right by them a second time.

THOUGH LEXIE CONTINUED to resist Simon's attempt to move in with her, deep inside she was tempted to let him. It wasn't the promise of protection, but the feelings for him that she couldn't resist. Obviously, he still had feelings for her, as well, or he wouldn't be so insistent.

Suddenly she remembered her attacker's threat. "I don't want Katie involved in any of this."

"Of course not," he said.

"He said he was going to wait for her to get home and get the information from her." Lexie's pulse picked up at the thought that he could get to her daughter. "Katie doesn't know anything, Simon. And for the moment she's at her grandparents', but what if—"

"She'll be fine." Simon pulled out his cell phone. "Within the hour, I'll have someone watching your parents' house and following Katie wherever she goes."

Lexie wanted to object, but this was her daughter they were talking about. She couldn't jeopardize her child's safety because of her own stubbornness.

"All right," she agreed. "In the meantime, I'll call Mom and make sure they're not going anywhere this morning. I won't tell her about any of this, though. I don't want her worrying."

"Sensible."

Simon moved into the next room to make his call and, heart fluttering, Lexie dialed her parents' number. It was just about eight. Early, but not so early as to be suspicious.

Her mother answered on the third ring. "Hey, Mom, how are things going over there?"

"Fine, Lexie."

Lexie could hear the questioning note in her mother's voice. "Don't worry, Mom, I'm not going to crash your cookie-making party. I only wanted to know what was going on. Have you already started this morning?"

Sounding relieved, her mother said, "We just finished breakfast. As soon as I get off the phone, we're going to make those Christmas bells Katie loves so much."

Lexie was relieved, as well. "Great, Mom. Is she there?"

"Of course she's here. Do you want to speak to her?" Without waiting for an answer, she called, "Katie…your mother wants to talk to you."

She could hear Katie's irritable voice from a distance. "Tell her she's ruining my life, Nana. And that I'm not planning on trying to talk you into letting me go to that party, so she can relax already and just leave me alone."

Lexie actually smiled. "Let it go, Mom. She's still angry with me."

"Like daughter, like mother."

Lexie had to laugh. "Okay, okay, you can stop rubbing it in now. I love you, Mom. Tell Katie I love her, too."

She was hanging up the phone when Simon returned, carrying a framed photograph of her and Katie taken the summer before at the Fourth of July picnic her family always had. Katie still had long hair in a ponytail and her body hadn't started filling out yet, but she didn't look much different now. Their arms were around each other and they held one big piece of watermelon between them.

"She's beautiful," Simon said, his voice even, as though he were controlling it. "Just like you."

"We made a great kid, Simon."

But the idea of introducing them still didn't sit well with her. He hadn't come back for them…for her. He'd come back to settle his own score and they just happened to be there.

Simon set the photo down on the counter. "So you talked to your mom. Is Katie okay?"

"As well as a preteen can be."

Though his expression was puzzled, he didn't ask her to explain. "The cavalry is on the way."

Lexie got a bowl from the cabinet and started to crack eggs for an omelet. "Good. Now, about the key…"

"We need to figure out what it opens."

To Lexie's surprise, Simon pulled a frying pan from the rack and, opening the package of bacon, started laying down strips in the pan.

"It's so unusual," she said, adding three more eggs to the bowl, "it must belong to an old cabinet or file drawer, something likely owned by one of the Drakes. Drake Enterprises was implicated in the human trafficking ring. The fiancé of one of the victims said they were brought over on a Drake cargo ship. He was crazy with grief over her death, though, and now he's dead, too."

"Hard to say if he actually knew anything or was just making wild accusations."

"Right. So far, the authorities haven't been able to come up with any kind of connection."

"Let's assume Drake Enterprises *is* somehow responsible," Simon speculated. "That would mean either Brandon or Cliff is involved, right?"

"Not Brandon," Lexie said. Surely Marie's fiancé would have nothing to do with anything illegal.

She popped bread in the toaster and started cooking the eggs.

She said, "I don't see it being Cliff, either. He's not the type to get involved in anything serious. He's into yachts and partying and women who are too young for him."

"Then who is the type?"

Lexie thought about it for a moment. "Maybe Doug Heller. I don't know." When it came right down to it, she hated to implicate anyone.

"Heller... Who's he?"

"Cliff's manager. Basically, he's in charge of the Drake properties on the Eastern Shore."

"Right, I think I remember him."

Heller was pretty much a loner, so Lexie didn't know him

well, but she didn't want to point fingers. "I don't think he has anything to do with the shipping arm of the company, though."

"Well, someone has to be guilty," Simon insisted. "Someone responsible for bringing the victims here, where their organs were harvested. And if that was done with Drake ships, who else could it be?"

"I hate this," Lexie said, not wanting either Brandon or Cliff to be guilty. Heller was the wild card, as far as she was concerned. "But I hate what happened to a bunch of innocent people even more."

"Not as much as I do," Simon said, his voice grim. "This is going to sound…well, crazy, I guess…but I saw one of the victims last night."

"What are you talking about?"

"The kid who was shot in the woods. He led me to the cemetery. To the gravestone with my name on it."

"You mean a ghost?"

Simon nodded.

Lexie shivered. "I don't think you're crazy. I have a hard time believing in ghosts myself, but other people around here have claimed to see them lately, too. Maybe it's because they want the people who did this to them brought to justice."

"That's what I want, what I intend to make happen," Simon said, something in his tone sending a spear of ice through her. "Seeing the kid made me wonder how three grown men would react if *they* were visited by a ghost from their past."

"You mean you. But whoever put you on that transport knows you aren't dead."

"But I wonder how they would react if they saw me."

As they ate, Lexie wondered what would happen if they solved this mystery and Simon settled the score. Would he want to stay in Jenkins Cove with her and Katie?

Her heart ticked a little faster as she considered that possibility.

But no matter what she might want for herself, she had Katie to think of. She couldn't allow her daughter to be hurt. Not physically. Not emotionally. If Katie met Simon, she would probably fall for her dad as much as Lexie had. Before she introduced father and daughter, Simon would have to prove himself, convince her that he could be trusted and care for Katie as much as she did.

Lexie simply couldn't imagine Simon putting down roots here. More likely, he'd just leave Jenkins Cove in search of the action he'd gotten so used to. Then what would she tell their daughter?

Chapter Seven

On the way back to his digs at the fishing shack, Simon donned an earpiece and called Bray Sloane on his cell. "Any problems getting your men here?"

"None. The one watching the grandparents' home knows that if your daughter leaves for any reason, he isn't to let her out of his sight."

"I saw your other man when I left Lexie's place. You're sure she won't spot him?"

"He'll be invisible."

"Listen, Bray, I owe you."

Bray laughed. "Don't worry, you'll get my bill." And then his voice sobered. "Afghanistan was hell, but a hell I signed up for. What happened to you and those poor people who came to the United States thinking they were going to get a new, safe life…no one deserves that."

"Yeah." Simon didn't know what else to say.

"I've got to see a potential new client later this morning, so I'll be in Easton, about twenty minutes from Jenkins Cove. If you need me for anything, give me a call and I'll be there as soon as I can."

"I'll keep that in mind. Thanks, Bray."

He ended the conversation just as the narrow asphalt road to the hiding place for his truck came into view. Halfway there, he switched from asphalt to dirt and soon turned into a thick stand of pine trees where he parked and left the truck. He needed to catch a few hours' sleep before putting his plan into action.

His thoughts wandered from ghostly pursuits to Lexie to the daughter he'd never seen. A daughter who looked like the woman he loved. Who had his eyes. A yearning came over him and Simon had to shake it away. He needed to stay focused. Emotions were messy and would make him sloppy. Sloppiness could get someone killed…not necessarily him.

He'd seen enough death to last him a lifetime.

The only deaths he wanted to see were those of the people responsible for ruining his life and the lives of so many others.

As he neared the swampy area, Simon's mind wandered back to the wars he'd fought, and he didn't at first hear the voices until he was almost exposed.

"You're sure you don't own this land?"

"Perry, you're becoming a nuisance."

Simon stopped himself from stepping into the clearing. He stayed within the protection of the pines and the shadows they provided. This Perry guy was of medium height with brown hair combed to the side—no one familiar to Simon. But the other guy—dark-haired, tall and thin—seemed familiar, though his face was scarred and he was leaning heavily on a cane as he walked toward the two vehicles parked nearby.

"If you tell me who owns this land, I'll stop bugging you about your waterfront property."

"You can't build here anyway. It's a graveyard, for Pete's sake."

Simon realized that, again, there was no cop on site. Considering that the holidays were upon them, the police were probably shorthanded.

"They'll get all the bodies out," the guy named Perry was saying. "No one else will have the guts to buy it. I can get it cheap, and once I get a development going, no one will even remember what went on here."

"I've told you before that your schemes don't interest me. Now I'm even more certain."

"Look, Drake, if you don't cooperate one way or the other, I can ruin things for you."

Drake? Simon started. This was Brandon Drake. Scarred and on a cane!

What the hell had happened to him?

Simon had known Brandon since he was a kid. Four years older than Simon, Brandon had been one of the high school leaders for summer programs meant to keep the Jenkins Cove kids out of trouble. Simon remembered him being a little too overbearing. Or maybe he'd just seemed that way to a kid who resented anyone telling him what to do and who already had a chip on his shoulder because of his crappy home life.

"What? Now you're trying to blackmail me?" Brandon's outraged question was barely discernable as they neared the vehicles.

"I need this deal! You sell me that shoreline property I want and I won't talk."

Simon couldn't hear Brandon's response. He stayed hidden until the men drove off.

He stepped away from the trees and considered what he'd heard. This Perry guy seemed way too desperate to buy land; he didn't even care if it was a mass grave. What was up with that? And Brandon Drake most certainly was hiding something. What could Perry know about Brandon that he could use as blackmail?

And did it have something to do with Drake Enterprises being involved in human trafficking?

WHEN SHE APPROACHED the gated entrance that led up to Drake House later that morning, Lexie was wondering about the non-descript silver sedan that seemed to have been following her for several miles. She turned through the opening between the pillars and onto the drive, and glanced up into her rearview mirror. When the other car kept going without slowing, Lexie took a relieved breath and relaxed.

For a few moments, she'd thought her assailant was back for attack number three. This time, Simon was nowhere nearby to save her butt.

The thought jogged her into thinking about Simon, seeing his face in her mind, remembering how good it felt to be in his arms even on a hard floor in front of a woodstove. It also made her wonder what she should do about Simon in relation to their daughter. Should she let Katie know her father was alive?

It was a decision that could wait until later.

Her crew arrived right behind her. Lexie got them organized, hauling in the truckload of mums, gerbera daisies and more greenery right away. She glanced up at the burned part of the mansion, the reason for the flowers. She might be able to hide the remaining scent of burned wood, but she wouldn't be able to hide the visual evidence. Thankfully, guests wouldn't be arriving for the ball until after dark.

All the basics had to be in place before they left today, Lexie thought, on her way to the entry. The next day would be spent decorating the second-floor parlors and the outside entry to the house. Then there shouldn't be much more to do on the day of the ball than to haul in fresh flowers and cover the tables with linens and candles. Not that there wouldn't be a few last-minute details that needed to be taken care of, but that was always to be expected.

Lexie was just about to the front door when her cell rang. Checking the ID and seeing that it was Simon, she decided to stay outside a few minutes longer to take the call so that she could have some privacy. Circling along the drive toward the bay, she flipped the cell open.

A little thrill running through her, she said, "Hey. I thought you were going to get some sleep." Something she could use herself.

"I will, but I just overheard an interesting conversation between Brandon Drake and some guy named Perry."

"Where?"

"The mass grave."

"What the heck was Brandon doing out there?" And with Ned Perry, of all people.

"Something I wondered myself. This Perry guy wanted to know who owned the land."

"I heard he's been bugging people about it," Lexie said, gazing onto the bay whose shore was barely dotted with large houses and mansions, keeping the area from being overpopulated. "He can't get anyone else to sell him shoreline land so I guess he figures that since that land has partial access to the water, he could build his development there."

A shiver shot through her. If Ned succeeded in finding the owner and convinced him to sell, would future condo buyers be warned they were going to be living over a former mass grave?

Simon broke into her thoughts. "That's not actually why I called, though."

"What's up?"

"Brandon is hiding something."

"As in?"

"Don't know. But Perry was putting the squeeze on him."

"What kind of squeeze?"

"Blackmail."

"I don't believe it." Simon didn't respond and Lexie realized that he was serious. "You think it could be about Drake Enterprises involvement with the human trafficking?"

"What else?"

Lexie's stomach clenched. She didn't want to believe that Brandon had been involved or that he was hiding something to protect the family name. But as they had discussed earlier, Brandon had to be considered a suspect, along with Cliff and Doug Heller. She turned and gazed at the east wing again, the visible damage from the fire an immediate reminder that someone else had thought Brandon was involved with the human trafficking operation.

"All right," she said, then glanced around to make sure no one was around to overhear. "I have the key with me. I'll see what I can find out."

The lighting team had arrived. They would create pools of light to accentuate particular areas of the ballroom—the fireplace, the trio of trees, the silent auction area, among others—plus they'd create a special effect so that it would seem as if it were snowing inside. The first thing they needed to do was to figure out the power situation in case they had to add a generator.

"Can we see the breaker boxes?" the older man named Rick asked.

Isabella had entered the room and Lexie waved the maid over. "Rick needs to check on the electrical situation. Can you show him where the breakers are?"

Isabella gave her a sour expression, but said, "This way," and moved off, Rick and his young assistant following.

The high school kids arrived, and Lexie got them started decorating the already-lit balsam trees with white icicles and red and gold ornaments.

Another crew arrived with the tables and chairs. Food service would be confined to two other public rooms—the re-

:eption parlor for the buffet and the grand dining room for :eating the festive meal. Lexie handed them computer printouts that showed how to set up the myriad tables.

Everyone was hard at work, and everything seemed to be going smoothly. Lexie relaxed a little, certain all would be ready in time for the ball the next evening.

Good, because she had some snooping to do.

Brandon had been gone when she arrived and Marie had left the house to run some errands, so there was no time like the present.

With her unlimited access to Drake House, Lexie could move through any of the rooms in the public wing without raising suspicions. When Marie had turned over the key to her, she'd said it didn't fit any of the doors in the house, but she had probably just checked the key against the room doors, not against the furniture.

Lexie started with the first-floor rooms she'd been hired to decorate and checked for locked cabinets. No luck until she found a buffet with a drawer with a lock. Unfortunately, the key barrel was too big to insert.

She strolled through the kitchen, which at the moment was empty. Did she dare check out the rooms Marie's father had used before his death, which now were occupied by the housekeeper?

Lexie's hand was on the door handle when she heard a noise behind her and whirled around guiltily.

Shelley Zachary had just come from one of the back rooms used for laundry and storage. The housekeeper was balancing a tray filled with crystal serving dishes that she put on a stainless steel counter.

"Can I help you with something, Lexie?"

"I was looking for you, actually," Lexie lied, her heart thundering. "I just wondered if you knew when Marie was going to be back."

Shelley's narrow face pulled tight and her penciled eyebrows rose, making her look suspicious. "Why don't you just call her on her cell?"

"I tried." Lexie hated lying and wasn't very good at it. She only hoped her voice sounded steady and convincing. "Signal's not going through or something."

Shelley stared at her for a moment, then started moving the crystal serving pieces from the tray to the counter. "I imagine Marie will be here within the hour. Not that I keep track of her comings and goings."

While Lexie said, "Thank you, Shelley," she was aware that the housekeeper was keeping track of everything that went on in this house. And in town. According to Marie, the housekeeper was quite a gossip. "Back to work," she said softly as if to herself.

She felt Shelley's eyes follow her to the ballroom door.

Shaking off the feeling undoubtedly caused by her own guilt, Lexie reconnoitered. She knew the second-floor parlors overlooking the ballroom had only a few tables and seating arrangements, so she didn't need to check them.

Entering the empty foyer, she hesitated before going upstairs, to the third-floor rooms Marie and Brandon were using until the roof and other damage to the east wing was repaired. If she was to go up there, she needed a plausible explanation to cover her furtive actions.

Then it came to her. She grabbed extra greenery and a couple of plants that hadn't been set out yet. If anyone saw her, she could say she was simply spreading some of the Christmas cheer to her best friend's private quarters. Halfway up the staircase, she felt the small hairs at the back of her neck tickle and got a weird feeling that made her stomach do a flip. Had Shelley Zachary followed her from the kitchen? Though she glanced down, Lexie saw no one in the foyer.

She was probably feeling weird because of her friendship with Marie and therefore with Brandon.

What would her friend think if she caught Lexie in her private quarters and didn't buy the decorating excuse? Pulse humming, she rushed up to the third floor. Surely Marie would believe her cover story, especially since she planned to spruce up the sitting room.

Lexie hadn't been up here since she was a kid. She and Marie used to explore the house and play hide-and-seek and other games in the big rooms. Then one day Edwin had caught them. Marie's father had been very big on propriety and had told them they were quite out of line going where they weren't invited. She'd been scared straight then, but now thinking back on it, Lexie wondered if he hadn't been secretly amused...

She entered the sitting room first, placed the gerbera daisies on the side table next to the sofa and the mums on a table between two chairs before the fireplace. After arranging the greenery on the mantel, she went back to her real purpose. She found only one lock on the cabinet holding crystal glasses and pitchers and bottles of liquor. The key proved too large for the opening.

Getting that feeling again, like interested eyes were following her, Lexie rechecked the foyer, thinking that if someone spotted her, she would have to give up the search and go back downstairs.

The foyer was clear. But not her sense of being watched. Guilt certainly put her imagination on overdrive.

Shaking away the unsettling feeling, she continued her search.

No furniture in the bedroom Marie and Brandon were now sharing required a key. Thankfully, Lexie thought, not wanting to invade her friend's privacy any more than she had to.

In the rear of the wing, there were a couple of storerooms, one for linens, the other filled with boxes. Nothing that required a key in either.

Relieved, Lexie was about to return to work downstairs when she realized she needed to check the east wing, as well. Doing so might be dangerous. She didn't know how extensive the damage was or how safe entering those rooms would be. But she couldn't let it go unsearched.

The sense of being watched followed her down the stairs and across the gallery as she moved from one wing to the other, but no matter how intensely she searched for prying eyes, she saw no one, nothing out of place.

The damage was worst in the rear where the roof had collapsed. The fire had started in the second-floor nursery. Lexie couldn't check that room, the one adjacent or above it, but she figured she could manage the rest. Even though she started at the front of the wing, she was more aware of the smoke damage than she was down in the ballroom, despite the clean-up crew that Brandon had brought in. She guessed the wing would need a new roof and possibly some new walls and flooring before the smell would be obliterated.

Just being in this part of the house now gave Lexie the creeps and she asked herself why she was doing this. Because she wanted to eliminate Brandon as a suspect and this was the only way she could do that. She kept thinking about the dead man who'd set fire to the east wing out of a need for revenge. He must have had some reason to suspect Brandon. Maybe he'd found something…something that, should she find it, as well, would lead *her* to the real killer.

That decided, she got to work.

An antique cabinet in a parlor had a lock, as did a walnut armoire in what she assumed was Brandon's bedroom. Neither was a match to the key. She used the side stairs to get to the third floor, but stopped halfway up when she realized she was putting herself in physical danger. So she headed back down and continued investigating the abandoned first-floor rooms. No better luck there.

Soon, there was only one room left that she could get at, other than Shelley's new quarters. Brandon's office sat directly in plain sight of the foyer.

Just as she thought it, the entry door opened and Marie came in, carrying several packages. Before her friend could see her, Lexie backed up and around a corner to avoid the other woman, who headed directly upstairs. Thankfully, she hadn't done so while Lexie was up there.

Waiting a minute to make certain the coast was clear, Lexie approached the door to the office. Just to play it safe, she knocked. Perhaps Brandon had returned and was sequestered in there.

No answer.

Even so, her pulse was racing as she tried the handle. It turned easily. She slipped inside, pulling the door closed behind her before feeling for the light switch.

Brandon's office looked just as it must have when his grandfather had first furnished it. The floor was covered with an old Oriental carpet and the furniture—serpentine partners' desk with leather top, chest of file drawers with marquetry detail and matching credenza—were all of mahogany with brass accents, including locks.

Lexie tried the desk first. The lock on the middle drawer was old-fashioned, the kind that would take a key like the one found on the grounds. She tried to slip the key in the lock, but it didn't quite fit.

She moved to the cabinet with file drawers and her pulse sped up as did her breath when she noticed that the leaf pattern in the veneer trim matched the pattern at the end of the key. Taking a deep breath, she inserted the key into the lock. It slipped in easily, but didn't turn. The fit was close enough, however, for her to believe that her key would fit a similar cabinet.

Undoubtedly, the cabinets had been bought by the same Drake—Brandon's grandfather Henry. The matching file cabinet then would most likely be found in one of the Drake Enterprises offices.

Lexie had just taken the key from the lock when she realized she wasn't alone. Palming the key, she turned to face Isabella.

"Can I help you with something?" Isabella asked as if she were the mistress of the house rather than the maid.

Considering that she hadn't brought any plants or decorations into the office, Lexie figured she couldn't use that as an excuse, so she said the first thing that came to mind. "I lost something yesterday and thought it might be in here."

"Hmm, I don't remember your being in Brandon's office yesterday."

Lexie raised her eyebrows. Isabella did have an inflated sense of self-importance.

"I didn't realize you were keeping track of my every move."

Isabella ignored the dig. "I can help you look for whatever it is you lost."

"That won't be necessary."

"No trouble."

"You have more important things to do."

"Not at the moment."

"Then perhaps you should ask Marie for something to do."

"I don't work for Marie."

Getting more irritated with Isabella by the second, Lexie said, "Then find something else to do…away from here."

Finally Isabella backed down and gave her a sulky expression before leaving the room. Lexie sagged against the desk and slipped the key into her back pocket.

She had more than one reason to be relieved. While she couldn't say for certain that Brandon was innocent, the fact that she couldn't open his file drawer with the key meant it belonged to a different if matching cabinet, one that undoubtedly would be found at the Drake Enterprises offices.

And the person really in charge of the business was Doug Heller…

Chapter Eight

"Your daughter's on the move, Mr. Shea," the bodyguard assigned to watch Katie informed Simon.

A call from Bray Sloane having woken him up a short while ago, Simon was getting ready to go into town to meet the man. "With whom?"

"Alone. She's on foot. Looks like she's heading for Main Street."

"I'm ready to leave now," Simon said, shrugging into his leather jacket. "I'll be in Jenkins Cove in ten. Call me back when you know where Katie's going."

"Will do."

Simon shoved the cell in his inner jacket pocket, grabbed his car keys and left the fishing shack. He pulled on his gloves as he ran to the truck, which he'd parked on the other side of the camp, since again there had been no patrol car parked at the mass gravesite.

A sense of excitement filled him as he clambered into the truck, put on his sunglasses and a brimmed hat. The day was as bright as his sudden change in mood.

He couldn't help himself. Couldn't keep himself from grinning.

Katie…his daughter…

He still had trouble fathoming that he'd fathered a child. A child he would finally get to see in a few minutes. Not just a photo like the one of her and Lexie, but Katie herself. Not that he would actually introduce himself. He just wanted to get a look at her, even if from afar.

He started the truck and edged out of the stand of trees and headed for town.

For so many years, he'd been without family. He was an only child. His mother died when he was still a kid and his father was usually too drunk to know he existed, other than to make his life miserable. Once Rufus Shea had loved him—Simon was sure of that—but it was as if he'd blamed Simon for his wife's death. That's when his father's drinking had gone from social to serious. That's when Simon's home life had collapsed.

How desperately he'd been looking forward to starting his own family with Lexie that Christmas Eve thirteen years ago. Unbeknownst to him, he had. Sort of. If Katie wasn't aware that he was her dad—if he wasn't allowed to know her, to influence her as she grew into a lovely young lady—did his having fathered her count?

He would take what he could get. When this was over, he wouldn't deserve more.

His cell rang when he was about a minute from town. The ID told him it was the bodyguard.

"So where is she?"

"Katie headed straight into the supermarket. Just went inside. Do you want me to take off when you get here?"

"Not at all. I just want to see her for myself, you know, so that I can be sure she's okay. And then I have a meeting with your boss."

"Bray's in town?"

"He will be shortly. You keep an eye on my girl. Don't let anything happen to her."

"Check."

Simon drove past the bodyguard's car on the street across from Jenkins Cove Market and pulled into the parking lot. His pulse ticked faster as he left the car and went inside, still wearing the dark glasses and hat so that he wouldn't be recognized…if anyone still remembered him after all these years.

Christmas music blasted him as he grabbed a cart and raced down the aisles, looking for Katie. He found her in the aisle with baking goods. She was just putting a bag of sugar in her cart. Slowing, he pretended to be looking for something when he really was checking out his daughter. She was beautiful, a young Lexie. He couldn't stop looking at her.

She was tall for twelve—maybe five-six—and slender. Her short, dark hair was fashionably spiked, but her face was free of makeup, leaving her with a clear complexion and natural color in her cheeks. She looked up and even from a distance, he could see the clear green of her large round eyes.

His eyes.

Apparently sensing that he'd been watching her, Katie froze and gave him a weird look. Not wanting to freak her out, he picked something off the shelf, threw it in his cart and headed for the checkout.

As he passed her, from the corner of his eye, Simon saw Katie move away slightly. Damn! He hadn't meant to scare her. He'd just wanted a close-up look at his daughter without her having to know who he was, and now he'd ruined it. He fought the urge to look back at her.

"Will that be all, sir?" The kid at the register raised his voice to be heard over the piped-in Christmas music.

Simon grunted and looked down to see what he'd thrown in

his cart. Cherry pie filling. "Yeah," he muttered, placing the can on the counter and pulling out his wallet.

As much as he wanted to glance back, to see what Katie was doing, he kept his focus where it belonged.

His heart hurt for the years they'd missed. Surely there was some way he could be in his daughter's life. He was already regretting severing his relationship with his own father. He should have tried to help the old man get over his alcoholism instead of running out on him.

If he had, he would never have been forced to fight in a war he'd wanted no part of, would have a totally different life now.

On the way out of the market, Simon spotted a Christmas food drop for needy families and added the cherry pie filling to the cans and boxes already there. And then he kept going, to the lot, to his truck, never once looking back just in case Katie was there.

He headed straight for the diner at the east end of town in hopes that there would be fewer people who might recognize him. The place wasn't fancy, though there were Christmas lights in the window and a small tree near the register. Bray was in a back booth waiting for him. Simon waved, but stopped at the counter where a redheaded waitress with a big name tag identifying her as Wanda was giving one of the customers his check.

He got her attention. "Morning, Wanda. I could use coffee and breakfast if you're still serving it."

"We're still serving it, sugar. What's your pleasure?"

"The works. Surprise me. I'm about hungry enough to eat a snake."

"We serve snakes here, but we don't feed snakes to our customers." She laughed at her own joke and poked her head through the window to the kitchen to order a breakfast. "Hey, Sam, one Lumberjack!"

His stomach already growling, Simon moved to the table and

gave the big man there the once-over. His dark hair was spiked, his gray eyes seemingly free of the nightmares they'd once reflected, his body muscular.

"Bray." He held out his hand and the other man stood to take it. They were of equal height and strength. "It's been a long time."

"A lot of years," Bray agreed.

They both sat as Wanda arrived with Simon's coffee. "Brought you boys a pot," she said, setting it in the middle of the table and a mug in front of Simon. "That breakfast will be up in a few minutes."

"My stomach's already growling," Simon told her. Then, when she left, he turned to Bray. Before he'd left Afghanistan, Bray had been a mess. His eyes had held that look identifying him as a man on the verge of a breakdown. Not anymore. Simon would bet Bray's wife, Claire, had everything to do with that. "Good to see you."

"If only the circumstances were better," Bray said, keeping his voice low.

"Hopefully, when I'm done with this town, they will be." But did he want to be done with the town if that meant he was done with Lexie and Katie? Did he want to take the kind of revenge that would push them away forever? Not wanting to complicate things right at the moment, Simon focused on the reason for the meeting. "So what do you have for me?"

"Claire got a response to her ad. A Hans Zanko claims to be one of the survivors. He's in Annapolis, not too far from the Five Star Security offices." Bray handed Simon a folder. "Do you want Claire to follow up and interview him about what happened? He wants to be paid $10,000 for the information. He checks out as far as we can tell, but of course there aren't any records to prove his claim that he was brought over for his kidney. He could be in it for the money."

"That what you think?" When Bray shrugged, Simon opened the folder to find a photo and contact info for a man who looked to be in his forties.

"He didn't send that photo, by the way. Claire got it off the Internet."

Which seemed to legitimize Hans Zanko, though Simon was still uncertain. "I would have guessed they would pick someone younger to be a donor. Like in his twenties, not forties."

"Except we don't know how long ago the operation started. Some of those bodies they've dug up from the mass grave go way back. This guy has been in the country for a dozen years at least."

"I'll check it out myself. If this Zanko is legit, I may be able to get more out of him, since I do have something in common with him. You just get me the cash from the account as soon as you get back to the office." Simon had put $25,000 at Bray's disposal for expenses and could move money into the account electronically. "And thank your wife for this."

"I'll do that. I know you're in an odd situation, what with everyone thinking you're dead and all. You might need some backup other than from me. Someone in the system."

"A lawyer?"

"A cop. A detective for the state police. *The* detective, actually."

"You mean the one investigating the victims…the mass grave site?" When Bray nodded, Simon asked, "How do you know him?"

"He's my brother-in-law, Rand McClellan. He's good. He's fair. And he knows that things aren't always what they seem," Bray said, his tone odd enough that Simon took notice. "He can keep things under wraps until the time is right."

"I'll think about it. So why did you really want to see me?" Simon asked. "You could have sent me Zanko's photo and contact information. You could have told me about your brother-in-law in a phone conversation."

"Well, uh…"

"C'mon, Bray, what gives?"

"I only hesitate because you might find this hard to believe," Bray began. "My former partner at Five Star Security and I had a contract with a scientific company working for DARPA. There was a lab accident—an experiment that was aimed at developing a new biochemical warfare weapon. It left me without my memory for a while…" Bray looked around as if making sure no one could overhear. "…and gave me an ability I didn't have before."

"What kind of ability?"

"I can, uh…when I touch something, I can see something that happened to the object in the past. If I touch something connected to the murders—that key you told me about—maybe I can give you a lead that'll help."

Simon didn't immediately respond. He was wondering if his old acquaintance was in as good a condition as he'd first believed. Bray spoke up again. "Let me show you how it works. Give me something of yours and I'll tell you what I see."

Simon thought about it for a moment and pulled out his wallet. From it, he took a flat piece of metal with a picture of a crab. It had once been a pin, but cheaply put together, it had come apart. Still, Simon hadn't been able to get rid of the souvenir.

He handed it to Bray and watched the other man's forehead pull into a frown of concentration.

"A carnival of some sort…food…corn on the cob…crabs…"

"You could get that from the picture."

"A ring tossing game…a young woman…long bare legs… dark hair in a ponytail…big smile. She's determined to win…"

Suddenly Simon saw it all again—him and Lexie at the

Eastern Shore Crabfest, the day he'd fallen head over heels for her. He'd loved her ever since they were kids, but this one perfect day in August with her had made him see what life could be like if they could spend it together. It had made him want something he'd never had.

The day had been magic. *Lexie* had been magic. She'd cast a spell on him. So when she'd won the ring toss and had insisted on giving him her prize, the pin had taken on a value far above its true worth.

I'll keep this forever, Lexie. No matter where I am, it'll remind me of you.

Simon still remembered his exact words. And he'd been true to his vow. He'd kept the pin, had taken it out to feel closer to home—to her—even in war.

"She won the game and gave you the pin," Bray said, seeming as if he were coming out of a trance. "And you said you would keep it forever."

Simon cursed under his breath, but before he could say anything, a platter landed on the table before him.

"Hope it'll do you," Wanda said.

A glance at the plate of pancakes and eggs and potatoes and bacon and sausage and toast was enough to make Simon's stomach growl.

But when Simon looked at Bray and said, "I hope it'll do me, too," he wasn't talking about the food.

Chapter Nine

"We're done for the day," Lexie told Marie late in the afternoon just after her crew had cleared out.

"You've really done a fabulous job on this place," Marie said. "Better than I even imagined."

Lexie glanced back into the ballroom and admitted that it did look pretty good, definitely the holiday wonderland her friend had requested. The scent of pine wafted from the room that now was unrecognizable in gold and red and green splendor. The lights weren't even on, nor the special snow effect, and still it was transformed into a fairy-tale setting.

In two days her mood had shifted as greatly as the ballroom had. The Grinch was hiding somewhere, chased away by a sense of expectancy.

But it wasn't the holiday that had gotten to her.

Being with Simon again had lifted her spirits, if only for the moment.

Knowing she couldn't share her secret with Marie without betraying Simon's wishes, Lexie decided she'd better leave fast before she folded and gave it up.

"I'm glad you're pleased."

"I hope it lightens Brandon's mood," Marie said. "Something's been bothering him and he won't talk about it. Says it's business and he wants to forget about business when he's with me."

A curl of anxiety tightened Lexie's stomach. "That's good. Isn't it?"

"I guess." Marie shrugged. "Although I hate being shut out when I might be able to help him."

Lexie prayed that Brandon didn't know anything about the human trafficking operation. "I'm sure his mood will even out. Give him time to get used to your being around and believing he can share things with you."

"You're right."

Hoping she was, Lexie gave Marie a big hug. "See you tomorrow."

Lexie left and hurried out to the car. Brandon had to be innocent. Surely his mood had shifted because of some business pressures that had nothing to do with the horrific acts that had been going on in Jenkins Cove. If he was guilty or even knew something about the operation that he hadn't revealed to the authorities, Marie would be devastated.

Having gotten a call from Simon just as she was wrapping up for the afternoon, Lexie took off and headed for town to meet him at the diner. When she'd asked him what was up, however, he'd been all mysterious. She expected there was more than a fast dinner together involved. He must have gotten some information.

Halfway there, Lexie realized that the same vehicle had been behind her since she left the estate.

From a distance, it looked like it could be the same silver sedan that she'd seen that morning. Surely not. Surely her imagination was working overtime. Wanting to know for certain, Lexie slowed her SUV to let the other vehicle catch up. It slowed, as well.

Her pulse fluttered. What if someone really *was* following her? Her assailant?

She stepped on the gas, now wanting to get away from the car, but the other driver did the same, keeping the same distance between them, just far enough back so that she couldn't be sure of anything. If only it would get closer, she could use her cell to take a photo, maybe get a shot of the plates that could be blown up.

When she entered Jenkins Cove, she made a couple of unnecessary turns. The other vehicle did, as well. The car was close enough now that she could see that it was a silver sedan. Still too far away to get a good shot on her cell phone.

When she turned back on Main Street, Lexie stepped on the gas and headed straight for the diner where Simon was waiting for her. Parking the car right out front, she ran into the diner, pulling her cell from her pocket, then stared out the window, waiting for the car to pass.

It didn't.

"Lexie, over here."

Simon's voice pulled her attention from the window. She turned to see him sitting with another man at a back booth. How weird, considering he didn't want his presence known. After glancing back through the window, she joined them.

As she approached the booth, Simon frowned at her. "What's wrong, Lexie?"

"I think I'm being followed."

Simon and the stranger locked gazes, and getting a sick feeling in her stomach, Lexie sank down into the booth. "Why do I get the feeling you know something about this?"

"Because he's my man," the stranger said. "I'm Bray Sloane."

Lexie turned to Simon and couldn't keep the accusing tone out of her voice. "You decided to have me followed and didn't tell me?"

"He's a bodyguard," Simon told her, "doing what you

wouldn't let *me* do. You agreed it would be a good idea to keep Katie safe."

"But you didn't say anything about hiring a bodyguard for *me!*"

"You need protection, but I know you would have refused if I'd mentioned it."

"Apparently you know me well." She turned to Bray who sat in silence, but with a knowing expression.

"Tell your man his services won't be needed anymore."

"Don't tell him any such thing," Simon countered. "Unless…"

"Unless what?"

"You agree to let *me* protect you until the situation is resolved."

"You mean move in?" Lexie's pulse quickened but she said, "I don't want to confuse Katie."

As if Katie were the only one who would be confused by Simon's presence…

"You told me she was staying at her grandmother's for a few days."

"Yes, but then what?" Lexie asked. "What happens when she comes back home?"

"We can renegotiate…if the situation isn't resolved before then."

Lexie gritted her teeth. She knew Simon would insist that she have protection, no matter what she said. In truth, he was right. She'd been attacked twice. She definitely could see the advantage of someone watching her back. Part of her wanted it to be Simon himself. Though her feelings about him and about his staying away from her were ambiguous, she wanted the chance to sort them out. She simply didn't like someone else suddenly making decisions for her.

Not even a ghost.

Sighing, she finally said, "Fine. You can move in."

"Fine?" Simon's brows shot up, showing his surprise at her easy capitulation.

"But you sleep on the couch."

"Fine," Simon said again, then turned to Bray. "Take the bodyguard off Lexie, but not off Katie."

"Will do."

Not liking being manipulated, Lexie took a big breath before asking, "So what did you want to see me about?"

Simon gave a quick look around the room before asking in a low voice, "The key. You have it on you, right?"

"What about it?"

"Bray would like to see it."

Lexie looked from Simon, to Bray, back to Simon again. "Why?" Did he think Bray would recognize it?

"Trust me. Just hand it over."

Lexie fished the key out of her back pocket and held it out to Bray. He took it from her and his head jerked slightly. His gaze locked on the key, he sat frozen.

"What—"

Simon's kick under the table stopped her from finishing. Bray was obviously in some kind of trance. His pale gray eyes had gone kind of weird, like they were in some other place. Her pulse sped up and she held her breath until he seemed to snap out of it enough to speak.

"The key fits an old file drawer," Bray said, his expression intent. "The drawer is part of a wood cabinet with leaves embossed in the trim."

Lexie started. He was describing the cabinet she'd found in Brandon's office.

"Someone is unlocking it…a man, from the hands. He's sorting through the files… Wait, he's stopping, pulling one out…Lala Falat."

Lexie started. Seeing Bray's eyes come back into focus as if he'd just come out of a trance, she said, "Lala Falat is one of the women whose kidney was taken. She died later, of complications." And her fiancé had plotted revenge against Brandon. "Did you see any of the other names?"

"A few. Anna Bencek…Franz Dobra…Tomas Elizi… That's it, I'm afraid."

"The face?" Lexie asked. "Did you see the man's face?"

Bray shook his head. "I saw through his eyes, just as if I were the man in question. Sorry I can't give you more, that's just how it works."

He handed back the key.

Lexie might have disbelieved Bray if he hadn't described the cabinet so accurately.

"So what do we do with this information?" she asked Simon.

"See if those other names are of people who survived."

A QUARTER OF AN HOUR LATER, Simon squared the check with the waitress and gave her a big tip.

"Nice waiting on you, honey," Wanda said, obviously pleased. "You come back any time."

"I was never here," Simon said, handing her another bill.

Her eyebrows shot up but she didn't miss a beat. "Never saw you before, stranger."

When the waitress left, Bray rose from the booth. "Nice to meet you, Lexie."

"Thanks for your help."

Simon took another look at the names he'd written down—those Bray had picked up from the folders in his vision, as well as the one who'd contacted Claire. Trying to track down these people was someplace to start, even if he had to pay for information that could lead him to the truth. He certainly could afford it. And he would start trying to reach any survivors as soon as he moved his things into Lexie's house.

As they left the diner, Simon stuffed the list in his pocket and said, "We need to stop at the fishing cabin before going to your place."

"You can meet me there."

"And let you out of my sight? Not a good idea. Not part of the deal."

"Surely you don't think I agreed to have you shadow my every movement."

"Only the ones that could get you into trouble. Truth is, my instincts tell me to get you the hell out of here. You and Katie."

"That's not going to happen."

"I can make it happen, Lexie. And I will if I have to…if you don't cooperate."

He could see that Lexie was still fighting the idea, that she didn't like being told what to do, but in the end she nodded. "All right."

She led their little procession straight to the fishing camp, while he followed close enough that no one could get between them.

He wondered if he was doing the wrong thing getting so personally involved with her again. Yes, he loved her, yes, part of him wanted to think there was a way he could have some kind of life with her and Katie in it. But the other part of him—the dark part, fostered in a country halfway across the world—wanted revenge for what had happened to him, and he wasn't certain which emotion was stronger. He wasn't certain he would be good for Lexie or for their daughter, not only because of his past, but because of his planned future.

If Lexie knew the kinds of things he'd been forced to do—the kinds of things he would like to do to repay whoever had set him up—he couldn't imagine that she'd want him in her life. Certainly not in Katie's. But after the life he'd been coerced into, how could he let go of the past until he'd seen that justice was served?

Five minutes at the fishing camp and they were off again. Though Lexie's remote home had made her more susceptible to her assailant, the place had its advantages. No one would know that Simon was there.

Once he got his stuff inside and made sure the premises were safe, Simon moved his truck into the wooded area where he'd parked before. Then he jogged back to the house.

Lexie was standing at the kitchen door, watching for him through the window. Simon's heart began to jog faster than his legs. With her dark hair spilling around her pale face, her expression at once worried and welcoming, she was a sight any man would be glad to come home to. He just didn't think that man could be him.

"I put some coffee on," she said after opening the door to let him inside. "If you could drink another cup."

"I can live on coffee." He didn't tell her there were times when he had, when in the field food had run out and they'd used coffee grounds a second and third time to have something warm to drink at night.

"So where do we start?"

"Computer. I'm going to do searches on all four names, see what I come up with."

"You mean addresses?"

"And telephone numbers. And hopefully other information, as well. The more we have, the better off we'll be."

"I can help you with that. I have my laptop here."

Then he told her about Bray's wife getting a response from a possible survivor named Hans Zanko.

"He wants to sell you information? What about justice?"

Simon shrugged. "Justice wouldn't pay the bills or feed his family. Who knows his circumstances? He might never have really recovered from what they did to him."

As he himself hadn't recovered, Simon thought. *Maybe he never would.*

"Well, I still think it's horrible." Lexie poured two mugs of coffee and handed one to him. "Let's get started with that research."

Sitting at the kitchen table, Simon worked on his laptop, while Lexie worked on hers. Good thing she had installed a home networking system. Simon had found his wi-fi to be fairly useless when he'd been at the fishing camp, but it worked great here.

He started with Franz Dobra, she with Tomas Elizi.

Simon found a Frank Dobra. When he called the number and explained why he was calling, the woman at the other end agreed that her husband's name really was Franz, but everyone called him Frank. She also said that he'd left her for some floozy and she had no clue where to find him. Then she hung up on him.

The only Tomas Elizi Lexie found was in Europe.

"I don't know if it's me or if he simply doesn't exist," Lexie said. "He could have changed his name, moved like your Frank/Franz Dobra did."

"Or he might not have made it," Simon said, thinking of the bodies from the mass grave that might never be identified.

"Or that."

Trying not to be discouraged, Simon said, "I'll get hold of Hans Zanko and set something up. At least he's willing to talk. Claire got his cell number."

"Okay, I'll start a search on Anna Bencek."

Simon pulled out his cell and hit paydirt when the man immediately answered, "Zanko here."

"Mr. Zanko, I'm the one interested in getting information on the human trafficking operation run out of Jenkins Cove."

"I would be happy to speak with you in person. What did you say your name was?"

"I didn't. It's Madison. Jake Madison." Until he was ready, Simon wasn't about to give out his real name to anyone, not even to a survivor.

A heavy pause was followed by Zanko saying, "All right, Mr. Madison. You can meet me at an abandoned boatyard near Annapolis at nine this evening." He gave Simon the address. "And don't forget your part of the bargain."

"Don't worry, I'll bring the money."

By the time Simon hung up, Lexie had had some luck.

"An Anna Bencek has a dress shop in Easton. Here's the address and phone number."

Surprised that she'd possibly located a survivor so close, Simon immediately followed up, but was met with a recording. He hung up. "She's out to lunch or something. Let's go meet Bray to get that money. We can stop in Easton on the way to Annapolis. Hopefully, we can catch the Bencek woman."

Chapter Ten

They left a short while later, Simon driving Lexie's SUV. On edge, she kept a sharp eye on the sideview mirror, but saw no one following them. Not until they were on the road heading north to Easton did she allow herself to relax. The drive was all too short.

They went directly to the Dover Shopping Center where a Christmas carol blared out over the lot. The dress shop was at the far end. As they approached the store on foot, Lexie looked at the holiday window display. Another reminder of the day both of their lives had changed forever. But for some reason, it didn't bother her as much as it might have mere days ago.

Simon opened the door and placed his hand on Lexie's back to guide her inside. His touch made her catch her breath, so she quickly put some distance between them. She had to keep her mind on their mission, not on Simon himself. A look around revealed one woman looking at a display of accessories, another sorting through a rack of dresses.

A too-thin, midthirties blonde came from the back with a purse in hand. "I find it."

The customer at the accessory display immediately joined her and bought the purse. As she left the store, the woman who'd been browsing through the dresses walked out, as well, leaving Lexie and Simon alone with the owner.

"Can I help?" she asked them with a big smile, her words tinged with a faint accent reminiscent of Eastern Europe.

"Anna Bencek?" Simon asked.

"Yes." Her smile wavered a little and caution reflected from her pale blue eyes.

"My name is Simon Shea and this is Lexie Thornton…from Jenkins Cove."

The smile disappeared altogether. "What you want with me?"

"Who are you afraid of?" Simon asked.

"I—I don't understand." The woman's hands shook slightly as she looked away from them and straightened a display. "If you don't make purchase, please leave. I—I close up now."

"Simon may have come on a bit strong," Lexie said, her voice soothing. "We mean you no harm, Ms. Bencek. We're hoping you can help us."

"To find dress?" Her voice was stronger now. Angry.

Simon said, "No—"

Lexie touched Simon's arm and gave him a look that said, *Let me handle this.* "We need information…about the people who brought you to this country and hurt you."

The Bencek woman shook her head. "You leave now."

Taking his cue from Lexie, Simon softened his approach. "Please. They hurt me, too. They took me from my home across an ocean, just as they did to you. They didn't take my kidney, but they put me to work as a soldier in a war I'd only heard about, and all because I saw a young man murdered. A young man who was trying to escape them, maybe even someone you knew. I was held prisoner for years. And now I want to find out who was responsible."

"I—I can tell you nothing."

Did she mean she couldn't identify anyone or that she didn't know if she should help them? Lexie sensed Simon's frustration.

"Please," Lexie said softly. "The people responsible for the human trafficking operation shouldn't get away with what they did. Maybe they'll do other terrible things. I'm sure you've heard about the mass grave—"

A choked sound came from the other woman and she grasped her throat. "My friend Bernice…she disappeared… when I heard about bodies…"

Simon said, "Perhaps you could close up and we could go somewhere private?"

The shop owner resisted for a moment, and then she nodded. A few minutes later, they sat in the back room, a combination office and storeroom filled with cartons. Anna Bencek sat in her desk chair, hands gripping the arms, while Simon took two chairs from a stack and set them down for him and Lexie.

"Anything you remember might be of help."

"Ten of us came to United States. We pay for passage and papers to work. When we get here, they say not enough money. Pay again. We have no money. So they say we pay with kidney or go back."

"How horrible," Lexie murmured.

"How *did* you get here?" Simon asked.

"Boat…cargo ship. We have cots below. People sick. They gave medicine. We sleep. Then one day, they tell us we are here. No port. Only water."

"They transferred you to a smaller boat?"

She nodded. "A yacht."

Lexie stiffened. "A yacht…a sailing yacht?"

"No sails, motor. Big yacht."

"The name—did you see it?" Simon asked.

Again, the woman nodded. "I never forget. *Drake's Passage.*"

Feeling sick, Lexie half tuned out as Simon continued to question the woman.

"Where did the yacht take you?"

"To warehouse where we wait like jail. Then to place for surgery, then back to warehouse for a few days until is okay to go."

Lexie was only vaguely aware of Simon's further questions and the fact that Anna Bencek had nothing further of value to tell them.

When he was done, they thanked the woman and headed for Annapolis and Five Star Security, where Simon was going to collect the money to pay Hans Zanko for information.

"So what do you think?" he asked as they got on the road.

Lexie swallowed hard before saying, "*Drake's Passage* is owned by Drake Enterprises."

Now there was no doubt Cliff or Doug Heller was involved. Brandon just couldn't be…

"So is Brandon into boating?" Simon asked.

"No…no!"

"Why the emphasis?"

"He didn't do it. I told you the key didn't fit the file drawers of his cabinet."

"I assume he has keys to the corporate offices."

"I suppose so," she said grudgingly.

"And access to the yacht."

Lexie sighed. "He used it a couple of times last spring and summer. I know because he ordered fresh flowers for the cruises. Something about a thank-you to big contributors to the Drake Foundation. That's a far cry from importing illegals for their kidneys. After his wife, Charlotte, died, I thought it was odd that Brandon continued the practice, because he became something of a recluse…"

"And there's the matter of Perry trying to blackmail him," Simon reminded her. "So we can't eliminate him as a suspect, after all. The three men who would have access to the yacht are Brandon and Cliff and Doug Heller. Right?"

Lexie didn't argue. She had no proof of Brandon's innocence. Instead, she sank into a depressed silence.

BRAY WAS WAITING for them at the front counter of Five Star Security in an Annapolis strip mall. "The money's in the office. Do you need backup?" he asked Simon.

"Probably not a good idea if I don't want to scare the guy off."

Simon hugged Lexie to him as they followed Bray down a hallway to an office. She leaned in to his side and her pulse suddenly accelerated. She wanted him to hold her this way forever, but she knew that was highly unlikely. She would take what she could get.

Bray led them to a desk and picked up a small leather case. "All hundreds."

"Thanks, man." Simon took the case and shook Bray's hand.

"Anything else you need," Bray said, "just call."

"Will do."

With that, they left, Lexie wondering if they were crazy. Shouldn't they just leave this whole investigation to the police? She wanted to say so, but she didn't dare. Simon was on a mission and he had the chops and the skills to pull it off. If she tried to divert him from his course, he would simply leave her behind.

Again…

Still, when they arrived at the abandoned boatyard and got out of the SUV, Lexie felt a cold lump settle in the pit of her stomach. No other vehicle was in sight.

She didn't like the creepy feeling the place gave her, nor the location or the fact that the area wasn't lit. Still, the moon was bright enough for her to see hulls of boats in all states of decomposition and rust in the weed-strewn land all the way to the waterline. A couple more boats stuck out of the water near a collapsed pier. Added to the derelicts were a graffiti-covered building half-collapsed on one side, two abandoned cars and something that looked like a horse trailer.

Why had Zanko wanted to meet them here?

The place was surrounded by a chain-link fence, but parts of it seemed to have crumpled to half the original six-foot height. Simon vaulted over the fence with ease, then reached out and helped her over it, too.

Lexie landed against Simon's chest and his arms snaked around her back. Her heartbeat sped up, but she wasn't sure if it was because of Simon or because of the hairs rising at the back of her neck. She didn't like this place—not at all. Breathless, she pushed away from him.

"So where is he?" she gasped, looking around wildly when she heard a sharp crack.

Even as dirt at her feet churned, Simon threw himself on her and pushed her to the ground, then rolled her into the shadow of one of the derelict boats. More shots rang out and wood splintered.

"Why is he firing at us?" Lexie whispered. "Does he think you're one of the bad guys?"

"No." Simon reached inside his jacket and pulled out a handgun. "I think *he* is."

"What do you mean?"

The moon bathed Simon in its silver-blue glow, and Lexie could see his face clearly. Her heart thumped against her ribs and her mouth went dry. His expression was so hard, he was unrecognizable.

He looked nothing like the man she loved.

"STAY HERE," Simon ordered, getting into a crouch.

"You're not going to leave me here alone?"

"I'm going to get him before he gets us." Something he was proficient at.

"Get him? You don't mean kill him?"

Hearing the horror in Lexie's question, Simon didn't answer. "Stay. Don't so much as poke your head out to see what's going on until I give you the all clear."

With that, he scrambled to the next wreck and then to the next. It took Zanko that long to realize he'd moved. A couple more shots followed. Simon was able to figure out that they came from what was left of the building. He was close and yet so far. If he didn't distract the man before making his run, he would be an easy target.

Looking around, Simon spotted what looked like a piece of loose board behind him. He snagged it with his foot and edged it up a little at a time so that it didn't leave the protective shadow of the hull. Finally, he was able to fully grasp it in his hand. A deep breath and he was ready. First he flung the board as far as he could to the other side of where Lexie still hid, then he ran.

Gunfire hit wood and metal in that opposite direction, but stopped just as Simon got to the outside wall of the building. He pressed his back against the boards and adjusted his breathing the way he'd learned so that Zanko wouldn't hear him. Barely a yard away, the opening that had once held a door awaited him.

Movement from the wreck where he'd left Lexie made him want to curse aloud. She was going to come after him. Damn it! He had to get Zanko before the bastard could get her! The supposed survivor would kill her, if he could. He would kill them both. They'd been set up by whoever had been running the operation, and Zanko—if that was even his real name—had been hired to get rid of them.

Simon threw himself through the doorway and rolled. Shots chewed up the flooring around him, but he got behind a collapsed table unscathed.

"You might as well give up now," he said. "If the man who hired you told you anything about me, you know I was trained by the best. Your life for a name."

In response, he earned a curse and another round of gunfire that pinned his location for Simon. He didn't want to kill the man—Zanko couldn't talk if he was dead—but he would if he had to, if it meant saving his own or Lexie's life.

Tuning into the night, Simon caught every sound, would be able to see every movement, no matter that the space was dark but for the faint moonlight cutting through the doorway and the glassless windows. He remained still, his breathing easy and shallow, but his quarry didn't have the same training. Zanko was making slight movements, probably looking for a way to get to Simon. His clothing rustled. He expelled his breath in little puffs of anxiety.

Simon shoved his gun in its holster and grabbed the legs of the table sheltering him. His muscles coiled in expectation and when the man made his move, so did Simon, lifting the table and using it as a shield as he plunged forward and smacked the other man hard.

"Aak!" Zanko jerked backward, the gun flying out of his hand and hitting something with a sharp thud.

Zanko was a big man, bigger than Simon, but definitely not as toned. Throwing what was left of the table to the side, Simon got his hands on the bastard and threw him, too, so that he hit a rotten support that broke with a sharp crack. The ceiling started sifting down on them, but that didn't stop Simon.

"Who hired you?" he demanded, ignoring the debris falling on him and dragging Zanko back up to his feet.

Eyes dark enough to look black in a puffy, beard-stubbled face glared at him. The man tried kneeing him, but Simon stepped to the side, at the same time catching Zanko's leg and twisting. Zanko rolled and flew into the wall, his arm punching through the rotting wood to the outside. He struggled to free himself, but didn't succeed until Simon grabbed the front of his jacket with both fists and gave a sharp pull.

"I don't intend to kill you," Simon growled. "But I intend to get a name from you."

Zanko spat and Simon ducked to the side, then twisted the other man's arm until he screamed.

"I was trained to get information from reluctant people," Simon said. "I know how to make you hurt, how to make you suffer. I don't even have to break anything to do it. I can even do it without leaving any mark on you." He had never tortured anyone, but Zanko didn't know that. "You can make things easier on yourself if you talk, Zanko. Give me the name of the man who hired you to kill us."

Just then Lexie slipped through the doorway and though Simon didn't so much as look her way, he sensed her, and the distraction of knowing she was there was enough to throw him off just a hair, just for a millisecond. Zanko struck out, gut-punching him this time, then hooking a foot behind Simon's knee and giving it a sharp tug. Simon went halfway down and though it only took seconds for him to recover, Zanko was on his way to the door.

Simon regained his footing too late. Zanko had already grabbed Lexie and spun around, using her as a shield.

"I, too, know how to make people hurt," he said, his accent distinctly East Coast. "Don't move or I'll break something."

Simon's heart thudded hard against his ribs as Zanko backed out of the shack and Lexie's expression turned horrified as she tried to fight the man off. It was like watching a fly beating its wings against a predator. Simon thought fast, but he couldn't see a way of getting to Zanko without the bastard doing something nasty to Lexie.

"You can be sure that if you so much as cause her the slightest harm," Simon growled, "your life will be worthless, Zanko. I'll hunt you to the ends of the earth if I have to. I'll gut you and skin you and hang what's left of you out to dry!"

Zanko was backing Lexie down the beach now, toward the fallen pier. What the hell was he up to?

Though Simon followed, he didn't dare rush the man, lest he carry on with his threat against Lexie. He kept his distance, yet matched Zanko stride for stride.

Lexie wasn't stopping, either. She kept struggling in Zanko's arms, working her face over to his bare hand.

Knowing she was planning on biting the man, Simon whispered, "Don't do it, Lexie." But he knew she would and his muscles once more coiled for attack.

Suddenly, Zanko yelled, the sound cutting through the night. He lifted Lexie off her feet and tossed her as he might toss a piece of trash. Limbs flailing, she went flying at the broken wood of the downed pier. No contest about which of them to go after. Simon had to see to Lexie, to make certain she was all right.

In the water now, she was thrashing around in an attempt to free herself from the debris.

"I'm all right. Go after him!" she screamed.

But he was already reaching down to help her.

"Go!" Getting to her feet, she literally pushed him into moving.

Drawing his gun, Simon negotiated the pier, using it for cover in case Zanko had another piece. Then a motor cut through the night and Simon threw caution to the wind and raced around the wooden piles only to see a speedboat take off.

Simon aimed and took a couple shots, thinking to wound the man, maybe toss him out of the boat. But the motor revved and the speedboat practically went airborne.

Cursing, he lowered his gun even as Lexie joined him.

"Are you all right?" he asked.

"Shaken and maybe a little bruised is all."

Simon took her in his arms and held her, steady as rock. Inside he was shaking. He knew what atrocities humans could do to one another. Awful memories flickered through his mind like a photograph album from hell.

Though Lexie had gotten away relatively unscathed, the mere threat to her gave Simon one more reason to thirst for justice to be wielded by his own hand.

Chapter Eleven

As Simon drove back over the Bay Bridge toward Jenkins Cove, his threats against Zanko haunted Lexie, who had heard every chilling word.

They were just threats, she told herself, wrapping the blanket she luckily carried in the SUV more tightly around her. She was still wet from that dunk in the bay, but the dry cover and the heat blowing on her were keeping her warm enough physically.

It was her heart that had gone cold, and Lexie was trying to rationalize Simon's words.

He'd simply been trying to find a way to make Zanko talk, then to make certain the man didn't hurt her. But Lexie knew that wasn't really true, that there was a part of Simon that was damaged and downright scary. Not that *she* was threatened by him.

Even so, Simon scared her in a more visceral way.

Tonight had given her more of an idea of his experience as a mercenary. Had made her wonder if there was any coming back from that kind of psychological damage. Even though the choice to become a soldier for hire hadn't initially been his, he'd continued working for Shadow Ops and the CIA when he'd no longer had to.

Had Simon really felt he couldn't inflict himself on her—

his excuse for staying away—or had that violent way of life become ingrained in him?

Simon had reason to be angry, to seek some kind of justice, but Lexie feared the only justice he really understood, really appreciated, was one linked to violence. A thought that made her shiver.

A fact that Simon noticed.

He broke the uneasy silence. "Lexie, are you sure you're all right? I can still get you to a clinic if there's any doubt."

They were about a mile from Jenkins Cove and all Lexie wanted to do was get home, get in the shower and then get into dry clothing.

"I'm fine. Just a little worse for wear, but I'll manage."

Simon went silent again, then, as they passed the diner where they'd met Bray, said, "You realize that we were set up, right?"

"It's pretty obvious, even to me."

"Which means whoever ran the human trafficking operation is onto us," he said. "That person must have caught the ad Claire ran, asking for any survivors to contact her. Zanko was the only one who did."

"But you don't think he's the one we've been looking for, do you?"

"He was a hired gun, Lexie, a professional. He may have been part of the operation. My instincts tell me what's left of it is bigger than one man. It couldn't just have been the three of them—the nameless head, the doctor and his assistant who hanged himself."

Lexie nodded. "Anna Bencek said ten people came to the United States together, too many for Dr. Janecek and Kreeger to handle by themselves."

"So it makes sense that they had help, whether from hired guns like Zanko or from other locals."

Locals—more people she knew. The thought left Lexie breathless.

"You're talking about the average person? You think just anyone might be involved?"

"Anyone who needs money and can use whatever is in it for him to clear his conscience."

Not wanting to think people she knew were guilty of propagating such horror, Lexie put it out of mind and thought again about the survivors, about what they'd learned and experienced that night.

"We should have known that no one who'd gone through what the survivors had been through would want to come forward voluntarily," Lexie said. "Zanko's asking for money made him more believable somehow." Remembering that Simon hadn't given away his name during their phone conversation, she asked, "But why would these people want to kill us when they didn't even know who we were?"

"They simply didn't care. The fact that anyone was onto them and was looking for information by finding survivors was enough. They couldn't chance our finding a real survivor who might talk."

Lexie's mind whirled with that thought. *Then what about the survivors themselves? Would the head of the operation get rid of any potential witnesses he could find?*

"Anna Bencek… Oh, no." A cold lump settled in Lexie's stomach. "What if we put her in danger?"

Simon cursed and immediately made a call on his cell. "Bray, we have a problem."

Simon then told Bray about the ambush that had been awaiting them and the possibility that someone could get to Anna Bencek.

Lexie sat stunned. She hadn't so much as guessed it would

come to this. She'd never meant to put anyone else in danger, certainly not a woman who'd already been through so much. And she didn't want to be in danger again herself.

Three attacks in as many days were enough to send her running...but to where?

Her whole life was in Jenkins Cove.

Her business...her family...her daughter.

Wanting in the worst way to call Katie, to make sure her daughter was safe, Lexie felt even more frightened and frustrated when she realized it was hours too late. Her parents went to bed early. If she called now, they would know something was wrong.

Closing his cell, Simon said, "Bray will put someone on it immediately. One of his men will keep an eye on the Bencek woman until this thing is settled."

"Thank God," Lexie said, still edgy. "I would never forgive myself if..." She forced herself to stop thinking that way. Anna Bencek would be all right. Bray's man would see to it. "Simon, can you call Katie's bodyguard? I just want to make sure she's all right."

"He would have called me if anything suspicious had happened, but if it'll make you feel better, of course I'll check."

He immediately made the second call just as they pulled into the driveway outside her house.

Lexie barely swallowed until Simon nodded at her and said, "Good," to the man at the other end. "We had some problems tonight. Be prepared, just in case." He hung up. "Lights went out about an hour ago. All is well at your parents' house."

"Thankfully." She sighed in relief.

"Now let's get you inside where you can get warm."

"I'm warm enough," Lexie countered, but she didn't stop Simon from wrapping an arm around her back and rushing her to the front door.

By the time they got inside, she was hot and not from the room's temperature. Pulling away from him, she dropped the blanket and took off her wet jacket, which he took from her.

Kicking off her equally wet boots and socks and dropping them by the door, she said, "I'm heading straight for the shower."

"Good idea."

She thought he meant good idea *for her* until a few minutes later. As she stood in the shower, just letting the hot water pound her, a nude Simon opened the glass door and slipped inside.

"Simon…"

This wasn't part of the deal. He'd agreed to sleep on the couch. So why couldn't she make herself remind him of that promise?

"I just want to check you for injuries," he said, "since you were too stubborn to go to an E.R. or clinic."

The way he was inspecting her body made Lexie's toes curl, and something warm and fluid unfurled inside her. She didn't want to be alone. She wanted safe arms around her and assurances that everything was going to be all right.

He was thoroughly wet now, and the water made his skin gleam and accentuated the incredible sculpted musculature of the body she'd once known nearly as well as her own.

"What makes you an expert?" she asked, meaning to tease him.

"Field experience."

He was serious.

She felt heartsick for him.

What Simon must have endured for more than a decade was something she couldn't fathom. Having to play doctor for his comrades out of necessity seemed unreal to her. By comparison, her life with all its daily dramas had been a picnic. She'd always had her family to love and support her. And she'd had their daughter.

While Simon had been caught in a living hell.

Now under the water with her, he turned her around, checked her body gently but thoroughly for any injury. The more he touched her, the less likely Lexie thought it would be that he would spend the night on the couch.

Why should she push him away from her when being with him was what she wanted? What she needed. What *he* needed.

The danger they'd shared had bonded them in a way she didn't quite understand. Even while part of her was frightened of what Simon might have become, there was a stronger-than-ever attraction to him. That scary part of him had protected her, she reminded herself, would keep her and their daughter safe until they found the answers that would bring down the perpetrators of the horrendous human trafficking operation.

He turned her again, ran his hands over her ribs.

Suddenly consumed by physical hunger, she couldn't meet his eyes, but looked down and realized that examining her had exactly the same effect on him. Thrown back into the past, she remembered the things they'd done for months until finally giving in to their passions and sleeping together that one magic night.

Before she could stop herself, she was touching him… lowering herself to her knees…kissing him…tasting him. Water drummed against her back as she took his soft tip into her mouth, loving the salty taste of him.

He groaned and threaded his fingers in her hair, and held her head tight up against him.

At seventeen, she'd become very practiced at this with him, but now at thirty, she felt like an amateur, wasn't sure if she was taking him deep enough or sucking hard enough or using her tongue cleverly enough to please him.

"Oh, Lexie, baby," he growled, pulling her up and lifting her off her feet.

The next thing she knew, her back was against the wet, slippery tile and her legs were wrapping around his hips and he was homing in on her like they'd done this on a regular basis for the last thirteen years. She was already drenched inside and he slipped in easily. Opening wider, she urged him in deeper until she had all of him.

"This is where I want to be," he murmured in her ear.

"This is where I feel safe," she admitted softly, trying to erase the memory of what had happened, of the fear she'd tasted, barely an hour before. She touched the scar on his chest, wondered if Simon ever really felt safe anymore.

They held each other, shower water raining down on them, and didn't move until the anticipation built and built. Finally he withdrew a little and pushed back inside. Her back was pressed against the wall, and he let go of her, found her breasts, tweaked her nipples the way she remembered he used to do.

"Touch yourself," he whispered in her ear, leaning back to give her access.

Her breath caught in her throat as she slid a hand between them. While they'd only slept together that once, they'd tried just about everything else beforehand. He'd loved it when she would touch and stroke herself and let him watch.

He was watching her now, his features tense with his desire. Sensation swirled through her, growing more urgent with each stroke.

"Rub harder," he whispered, and make his strokes last longer. "I want you to come with me. I'll try to hold on."

Then he leaned over and kissed her openmouthed, and it didn't take her long to reach the frenzy he sought. Pressing his hands against the wall on either side of her head, he rocked into her faster and harder so their rhythms matched, until, at last, they reached the pinnacle, crying out, kissing each other like it might be the last time.

Which indeed it might, Lexie realized, wrapping her arms around his neck and holding on tight as if she would never let him go.

Zanko or another gun for hire could get to them.

Or Simon could simply realize he'd made a mistake in coming back to Jenkins Cove and take off for parts unknown.

This might be the last night she would have with the man she loved—a reason to make it memorable enough to last her for a lifetime.

LEXIE ARRIVED at Drake House the next morning in the garden center's delivery truck. Phil Cardon was driving. She wondered if he'd noticed that they were being followed.

She glanced back just once to see Simon's truck ease by the gate. He'd insisted on following her, had made her promise that before she left Drake House, she would call him on his cell so that he could come back to do the same.

Having spent the night in his arms, she had soft feelings for Simon. A yearning that wouldn't go away. She wanted to believe that he would stay for her. For their daughter. Give her a real family of her own. But another part of her thought that would be highly unlikely, especially in light of the Simon she'd seen in that abandoned boatyard.

Phil parked the truck and they got out, then began unloading the greenery from the back.

"Hey, did you ever find the owner of that key you showed me the other day?" Phil asked as they hauled out a couple of small balsams for the upstairs parlors.

The mention of the key jerked Lexie to attention. "No. Why?"

"Just wondering. So what did you do with it?"

Pulse thudding, she kept her voice even as she lied. "I threw it away."

"But it belonged to someone. You didn't turn it in to Chief Hammer?"

"It was only a key."

"Still. The owner's probably pretty peeved he lost it."

She'd bet he was. *But what was Phil's interest in something so seemingly minor?* she wondered as they each carried a tree into the foyer and up the stairs. She couldn't believe he hadn't forgotten about the key the moment he'd said it wasn't his and he'd never seen it.

Unless *he'd* been lying…

Could something other than curiosity underlie his interest? Had he told someone about the key? The owner who'd then come after her twice? Or had her assailant been Phil himself?

Phil had never had a regular job since moving to Jenkins Cove several years ago. He'd taken odd jobs, worked for her during the holidays and on big landscaping jobs. And yet he lived in a decent house, never actually appeared to hurt for cash.

Because he had a secret job that paid him well?

Human trafficking?

Were all his side jobs just a cover?

Lexie shook herself as the reached the parlors. What was she doing, trying to pin something so awful on Phil just because he had asked about the key?

Apparently the conversation with Simon the night before had set her up to be suspicious of everyone. Who would she think was guilty next?

Needing some respite from the trauma of the attack in the boatyard—a trauma eased but not erased by a night spent in

Simon's arms—Lexie determined to put the human trafficking operation out of mind, at least while she was working at Drake House.

AFTER MAKING SURE that Lexie was safe at Drake House, Simon decided to do some investigating on his own. He drove back out to the mass grave. No patrol car idled there—Lexie had told him that she'd heard Chief Hammer had stopped trying to cover the area, not only because he was shorthanded, but because no one wanted to go near the place. Even so, Simon made sure to hide the truck, just in case a patrol car drove by.

Stopping in front of the swampy area, he paused and looked around, wondering if the ghost of the dead kid made daylight appearances. There was mood lighting, courtesy of a sky that had grown gray with the threat of rain or snow, but there was no fog, no ghost. A wry smile played on Simon's lips as he moved on, around the area in a direction he hadn't yet taken.

There was a road down to the pier and warehouse where the surgeries had been performed, but not knowing if anyone might be wandering around down there, a cautious Simon had determined to go on foot, to stay within the treeline, to remain a ghost.

Lexie had told him the warehouse was probably a half mile or more off the main road, but that was an easy five minutes or so for a man as fit as he was. The sun had melted off the snow most places, but the woods were protected, and patches remained here and there. From what he remembered, snow never lasted that long here. Not cold enough.

As Simon jogged down a path through the trees, he thought about the night before, about the promise of a different life—one filled with more nights like that. With happiness. With that family he'd always wanted. What would Katie think if she suddenly learned that she had a father she hadn't known was alive? Would she recognize him from the market? Be freaked out? Or be happy that he existed?

Katie wouldn't be happy if she knew about his past, not any more than Lexie was. Not that she had said so. But she'd overheard his threats against Zanko and had seen him in action. That gave her some idea of what he was. While she'd made love to him, had held him as if she would never let him go, he was certain that in the end she would do so, if not for her own sake, for their daughter's.

Katie was Lexie's number one concern…just as it should be.

And as it should be for him. Both mother and daughter were his concern, and as such, they would be better off if he left after he made sure that justice was done.

Not wanting personal thoughts to distract him as he neared his destination, Simon turned off that part of his mind and tuned up his senses. A moment later, he heard voices, though he couldn't make out what they were saying, since the forest muffled any sound.

Slowing, Simon moved to the tree line where he could better see the road leading to the warehouse, which was practically within spitting distance. The decrepit old building was made of weathered wood, with boards missing on both sides. It hung partly over the water as if growing from the cattails that lined the shore. He could see yellow crime scene tape flapping in the wind.

Closer to him, two men stood out on the pier, one decked out in a wetsuit, hood, gloves, boots and full face mask, an air tank strapped across his back.

What the hell? Did he really mean to go into the water at this time of year? For what purpose?

The man jumped off the pier backwards, while the second guy watched. With close-cropped, sandy-brown hair and a weather-beaten, jowly face set in a scowl, the man on the pier looked familiar to Simon. He was dressed like a workman in jeans, heavy boots and a canvas jacket. It took Simon a while to identify the guy, but suddenly his memory kicked in.

Doug Heller. Cliff Drake's right-hand man and one of their prime suspects.

What the hell was *he* up to?

Simon wanted to go out there and *make* the man talk, but he held himself in check. He had to remain a ghost for a little while longer.

But a little while stretched into minutes, then into nearly half an hour. The water couldn't be very deep here along the shore, so the tank would last quite a while. Heller edged up and down the pier, apparently watching the diver's movements. The sky was getting darker and wisps of fog were rolling in over the water. Heller couldn't hide his impatience and began stomping around the pier, once taking a cell call, his voice too low for Simon to hear his conversation.

Finally, a dark shape broke the water's surface. Heller threw the other man a rope and hauled him up out of the water and onto the boards. His back was to Simon as he removed his gloves, mask and hood. He was empty-handed, which seemed to drive Heller into a fury.

"What do you mean you didn't find it?"

Simon tuned in, barely caught the shouted words.

"…telling you…wasn't there."

"…has to be."

"Then you go…find…"

"…through with…"

Simon caught enough to get the drift of the argument.

The man stomped toward the warehouse and only when Heller yelled, "Wait a minute!" did he turn back.

Simon immediately recognized the puffy, beard-stubbled face. Hans Zanko!

There it was, proof of collusion between the man who'd tried to kill Lexie and him the night before and Doug Heller, one of their suspects.

Simon quickly took out his cell phone and snapped a couple of photos of the two as Heller caught up to Zanko and spoke in a tone too low for Simon to hear.

Both men disappeared into the warehouse, leaving Simon playing twenty questions with himself about what the hell they'd been up to.

He knew he had to find out.

He settled down, his back against a tree trunk, to wait and to think things through.

All along, Lexie had maintained that Heller had to be the guilty one. Apparently, she'd been correct.

But how to prove it to the satisfaction of the authorities?

Maybe whatever Heller had expected Zanko to find in that water would provide a clue…

Chapter Twelve

After the men drove off, Simon waited awhile, then cautiously approached the warehouse. Dismantling the lock only took a minute. Still careful, Simon entered and focused his senses. No one else here. Closing the door behind him just in case some cop on patrol came along, he waited for his eyes to adjust to the dark before moving around inside. The only shafts of light came through the high windows.

The foundation was cement, weeds growing through cracks here and there. The place looked empty but for a padded table that might belong in an operating room. The place was drafty, with odd cold spots that sent a chill up Simon's back.

How did he know it wasn't haunted by the people detained there who hadn't made it out?

Hardening himself against the sheer inhumanity that had gone on in this place, Simon looked around until he spotted a sheltered area in one corner and headed for it, only to find the wetsuit hanging on a pipe over a drain. The rest of the gear had been laid out on a table. He checked the tank. About twelve minutes of air left.

It would have to do.

Simon wasn't looking forward to getting into near-freezing

water, but he'd been trained to deal with any conditions, and he'd been trained to scuba dive—he'd even done so on a couple of missions. Searching for some lost object in shallow waters would be easy by comparison.

Quickly, he donned the Thinsulate underwear that went under the wetsuit, then the suit itself. Zanko was a stockier man than he and, as Simon had expected, the neck seal especially was a tad loose. Nothing he could do about that, he thought as he pulled on the boots and then the hood, except pray that the gap wouldn't let too much cold water inside the suit or he would be vulnerable to hypothermia. He added weights and a buoyancy compensator and the tank, then grabbed the face mask, regulator and underwater light and left the warehouse for the pier.

Where to go in?

Heller had been a pretty accurate marker as to where Zanko had searched. He hadn't quite gone to the end of the pier, so that's where Simon chose to begin. Undoubtedly, they'd been looking for an item someone had dropped. Now if only he had a clue as to what that might be...

Simon secured the face mask, checked over the rest of his equipment, then jumped into the water, which was only about twelve feet deep here. Even so, a trickle of icy water oozed its way in through his loose neck seal.

Starting at the very tip of the pier, Simon turned on the underwater light and inspected every square foot. The only things that immediately caught his eye were plastic beer can holders and pages of a newspaper that hadn't yet dissolved. As he went on, he found more garbage dropped by careless humans. Certainly nothing of value.

The bay's water continued to trickle down inside his wetsuit. His discomfort growing, Simon checked his air supply time.

Five minutes left.

As he inched along the pier back toward the shore, he thought fast. If Heller had believed the lost object was still here somewhere, then Simon figured it was something with weight. And if the object had dropped from the pier, it should still be around. Tides moved things, even heavy things. But an object with weight shouldn't have gone far.

Four minutes...

Though he kept checking at every piling, turned over anything that stuck out of the bay's bottom, Simon was getting closer and closer to the area near the shore where Zanko had spent the most time searching.

But Zanko hadn't searched where the warehouse hung over the shoreline.

Three minutes...

Simon tried to ignore the blossoming cold inside his wetsuit as he finished checking the length of the pier. That brought him into shallower water, where he turned his underwater light along the shoreline. Part of the warehouse hung over the water's edge that was lined with cattails. All kinds of things were caught in the stalks, which grew to more than six feet.

Two minutes...

Clenching his jaw so his teeth wouldn't chatter, he moved under the edge of the warehouse and searched and pulled at things woven into the shoreline vegetation. Frustration ate at him as he struck out again.

One minute...

And then he spotted something big and shiny near the edge of the warehouse, close to where the road above ended. He raced to the spot.

Zero minutes.

Simon surfaced and gasped, tried to shake off the chill

now affecting his efficiency. Tempering his breath, he took a deep one and dived. He got a gloved hand on the object that was long and heavy, but the cattails seemed to have grown around it, clutching it. He started ripping at the vegetation, but before he could free the object he had to come up for more air.

Down he went a second time and nearly managed to pull the object free.

A third dive and he succeeded, taking possession of a metal object shaped like a long cup.

Surfacing with no air to spare, Simon took a moment and simply breathed. Tendrils of fog snaked along the water and up over the shoreline. The outside air had changed, hitting him in gusts. About to climb out onto shore, he stopped when he heard a vehicle moving toward him. Grasping the trophy to his chest, he threw himself back into the cattails close to the warehouse and listened, ready to sink below water level if necessary.

The vehicle crept closer and Simon's pulse thundered, the extra adrenaline warming him. Had Heller and Zanko returned to renew their search for the trophy? Or had someone else come out here to look for it?

Simon waited chin-deep in the water for what felt like forever, but was actually only a few minutes. The vehicle never stopped, merely circled and moved away. Simon moved, too, so he could get a look at the vehicle that turned out to be a Jenkins Cove patrol car. Apparently, the local cops were still on the job, after all.

Heaving a sigh of relief that he hadn't been discovered, Simon lifted the trophy to see exactly what the hell he'd found. Inscribed on the base of the cup was the name of the race— UK Challenge Cup—and the name of the winner.

Clifford Drake.

"WHAT ARE YOU DOING HERE?" Lexie asked when her mother walked into the ballroom with Katie in tow.

"Nice to see you, too, sweetheart."

Lexie hugged her mother, who was several inches shorter with a soft, round body. Her glasses were pushed up into her dark hair threaded with gray, and she wore a smear of flour on one cheek.

"It *is* nice to see you. Just a surprise." One Lexie didn't appreciate at this moment, considering the circumstances. Besides, she was just about to call Simon again. He hadn't picked up the last two times she'd tried to get him and she was worried. She hugged her daughter and reminded herself that at least Katie's bodyguard had their back. "Hey, kiddo, how's the cookie-making?"

"This morning, Nana showed me how to make six kinds of cookies from one dough recipe."

"Well, good. I expect you'll keep us well-stocked with goodies from now on." She looked back to her mother. "So what's going on?"

"We decided to take a break from baking. Katie wanted to stop at home so she could get her iPod and some fresh clothes. And then she insisted that we come here so she could get a sneak peak at what you've done with the place. I was curious myself. You've outdone yourself, Lexie. It never looked this good when Jonathan was alive and your dad and I did the decorating."

Lexie gave her mother another hug. "You exaggerate, but thanks."

"This looks really rad, Mom." Katie twirled and dipped in the center of the ballroom as if she were dancing with an invisible partner. "Next year you've got to hire me to help."

Lexie started. "You're asking me for a job?" Her daughter was growing up way too fast. "Aren't you a little young to be worrying about working?"

"I *will* be a teenager by then," Katie reminded her, her snub ose in the air. "Teenagers have needs that allowances just on't cover."

"Okay," Lexie said, holding herself back from laughing, "I'll keep that in mind."

She spent the next ten minutes showing her mother and daughter every public room so they could see everything. She even had one of the lighting guys turn on the snow effect.

But all the while she had to hold her anxiety in check. What was Simon up to? Had he gotten into the warehouse?

When Mom and Katie left with hugs and kisses all around, Lexie pulled out her cell and tried again.

No answer.

A chill settled in her middle and she was suddenly afraid that Simon had gotten more than he'd bargained for.

What in the world was going on?

THOUGH SIMON DIDN'T KNOW the significance of the trophy being in the water, he was certain it was what Heller had sent Zanko down to find. Thinking it wouldn't do to mess with any prints on the metal, just in case they would prove to be significant, he kept the diving gloves on until he got back into the warehouse and shoved the trophy into a ditty bag that had been left with the diving gear.

Then he stripped, dried himself off as best he could, and dressed in his blissfully warm clothes. Even so, he was cold to the core and trying not to shake inside. A jog back to the truck should warm him.

Not wanting anyone to figure out what he'd been up to, he put everything back the way he'd found it. Hopefully, the damp undergarments he left folded on the table wouldn't give him away.

Then, after making sure he was still alone, Simon left the

warehouse, resetting the door lock, after which he made for the tree line, ditty bag in hand.

What the hell should he do with the trophy until they figured out what part it had played in things? he wondered. Too risky to leave it in the back of his truck or to store it in Lexie's house. Better if he hid it someplace in the open. Someplace where no one would think to look. Like somewhere in the swamp.

Thinking he'd find a good spot in the area where he'd parked, he started for his truck.

The wind had picked up, as had the cold. Rather, cold spots. They followed him into the woods. Gusts brought with them fine sprays of snow, though he hadn't thought it was supposed to snow until later. A shiver raced through Simon and he tried to blame it on his time in the water. But there was something different about the way this felt, as if the air pressure itself had changed. Similar to the way he'd felt the other night. He stopped and peered into the gloom between two trees where he focused on waves of energy that stretched and whirled and morphed into a figure that appeared to be human.

The ghost had returned.

"What do you want me to see this time?" Simon whispered, the cold suddenly taking him in its grip.

He felt an urgency, a force even, pushing him toward the faint apparition that seemed to be taking on substance. The kid appeared in his thin leather coat, the mop of pale hair falling into his face. His dark eyes were sorrowful, his mouth an angry slash in the too-pale face.

"What is it?"

The kid seemed agitated as he waved for Simon to follow, then whirled and pressed deeper into the woods, and Simon couldn't have stopped himself from following the spirit if he'd wanted to. It was as if invisible strings were tugging at him,

onnecting him to the dead kid, making him subject to the will
f someone who didn't even exist on this plane.

Instead, he followed a swirl of mist that, to him, seemed to
be full of fury.

Why? Simon wondered.

Suddenly the kid stopped, twisted around to face Simon as
f trying to tell him something. Or show him something. The
apparition was losing substance by the second.

Simon jogged across the short expanse, but the closer he
got, the fainter the wraith became. It hovered for a moment,
then seemed to dissolve into the blowing snow sweeping
through the woods.

"What the hell?"

Simon stopped short. Why had the ghost appeared to him
again, only to disappear before there was anything to see? Or
was something there and he just had to look more closely?

He stepped forward, putting one foot in front of the other
like a robot, unable to stop himself until he was within a yard
of where the ghost had disappeared. What now? He turned, examining the trees around him as the fog mysteriously rolled
back on all sides, as if framing the suspect area.

Nothing!

What the hell?

About to give up and go back to the truck, Simon felt the
earth beneath his foot give a little. He looked down. The ground
where he stood had been newly turned. No traces of pine
needles or leaves covered it. None of the snow that limned the
ground around it, delineating the small area.

Had something been buried here?

Wishing he had a shovel, Simon started pushing at some of
the soft dirt with his foot. It scooped away easily. A strange
feeling shot through him as he gauged the length and width of

the patch of nude earth. Hesitating only a second, he put the ditty bag down, got to his knees and started scooping with his hands. Within seconds he uncovered part of what was buried there.

A man, the side of his head bashed in and bloody, stared up at him through lifeless eyes.

Simon hadn't officially met the man, but he recognized him. Ned Perry, the land developer so desperate to get his hands on shoreline land, even one with a mass grave. The man he'd overheard trying to blackmail Brandon Drake.

His heart thundered as he inspected the wound as best he could without touching the guy. He'd seen fatal wounds like that before—rubble falling on his comrades, cracking open their heads like fragile eggs.

But this wound hadn't been caused by rubble, but by a directed strike—he was certain of it. It looked like someone had taken a baseball bat to Perry's head.

Or a big metal trophy...

Simon swore. Had he really been dragging around the murder weapon?

Opening the ditty bag, he stared at the cup without touching it. No blood, of course, not after being in the water. He didn't even know if prints would hold up.

He had a body and undoubtedly the murder weapon.

What now?

Could he trust the local cops to get it right?

Figuring Perry's death somehow had to do with the human trafficking situation, Simon first called Bray and gave him the scoop, asked him to call that state detective brother-in-law of his and get him down here fast.

"Just don't mention my name," Simon added before hanging up.

He wiped the ditty bag to get rid of his own fingerprints, then dumped the trophy a short distance from the body—near enough to be found, far enough away not to be obvious—then jogged to the truck. Only when he was in it and on the road away from the site and heading toward Drake House did he call the Jenkins Cove Police and ask for the chief.

"Hammer here," came a drawl on the other end.

"I'd like to report a murder."

"Who is this?"

"Someone who doesn't want to get involved." Simon wasn't about to identify himself—not yet, not before they got more answers.

"Is this some kind of a joke?" Hammer demanded. "Who put you up to this?"

"I was taking a walk through the woods and nearly stumbled over the body. It's near the mass grave."

"Another one of them." Hammer sounded bored.

"No, this one's fresh. The victim is Ned Perry. You'd better get down here, Hammer, if you want to keep your job. The state police have already been informed, and Detective Rand McClellan is already on his way."

Chapter Thirteen

"Why are we leaving now?" Phil asked, when Lexie insisted they stop for the day. "We still need to finish the last couple strings of outside lights."

"The sun is already down. It'll be dark soon," she said by way of a plausible excuse. "They can wait until tomorrow morning. I've already told Marie we're heading out."

Lexie chose to leave it at that, not embellish. The fancier the story, the more likely it would raise suspicions.

Phil shrugged and got behind the wheel of the truck and pulled down the drive. Though she looked for Simon's truck near the gate, Lexie didn't see it until they were on the road and she caught a glimpse of it in the sideview mirror.

His call had at first relieved her—she'd begun to fear the worst, that something terrible had happened to him—then had made her tense. Ned Perry dead. He'd been obnoxious, but that wasn't enough reason for someone to want to murder him. What had he been up to?

The plan was to go back to the shop, get her SUV and then rendezvous with Simon at her place.

But as they headed for town, two local police cars and one unmarked police car, all with lights flashing, were cutting onto a gravel road that led into the woods not far from the mass gravesite.

"Hey, something's up. Let's see what's going on," Phil said, following before she could stop him.

She threw an apprehensive look over her shoulder. This wasn't part of the plan. What would Simon do?

He kept going on the main road.

Now she was really anxious. Why in the heck had Phil done that?

Suddenly she realized that the police cars ahead had been abandoned, along with several other state vehicles and an ambulance. Uniformed and plainclothes officers were on foot, gathering around a spot a hundred yards away.

Phil pulled over. "Something big must be going on. Let's go see."

Again, before she could object, he acted. He flew out of the truck and jogged through the trees. What did he think he was doing? The police weren't going to let him anywhere near the crime scene.

Lexie stayed behind and used her cell to call Simon. When he answered, she asked, "Where are you?"

"Down the road on the other side of the grave. What happened?"

"Phil took things in his own hands. Literally."

"Get in as close as they let you, see what you can overhear. I'll be around, but out of sight."

Wishing they could be together, that she could feel Simon's supportive arm around her, Lexie approached the knot of officials, but didn't want to get too close, even if they let her. She didn't want to see Ned Perry with his head bashed in.

Chief Hammer was consulting with the state detective, Rand McClellan, whom Lexie had seen before but not met. A crime scene investigator, a couple of EMTs, and a few reporters were on the spot, too. She figured it wouldn't be long before a television news crew showed up.

Phil Cardon was nowhere to be found, making her wonder where he'd disappeared to, why he'd been so hell-bent on following the police cars to a crime scene, only to disappear.

Still looking for him, Lexie hung back, not wanting anyone to notice her and make a big deal about her being where she didn't belong.

"Looks like he was murdered sometime last night," came a deep male voice from the knot of people. "Struck with an unusually shaped object…could be something round."

"Start looking for anything that might be the weapon," McClellan told the uniformed officers.

Lexie backed off, circled the investigation team and quietly wandered off in the direction Simon might be hiding. The woods were gloomy. It would soon be dark. She wished things didn't have to be like this, that Simon could be out in the open, that she could be seen with him rather than sneaking around to find him.

A "psst" got her attention and she looked to her right.

Standing in the shelter of a tree, Simon indicated they should move farther into the woods, away from the activity. She quickly complied and they backed off another dozen yards.

"So what did you hear?" he asked, keeping his voice low.

"Only that Perry was probably killed last night. The question is why."

"Considering how I found him, I would guess it has something to do with the human trafficking operation."

"How *did* you find him?"

"It was the kid again, the one I saw murdered. He led me right to the grave."

The ghost again. Simon was a rational man. Marie and

Chelsea were both rational, too, and yet they'd both had experiences with the afterlife. And what about Bray? His touching the key had led them to Anna Bencek. If Simon thought he saw a ghost, Lexie believed it.

"But Ned Perry?" she murmured. "I mean if he *was* involved in the trafficking, he should have been well-off. He was so desperate to make money he was even willing to buy land that had been a mass grave."

"I didn't say he was directly involved. But he could have found out something. Maybe something about that land. What if he was blackmailing the wrong person?"

"You mean Brandon," Lexie said, remembering the conversation between the two men that Simon had overheard. "I don't believe that, either."

"You don't want to believe it. And you're probably correct," he conceded.

Simon told her about his morning's activities, about Doug Heller's connection to Hans Zanko, about finding Cliff's racing trophy, which the men obviously had been searching for.

"Zanko tried to kill us, and he was looking for the trophy that was undoubtedly the murder weapon used on Perry. And right after I found it, the ghost led me to his body. It all has to be connected."

"The trophy...I heard them say Ned was struck by a round object."

"I dumped it in the area for them to find. Are you familiar with it?"

"I've seen it. Cliff kept it on *Drake's Passage*," she admitted, then hastily added, "which doesn't mean Cliff did it."

Simon nodded. "It's looking like Heller is our man. Now we just have to prove it, get our hands on those files before he decides to destroy the evidence. His prints are probably all over them."

"We just have to find the cabinet the key unlocks," Lexie said. "Which means we have to get into Drake Enterprises." Though she was reluctant to leave him, Lexie said, "I'd better get back, before Phil comes looking for me."

Simon whipped her against him for a quick kiss that left Lexie breathless.

"I'll be watching you," he promised.

Reminded of the way he'd been watching her the night before, Lexie flushed as she made her way back to the crime scene. Simon was becoming more and more real to her, and she was less and less willing to give him up. What could she do to keep him? To satisfy the part of him that had changed? To keep him from carrying the justice thing too far?

Halfway to the crime scene, she noticed a furtive movement ahead in the descending dark and slipped into the shadow of a large tree to see what was going on.

Phil Cardon was skulking away from the crime scene, something bulky under his jacket. About to confront him, she stopped when she realized he was being followed.

"Cardon, what do you think you're doing there?" Chief Hammer caught up to the man, grabbed him by the shoulder and spun him around. "Let me see what you're hiding."

Hammer didn't wait for Phil to cooperate, but opened Phil's jacket and pulled a large bag free from where the other man held it to his chest.

"Hey, you can't do that!" Phil said.

"I just did." Hammer opened the bag. He reached inside and hauled out the trophy. Then a look of comprehension colored his expression. "What the hell are you doing with this?"

"Hey, I found it. I figured it was worth something at a pawnshop. You can't blame a guy for trying to make a few extra bucks where he can, especially during the holidays."

Hammer grabbed Phil's arm and whirled him back toward the crime scene, saying, "We need to have a little chat."

Lexie stepped into a clearing and watched Phil try to squirm his way out of going with Hammer. The police chief had him in a tight hold and didn't seem about to let go.

What had Phil been doing with the trophy, undoubtedly the murder weapon? Why had he been trying to remove it from the scene of the crime?

By the time she got back to the crime scene, Ned's body was bagged and being carried to the ambulance. One of the officers was pushing Phil into a squad car. No doubt they were taking him in for questioning.

Did he have something to do with the murder? With the human trafficking?

Lexie didn't know what to think, but everything was coming to a head. They needed to find those files.

Before she could slip away, a man stepped in front of her. She stared at the finely cut overcoat for a few seconds before lifting her gaze to that of Detective Rand McClellan.

"What are you doing here?" he asked.

"I was hijacked," she said, her stomach doing a fast twirl. Thinking Bray Sloane had told his brother-in-law about Simon and her, she was tempted for a moment to confide in the state lawman. She wanted nothing more than for the state authorities to take over the investigation. "One of my seasonal workers was driving the truck. We were on our way back to the garden center when he saw the squads and decided to follow them."

"So where is this guy?"

"Chief Hammer has him."

A look of understanding crossed his face. "Ah."

"I'm Lexie Thornton," she said. When he didn't react, she realized Bray hadn't said anything to him. And she knew she couldn't, either. If she did, she would betray Simon. Disappointed, she asked, "Can I go now?"

McClellan nodded. "Sure."

Getting into the truck, Lexie sped away from the crime scene as fast as she dared. Once on the main road, she headed for town and looked for Simon, but he didn't seem to be following, probably because some of the police cars were heading out, as well.

She called him. "I'm heading for the garden center to pick up my SUV."

"I'll meet you at your place. Don't go inside until I get there to go in with you."

"You'll be there ahead of me. I'm going to pick up dinner."

"Lexie—"

"Unless you want peanut butter and jelly sandwiches."

"Don't take any chances."

Lexie called in to a local café and ordered a couple of the blue plate specials—meat loaf, mashed potatoes and green beans—so they'd be ready by the time she got there.

Thornton Garden Center was already closed for the night and Carole was gone. Lexie traded the truck for her SUV and headed for home.

Waiting for her, Simon led the way inside, checking to make sure there hadn't been a break-in, before they sat down to eat at the kitchen table.

Lexie told him about Phil Cardon.

"He could be an accomplice," Simon said, "trying to get rid of evidence."

"Something I was wondering myself," Lexie said. She even wondered if Phil could have attacked her, but fearing Simon's reaction, she didn't voice the question. "If he's not arrested, I'm not sure I want him working for me."

"Does he have to work for you? Legally, I mean?"

"He's seasonal. I guess after we finish Drake House tomorrow morning, I can let him go. But what if his story about wanting to hock the trophy is true?"

"You are too trusting."

At least he didn't say naive.

"Drake Enterprises is officially locked up until Monday morning," Lexie said. "So how do we get in?"

"Leave that to me. No problem."

Another reminder of Simon's past. The mouthful of food nearly stuck in Lexie's throat and she washed it down with half a glass of water. Would Simon ever be satisfied living a normal life again? She couldn't imagine it.

"So we're going to check out Drake Enterprises tonight?" she asked.

"That's the plan."

A thrill shot through Lexie as she realized they might find their answer tonight. Then what?

"If we find the files, will that be enough proof for the authorities?"

"I don't know. It'll be enough for me."

Lexie wanted to ask what he meant by that, but she was afraid she might not want to hear the answer.

They finished eating in silence, after which Simon said, "I'll clear."

"I'll get the key."

Even as she left the kitchen, Lexie had some doubts about what they were doing. This kind of a search should be left to the authorities. Then again, she doubted that Chief Hammer believed in ghosts or in psychic abilities like the one that allowed Bray to see the names on the files.

Even if they found the files, how were they going to explain everything?

Maybe she never should have kept the key. But a lost key wasn't exactly something the police would want to be bothered with. Scary how everything had escalated so quickly.

Lifting the finial off the newel, Lexie looked inside and gasped. The key was gone.

Chapter Fourteen

"Whoever got in and took the key is really good," Simon said. "I didn't see any sign of a break-in."

Suddenly it hit Lexie. "Katie! Mom brought her by the house to pick up some clothes earlier. She must have found it."

Lexie hurried to the phone and called her parents' number. Her mother answered.

"Mom, I need to speak to Katie."

"She's up in her room. She said she was tired and wanted to go to bed early."

Was she getting sick? Katie never wanted to go to bed early. "Can you get her, please?"

Lexie covered the mouthpiece and met Simon's gaze. "Why would she have taken the key?"

"Maybe she looked to see if you left a note…and thought the key was for her."

"That makes sense," Lexie agreed. "We'll have to stop at the house to get it from her."

Her mother came back on the phone. "Honey, I don't know how to tell you this but…Katie's not there. I—I think she left the house."

"What?" Panic gripped Lexie—had someone kidnapped

her daughter? She looked to Simon. "Where would she go—and at night?"

Simon immediately flipped open his cell and walked to the other end of the room, undoubtedly to check with the man who was supposed to be guarding their daughter.

Then her mother said, "That party you wouldn't let her go to…it's tonight. Maybe she went despite your telling her she couldn't go."

That had to be it, Lexie thought. Better that than where her mind had started to take her. "What was the name of that boy?"

"Josh Pearson. He lives a couple blocks east of me. I'll go there right now."

"No, I'm her mother." Lexie grabbed a pad of paper and pen. "Where does he live?" She made note of the address and hung up at the same time Simon closed his cell and cursed under his breath.

"He didn't see a thing."

"I don't understand how she slipped by him, unless he was asleep," said Lexie, annoyance, anger and fear suffusing her voice.

"She must have gone out the back door. He simply couldn't be in two places at once."

Lexie nodded and headed for the door. "We're going to a party."

They threw on their jackets and left the house. Lexie went directly to the SUV and Simon climbed into the passenger seat. Lexie's stomach clenched at the thought that Simon and Katie would meet face-to-face.

"What are you doing?" she demanded.

"Making sure my kid is okay. You can introduce me as your date."

"She'll know that's a lie." The moment the words were out of her mouth, Lexie flushed. Simon didn't have to know she didn't date, but it was too late to take it back.

"You can tell her there's a first time for everything," he said as she started the engine.

Truth be told, despite her doubts about putting father and daughter together before they'd worked anything out, before she'd had time to prepare Katie, Lexie was glad Simon was with her. She could use his strength, and his sense of calm was catching.

Ten minutes later, she double-parked outside a house that was obviously the scene of a party. All the lights were on and music and shouts drifted out to the street.

Turning on her flashers, Lexie said, "Wait for me here," and jumped out of the vehicle.

As she ran up the steps, she looked through the front bay windows, but didn't see Katie. A knot formed in her stomach. Katie had to be there. She *had* to be.

A sign on the door said to COME ON IN—IT'S OPEN, so she did. Heart pounding, she looked around at kids who were eating and talking in one room, dancing in the other. She recognized only a few of them. She didn't know many of the high school kids. When she didn't spot Katie right away, her pulse began to race.

What if they were wrong and Katie wasn't here, after all?

What if someone had gotten into the house and had taken her?

Just then she spotted a girl named Megan, an older friend of her daughter's.

"Megan, hi," she said, forcing a smile. "Have you seen Katie?"

"I think she's in the kitchen." Megan pointed her in the right direction.

Relieved, Lexie said, "Thanks," and moved through the crowd to the kitchen.

She spotted Katie immediately. Rather than being with the high school kids she'd wanted to be part of, Katie was with adults. Two women were getting food together and Katie was helping them by placing sandwiches they made on a tray. She had a big grin on her face and nodded at something one of the women said.

Lexie waited until her system righted and called, "Katie!"

Katie's head whipped around and her eyes went wide. "Mom?"

"Let's go."

A mulish expression settled on her daughter's face and she didn't budge. The two women looked distressed but didn't interfere.

"Katie, *now.*"

Suddenly Katie rushed across the kitchen, eyes bright, and sailed right past her. Lexie nodded to the women, who gave her sympathetic looks, then followed her daughter, who grabbed her jacket from a coat tree and stormed straight out of the house and down the front steps.

"Get in the backseat."

"What? Why?" Katie demanded.

"Because the front seats are occupied."

Katie did as she was told and slammed the door.

Lexie slid behind the wheel and gripped it for a moment. "I'm disappointed in you, Katie Thornton. You scared Nana to death. You scared me. You deliberately disobeyed me. What were you thinking?"

"That I didn't want to be an old stick-in-the-mud like you. I wanted to have some fun in my life. But it looks like you were doing that, too, behind my back."

"Don't speak to your mother that way," Simon said, his tone flat but firm. "You owe her your respect. She was very worried about you and with good reason."

Lexie thought Katie might argue with Simon, but the girl didn't say a word as they pulled away from the curb.

"I'm taking you back to your grandparents' house, Katie. I don't want to disappoint them because they were looking for-

ward to spending time with you. But if I do, I want to know
that you won't act without permission again."

Katie's voice was sulky as she asked, "You're not ground-
ing me?"

"I didn't say that, but that can wait until you're back home.
In the meantime, I want you to promise me you won't try to
sneak off again."

"All right. I promise!"

"One other thing…do you have the key that I left in the
newel post?"

"I thought you left it for me." Katie's voice rose defen-
sively. "Like it was some kind of puzzle I was supposed to
figure out."

"No, Katie. I just put it there for temporary safekeeping."

"Safekeeping? Why?"

"I just didn't want to lose it," Lexie hedged, holding out an
open hand by her shoulder. "May I have it, please?" She felt
the metal press into her palm and let her fingers curl around it.
"Thank you."

"You're not mad about the key, too, are you?"

"No, honey, I'm not angry about the key."

When they arrived at her parents' house, Lexie walked Katie
inside and assured her parents that everything was all right and
that their granddaughter had promised not to scare them again.
Katie couldn't look at her, wouldn't speak to her, not even
when Lexie gave her a one-armed hug and kissed the top of her
head. Silently apologizing for any scares she'd given her own
parents, she kissed them, too, before leaving.

When she got back into the SUV, she just sat there for a
moment, trying to regain her equilibrium.

"Everything okay?" Simon asked.

"Fine. Is Katie's bodyguard out here?"

"In the dark car across the street."

"Good. Then we can go."

As she started off for Drake Enterprises, Lexie couldn't help but worry. Katie had been asserting herself more lately, had even openly defied her, but she'd never gone behind Lexie's back before. Or attacked her personally.

Remembering how Simon had stepped in, how Katie had responded to him, she said, "You surprised me before. You sounded like a father."

"Maybe because I *am* a father and I want to be part of our daughter's life."

Lexie had nothing to say to that.

SIMON HADN'T MISSED the way Lexie avoided the *father* reference. Because she didn't believe him? Or because she didn't want him to be a father to Katie?

He also hadn't missed that she hadn't introduced him to their daughter. Then, again, what could she have said about him under the circumstances?

The whole situation had simply been awkward.

What he got from the incident, though, was to see firsthand a mother's love. Lexie was tough and focused, a lioness with her cub, even in the face of their daughter's temper. Katie had been a little snot to her, as kids could be when they didn't get their own way. Though he'd interrupted, he hadn't said what he'd longed to say—that Katie should appreciate what she had because she could lose it any time.

Just as he had.

Simon forced his mind away from the personal and concentrated on the task ahead.

"Have you ever been at Drake Enterprises at night?"

"Several times. We do their Christmas decorations. And

then I went with Marie once. She was meeting Brandon there after a board meeting."

"What about security?"

"No one mans the security desk after hours," Lexie said, "but there is a guard that makes rounds every so often. Maybe once an hour."

"We should be able to avoid him." At least Simon hoped they could. He didn't want to have an altercation with some poor guy just doing his low-end job. "So you know the layout of the building."

"Somewhat."

"The executive offices?"

"They're on the second floor. I've only taken an elevator up, but there are at least two sets of stairs, as well."

"We'll take the stairs then." The elevator would create noise and bring the security guard running.

Just outside of town, Lexie pulled onto Yacht Basin Road, and when it split she took the right branch. Drake Enterprises was straight ahead, overlooking the water. She pulled the car over to the side of the drive under a stand of trees just before they reached the two-story brick building.

She said, "I figure the security guard won't be looking for anything back here."

"Good thinking."

And good that trees lined the road and provided them with cover all the way to the building.

Simon led the way, fine-tuning his senses to any noise or movement. The only thing he heard was the water washing against the shoreline. Nothing in sight moved.

"We'll get in through the loading dock door," he told Lexie. And prayed there would be nothing extraordinary about the locks that protected it.

A moment later they were on the dock, under the shelter of a canopy. Noting the alarm system, Simon removed some tools from his pocket and disabled it. Then he started working on the door locks.

"Is all this something you learned to do in your former life?" Lexie asked, her uneven voice revealing her nerves.

"I had to learn to do a lot of things that I never thought I would do," Simon returned. Breaking and entering were among the least offensive of the skills he had been forced to learn. "When we get inside, we'll have no idea where the security guard is, so we'll need to be silent. Use sign language."

The lock clicked and he put a finger to his lips, then cracked the door and listened intently for several seconds before opening it fully and showing her inside. It was dark, but Lexie indicated that they needed to go down the long corridor to a set of double doors inset with small windows that glowed softly against the black corridor.

When they got to the windows, Simon looked through one to the lobby where a few fixtures were dimmed, allowing him enough light to view the whole space. A young man in a gray uniform trimmed with black stood by the front windows, looking out. Simon held a hand up to tell Lexie to wait. A moment later, the guard moved off, crossed the room and went through a door on the other side of the security desk.

Simon opened the door slowly, concentrating on making no sound. He urged Lexie through and, with only the equivalent of an emergency light to guide them, she went straight for the stairs. Simon followed, then once in the stairwell moved past her.

At the top of the staircase, he stopped and listened, then cracked open the door to darkness. No light here. He looked to Lexie, who indicated that they should go to the left.

Simon nodded, took Lexie's hand and let her take the lead

until a door slammed open down the hall. His pulse kicked up. The last thing he wanted was a confrontation. The young security guard was no Hans Zanko. Simon certainly didn't want to hurt him, which would surely happen if he didn't avoid the man, who must have come up that second set of stairs.

The dark down the corridor was suddenly broken by a strong beam of light that moved from side to side. Simon squeezed Lexie's hand to warn her, and immediately felt for the nearest doorway. He opened the door carefully so as not to make any noise, then pushed Lexie inside. He followed even as the corridor lights went on.

Simon felt another door just inside the first, opened that one and stepped inside, pulling Lexie with him. There was hardly room for both of them in what was a closet, hardly room to breathe. Coats and other clothing crushed against them, cocooning them together. Though the situation was tense, with Lexie's derriere pressed against him, Simon couldn't help but respond physically. When Lexie audibly caught her breath, he knew she noticed, and he suspected that she was equally turned on.

Fighting the distraction, he closed his eyes and listened intently as the sound of doors opening and closing echoed along the corridor. The security guard was doing more than a cursory job. He was taking careful inventory. Simon prayed he wasn't looking into every closet, too.

When he heard the office door open, Simon tensed, tightened his arm around Lexie. The guard was moving around… stopping…standing still for what felt like an interminable amount of time. Then he moved again and the office door closed behind him.

Simon didn't move. He listened to the security guard's progress as he made his way slowly down the corridor.

"What do we do?" Lexie whispered.

"Wait."

It was several minutes before the security guard strode back down the hall, stopping halfway. The mechanical groan and whir of the nearby elevator relieved Simon, who'd thought the man might have suspected they were there, hiding from him. He listened harder, made sure the doors swished open and closed and the elevator descended, before relaxing.

"Let's wait a minute longer to be sure," he whispered into Lexie's ear.

She nodded, her hair moving against his skin, and at that instant, Simon knew he'd never wanted her more. Not that he could have her, not here. Each minute he waited was torture, but each minute was necessary to keep from being found out.

Finally deciding that the guard was truly gone, that it was safe to leave the closet, he opened the door. They practically fell out together.

"That was close," Lexie whispered.

"Too close. Let's do this."

Leaving the office, Simon let Lexie lead him all the way to the end of the corridor. She stopped, felt around. Simon heard the sound of the doorknob being tested. Then the door swung inward and Lexie led him inside.

"This is the executive suite," she whispered in his ear.

Simon thought to tell her they could talk in low tones now, but the sensual vibes he was getting from her breath and sheer closeness stopped him from spoiling the moment.

"The receptionist sits out here. Cliff's office is to the right. Heller's office is to the left. Both overlook the water, of course."

"What about in between?" he whispered in return.

"The boardroom. Cliff's administrative assistant and Heller's secretary have offices outside the suite."

"Let's try Heller's office first." Holding her hand, he pulled er inside, closed the door and turned on a small desk lamp. "I think it's safe to talk now."

Lexie was examining the three file cabinets in Heller's office. "These are similar, but not identical." She tried to insert the key. "Nope. Doesn't even fit. I don't understand. We were so sure it was Heller."

Simon clenched his jaw. He'd been hoping to hit pay dirt, but apparently it was too much to expect on the first try.

"Cliff's office," Simon said, noting Lexie's dismayed expression before turning off the light.

But Cliff's cabinets were identical to those in Heller's office.

Lexie appeared relieved.

"There's still the boardroom," Simon said.

Lexie's relief seemed short-lived. "If it's in there, it could be either one of them."

Indeed, one end of the boardroom was an entire file and storage system. Both file drawer and door cabinets were decorated with the requisite leaf marquetry.

When he noticed Lexie staring at them as if she couldn't take a step forward, Simon asked, "You want me to try?"

She handed over the key.

Simon tried the first lock. The key slid in easily but didn't turn. He tried the second…third…all. The key opened none of them.

Frustration turned him rigid, made him want to beat on something. Someone.

A gentle hand on his arm startled him. He whipped around to face Lexie. "I don't get it," he said. "Can there be more of these cabinets in other offices?"

Lexie shrugged. "I wouldn't think so. I can't see just anyone having them."

Even so, they backtracked down the hall, checking office after office and finding nothing even close to a match.

They left the building the way they'd come and with as much care as they'd taken when they'd entered it. The only sign that they'd been there was the disabled alarm.

Not wanting anything to go wrong before they got out of the area, Simon left it unarmed, knowing it would warn the villain that his time of going undiscovered was drawing to an end.

LEXIE LOST HERSELF in the silence on the way home. Simon was driving. Just as well. Her mind was dizzy with the thoughts running through it.

How could they not have found the cabinet with the file drawer containing all those folders? She tried convincing herself that Bray's vision might have been off. Or that he might be a con man himself.

Only she didn't buy it.

Simon believed in Bray and his vision, so she had to.

The cabinet and those files should have been at the Drake offices where Heller could easily get at them. She couldn't imagine that Heller had personal possession of one of the antique cabinets originally owned by Henry Drake, Brandon's grandfather and Cliff's father.

That left only one place to search.

An option she didn't want to think about…

As they turned onto the gravel road leading to her home, she glanced at Simon, got a glimpse of his closed expression and could only imagine the thoughts going through his head. She could almost feel his roiling emotions reach out to her. Simon had even more reason to feel let down than she had, and Lexie sensed that his disappointment was deeper, darker, more dangerous. He was gambling part of himself on this mission of theirs, and he was losing.

A shiver ran through her.

Simon parked and they got out of the car without speaking. When he took her keys, Lexie felt an untapped energy emanate from him, leaving her uneasy and a little breathless to see how his mood played out. Once inside, he relocked the door and threw the keys on a nearby table. They stripped off their outer clothing and boots.

Then, without warning, Simon pulled her to him and held her for a moment so tightly she could barely breathe. He kissed her hard and drove her backward toward the stairs. She stumbled, but he caught her, brought her down easy on a step, then came on top of her, all without taking his mouth from hers. He ripped the front of her jeans open and plunged his hand inside.

Lexie gasped. There was something different about this Simon. Something as far from soft and gentle as she could imagine. Even so, as he slid his fingers in her, never letting up on the kiss, she lit up like a bottle rocket from the inside out.

As if frenzied by her cry of pleasure, he stripped off her jeans and panties.

Wanting to know what came next, Lexie couldn't move as she watched him unzip his fly and step out of his jeans.

Then she didn't have time to think at all when he spread her legs and slid inside her, taking her like some demon was driving him. Embracing him with her legs, she thought simply to let him spend himself on her, but got caught on the wave of his passion and hung on for dear life.

Chapter Fifteen

The next morning, Lexie awoke in Simon's arms. She never wanted to leave their shelter, would spend a lifetime wrapped up in them—in him—if only fate would permit.

Truthful with herself, she was tired of going it alone, but she didn't simply want a man. She wanted *Simon*—the love of her life, her soul mate. She wanted to make a life with him. She wanted to believe he would make a good partner for her, a good father for Katie, but her doubts kept her from trusting him completely. He was used to living on the dark edge of life, which was the reason he was here in Jenkins Cove now. Could he settle down in a small town once the mystery of the human trafficking operation was resolved?

And what was his idea of resolution?

She simply didn't want to go there.

They'd spent half the night making love, but Lexie couldn't help but wonder if Simon's passion had been more to erase the frustration at hitting another brick wall than it had been due to his feelings for her.

It wasn't that she didn't believe that he cared for her. She simply didn't believe that she was the most important thing in his life at the moment. She didn't know that she—or their daughter—would ever be. Simon claimed that he wanted to see the perpetrators of the human trafficking scheme brought to justice, but she feared that he was simply driven by the need for revenge.

"Hey, you're awake," Simon said sleepily, a smile softening his face as he ran his hand down the small of her back to her naked butt.

Need immediately gripped her insides at the intimate touch; nevertheless Lexie scooted away from him and rolled out of bed.

"It's B day," she said, her heart pounding. She couldn't look at Simon, not after the thoughts that had been playing havoc with her emotions. "The Drake Foundation Christmas ball starts at six. There's still some work to be done and it's…" She checked the clock. "Good grief, it's almost ten! I need to have the fresh flowers in the truck and be at Drake House at eleven." Then it hit her. "Phil Cardon was supposed to help me finish. I don't even know if he's in jail or not."

Throughout her long-winded spiel, Simon lay there staring at her. He kept whatever he was thinking to himself, but his smile had faded, to be replaced by a neutral expression.

"Whatever you need to do," he said.

Lexie showered in record time. This time Simon didn't even try to join her. He waited until she was dressed and scaring up a fast breakfast of coffee and toast with peanut butter and jelly—her specialty.

Then she called the police and asked if Phil had been arrested. He hadn't. Though she wasn't sure how to feel about that, she hoped Phil would show at the garden center or she would have to get someone else fast.

Simon came downstairs, his very presence making her pulse speed up.

"Breakfast," she said, in the middle of eating hers.

"Thanks. None for me."

The way he was looking at her—as if he knew what she'd been worrying about that morning—made her uneasy. She washed down the mouthful of peanut butter and jelly with a slug of coffee. A lump sat in her throat. Knowing she couldn't finish, she threw away the rest of the toast.

"We're not done, you know," he said finally. "With the key. There's still Cliff Drake's place."

The thing she'd tried to put out of mind. "You mean the Manor at Drake Acres."

"Since you say he's so competitive with Brandon, he undoubtedly has more of the file cabinets that once belonged to his father."

Lexie knew he was right, but she hadn't wanted to think about it. "I really don't have access there, and the place is well-staffed."

Simon raised his eyebrows. "What about tonight? Won't everyone including staff be at the ball?"

"I—I suppose so. I need to be there myself, Simon. You know, in case anything needs my attention," she said, then quickly added, "My parents and my sister, Carole, and Katie will all expect me to be there with them."

Simon stared at her as if he were trying to read her mind. "You don't have to go with me this time," he said, his voice even. "I'll get in on my own."

More silence. The air was thick with things that remained unspoken between them.

Finally Lexie whispered, "I hate this!"

"What is it you hate exactly? Playing detective?"

From Simon's expression, Lexie swore he expected her to say she hated *him*.

"Thinking it could be Cliff," she said. "He's always been good to me and my family. The work he gave me saved the business a few years back. I just don't want to believe he would do something so awful. Heller has to be the one."

"I hope you're right, but I have to be sure."

"Why, Simon?" She had to get her doubts into the open so he could ease them. "What are you going to do with the information if you find it?"

A big pause was followed by his saying, "I don't know yet."

"That's what I'm afraid of. Call Bray, have him put you in touch with his brother-in-law. We can tell him everything we know. Let the authorities handle the investigation."

"Where is this coming from?"

"From fear, Simon."

"You're afraid of me?"

"I'm afraid of what you'll do. What you won't be able to undo. It's not too late to let Detective McClellan in on what we've learned. Remember, Bray said his brother-in-law would be understanding. Maybe it's time you trusted someone other than yourself to get the job done."

"I've trusted *you*."

And now he didn't? Is that why he was so closed off, so distant?

"It's you who don't trust *me*," Simon said flatly. "Not with you. Not with our daughter. Not even with a murderer."

"I *do* want to trust you, Simon, but trust takes time, has to be earned. I don't know what you would or wouldn't do. I don't *know* you anymore," she said truthfully.

"So that's it."

His tone had a finality to it that sent a chill through her.

What did he expect of her in so short a time? After spending only three days with him, how could she know him and what he would or would not do?

"Simon—"

"Let's not argue, Lexie. You'll be late for work."

And that quickly she felt an invisible wall go up between them
One she wasn't sure she could breach, even if she tried.

SIMON PLAYED BODYGUARD until he saw Lexie safely arrive at
Drake House. Then he hightailed it out of there and headed for
town.

He didn't know why he felt so let down. He'd known he was
no good for Lexie, had told himself so a hundred times before
he'd come face-to-face with her.

But once he had…

Wishing would get him nowhere. Nor would regret. How
could he regret the time he'd spent with the woman he loved?
How could he regret meeting his daughter, even if Katie didn't
know he was her father?

But maybe he would have been better off.

Expecting his return to Jenkins Cove would be short-lived,
especially if he found the files tonight, Simon figured he had
today to make his peace with his old man, something he felt
compelled to do. He could just leave without ever revealing
himself, but Simon hadn't liked the way things had ended
between them. And it seemed his father was a changed man.

If his father could change…

Driving straight for the Duck Blind, Simon was relieved to
note that it hadn't opened for the day yet. Only one vehicle was
parked in the lot, in the owner's spot.

He went inside.

The Duck Blind was a combination bar and restaurant with
wood-paneled walls and a floor of wide pine planks. Tables
in the center of the room were lit by lamps with fake stained-
glass shades.

Rufus Shea was behind the bar, his back to Simon. Apparently sensing another presence, he turned, and when he saw

Simon, he said, "It's Sunday. Sorry, but we're not open yet. You'll have to come back in an hour."

Simon took a good look at his old man. He'd aged, of course, his thinning hair and scraggly beard now threaded with gray, but he was still wearing a plaid shirt and an apron, just as he used to.

Suddenly his father's brow furrowed, the wrinkled skin around his eyes tightening. "You look familiar. Do I know you?"

Simon removed his hat. "You used to…Dad."

"S-Simon?"

Simon nodded. "I'm alive. I don't know the name of the poor kid you buried, but it wasn't me."

His father's face crumpled. Gripping the bar with both hands, Rufus lowered his head and wept, sobbing, "You're alive. My boy is alive."

Simon hadn't known what to expect, but it wasn't this. Something inside him threatened to break. He wasn't prepared. Didn't know how to handle the emotions suddenly crashing through him. So he waited until his father cried himself out and then told him an edited version of what had happened to him thirteen years before.

Rufus used a napkin to dry his tears. "I should've known it wasn't you who'd died. They wouldn't let me see your body, said better the casket remained closed. I was so sorry about the way things ended between us, boy. I was no good to anyone then. I couldn't take care of you the way a father should. I couldn't take care of myself. I'm so ashamed."

Giving into the regret he'd bottled up for years, Simon said, "Drink made you hell to live with, but you're sober now. You changed."

"I'm a different person," Rufus agreed. "I'm just sorry I didn't sober up when you needed me."

"We always need our parents," Simon told him. "That was

the last straw, you know—your saying I was no son of yours. That's when I decided to run."

Rufus didn't say anything. Suddenly he couldn't meet Simon's eyes and Simon's gut quaked. What the hell?

"What is it, Dad? What aren't you telling me?"

Rufus didn't answer immediately, but finally he said, "I-I love you as much as any father could love a son." He still was averting his eyes. "You got to believe that."

"All right."

"But I wasn't able to give your mother a child… The disappointment nearly killed her. We had some problems with the marriage over it. Then she got pregnant. Not by me." Finally he looked up, locked gazes with Simon. "She never told me who he was. She said it was okay if I wanted to leave her. I didn't though. I loved her more than anything. Her death nearly killed me, too."

It was taking Simon some time to process this. "So you're *not* my father?"

"I *am* your father in every way that counts!" Rufus said. "I couldn't have loved you more, boy, since before you were born. But I was weak and jealous of your mother. I found comfort in the bottle every time I thought about her and another man, not that she catted around on me. It was just that once. She swore it, and mostly I believed her. And then when she died…"

"You forgot about me."

"I didn't forget about you, Simon. Never. Not once in the last thirteen years." More tears rolled into his beard. "I never stopped regretting denying you that last night when all you were trying to do was stop me from taking another drink. I love you, boy. I always have."

Simon couldn't help but wonder who his biological father might be, but he knew he loved Rufus Shea, no matter what.

He settled down at the bar and talked with the old man until it was time for the Duck Blind to open.

Only then did he reluctantly leave, promising to be back.

His thoughts filled with the way Rufus had turned his life around, Simon wondered if it was possible for someone as damaged as he was to do the same.

Chapter Sixteen

As the sun set and the snow started falling in big fat flakes, the first of hundreds of guests arrived for the Drake Foundation charity ball, and Drake House lit up like a beautiful Christmas tree.

Having arrived early and alone, Lexie thought to keep herself busy, rearranging plants and tweaking the vases of flowers. Eventually, she acknowledged that the decorations already looked perfect and found a niche just inside the ballroom where she could see everyone as they came in.

Marie and Brandon stood together in the middle of the foyer, greeting each new arrival. Marie looked spectacular in an off-the-shoulder green velvet gown and made the perfect partner for Brandon, who could have been born in a tux. For once he was smiling. That she'd even had the smallest doubt about him made Lexie's heart twist in regret.

Shelley Zachary stood to one side, taking people's coats and handing them off to Isabella and another young woman to hang on specially set up racks just inside the private wing. Wearing what was obviously a designer black dress, Isabella looked ready to join the ball. From her expression, Lexie guessed that Cliff hadn't invited her to be his date, and Isabella wasn't at all happy playing maid tonight.

So far, a few dozen people had entered the ballroom, oohing and aahing that they'd never seen anything quite so beautiful. Lexie knew she should take more pleasure in the approval, but the Grinch was back.

She blamed Simon for her dark mood.

Oh, he'd seen to his duty as her bodyguard when she'd finished at Drake House earlier, then had followed her back here this evening. For the few hours in between he'd barely spoken to her, hadn't noticed her red silk chiffon gown with its ruched and beaded bodice and a studded bow at the hip. Indeed, he'd seemed preoccupied with his own thoughts.

Had he been making plans to break into the Manor at Drake Acres or plans to leave Jenkins Cove? Maybe both, she thought sadly.

"Lexie, there you are!"

"Mom, Dad." Lexie focused on her parents. Her mother was wearing a new deep blue cocktail dress and her father his old tuxedo. "You two look great. Where's Katie?"

"With Carole. They'll be along in a minute."

Her father kissed her cheek, saying, "My, you look glamorous."

"Thanks, Dad." She forced a grin. "Nice that *someone* noticed."

Katie and Carole entered arm in arm. Rather Carole had her arm linked with Katie's as if she were pulling her niece inside against her wishes. Apparently still miffed at being dragged from her party the night before, Katie was wearing a green dress that matched her eyes—Simon's eyes—as well as her best mulish expression.

Noticing that Katie had also worn the pendant that Lexie had given to Katie for her birthday—a gold abstract representing a mother and daughter with a square-cut emerald the color of her eyes in the middle—Lexie decided to act like nothing was wrong. She moved to the other side of her daughter, where she linked arms.

"I picked out a table for us." She indicated a large round one not far from the door. She needed to be easily found, just in case.

"It's so nice to have the whole family together outside of home or the store," her mother said.

But the whole family wasn't together. Lexie thought as they took their seats. Simon wasn't here with them and probably never would be. Their argument had crystallized things she hadn't wanted to face.

As the tables filled up with guests, Lexie looked around the room, transformed with plants and decorations and lighting special effects. The ballroom looked like a setting in a fairy tale. Kind of like the story she'd been trying to tell herself about her and Simon.

Not wanting to spoil the evening for her family, Lexie temporarily set aside her heartbreak and concentrated on them. She checked out the buffet with her mother, who put her seal of approval on the menu. She examined the silent auction contributions with her sister, who made bids on several items. She danced with her father, who tried out new steps he'd learned in the weekly class he took with her mother. She tried to get Katie interested in anything about the ball, but her daughter was stubbornly silent, refusing to interact with anyone any more than she absolutely had to.

"You know, there are other young people here," Lexie said. "A couple of cute boys your age. They came with their parents, too. I bet you know some of them."

Katie simply sighed and did her best to look bored. Carole rolled her eyes at Lexie, who bit the inside of her lip so she wouldn't laugh. She was trying to figure out how to handle her stubborn daughter when Katie suddenly reminded her of Simon.

Feeling a little too vulnerable, Lexie excused herself and

wandered over to the windows that overlooked the terrace and gardens and faced a small cove on the bay. The wind had picked up and the snow whirled and swirled in delicate patterns. On the other side of the inlet on another promontory, soft light made every window at the Manor at Drake Acres glow. Lexie felt as if she were looking out at a Christmas card.

That Simon had probably already broken in to the Christmas card seemed ludicrous to her. And frightening. How long would it take him to learn that he was wrong? she wondered.

Or that *she* was?

Just then, the band at the far end of the room stopped playing and Brandon and Marie stepped up onto the stage. Lexie hurried back to her seat at the family table.

Her daughter wasn't there.

Her pulse picking up, Lexie asked, "Where's Katie?"

"Said she had to go to the powder room," Carole whispered.

Lexie relaxed as Brandon and Marie stepped up to the microphone on a stand.

"Welcome to Drake House," Brandon said, leaning more lightly on his cane than usual. "Marie and I want to thank you all for giving your support to the Drake Foundation."

"Remember that we have some exciting items contributed to the silent auction," Marie said, "so don't forget to put in your bid. The winners will be announced at midnight."

"Ah, winners..." Brandon said. "My Uncle Cliff has an announcement to make." He indicated that Cliff should come up to the microphone, then, with his arm around Marie's waist, left the stage.

As usual, Cliff was one of the handsomest men in the room. Certainly, he was the best dressed in a designer black tux and black silk shirt, Lexie thought, trying to push out of mind the idea that he could be a mastermind of evil. She looked around for Doug Heller, but couldn't find the operations manager among so many people.

Holding a large envelope in one hand, Cliff stepped in front of the mike. "As you know, every year the Merchants' Association sponsors a contest for the best and most tasteful holiday display. They asked me to announce this year's winner." He went on to read the list of nominations before opening the envelope. "And the winner is…Sophie Caldwell, owner of House of the Seven Gables Bed-and-Breakfast! Sophie, come on up here and say a few words."

Lexie heard the announcement as if through a filter. She couldn't help it. She barely saw Sophie's beaming face as she left the table with her niece, Chelsea, and Chelsea's fiancé, Michael, and stepped up to the mike. Though she wanted to put everything but the here and now out of mind, Lexie simply couldn't. She scanned the crowd for Doug Heller before looking back to the stage where Cliff was handing Sophie the envelope.

Staring at Cliff, she tried to see through the outer facade, tried to discern the face of evil.

If it was there, she simply didn't recognize it.

Would Simon find something to prove otherwise?

IN POSITION FOR SEVERAL HOURS, using night-vision binoculars, Simon had watched the occupants of the Manor at Drake Acres abandon it. The cars had left one at a time until none but a few high-priced toys in the main garage were left. The snow was coming down more heavily now, and it was getting more difficult to discern details. Certain that the grounds were truly empty, though, he made his run from the tree line to the redbrick buildings that comprised Cliff Drake's home.

In addition to the main house, with its three-story white pillars and the nearly-as-tall white-cased windows and balconies on each floor that overlooked the water, there were two garages—one for Cliff, the other for the servants—a guest house, a cabana and outdoor pool, and farther back from the water, the stables. At the water's edge, there was also a large boathouse and a pier jutting from it, a high-performance boat docked there despite the weather.

Did Drake Enterprises really make Cliff enough money to support such ostentatiousness? Or did a secret source of income provide him with a lifestyle most people only dreamed of? Simon guessed that the latter was more probable.

Rather than trying to breach the main house directly, he decided to approach from the rear. Overriding the security system, he didn't even need a key to open the door. He slipped inside the largest kitchen that he'd ever seen in a private home. Several doors lined the opposite wall. The first one he checked was a pantry. The second a half bath. He went straight out the third and down a hallway that led to a two-story atrium at the front of the house.

Lights were on all over the house, as if leaving him a trail of breadcrumbs to the first-floor office located off the atrium.

Once inside, he spotted the file cabinets immediately.

They were the wrong ones.

Not only were they modern, rather than antique, but the key wouldn't go into the locks.

"What the hell?"

He'd been so sure he would find the fit to the key here, but it looked as if Lexie had been correct. Then where would the damn cabinets be? What if there weren't any others?

Or...

What if he hadn't been wrong and had simply looked in the wrong room?

The manor was certainly big enough to house more than a

single office. This one was situated in a high-traffic area, accessible to anyone coming in the front door. Not a good place to store valuable documents, especially not ones that could mean a prison sentence.

There had to be another office, so Simon vowed not to leave the building until he'd checked every room.

He started on the first floor and found another office, smaller than the first, but this one didn't even have file cabinets.

The second floor held a third office, but no luck there, either.

As he went through the house, Simon realized that unlike what Lexie had said about Drake House, all the furniture here was ultramodern, the artwork abstract, as if Cliff had purposely made the Manor at Drake Acres as different from Drake House as he could. Those old file cabinets simply wouldn't fit in here.

Admitting he'd run into another dead end, Simon stood in the atrium for a few moments, looking out into the snowy night. A night transformed by wind and fog like the one when he'd been taken from Jenkins Cove and thrust into a world he hadn't imagined.

An unexpected chill shot through the atrium, pebbling Simon's flesh. For a moment, he could hardly breathe.

He felt the weight of the dead on his shoulders.

Of the injustice.

Felt as if myriad ghosts were pleading with him not to give up.

Looking deep into the fog curling up to the house, he could almost see them—men, women, the kid he'd seen killed. Did he really see them or was it an illusion? He blinked and when he looked again, they were gone. But the weight of their deaths wasn't. He felt it like a tangible thing, knew their souls wouldn't rest—that *he* couldn't rest—until he avenged them all.

But at what cost?

Had he already lost Lexie? She didn't trust him, but could he blame her?

He'd known from the beginning that what he'd been through had turned him into a man she wouldn't want to know. He'd lived on the edge his entire adult life, long enough that he didn't have any idea of how else to be.

His father had changed, he reminded himself. No matter that he'd learned another painful truth that afternoon, Rufus Shea would always be his old man. And if his father could choose to straighten up his life and be a man a kid could be proud of…

Shaking his head, Simon left the house the way he'd come. Only when he was about to make his way back to the road did he stop and consider the other buildings on the property. Primarily the guesthouse.

Was it really?

Suddenly an arctic cold whipped through him and he felt invisible hands pushing him, urging him toward the guesthouse. Simon acquiesced.

As he crossed the back of the property, the cold followed. His inner ghosts filled him with tension. He gazed around, on the lookout for trouble. The small hairs at the back of his neck stood up, but he saw no reason for it. He checked the ground. For as far as he could see through the snow, the fresh white cover remained undisturbed by recent footprints except for the ones he was leaving.

Only him and the ghosts, he thought, his mood darkening.

Upon reaching the guesthouse, he was surprised to find the security system unarmed. Edgy now, he tried the door handle. It turned and the door swung open. Too easy, he thought, unless there was nothing here to protect. Stepping inside, he turned on the light.

The place looked occupied, as though someone was living

there. Furnished in a combination of comfortable couches and chairs and some antique wooden pieces, it had a totally different feel from the main house. The artwork was different, too—all related to the Chesapeake Bay and the Eastern Shore, from the framed watercolors on the walls to the metal sculptures of bay creatures decorating the various old end tables and a hand-carved buffet in the dining area.

Assuming that Cliff had guests for the holiday, Simon was about to leave when a cold breeze shot down his spine. He stopped and examined the room again. A briefcase lay on the coffee table. He drew closer, and saw the initials *DH* engraved on the metal clasp.

DH for Doug Heller?

The briefcase was filled with Drake Enterprises work. Why else would Heller have left it in the guesthouse if he hadn't made himself at home here?

Simon gazed around the room. Instincts buzzing, he headed for a closed door and opened it to a bedroom. A familiar canvas jacket—one he'd seen on Doug Heller—was thrown on the chair across from the bed, making Simon think the operations manager did live, or at least work, in the guesthouse.

So where were the damn file cabinets? Simon wondered as he left the bedroom.

Another door on the other side of the living area called to him. A rush of sound like wails of pain and grief unnerved him, but Simon knew it was all in his own head. He crossed to the door. His hand actually tingled as he gripped the knob. Swinging the door open, he turned on the room light to face another office.

Against the opposite wall was a file cabinet with leaf marquetry. Simon crossed the room, pulled out the key and tried the lock.

A match.

He could hardly breathe as he opened the drawer. Inside were file folders with names written across the top. Inside his head, the victims chanted their names…*Anna Bencek…Franz Dobra…Tomas Elizi…Lala Falat…*

Exactly as Bray had seen when he'd touched the key.

Simon pulled Anna Bencek's folder, which held proof of a medical check and blood workup and Anna's signed statement that she was voluntarily donating a kidney for transplant. It also held her current information—address, phone number, name and address of her shop.

The other folders gave up similar information, a folder for each transplant donor.

So Heller knew where to get to these people…

The middle drawer produced more folders with similar information. But these held information on the recipients, including who each person's donor had been and how much the recipient had paid to skip to the head of the line for a new shot at life.

Doug Heller had used his position with Drake Enterprises to run his own illegal business, and right under the nose of his employer. How had he gotten away with it all these years? Simon wondered.

Well, Heller wouldn't get away with it anymore, Simon thought as the cold seeped through him once more, straight into his bones, into his soul.

Time to mete out some justice.

Simon was so engrossed in his dark thoughts that he didn't hear the whisper of footsteps until they were practically upon him. Even as he whipped around, he heard a pop followed by an incapacitating pain.

He barely caught a glimpse of the two wires connecting to him…and then he saw nothing at all…

Chapter Seventeen

When nearly a half hour had passed and her daughter hadn't come back to the table, nor had Lexie so much as caught sight of her, she started to worry.

"I'm going to go look for Katie," she told her sister.

"She's probably with some other kids her age," Carole said. "She won't appreciate your interrupting."

An uneasy sensation in the pit of her stomach wouldn't let Lexie back down. "If she is, I'll keep walking without bothering her. I just want to make sure she's all right."

Making her way through the crowd was a feat in itself. People were shoulder to shoulder and more were arriving all the time. Lexie looked everywhere—the ballroom, the buffet, the dining room, even the upstairs parlors—but couldn't find her daughter. That uneasy sensation blossomed into something akin to panic. She began to ask people if they'd seen Katie in the last half hour, but no one had.

On her way back to alert Carole and her parents, Lexie heard her name. Pulse fluttering, she stopped and turned to see who was calling her.

"Cliff."

His usual jovial expression was missing. "I need to talk to you."

Cliff gestured that she should follow and, not knowing what else to do, Lexie did. He crossed the foyer and passed the racks of coats into the front room of the personal wing.

Facing her, he said, "First, let me say Katie is all right."

"Katie?" Lexie's heart began to pound. "What happened to my daughter?"

"Apparently, she took herself for a walk out of here and slipped and fell on the road." Cliff patted her shoulder. "She only sprained her ankle a little, that's all. She'll be fine."

"Where is she? Upstairs?"

"No, not here. Tommy Benson found her near his place so he took her home to ice the ankle. Then he called me. He didn't have your cell number, but he knew you'd be here. I'll take you to her. Let me get our coats."

The pressure in her chest easing a bit, Lexie nodded. "Thanks, Cliff."

Tommy Benson was a Jenkins Cove police officer. Good thing he'd found Katie or she might have been out in the snow for who knew how long. What was she doing out on the road? Rebelling against being here and going home in protest? After what Katie had pulled the night before, Lexie wouldn't doubt it. She figured she was in for a lot more worry over her daughter's escapades during the next few years.

Thinking she should let her family know what was going on, she pulled her cell phone from her purse just as Cliff came back with the coats.

"Here you are." He held out Lexie's coat for her.

She slipped her arms into it. "Thanks. I should call Carole, so she doesn't send a search party after me."

"Maybe you should wait until after you see Katie for yourself. That way they won't worry like *you're* doing right now."

"Maybe you're right."

She put her cell back in her purse. Even with Cliff's reas
surance that Katie was fine, Lexie couldn't help but feel off-
kilter. Knowing she wouldn't feel better until she saw Katie
herself, she quickly followed him out of the house to the BMW
one of the valets had already pulled up front. Cliff tipped the
man who ran around to the passenger side and opened the door
for Lexie.

"Try to relax," Cliff said as they fastened their seat belts.
"We'll be there in a few minutes."

Lexie nodded and took a deep breath. As they set off for the
Benson place, she couldn't help wishing Simon were here with
her. Sometimes it was so hard being a single parent, especially
where her child's welfare was concerned.

Suddenly it hit her…Simon…at Cliff's place… In her worry
for Katie, she'd forgotten about what he was doing. Surely he
was done searching the Manor.

So why hadn't he called? No matter what he'd found or
hadn't found, he would call to tell her about it, even if he was
still angry.

Great. Now she had two people she loved to worry about.

Suddenly she realized they were slowing and she looked for
Benson's house, but only saw twin redbrick pillars with
wrought-iron gates decorated with a fancy *C* and *D*.

"This is the entrance to the Manor," she said, keeping her
voice even, though her pulse jagged a warning. "I thought you
said Katie was at Tommy Benson's place."

"I need to stop for something. It'll just take a minute." He
completed the turn and started on the long drive, but he didn't
stop in front of the door.

Her pulse picked up and rushed through her head so that she
could hear it. "Cliff, I'm really concerned about Katie—"

"You'll see her soon enough."

But Lexie didn't think so. Had Simon been caught? Was the game up? Was that why Cliff had brought her here? Had she been wrong about him all this time?

Cliff stopped the BMW near the guesthouse. Thinking she could run, then call the police, Lexie tried the door handle.

"You won't get it open, Lexie."

"What are you doing, Cliff?" Lexie kept her voice as even as she could. The words fought her as she spoke. "Where's Katie?"

"Katie?" He opened his door and hopped out. "At the ball, I assume." Slamming the door, he walked around to the passenger side and opened her door. "Get out."

"No. Take me back, Cliff." She stiffened when he grabbed her arm. "I don't know what you think you're doing—"

Her words were cut off when he jerked her out of the car. Lexie fought him, but despite his playboy persona, Cliff was every bit as strong as Simon.

"Why are you taking me here?" Pulling against him only meant she tripped as he dragged her to the guesthouse. "What's going on, Cliff?"

"I don't have to tell you, Lexie. You already know."

Simon… Dear Lord, he'd been caught!

Suddenly breathless, she stopped fighting and stumbled after him. Once inside the guesthouse, she saw Simon in a chair facing the door. He didn't even look her way. He was slumped in his chair, hands behind his back, and his head lolled to the side. His eyes were only half-open.

Directly opposite Simon, Doug Heller held a knife as if he knew how to use it.

Feeling like a fool for believing in Cliff, she looked to him, unaffected by his regret-filled expression. "You're in on this together?"

"Not exactly."

"Old Cliffy works for me," Heller said.

"Not exactly!" Cliff repeated, this time with more emphasis

"Oh, right. We're *business* partners. I do all the work and he takes half the money in exchange for access to his ships and yachts and properties."

So they'd done it, Lexie thought. They'd nailed the heads of the human trafficking operation.

Now the question was this: would she and Simon live long enough to tell the authorities what they'd learned?

THAT HELLER WAS TALKING so freely made Simon's gut roll. The killer wouldn't be admitting to anything unless he planned to get rid of both him and Lexie.

Not that Simon would go down without a fight. He'd stop the bastard any way he could, and if he went down with Heller, so be it. He probably deserved to die.

Why hadn't Heller killed him already?

What was he waiting for?

Heller had used a Taser on him—the reason he hadn't been able to get his hands on the man. Simon remained half-slumped in the chair, his eyes at half-mast, so Heller wouldn't realize that he was starting to recover from the powerful shock. For several minutes now, he'd been working at the knot in the rope that tied his hands behind his back, and it was starting to loosen.

"What are you going to do to us, Cliff?" Lexie asked. "Kill us?"

"The two of you pose a real problem, Lexie." Cliff shook his head. "I saved Simon's hide once, but I don't know if I can do it again."

"You saved my hide?" Simon echoed, making his voice sound unsteady, as if he were still weak from the Taser blast.

"I wouldn't let Heller kill you. I agreed to let him ship you ff to be part of a paramilitary army that would keep you busy and away from here for a few years. He arranged everything."

Though he was sure he already knew, Simon asked, "Why?"

"I didn't want you to die. I figured you didn't see anything really, and by the time you came back to Jenkins Cove, any evidence would be destroyed and your memory of that night would have faded. Killing people wasn't part of the deal."

"But people did die...*Dad.*"

Cliff locked gazes with Simon. "Wh-what?"

Though he appeared shocked, he didn't deny the relationship, making Simon's gut tighten.

"Rufus and I had a heart-to-heart this morning. He spilled his guts." But Rufus hadn't known the identity of Simon's biological father, and now Simon wished he didn't know, either. "So, you couldn't kill your own flesh and blood?"

"No! I never killed anyone, Simon. I swear to you, my hands are clean."

"Clean? You knew what was going on. You made money on people's misery!"

"They wanted to come here, to live in this country. They have better lives here. They're happy—"

"Maybe those who are still alive. What about the ones who didn't make it because they didn't have the proper medical follow-up? Who died of complications, like Lala Falat? Or those who were shot to death like the kid in the woods? Or bludgeoned to death with a yachting trophy?"

"I wasn't responsible for any of that!"

"Stop whining," Heller demanded. "It doesn't suit you."

"Now I know why you've been so good to me and my family over the years," Lexie said to Cliff. "You knew Katie was your granddaughter. After all you've done for us, surely you won't let Heller kill us now."

Simon stewed inside. They *couldn't* kill Lexie. She wa
innocent. He'd gotten her mixed up in this. He couldn't let he
pay for his sins. Even as he thought it, the knot gave and the
binding holding his wrists together loosened. He worked one
hand out, then the other.

Cliff asked, "Simon, are you willing to drop this investigation
of yours and remain silent about what you've learned? I could
make this as financially rewarding for you as it has been for me."

Insulted that this man who was of the same blood thought
they were anything alike, Simon felt heat creep up his neck.
"No way in hell. Too many people were harmed or killed
because of you."

"All I did was rent my ships and properties to Doug and—"

"Knock off the sanctimonious act, Cliff!" Heller shouted.
"It's not going to get you a pass."

Cliff turned on his partner. "The human trafficking operation was your idea. You ran it!"

"But if the authorities found out about us, you'd be held
equally responsible for everything that happened."

"We won't tell," Lexie suddenly said.

Heller cocked his head and seared her with his gaze. "Now,
why don't I believe you?"

Simon didn't believe her, either. She was stalling for time.
What was she up to? Finally, his head clear of the effects of the
Taser and his hands free, though still behind him, Simon
gathered himself together and waited for an opportunity to
strike. Heller should have done a better job of restraining him.

His mistake.

"Really," Lexie said, inching closer to Heller. "I mean the
operation is over now, right?"

"For the time being. We don't have a doctor who can do the
surgeries."

Which sounded like he was planning on starting up again as soon as he found one, Simon thought. He wondered what Lexie was planning to do by getting close to Heller, who held the knife as if he was looking forward to gutting someone with it.

Too bad Heller had searched him and found the knife in his jacket, Simon thought. Too bad he had no other weapon on him other than his bare hands.

They would be enough, he vowed.

"Cliff, I'll make a deal with you," Lexie said. "I believe you when you said you never meant for anyone to be hurt. You don't have to go on letting this man use your resources. Agree to stop doing that and we'll forget everything we learned. You're my daughter's grandfather. I don't want to see you go to jail. Heller can take off, disappear to another country or something."

What the hell was she saying? Simon almost protested when she turned her attention to him.

"Cliff's your father, Simon. You don't want him in prison any more than I do, right?"

Though her words sounded like a capitulation, the tension in her expression and the denial in her eyes when she locked her gaze onto his told Simon otherwise. She was playing Cliff to get closer to Heller.

Simon's muscles coiled.

"This is bunk! Don't believe a word out of her mouth!" Heller said, charging to his feet and coming too close to Lexie for Simon's comfort.

The way he was handling the knife—like he was getting ready to use it on someone—made Simon prepare to launch himself at the bastard. But Lexie was too close. And Heller wasn't stupid. He kept a sharp eye on Simon.

"Lexie has never lied to me," Cliff argued. "She's the most honest person I know. Her child is my blood."

Simon indicated that Lexie should get out of the way. Though understanding colored her expression, she ignored him. Her eyes flashed to a nearby table.

"Then take her damn child!" Heller yelled at Cliff. "Adopt the kid. I don't care! But you're not going to let these two go. I'm not going to prison because you're a gutless wonder, as usual!"

As the men argued, Lexie reached for a heavy metal sculpture on the table—a Maryland crab.

"Watch what you say!" Cliff warned.

"Or you'll what? If you hadn't convinced me to let your bastard live thirteen years ago, we wouldn't be in this situation!"

Lexie grabbed the crab and swung it at Heller's knife hand. The man's sixth sense must have warned him because he stepped away and the sculpture barely brushed him. While Heller's attention was diverted, Simon lunged at him and made contact, knocking him back and away from Lexie.

Heller struck out at his gut with the knife, but Simon was faster and arched away so that it missed anything vital, only slicing through the leather sleeve of his jacket and nicking his arm.

Pain seared him, but Simon was blinded with hatred and the need to make this man pay, not only for putting him on that transport ship to hell, but for threatening Lexie's life, for taking the lives of people he didn't even know.

He kicked out and made contact, knocking the knife from Heller's hand. Heller tried to go after it, but Simon tackled him. They went rolling across the floor, trading punches. Heller was heftier and definitely strong, but Simon was trained for battle and a black rage coursed through him. Rolling on top of Heller, he hit the man in the face with a series of stunning blows, then grabbed him by the throat and put pressure on his airway.

"Do you have any idea what it feels like to know you're

going to die?" Simon demanded, totally focused on his enemy. He squeezed tighter so the other man was choking, trying to get air. "I do. I was certain of it day after day. I felt like I was already dead and living in hell. A place that will welcome you with open arms."

He increased the pressure on Heller's throat even more. The man's face turned red and he tried to say something, tried to pry Simon's fingers away, but he couldn't budge Simon.

"Simon, stop before you kill him!" Lexie's cry unnerved Simon just for a second. It was all Heller needed.

Heller ripped Simon's hand from his throat and knocked his arm on a nearby table. The knife wound came in contact with the table's edge and pain reverberated through Simon so that he saw stars and gasped for breath.

Heller threw him off, got up and ran straight through the open front door. By the time the pain lessened enough to allow Simon to get to his feet, the man was gone. His mind focused on only one thing, he stopped in the doorway to visually track the man's footprints, visible in the night. The snow had cleared and the moon was out. The footprints ran straight into the fog coming off the bay.

"Heller's headed toward the boathouse," he said, feeling invisible hands pushing him in that direction. He heard a silent chant in his head, urging him to stop Heller. "There's a speedboat docked at the pier."

"Don't go after him!" Lexie pleaded, hanging on to the back of his jacket. "What if he has a gun?"

An invisible struggle pulled Simon in two different directions. The dead wanted their justice. Lexie wanted him alive.

As he looked at the woman he loved, Simon felt the darkness and the voices in his head recede. He couldn't leave Lexie here alone with Cliff. He had to protect her.

Turning, he saw Cliff pick up something from the floor where Simon had attacked Heller. When the man straightened, his brow was furrowed. He crossed the room, holding out a delicate chain with a gold and emerald pendant.

"Wasn't Katie wearing this tonight?" he asked.

Lexie grabbed it from him. "Oh my God, Katie! Where is she?"

Simon's gut rolled. "Not here. Heller must have her." He made for the door. "He's headed for the pier."

"I'm coming with you!" Lexie said, rushing to catch up.

Cliff was right behind her, but Simon couldn't deal with the man right now, not when his daughter was in danger. He grabbed Lexie's hand and ran full-out, the chorus of ghostly voices in his head growing in urgency. They were three-quarters of the way to the boathouse when the door flashed open. Through the mists, Simon saw Heller drag Katie down the pier. She was a little spitfire, fighting him with everything she had, but she was just a kid.

His kid.

"Heller! Let go of Katie now!"

Ignoring him, Heller forced the girl into the speedboat, then jumped in beside her. Simon let go of Lexie's hand and raced for the pier so fast, his feet seemed to skim the earth as if he were about to take flight.

"Don't try to follow me and I'll let the girl live!" Heller shouted, starting the engine. "I'll even call you to tell you where to find her!"

The speedboat nearly jumped as it took off.

Simon reached the pier too late to climb aboard, but not too late to see his daughter's tear-stained, frightened face before it disappeared into the fog.

A face that would haunt his every waking moment…

Chapter Eighteen

Lexie screamed in horror as the fog swallowed her daughter, perhaps forever. For a moment, she remained frozen, her mind a void, as if she were dying.

But she wasn't dying and she refused to let Katie go without a fight. Whipping around to find Cliff coming up behind her, she shouted, "That new speedboat—the fast one—tell me it's here."

Cliff nodded and ran past her into the boathouse.

Lexie ran to Simon and as he turned to her, she saw an unfamiliar sheen in his eyes.

"Lexie, I'm sorry," Simon said. "I should have gone after that bastard Heller right away."

"You couldn't have known he'd stashed Katie in the boathouse. We'll get her back. We have to." The reassurance was as much for herself as it was for him.

"He won't let her go. She's seen his face."

Though Lexie already knew that, she couldn't lose hope. "We'll catch up to them."

"How do you think we can catch him with the head start he has?" Simon asked, even as an engine roared to life from the boathouse.

Lexie took Simon's hand and pulled him farther along the

pier, while Cliff edged the futuristic-looking craft out of the boathouse and toward them.

"That's how."

As the speedboat came alongside them, Simon leaped onto the hull then held out a hand for Lexie. She grabbed it and jumped, her stomach shaking as the boat rocked on contact. He helped her navigate the hull and climb into the seat behind Cliff, then jumped into the one next to her.

"Go!"

The speedboat practically flew into the fog. Lexie had no idea how Cliff knew where he was going or even what direction he should take as he ripped through the blinding wet cloud.

Dear Lord, let them find Katie…let them get their daughter back safely.

Lexie knew it was her fault that Katie was gone. If she hadn't distracted Simon, Heller would never have gotten away. But if she hadn't done so, Simon might have *killed* Heller. Simon had been so focused on the man, she'd feared he would do something he would regret. Killing in combat, even as a soldier in a private army, was a whole different thing from killing someone in civilian life.

Had Simon done that, he would have been held accountable. To the authorities. To her.

To himself.

For, no matter what he said about his past, Simon was truly a decent man. He had a conscience. Had he taken a life when he could have restrained Heller and handed him over to the authorities, Simon never would have rid himself of *that* ghost.

Right now, though, with Katie in danger, Lexie wondered if she hadn't made a mistake in stopping Simon. And if something happened to her daughter…Lexie could see how easily a person could get caught up in dark, dangerous thoughts like revenge.

A moment later, they tore through the fog into open water and rough seas. Through the remaining trails of mist, she could see the wake left by the other speedboat.

And then the boat itself.

Simon squeezed her hand and, tears forming in her eyes, Lexie met his gaze.

"We'll get her back," he promised.

She had to believe him. Had to believe there could be a happy ending, at least as far as Katie was concerned. Nodding, she forced down the growing lump in her throat and focused straight ahead.

Cliff guided them through the other boat's wake like it was child's play, yet the seas were rough, the ride nearly painful at times when the boat lifted into the air and then slapped down hard. Water sprayed her, but Lexie hardly noticed. She could see the people in the other speedboat now—her daughter huddled in a rear seat, Heller standing behind the wheel.

Heller kept looking back as they inched closer. Lexie could almost feel his panic increase as Cliff tried to bring their boat alongside his.

"Get as close as you can!" Simon shouted, letting go of Lexie's hand.

Simon then climbed over the front seat, over the windshield onto the hull, which rocked and bounced in the choppy seas. Even so, he stood firm, his knees slightly bent and acting like shock absorbers to his body as the boat slipped expertly along-side Heller.

Without warning, Simon leaped from the hull and Lexie's chest went tight as she stopped breathing.

HELLER'S FACE TWISTED in fury as Simon landed on the killer, the voices in his head screaming for vengeance. Heller had the advantage, however, and threw Simon off long enough to gun the boat's engine and pull it in such a tight circle away from the other craft that Simon couldn't get back up on his feet.

He threw a quick look at Katie and saw that while her eyes were swollen from crying, they were focused on Heller, and her expression was mutinous, as though she was ready to join the fray and attack the man who'd kidnapped her.

Getting her attention silently, Simon indicated that Katie should stay put, but he wasn't certain she would.

Suddenly, the engine stalled and the boat slowed and righted, allowing Simon to rise as Heller fumbled with his pocket.

When the killer pulled out a gun, Simon reacted, kicking out and hitting Heller's arm so that the gun tilted up, a shot going wild. And Simon knew that if he could, Heller would kill them all. The voices in his head urged him to stop Heller any way he could.

And he could see only one way…

Simon grabbed the other man's arm and they engaged in a bizarre dance, fighting for control of the weapon. Heller had to be stopped, no matter what it took. Instinct made him throw a quick glance at Katie, even as she rose from her seat.

"Stay there!" he yelled, finally getting hold of a pressure point in the other man's arm that allowed him to rip the gun from Heller's hand.

Simon didn't even have time to aim before Katie climbed onto the seat. As fast as she rose, Heller acted faster. With a sweep of his arm, he smacked her across the chest, tossing her off the boat. She hit the water with a scream that seared Simon's soul.

"Oh my God, Katie!" Lexie yelled.

Instinct drove Simon over the seat into the icy water after her. At the first shock of cold, he let go of the gun. Stunned, he cleared his head and focused, then grabbed for his daughter. Tossed by the rough seas like a rag doll, she eluded him and then went under.

"Katie!" Lexie screamed again.

No, it couldn't end like this! Katie couldn't be lost to him before he even got to know her!

Simon dived down after her, blindly reaching for her, his hand brushing against her but unable to get a grip. He came up for air and went down again, deeper. This time, he couldn't find her. Couldn't see her. Panic blossomed in his chest. She couldn't die. Not Katie! Not another innocent. Another senseless death.

Gasping for air, he surfaced to an explosion of sound. Lexie was screaming their daughter's name. An engine was turning over, but not starting. The voices in his head were urging him to dive again, to rescue Katie.

He went down for a third time and thought if he couldn't find her, there was no use his coming back to the surface. He couldn't face Lexie without their daughter.

Even as he thought it, the blackness of his surroundings lifted for a moment, as if a beam of sunlight shot through the water. Or as if a ghostly mist had dived deep with him. Suddenly he was able to see a fragile hand floating as if reaching for him. A surge of strength pulsed through him and he kicked and reached out until he caught it. Tugging hard, he pulled an unconscious Katie to him.

It couldn't be too late, he thought, arm around her middle as he kicked to the surface. Cliff and Lexie were frantically looking over the side of the craft.

"You've got her!" Lexie yelled, leaning out over the water, reaching for her daughter.

Cliff reached, too. "C'mon, Simon!"

His arm hooked over her chest, Simon was careful to keep Katie's head above water as a wave rolled toward the boat. He was exhausted and shivering. The cold water held him in a death grip. Even so, he mustered enough strength to lift Katie

up to her mother and grandfather. They caught the girl's arms
and pulled her up and into the boat.

"Katie, honey, it's Mom!"

Cold froze Simon's limbs and sleep called him. Or was it Cliff?

"Simon, give me your damn hand!"

Cliff was hanging over the side of the boat again, arm outstretched. Simon tried reaching for it, but he couldn't do it. He
had nothing left.

Then Lexie popped her head over the side of the boat.
"Simon Shea, fight. Your daughter is alive because of you. *I'm*
alive. We need you!"

Somehow, Simon found a kernel of strength to reach out and
grab hold of Cliff's outstretched hand. Cliff grasped him with
both of his, then slowly dragged him up out of the water. Lexie
grabbed hold of his jacket and with more strength than he'd
known she had, helped haul him inside the boat.

Simon immediately looked to his daughter. Wrapped in her
mother's coat on one of the rear seats, Katie was coughing.

Teeth chattering, he muttered, "H-Heller," then blinked and
focused on the other boat. "C-can't let him g-get away."

Simon blinked again as a familiar mist hovered over the hull
of the other craft. Lexie pressed into him, her hand gripping him
hard as if she saw the same thing he did.

"What in the world...?" Cliff whispered as the mist took shape.

The kid he'd seen shot materialized, the apparition making
Heller jump, his substantial weight whacking the side of the
boat and rocking it precariously.

"What the hell!" he shouted as a large wave tossed the craft,
tilting it nearly on its side.

Though Heller fought to stay upright and grab on to something—anything—he couldn't manage it. He was swept off the
boat and into the water.

Simon moved to the rail, ready to grab for the killer when he came up.

Seconds passed. A minute.

"He's gone," Lexie said. "Just like that."

Simon looked up to the hull of the righted boat.

Not only was Heller gone, so was the ghost.

DRESSED IN CLOTHING one of Cliff's former girlfriends had left at his place, Lexie felt uncomfortable, if dry and warm, as she sat and watched her daughter sleep in the emergency room bed. Even though Katie was safe now, the pressure in Lexie's chest had hardly diminished.

How could it when she had to see her child hooked up to all this monitoring equipment?

Needing to stretch her legs and get some air, she rose, kissed Katie's forehead and left the cubicle. She could hear Simon in the next cubicle giving his statement to Detective Rand McClellan, who'd already interviewed her.

She wanted to get home and shower and change, but she wasn't about to leave until Katie and Simon were cleared to go with her, which, according to the doctor, wouldn't be until morning. They would be monitored all night. She'd called her parents to let them and her sister know what had happened. They'd wanted to rush to her side, but she'd asked them not to come. She'd assured them that Katie would be fine and that she needed time alone to think things through.

Pacing in the hall, Lexie couldn't help but replay the nightmare in her head a dozen times.

She had to hand it to Cliff—he'd come through for them at his own expense. He'd gotten them back to land and into dry clothing while they'd awaited an ambulance. And then he'd called the state police and had turned himself in. He'd said he hadn't wanted to put the burden on her or Simon; they'd already been through enough because of him.

That she'd been wrong about Cliff deeply saddened Lexie, especially now that she knew he was Simon's biological father and Katie's grandfather.

Lexie started when she almost bumped into Detective McClellan.

"I'm done for now," he said. "I will have to talk to your daughter, as well. It can wait until she's home, though."

"Thank you. Bray said you were understanding."

"I might be, but parts of your story are going to be hard to sell the brass."

The ghost part, she knew. Not that he needed to put that in his report. A wave had tossed Heller's boat nearly on its side. Whatever he decided, Lexie would back him up and she was certain Simon would, as well.

"You'll be hearing from me, probably tomorrow afternoon. I'll give you a chance to get back home and settle in."

Lexie waited until he'd left before venturing into Simon's cubicle. Still covered with several warming blankets, he lay back in his bed, his eyes closed. She stopped to look at the face she so loved and, lump in her throat, wondered how much longer she would be seeing it.

His eyes fluttered open. "Katie?"

"She'll be fine. They just want to keep her overnight for observation. You, too."

"I'm all right."

"You're more than all right," she said softly, sitting on the edge of his bed so she could touch him. She ran her hand along his chest. "You're a hero. You saved our daughter's life."

"She wouldn't have been in danger if not for me."

"Where do you get that?" Lexie said.

"I stirred up a hornet's nest by coming back here."

"You're not guilty of anything but trying to find the truth. I'm the one who had the key. Even if you hadn't come back—"

"Don't go there."

She nodded.

"At least the souls of the dead here can rest now," he said. "And you and Katie will be safe."

"Because you'll be with us?"

He looked away from her. "I'm no good for either of you, Lexie. I wanted to kill Heller tonight."

She didn't tell him she'd felt the same when he'd tossed Katie over the side of the boat. "But you didn't."

"Because you stopped me from strangling him."

"You could have shot him once you got the gun from him, Simon, but when faced with the decision of getting revenge or saving Katie, you didn't even hesitate."

"I couldn't have done anything else."

"I know that now. I know there are things more important to you than vengeance. *People.*"

They locked gazes and Lexie wished with all her heart that she could be with Simon forever.

"I was thinking about my old man…Rufus…about how he's hanged. He couldn't have done it alone. I don't know that I can, either."

"You don't have to be alone. You have me. And a daughter who will adore you. And you can get professional help if you need it, Simon, someone who knows how to deal with the kind of memories and nightmares you must have. A man can change. You proved that tonight. Please, think about staying. You have a daughter. A kid should know her father, be close to him."

"You're sure you want that?"

"Only if you do," she said, smoothing the blanket over his

chest, feeling his heartbeat grow stronger. "Only if you'd be happy here. I keep worrying you'll miss the excitement and danger—"

"I've had enough danger for a lifetime. As for excitement..." He pulled her closer, wrapped his arms around her. "You're all the excitement I can stand. I love you, Lexie, and I want to stay and get to know you all over again."

Lexie felt herself open up inside. "I love you, too, and your staying would be the best Christmas present ever."

As they kissed, she couldn't think of anything she wanted more.

Epilogue

'Da-a-ad! Stop eating the Christmas cookies or there won't be any left for our company!'

"I can't help myself. They're terrific. I'm going to expect you to keep me well fed. Your mother has lots of talent, but not in the kitchen. Do you know she tried to feed me peanut butter and jelly for breakfast?"

Entering the kitchen to see Simon pop some powdered sugar on their daughter's nose, Lexie smiled. Katie had taken to her father as if she'd just been waiting for him to show up all her life. And from the loopy grin Simon wore, it was obvious he was in love with his daughter, as well as with her.

"Hey, everyone is asking for you two," she said, grabbing a plate laden with fresh appetizers.

Simon lifted the tray of cookies and Katie grabbed bowls of chips and dip and followed her into the living area, now decorated every bit as beautifully as Drake House. The three of them had turned the living room into their own winter wonderland just that afternoon.

Now it was Christmas Eve and Lexie's parents and sister, Carole, plus Rufus, Brandon and Marie were there for the evening. Michael and Chelsea and her Aunt Sophie had stopped by for a drink.

Marie handed out flutes of champagne to the adults and some sparkling water in a flute to Katie.

"To all of us and to Jenkins Cove," Brandon toasted. "This Christmas brings us the best presents of all—love and the resolution of the terrible crimes that have haunted Jenkins Cove for years."

They all clinked glasses and Lexie sipped her champagne. How had she ever considered that Brandon had anything to do with the operation? It seemed that Ned Perry had been trying to blackmail him over a property the foundation had wanted to buy for a women's shelter. Hoping to keep the price down, Brandon hadn't wanted competitive bidding on it.

Ned had been killed because he'd overheard Doug Heller giving Hans Zanko instructions to answer the ad for survivors. Zanko had been the one to attack Lexie at her house—he'd already been arrested.

Phil Cardon had turned out to be nothing more than a petty thief who'd planned to hock Cliff's trophy.

Isabella had tried landing Cliff for herself by spying for him. She'd told him and Doug Heller about the key. Her employment had been terminated.

"I went to see Cliff this morning," Brandon said. "At his request. Simon, he asked me to tell you that he planned to sign over his share of Drake Enterprises to you."

Simon started. "I thought the government was seizing his assets."

"All but the business. Cliff inherited his half, and the other half is mine. His dirty money went into the manor and his cars and boats. At any rate, I want to continue concentrating on the Drake Foundation. I hope you'll consider taking charge of Drake Enterprises."

For once, Lexie thought, Simon seemed apprehensive.

"I don't know anything about running a company."

"I can help there," Brandon said, "until you're up and running on your own. If we don't get it together fast, a whole lot of good people will be out of work."

"Give me at least a minute to think about it," Simon said, but he hugged Lexie to him and she knew this was exactly what he needed to feel useful.

"You'll do fine, boy!" Rufus said, raising his glass to Simon.

"I heard Cliff would probably plead out to get a lesser sentence," said Michael, ever the investigative reporter. "His final actions in saving you all—and the fact that he didn't commit any of the actual murders—will be considered in his favor."

"Which means the state won't go for the death penalty," Chelsea said.

Her Aunt Sophie shook her head. "Cliff was always a brash boy, looking for attention. Who knew how far he would go to get it. At least he wasn't directly responsible for anyone's death."

"Not that it exonerates him," Marie added.

Lexie was glad Cliff wouldn't be looking at the death penalty, which would have been an added burden for Simon and now Katie. After what their daughter had been through, she and Simon had told Katie the truth about everything.

Katie had taken it all in stride like the preteen she proudly claimed to be, Lexie thought, smiling.

"Happy?" Simon murmured into her ear.

"I couldn't be happier."

Simon pulled Lexie off into the hall under the mistletoe and kissed her soundly.

When they came up for air, he said, "I never stopped loving you. I want to start my life fresh, as if the last thirteen years never happened. I promise I'll never leave if you'll make an honest man of me." With that, he pulled out a ring with a very large

emerald. "I know a diamond is more traditional, but I wanted
something that would remind both of us of our daughter's eyes."

Lexie held out a slightly shaking hand, but Simon steadied
it and slipped the ring on her finger.

"When you agreed to stay," she said, grinning, "I thought I
couldn't be happier. I was wrong." Her pulse skittered. Finally,
she didn't just have to dream about being happy with Simon.
"I don't have nearly as spectacular a Christmas gift for you."

"You already gave me one." He looked to Katie, who shone
as brightly as any ornament on the Christmas tree. "But I
wouldn't mind if you gave me another one of those."

Simon kissed her again, and Lexie realized that her whole
life was about to change.

She couldn't wait.

* * * * *

MILLS & BOON®

Sparkling Christmas Regencies!

A seasonal delight for Regency fans everywhere!

Warm up those cold winter nights with this charming seasonal duo of two full-length Regency romances. A fantastic festive delight from much-loved Historical authors. Treat yourself to the perfect gift this Christmas.

**Get your copy today at
www.millsandboon.co.uk/Xmasreg**